House on October Hill

A Novel By

Leighton McCormick

authorHOUSE®

AuthorHouse™
1663 Liberty Drive
Bloomington, IN 47403
www.authorhouse.com
Phone: 1 (800) 839-8640

Published by AuthorHouse 01/05/2016

ISBN: 978-1-5049-6025-0 (sc)
ISBN: 978-1-5049-6026-7 (hc)
ISBN: 978-1-5049-6024-3 (e)

Library of Congress Control Number: 2015918405

Print information available on the last page.

Contents

To wife Patti, who has put up with me for 50 Octobers. And daughter Kate, who couldn't wait two days for October. Love and thank you, my ladies!

Also, I want to thank the Author House Team for making this book possible: Specifically, Dianne Hiatt, Joan Conners, Rebecca Prato, **Joseph Elas**, and Catherine Gomez.

"And when October goes
The snow begins to fly
Above the smoky roofs
I watch the planes go by
The children running home
Beneath a twilight sky
It doesn't matter much
How old I grow
I hate to see October go"

- Johnny Mercer -

Chapter 1

First Meeting

A WET FALL CLOTHED THE WOODED valley leading into Huntsdale in rich autumn hues of orange and gold. Here and there, rogue clusters of sassafras, persimmon and sugar maple flared vivid crimson, sprucing nature's fall wardrobe.

The red fox appeared almost motionless as she edged stealthily through the early morning, dew-laden underbrush. Her ebony-tipped ears cocked back, and incisors gleaming through curled black lips. Her moist nostrils tasted the scent of the rabbit nibbling gravel beside the road.

The fox paused, front paw suspended in mid-step and ears now perked. A sudden sense of peril gripped her; an unfamiliar threat approaching.

In the distance, automobile tires whined imperceptibly louder. The rabbit's ears twitched as it readied itself to dart from oncoming danger. Its back hunkered and senses straining.

Instinctively, it took three short hops into the dense foliage a few feet away. And nearly collided with the stationary fox. Which took immediate advantage of the meeting and quickly snapped the rabbit's neck with her powerful jaws.

The rabbit kicked convulsively for a moment, then hung limp. The fox darted through the undergrowth into a field of orchard grass paralleling the highway. Fresh meat would nourish her six cubs safely hidden in a nearby den.

The driver of the speeding Ferrari detected the fox's movement in his peripheral vision. At that precise moment, his car's rear tires broke traction on the weathered, sun-fried blacktop. He cramped the steering wheel hard left, and gingerly pumped the brakes. The sports car slid sideways and halted amidst the smoke and bellow of radial tires rasping on asphalt.

Matt Durham shifted to neutral and pulled on the hand brake. He pressed his forehead against the leather-wrapped steering wheel; beads of nervous perspiration water-marking the supple brown covering.

"Goddamnit to hell!" he hissed through the stainless steel yoke. He pushed back violently in the snug bucket seat, clutched his knees roughly and felt his legs trembling.

"Keep your mind on the road, dipshit! Or you'll scatter your beautiful Testarossa all over hell."

The man watched the fox bound up the field's slight incline, zigzagging through sumac clusters, the rabbit still dangling from her mouth. When his heart ceased its excited pounding he relaxed and settled into the comfortable seat. Then laughed to himself in the fox's direction.

"Here's to your beautiful ass, Ms. Fox," he said. "Bet I didn't frighten you any more than I did myself."

Matt opened the car door and pulled himself up and out. The fox loped to a juniper stand at the far end of the field. She paused and glanced back warily.

As the man limbered himself, an empty beer can clattered to the blacktop and rolled under the idling machine. He lit a cigarette and squintingly focused through the haze of exhaled smoke as the fox topped the crest and disappeared.

Matt had marveled at the red fox's beauty...or that of her predecessors... over the course of forty years. Hundreds of times, he expected. Seldom more than a mile from this spot.

Suddenly, anxiety arose within him. Nostalgia constricted his throat and clouded his eyes. And he experienced the feeling he had known months earlier in New York.

Then, a summer fragrance tripped the response. Lilting his nostrils and reminding him of childhood and freshly mown grass. And he, again a kid, peddling his paper route in New Haven, Connecticut.

"Christ, Durham, you're getting old," he muttered, taking another pull from the cigarette.

His left arm, tucked against his ribcage, trembled uncomfortably. He rubbed it briefly, then dropped the cigarette to the ground and crushed it under his foot.

He swung back into the throbbing vehicle, pulled the door closed and shifted into gear. He let out the clutch and the soft rubber tires growled and spat loose bits of asphalt. He spun the car straight and continued in his original direction.

Matt shifted effortlessly through the gears, and continued railing about the nostalgic interlude.

"Old and maudlin," he hissed scornfully. "Damned mind so chock full of memories anything sets it off!"

He accelerated along the smooth black swath, now bordered on one side by soybean stubble and the other by desolate rows of crackly, skeletal corn stalks. He couldn't shake the fluttery feeling that quickened his pulse on seeing the fox. And his thoughts raced the ten mile stretch to the end of the day's journey.

Matt's mind pictured the Indian Summer setting in which he would see The House after more than a year. Instinctively, he recalled first seeing it.

It was this stretch of season. He was twelve.

His father's car topped the hillcrest and his eyes instantly traveled the white gravel road; leading straight as a beacon's beam to the front of The House.

It beckoned, embraced by a copse of hardwoods, and he remembered his instant awareness that it belonged exactly where it stood.

As much a part of the landscape as the trees, grass and earth. And it could so perfectly blend with no other location.

The House stood framed by long strands of weathered split rail fencing, cordoning nearly an acre of thick bluegrass. The terraced yard tucked neatly and comfortably against the hillside. And the sight instantly and indelibly etched into his soul.

Through the middle of this manicured oasis swept the chalky gravel drive. It swung a gentle half circle in front of...and graciously carried visitors up to...the structure itself.

The building was grand, yet unimposing. Not like those gnarled Elizabethan types of Poe and Dickens. Its design and construction were clean and simple.

A well-crafted three-story frame with turrets capping its clapboard sides and green tarnished copper downspouts standing at its corners. Perfect for collecting leaves, acorns and walnuts, and for children to shinny up and slide down.

Moon-sliver shutters spread beside The House's windows, and its two large bay portals looked east and west. Still, its most impressive feature remained the panoramic backdrop. For The House stood regally in the middle of a wooded five-acre plateau, almost at the pinnacle of the highest bluff.

It overlooked Huntsdale Valley and the village to the southwest, and the Paginaw River to the east.

The House, nestled among a thick grove of walnut, sycamore, cottonwood and maple trees, complemented its surroundings as if it were part of nature's decree that it should exist in this idyllic setting.

Its owner, Doctor Damon Arthur Forsythe, had been Matt's father's closest friend since the two were fraternity brothers at Yale University. He inherited The House in 1934 when his father, also a doctor, died.

"Damon's grandfather built her shortly before the Civil War," Walt Durham informed his son. Outside, Matt heard the car's tires crunch the gravel approachway. "He was a tobacco grower and part-time riverboat captain. Fact is...during the War, Yankee and Confederate soldiers each confiscated The House a time or two. Used it reconnoitering ship traffic on the Paginaw. Damon says it's the lookout point where Union intelligence officers first spotted the Rebel's ironclad vessel...the Merrimack...undergoing sea trials."

"Gee," Matt gasped, casting a more appreciative glance at the oxbowing waterway a few miles distant. His mind conjured blue and grey military skirmishers defending their respective sides of the river.

"Damon's dad helped plant and harvest tobacco," continued Walt. "He really wanted to be a doctor, though. And eventually graduated from Yale's medical school. Practiced in New Haven."

Matt remembered reading that at the turn of the century tobacco emerged as a big cash crop in the area. Walt glanced to see if his son still listened, then continued.

"For the rest of his life, Damon's dad split his time about evenly between two locations and professions. I knew him and Damon's grandpa. Both true gentlemen, through and through. Like Damon."

Walt and Damon graduated from Yale in June 1917. In time to involve themselves in World War One.

Walt voraciously read every text on the new field of aeronautics. And enrolled in the few college courses available; knowing he would link his future with this exciting fledgling industry.

The instant he received his engineering degree, Walter Francis Durham joined hundreds of other Americans and enlisted as a volunteer pilot in the Canadian Air Force.

He went through basic flight training at Malton Airfield outside Toronto, spending countless hours in Curtiss "Jennies" flying practice formations and logging night-time patrols along Lake Ontario's shorelines.

In October 1917, Flight Lieutenant Durham and his cadre transferred to France. There, he flew small and fast French Nieuport Scout fighters.

A year later...as a captain...he commanded Squadron II of the elite LaFayette Air Corps, based in Moussons-Viex. And piloted the new French Spad.

Walt was a big man. Nearly six feet, three inches tall. He weighed two hundred and forty-five pounds. Early on, he experienced difficulty shoehorning into the tiny circular nacelles of the little French fighters. Over the months, however, disdain for French cuisine and a subsistence on wine, cheese, bread and sausage, helped him shave twenty pounds.

A slimmer torso, comfortable in the Spad's tidy cockpit, made flying even more enjoyable for Walt. And he loved being in the air. Night or day. Fair weather and foul. And tallied enough enemy aircraft to earn honors as an "Ace."

When the American Expeditionary Forces pushed their way into northern France, Lieutenant Colonel Durham immediately transferred to the allied Army Air Corps.

"Just for the cooking, though," he said jokingly.

Meanwhile, his comrade, Damon Forsythe, also went to war. After medical school, the doctor joined the Surgeon General Corps and served with the Expeditionary Forces in England, France and Germany.

Damon also was tall, though leaner than his friend. And his white blonde hair lifted in feathery wisps with the slightest breeze.

His narrow face was disarmingly handsome, and displayed the angular profile of a Roman tribune. His deep blue eyes, shining over high jutting cheekbones, beamed warm and friendly.

On first meeting the doctor, Matt understood his father's respect and brotherly love for the man. And at once realized the physician's life-preserving hands distinguished him from others. They were immaculate. Soft, gentle, yet strong. And as Damon spoke, his hands gracefully highlighted words' meanings, holding one's eyes captive.

Damon's daughter, Karen, inherited his attributes. The silken hair, crystalline blue eyes and prominent cheekbones. And, the delicate, graceful hands.

When World War One ended, Damon accepted a position on the surgical staff at Yale's School of Medicine. Walt hired on as chief engineer at Connecticut Castings Company; a pioneering manufacturer of aircraft engines and frames.

Walt retained his commission and flight status in the Army Air Corps Reserve. And when World War Two erupted, held the rank of brigadier general. As such, he commanded the Army Air Corps Training Center in Springfield, Massachusetts.

Where he learned to fly the quick and maneuverable P-51 Mustang and P-38 Lightning fighters.

In the fall of 1942, the general took command of an overseas combat wing. Which again meant flying hostile skies. And soon after the Christmas that lay ahead.

It was on this holiday leave...before ferrying with his squadron to England...that Walt first brought his boy to The House. They intended sharing father and son moments; probably the last for many months.

Walt also wanted Matt to meet and get to know his dear friend, Damon. It was crucial the two hit it off, for Walt asked the doctor to watch over his family should he fall in combat. Without hesitating, Damon vowed to safeguard the Durham clan as his own.

Matt's first trip to The House had another ulterior purpose as well. His father intended to introduce him to the East Coast's finest waterfowl hunting.

A large entry foyer inside The House opened onto a long passageway. Oriental carpets and throw rugs muffled the hand burnished oak plank flooring. And the warm gleam of afternoon sunlight poured through floor-to-ceiling crystal windows on both sides of the front door.

A spacious kitchen beckoned down the hall in the distance. Before reaching it, however, one first passed the visiting parlor, living and dining rooms on the left. To the right, a wide winding stairway rose to second and third floor bedrooms and baths.

The dining room contained a bay window opening onto the woods, bluff and farmland visible north of The House. Opposite the dining room was the study, a restful refuge replete with walls of shelves lined with well-worn, heavy hardbound books and medical journals.

To one side of the library stood a long oak reading table. Scattered about were several sturdy leather-cushioned chairs. At the rear reposed a roll-top desk belonging to the doctor's grandfather. It was immense, and contained dozens of hidden cubbyholes and panels. Damon joked his grandfather built The House around it.

The study smelled of the cool, heady fragrance of pipe tobacco. Merging wonderfully with the perfumes of rich wood, leather and lemon furniture polish.

This room boasted the other bay window. One commanding a breathtaking view of the Paginaw River Valley and, far in the hazy distance, several houses forming the village of Chester.

Karen was there when Matt first walked through the massive oak front door. She sat on a step midway up the tall staircase, peering at him through the ornate walnut balusters like a captive capuchin monkey.

Matt, at twelve, could not define his feelings on first seeing her. However, he became aware of a pleasant, inwardly unsettling sensation.

Strange, yet exciting. Unlike his indifference toward most other girls.

Her luminous eyes reflected the sun's glint. And a sudden dimpled smile caught him offguard. Instantly, however, he knew they would be immediate friends; and for a long time to come.

Karen stood gracefully, then skipped lightly down the stairs. She greeted and passed the two men at the doorway...shaking hands and patting each other's backs...and offered her slender hand to Matt.

"I'm Karen," she said, dimples accentuating the cheek bones.

He carefully took the dainty hand in his, and flashed surprise over her firm grip.

"Hi, I'm Matt," he stuttered, glancing quickly toward his father for reassurance. Then back to her.

She was taller than he had assumed when he saw her on the stairway. She nearly looked him eye to eye. Her smile creased warm and open, and she smelled of flowers. He decided that, as girls went, she was quite pretty. Then he realized he still clutched her hand, and flushed with embarrassment; causing her smile to broaden.

Walt touched his son's shoulder and gently turned him facing Doctor Forsythe. The young man reached out his hand and the doctor pumped it vigorously; clearly overjoyed by his daughter's spontaneous approval of the youngster.

And Matt's noticeable astonishment on meeting someone like her.

"Daddy, can Matt and I gather walnuts for the squirrels?" she asked, tucking her arm through her father's. Then, before Damon could reply, she turned to Matt: "Want to come outside and help me, Matt?"

Matt's total attention focused on her. Only now did he look dazedly into Damon's eyes. He snapped from his rapture when she repeated the question to her father.

"Oh, yes, go outside if you must," the doctor growled. He rolled his eyes upward for Matt's benefit, pretending aggravation over the repeated request.

"You'd better go with her this instant, Matt. Or she'll pester us mercilessly."

Boisterous laughs followed the couple down the long entrance hall as they raced toward the front door. The two men, arms on each other's shoulders, disappeared into the library; pleased with the positive results of their offsprings' initial meeting.

Outside, Karen and Matt created parallel trails dragging their feet through an ankle-high blanket of leaves that smothered the eastern side yard. They walked among the tall walnut trees alongside Magusett Creek. And their footpaths uncovered late summer shocks of vivid green grass that contrasted with the yellow mantle like emeralds against gold.

"It must be swell staying here...away from everything," Matt volunteered shyly as he stripped the dry shell of a maple leaf to its fragile skeletal frame. "It's like my grandpa's place near Hartford. That's where mom and I will stay. Leastwise 'til the Germans and Japs call it quits, and dad comes home for good."

"Daddy says your father is going overseas, Matt," she said. Then, turning to face him, suddenly serious and grasping his hand: "I'm truly sorry. Really I am. I'd hate it if my dad left us. Why does yours?"

"He's an army flier," he replied, turning and pulling his hand away to dab a tear. "He'll leave after Christmas. Go to England and fight the Germans."

She intuitively, gently, placed her hand on his shoulder.

"Don't worry, he'll be fine. I know. Dad says people like him will get us through this silly old war. And God will watch over him."

Matt turned, sniffling, and looked hopefully into her consoling eyes.

Her face glowed in the soft mid-afternoon sun, and now he noticed freckles sprinkled across the bridge of her nose and under the translucent eyes. Golden down glistened on her temples and neck, and her innocent beauty again caused an inexplicable throb in his chest. A strange fluttery feeling. And teary trails streaking his face didn't concern him.

"Gee, I hope so," he urged. "I hear mom crying all the time when he's gone. She doesn't know I hear...but I do. God needs to take care of him just for her. I don't know what we'd do without him."

She clutched his hand warmly again.

"He will. Just you wait and see. Everything will work out hunky dory. Hey, let's collect walnuts!"

Matt dried his eyes as they walked toward the artesian fed creek. Hundreds of large green wrinkled walnuts had fallen and lay hidden beneath the leafy crust. The two located the nuts by first stepping on them, then retrieving and tossing their finds into a burlap bag fetched from the tool shed.

"Autumn's the most beautiful time of the year," Karen said abruptly.

She took in the sunlight-swathed surroundings with a broad sweep of her arm, then fixed him with a funny, quizzical look. He didn't know then, but he would see that look hundreds of times throughout his life.

As if she were trying to settle her mind about something, and had not quite. And needed only a supportive sign to cement her conviction.

He gave it, nodding agreement. Hoping to draw her on.

"It's my favorite," she continued. "In autumn, everything comes to life. Trees dress in beautiful colors. The air smells and tastes fresher. People are friendlier. And think of the excitement of the season!"

His mind conceived the images she described.

"Halloween, Thanksgiving and Christmas! The quail, pheasant and duck seasons. Daddy and his friends almost live here during the hunting season. You'll hunt here too, won't you, Matt?"

"Gee, I don't know," he stuttered, words clipped anxiously. He recalled the fabulous hunts his dad described, and hoped this year the men would take him with them.

After all, he was nearly thirteen. Old enough to hunt with men. And well trained, at that.

Walt, indeed, had taught him about handling guns around others afield or in a blind.

They hunted geese, quail and pheasant together. The boy shot wisely and well, had a keen eye, and handled his gun safely.

Still, Matt intuitively knew the unspoken rule: youngsters don't hunt with other grownups until they reach a certain stage; when they react with deliberate judgment, commonsense and caution. Not a kid's show-off reflexes.

Although Walt had not told him, Matt had achieved that exalted state of hunterdom.

"Dad hasn't mentioned my hunting here," he continued. "However, he did say it was time I joined the October Club."

"Well, silly!" she exclaimed. "That's the hunting club our dads and Judge Corley started years ago. It was you they mentioned the other day! Because I heard the judge tell your dad they needed someone younger. You know, to paddle boats, fetch dead birds and straighten decoys. I'll bet that's you!"

"Oh, gosh, do you think so?"

Matt's feeling of ecstasy overpowered his fear of disappointment, and he grinned ear to ear. He recalled his dad and grandpa painting Huntsdale as the Garden of Eden for outdoorsmen.

"We hunted pheasants on a farm outside Chester last year," he could still taste the feast the birds had provided. "It was tops. We bagged limits by noon."

He looked hopefully into Karen's large eyes once more. His face still reflecting wonderment. Then, embarrassed by stretched seconds of silence, asked:

"You think we've got enough walnuts?"

He barely could heft the half-filled gunnysack.

"Sure," she flushed slightly, too, then glanced downward and again flashed the quizzical look. "C'mon, we'll tow it together."

The two dragged the bulging bag toward The House, chattering about various exciting events filling their respective twelve years to that minute. Walnut juice had stained their hands deep brown. Yet they were youthfully oblivious to the dye. More interested in what the other was saying.

They trudged through the rustling drifts of dry leaves. And soon, The House's outline took shape against the waning afternoon sun.

Matt realized then that he coveted The House and its surroundings. The hilltop vantage point. The color-clad valley. The warm, spacious, inviting structure itself.

And, probably, the gangly legged, freckle-faced girl grunting and tugging alongside him.

They halted a moment and gazed at The House silhouetted against the dying orb.

"I call it my House on October Hill," she gasped, short of breath from exertion and conversation. She noticed his steady, appreciative gaze, and smiled. "October is when this special part of the world comes to life."

He nodded silent agreement, his eyes fixed upon The House as it drew nearer. And thought to himself how exceptionally true her statements were. No other part of the world could possibly offer the beauty and allure that Huntsdale did at this moment in his existence.

They emptied the bag and spread the nuts to dry and blacken on the cement cistern cover near the woodpile by the back door. A broad happy grin contorted Matt's face and his entire body tingled. As if angels' wings fanned his heart.

At twelve, he had no way of discerning how this place would entwine itself around his life.

Chapter 2

October Club

DOCTOR FORSYTHE AND GENERAL DURHAM were enjoying afternoon highballs when Karen and Matt entered the front foyer. The youngsters were rosy-cheeked, walnut-stained, giggling and obviously enjoying one another's company.

"Welcome the wandering children," quipped the physician. "My Lord, Walt, look at those urchins' hands! Those certainly would make a grand impression in the operating room!"

"Oh daddy," she protested, hugging him around the neck with her forearms, and carefully avoiding smearing the brown dye on his canary cardigan sweater or favorite easy chair. She pecked his cheek and looked excitedly into his eyes.

"We nearly filled a bag with walnuts, so the poor squirrels should have food through the winter."

"Damon and I worried for a minute the squirrels had carried you two away, son," joked Walt, gently reaching and plucking a leaf from the young man's thick sandy hair. "By the way...now that you're back, we've got something to ask you."

Karen eased onto her father's knee and turned to face the others. She smiled her knowledge of what Walt was going to say.

Matt stood behind his dad and exchanged a secretive glance with her; putting a finger to his lips so she wouldn't speak.

The general turned and looked up at him.

"You already know, don't you Burrhead!" he said, tousling his son's hair, then continuing in mock indignation.

"Regardless...Doctor Forsythe, Judge Corley and I want to take you on as junior partner in the October Club. Would you like that?"

"Oh, yessir. I would!" Matt sputtered. He took his father's right hand and shook it vigorously. Then did the same with Damon's.

"You'll be glad you asked me. I promise. I'll pull my share, and never complain."

"Judge Corley's suffering from worn cartilage between two vertebrae in his spine," explained the doctor. "Almost paralyzed his right side. Especially his leg. If you're agreeable, Matt, it would be nice if you helped him around. You're young and strapping. Shouldn't slow you too much. What do you say?"

"I'd love to, Doctor Forsythe. I'd love to! And I won't mind a bit. Not in the least."

He was so overwrought with excitement he would have carried Judge Corley on his back from sunrise to sunset.

"Thank you both. And the judge, too."

"I'm sure he'll be thankful to you, son," Walt added. "Welcome aboard."

That first hunting season...staying at The House...rated as one Matt remembered vividly. And recounted and cherished many, many times throughout life.

It would exist in his mind through good times and bad. And each year, he would try to recapture and relive the joy and anticipation of those first hunts. Often, with great success.

Four weekends before opening of the duck season, the three men traditionally stocked The House with provisions and firewood. Walt and Damon repaired the duck blind and checked the boat and motor. The judge made sure the decoys were in good shape, and mice hadn't nibbled through weight cords over the summer.

For years, they situated their blind in a wide shallow pool formed by two willow-lined rock peninsulas. These dikes jutted into the current, and held part of the river captive.

Five miles farther south, the Paginaw emptied into Long Island Sound. The river's current was not as swift as that of many tributaries lacing Connecticut. Still, its capricious nature during the heavy rains and melting snow of the hunting season would snap frayed cords.

Throughout the waterfowling months, stray decoys regularly broke loose and drifted the main channel, eventually floating into the Atlantic Ocean.

With make-ready chores completed, the weekend before opening day heralded the arrival of Fall Festival. October Club members teamed with Huntsdale families to hunt squirrels, and then partake of a covered-dish luncheon; usually in the walnut grove beside The House.

Most of Huntsdale's townsfolk participated in Fall Festival, feasting on squirrel prepared various ways that appealed to all tastes. Deep fried, baked and barbecued squirrel were common delicacies. Although the traditional favorite was chunks of meat suspended in thick New England cream gravy, and ladled over homemade egg noodles or mashed potatoes.

Wives were invited to the Festival...and most attended. And marveled aloud over grown men enduring the miseries of arctic temperatures, icy water and male cooking to shoot waterfowl.

Doctor Forsythe and Judge Corley stayed at The House most of the hunting season. Fortunately, it always seemed a slack period for broken bones and crime. And before shipping out, Walt had opted for dividing his month's leave between New Haven and his wife, Claire, and hunting with Matt.

October rode into Huntsdale on crisp breezes that spurred winter to maturity in thirty-one days.

Old-timers made up the bulk of the small village's population, since the war effort siphoned away most of Huntsdale's young men. The elders blamed the European hostilities for the bitter chill.

They customarily gathered around the glowing potbellied stove at Arch's general store; their sacrosanct meeting place.

And one or two eventually would reflect: "It only got this cold, this early, back durin' the First War. Hey-yup."

A frigid gust slashed from the northeast and raked the spread of decoys bobbing on the water in front of the duck blind. It gathered force on colliding with warmer breezes from the Atlantic, and whipped directly into the rear of the camouflaged hut where the October Club members huddled.

The hideaway stood slightly above the water's surface on sturdy, deeply anchored pilings. A burlap and tarpaper outer shell afforded some protection. Still, winter's mist-laden breath snaked its way through cracks where the sides fastened. And the half open roof that enabled hunters to safely stand, aim and fire, also invited the elements.

Occasional wisps of snow welcomed the foursome the previous day when they placed and arranged the large spread of decoys that worked in front of the blind. They were directly offshore from Judge Corley's property.

Judge Winston Corley...plump, jolly and balding...came into his Huntsdale land as did Damon. His great uncle reigned as one of the village's first settlers. The man hailed from Virginia, and became a successful tobacco grower.

He sought rich soil, access to water for transport, and less competition. Huntsdale abundantly provided all three. So the judge's kin and their imported seedlings took root and thrived.

His great uncle also started Damon's grandfather planting tobacco. In exchange for prime starter plants and shared wisdom, he received free passage to market on the latter's riverboat. Their friendship and dependence upon each other over the years extended into the trout streams, bird fields and duck blinds.

The judge's five hundred acres of bottomland ran southward along the Paginaw for nearly a mile, and butted against the doctor's to the north. Access to the river was through the judge's property, and the boathouse they shared once was an interim tobacco barn.

Tobacco stacked there for curing often reached the rafters. During spring, the judge's uncle shipped it to ports on the Sound.

Law and duck hunting were the two things the Judge loved most. And he actively pursued both interests. Although in recent years, the painful lower back ailment nearly immobilized him.

He retired from the bench five years ago, but still acted as legal consultant for several New Haven companies. He probably would have forsaken his love for waterfowling this season were it not for Matt.

The sun tinged pink the blanket of grey clouds hanging overhead. More snow threatened. The four hunters were ready when Walt announced they could shoot legally.

Matt sat next to his father on the left side of the blind. Judge Corley and the doctor to the right. Out front, they heard the river lapping the hollow decoys that rode bill-forward on breeze-stirred breakers.

They listened in the early darkness to the whistling sounds of fast pumping wings as large flights of birds passed overhead. A lonesome mallard hen, fifty yards southward, squawked from her hiding place near the willowed outcroppings.

Small bunches of lesser scaup, teal and wood ducks had landed in the decoys shortly before daybreak, and now rafted among the blocks, facing into the gusts as if part of the spread.

As was the tradition, Judge Corley dug a pint of biting homemade blackberry brandy out of his canvas army knapsack. He unscrewed the cap and raised the bottle in a toast.

"Gentleman, to another fine hunt," he said. "Here's to excellent friends, and outstanding prospects. And welcome to you, my fine lad," he directed to Matt.

The Judge took a short nip of the contents and passed the bottle to the doctor.

Each hunter, in turn, performed the ritual; the tiny swallow of stinging sweet liquor burning its way to their bellies. Momentarily, through watering eyes, everyone felt his body temperature rise several degrees.

Matt soon learned this was the only time liquor appeared when guns were present. October Club rules permitted only a pre-hunt toast in the blind or afield.

"Alcohol dulls the senses and slows reactions," the Judge intoned. "Makes men take damned fool chances, and try long shots they normally wouldn't. End up crippling more game than they bring down."

He launched into a well-worn joke about a drunk shooting a goose with one shot after several sober hunters missed. The drunk proclaimed later: "Hell, out of a bunch like that I usually get three or four!"

Damon passed around tin cups of steamy coffee as the hunters loaded their weapons. Matt took three shells from a fresh box and inserted them into his pump shotgun. Almost immediately, he heard the "chukka chukka chukka" feeding call of mallards.

"Listen!" he cautioned in a low whisper.

The older men lifted their calls and mimicked the staccato sounds while Matt sat motionless, peering outward beneath the bill of his hunting cap.

A flight of about forty mallards sized the decoy arrangement, blue-notched wings whistling.

A mallard hen near the front of the bunch cackled and called to the counterfeit ducks on the water.

Then they heard the susurrant sound of feathered bodies passing overhead. Followed by frantic splashing and beating wings as birds settled onto the choppy surface.

The ducks swam skittishly among the blocks for a moment or two. Then Judge Corley barked: "Okay boys, let's get 'em!"

The four shooters stood in unison through the slit in the top of the blind, leveling their shotguns and tracking targets.

Matt picked a large drake stroking frantically for altitude. He eased the sighting bead above and slightly in front of the bird's greenish-yellow bill, and squeezed the trigger.

The twelve gauge slammed his shoulder. Over its barrel he saw feathers puff, and the drake cart-wheeled crazily into the water. A clean hit.

He led another greenhead swinging to his left, drew feathers on the first shot, and downed it with the second.

By now, Walt also had a pair floating on the water's surface. Judge Corley and Doctor Forsythe fired almost simultaneously, and two more drakes plummeted into the decoys.

When echoes from the shooting stopped reverberating down the river, eight drakes floated on the windswept pool in front of the blind.

"Well done, gentlemen," the Judge quipped happily. He shucked two spent shells from his trusty double barrel; bright purple Canadian ammo by which he swore.

"Nary a cripple or hen among them," he reported. "A splendid job, indeed!"

Matt and his father retrieved the straw covered johnboat from behind the blind, and paddled among the decoys collecting the downed birds. The young man marveled at the long lines, vees and clusters of waterfowl flying at various altitudes in nearly every direction. The sky over the shallow pool virtually swarmed with noisily quacking and chattering ducks and geese.

They flew in bunches of five or ten. Or in wavy feeding formations. Countless waterfowl plying the wintry sky, heading toward the patchwork soybean, corn and wheat fields that filled the rich Huntsdale bottomland that contained the Paginaw.

"Enjoy this while you can, son," shouted the general over the wind and din. He retrieved another plump drake from the frigid water and gently laid it in the bottom of the boat.

"It probably won't be like this when you're grown and take your son hunting. They're clearing too much land. Damming too many rivers. Driving wildlife into the open...which they don't like. Or, worse yet, into extinction."

They paddled slowly toward the blind.

"Plenty of changes have occurred since Damon and I first hunted these parts years ago. Then, you pointed a gun toward the sky any time and bagged a brace of birds."

For Matt, it still was the most awe-inspiring parade of waterfowl passing in review that he could imagine. The splendor of seeing so many beautiful, graceful species populating this little chunk of Connecticut was exhilarating. It nearly struck him breathless.

Widgeon and sprig whistled overhead. Black mallards and greenheads quacked on all sides. Everywhere else, scaup, ringnecks, wood ducks, bluebills and teal buzzed a few feet off the water.

Matt's eyes scanned the sullen wintry sky, as the diffused morning sunlight soaked the low hanging clouds in orange. And he thrilled to the patterns of birds crisscrossing back and forth across the horizon. He wondered if life ever could be richer, fuller, more invigorating or enjoyable than at this moment.

Walt sensed and empathized with his son's melancholy. Similar sights overcame him a quarter of a century ago.

He tenderly placed his hand on the boy's shoulder, and Matt turned and looked into his father's face.

"Makes you wonder what the poor folks are doing, doesn't it son?" Walt quipped.

At that instant, another flight of decoying mallards dipped low in front of the blocks. The birds cupped their wings, orange legs pawing for water, and close enough to the blind that those inside felt a breeze.

"Let's get inside pronto, Matt," said Walt. "These ducks have found a home, and they're liable to attack us here in the decoys!"

They quickly sculled behind the hut, Matt still combing the skies and admiring the endless flights of waterfowl. He wishfully daydreamed ahead to future hunts and experiences he'd share with his dad when the war ended.

He mentally weighed the prospects of owning property along the Paginaw. And vowed he would. Somehow. Someday. He'd have a place like The House. Right now, it embodied everything he wanted.

Contentment painted his face into a Cheshire grin as he stepped from the boat into the concealed shelter.

Chapter 3

Huntington High

THREE OCTOBERS SPED THROUGH MATT'S life. And a fourth dawned. With each, the hunting seasons proved better. Fall color schemes erupted more beautifully. The months passed quicker. And feelings shared by Karen and him grew much stronger.

Since first meeting as eighth graders, the two had grown inseparable. As seniors, launching their final year of high school, they thought and acted as one.

They were constant companions and steady dating partners. More important, they were close friends with no secrets from each other.

Doctor Forsythe's position as Dean of Yale's School of Medicine motivated him to find a residence closer to campus and City Memorial Hospital. He and his wife, Evelyn, had bought their home in West Haven in 1926, soon after marrying. Karen was born there four years later on a sultry June evening.

She and her mother often reflected on the love and sacrifices required to transform their small cottage into a comfortable home over the years.

After World War One, Damon served his residency and set up a practice. Soon after, the country writhed under the throes of the Depression. Doctor Forsythe often would not charge patients for services. Only for medicine. Even though his family frequently dined solely on wild game brought home from hunting and fishing.

Walt Durham also found the times stressful and challenging, but mostly pleasant. He believed he could square off to anything after the war.

He and Claire splurged on pot roasts, and invited the Forsythes over for homemade beer and hilarious rounds of Parcheesi. Although an infant then, Matt recalled the sight of four adults around the large walnut dining room table. They drank the volatile brew, played Parcheesi and shot cap pistols at each other, laughing hysterically.

As the general reflected:

"In a sad sort of way...they were happy, fun, yet inexpensive times. Like being in the military...you forget the bad and relive the good."

One war later, the general returned to the United States in the middle of his son's junior session. During twenty-four months in Europe, Walt flew more than a dozen fighter-escort missions. And two months before returning home, the commander of Supreme Headquarters Allied European Forces (SHAEF) grounded him.

His importance to SHAEF's mission, and value as a prized catch for the Germans, ended his flying career.

Walt long ago decided to retire when he no longer could pilot an aircraft, and closed his thirty-year career as a major general. He transferred back to the States in time for duck hunting, Thanksgiving and Christmas. And to see his son play football, and help celebrate the young man's birthday.

Connecticut Castings encouraged Walt's military leave of absence, and on his return promoted him to Vice President of Engineering. An unpleasant part of his new duties involved counseling three hundred people who were fired in the face of severe defense cutbacks.

Matt remembered his chore of kneading thick plastic bags of what seemed like white putty until it magically turned to yellow oleo margarine. The tiny color pellet inside dissolving under the massaging warmth of hands.

He also recalled completing homework while sprawled on the sewing room floor. Nearby, his mother worked the foot treadle on her ornate Singer sewing machine, singing or humming happily as she stitched clothes. Elsewhere in the room, a deep-voiced radio announcer hailed Franklin Delano Roosevelt as the thirty-second President of the United States.

Karen pleaded. Her mother urged. And Doctor Forsythe closed on a brick two-story in a woodsy section of New Haven.

Naturally enough, within walking distance of the Durhams who lived in Briarwood. Like Damon's ancestors in Huntsdale, three generations of Durhams grew up in the community.

Huntington High School was the more modern of two in New Haven. Karen and Matt enrolled there since they were within its district boundaries. Its late Thirties construction was underwritten by a grant from Samuel Huntington's estate. He had been one of Connecticut's four representatives to the Constitutional Convention, and twelfth to sign the

Declaration of Independence. He also achieved historical significance as one of the original city founders.

Huntington High School stood as a brick and mortar monument to post-Depression workmanship. Its tall Gothic facade featured three turrets. The middle turret contained clocks that were visible on three sides. Federal, state and school flags flew from atop the smaller side turrets.

The school rose three stories, with eighteen classrooms per floor. Located within its center was a gigantic auditorium. Which most of the time seated the students, faculty and guests attending assemblies, plays and special events. Constructed horseshoe fashion around the auditorium were classroom buildings.

At the back of the auditorium, separated by a ceiling high folding partition, were the basketball court and gymnasium. Beyond those were found the locker rooms and showers.

Behind Huntington High lay well maintained football and baseball fields, and an oval cinder track. These facilities occupied a lower level than the main building. The school's more stolid academic planners had a double purpose in mind for their design. One should look down upon athletics when in the classroom. And glance Heavenward from the fields when considering studies.

Highly polished, creaky oak floors catacombed Huntington High. Throughout the school year the interior reeked of pungent liquid wax and steam heat.

The Principal's and administrative offices reposed behind windows on the left side as one faced the front of the building. To the right was the library. Directly across a wide hallway from these spaces beckoned the auditorium.

Friday morning assemblies began at nine o'clock with the Pledge of Allegiance and school fight song. The senior class president and secretary traditionally led these recitations, voiced by most and mouthed by some.

Students presented skits, pageants and plays in the auditorium during Homecoming, Christmas and Easter. And May graduation exercises drew standing room only crowds, overflowing even this spacious gathering hall.

Matt and Karen enjoyed their sophomore and junior years immensely. As they entered twelfth grade at Huntington, it was clear they would complete high school as honor students. Both stood in the top five percent of their class of ninety-six seniors.

The junior class selected Matt for its vice president. Additionally, he quarterbacked the Hornet's football team. A slot he earned as a sophomore when the varsity play caller fractured his hip skiing. Like his father, Matt grew to good size. He stood over six feet, and pegged the scale at two hundred and ten pounds.

When he played exceptionally well, and felt too full of himself, Karen reminisced over his first game off the bench.

As he cocked to launch a pass to a receiver in the end zone, a large flight of Canada geese caught his attention. They hovered noisily overhead, grey underbellies reflecting stark white in the glare of ball-field lights.

During this moment of distraction, an opposing tackle slammed him hard, knocking the ball loose. The rival team captured it, and ran the field to a touchdown.

The coach's half-time berating affected Matt considerably less than his concern for disappointing teammates. And, embarrassing Karen...a cheerleader on the sidelines.

Later that evening, through tears of laughter rolling down her cheeks, she recounted the incident from a bystander's viewpoint:

"I didn't know what you were doing!" she exclaimed, catching her breath between chortles. "You just stood there, motionless. Arm crooked and ready to throw. Staring upward. Then I saw the geese and thought: 'Oh God, he's going to get slaughtered!' And sure enough... you did!"

"Ho, ho, ho," he replied sarcastically, pride pricked and acting indignant. "That's rich. I'm glad I amused you. God, I felt a buffalo herd stampede across my back when that big lug whacked me!"

In the second half, Matt redeemed himself by pitching two long touchdown passes. He also ran two TDs himself with minimal blocking.

More and more, the young man exhibited an affinity for writing and English. He cultivated an insatiable appetite for reading. William Faulkner, Jack London, Somerset Maughn, Paul Gallico and Ernest Hemingway counted among his favorites.

Matt joined the editorial staff of Huntington's yearbook, "The Harbinger." And continuously involved himself in creating, developing and supervising class fund-raising events.

Karen, to her father's dismay, nurtured an interest in art rather than medicine. Still, Damon recognized and admired her gift for merging color and form in pleasing compositions. He willingly acquiesced to her artistic bent.

In fact, encouraged her to attend summer art clinics. Which worked well, since Matt spent those months on a tractor working for Yale's agricultural department; a position arranged by the doctor.

Matt reaped high wages of seventy-five cents an hour. And stayed in football shape tossing around fifty pound sacks of seed and fertilizer, and bales of hay.

Karen worked closely with Matt as art director for "The Harbinger." And developed posters for his fund-raising events.

She was his perfect and inseparable counterpart. Junior class secretary. Cheerleader. And, president of Huntington's Art Honor Society.

Occasionally, Matt's writing and editorial style conflicted with Karen's dramatic eye-catching layouts. The true roots of disagreement stemmed from confining page sizes. And her desire to include as many sophomore, junior and senior faces as possible.

When these debates occurred, he weighed carefully her reasons for handling text and artwork in a certain manner. As executive editor, however, his word was final. Although she inevitably convinced him that class photos were crucial to yearbooks.

"Students want to see themselves and friends," she argued. "They'll recall faces all through life. Your writing's good, Matt, but it's not why they'll buy the books."

The concerted efforts of the young couple eventually paid off. Huntington High's yearbook swept annual statewide competitions for style and content. And finished second nationally behind New York City's Edison High. Which was not unusual. That school's editorial advisor also was Dean of the Columbia School of Journalism. He personally knew most of the judges responsible for selecting the top book.

Finishing second among thousands of high schools nationwide was heady praise for "The Harbinger" staff. And kindled Matt's journalistic fires.

Unlike his son, General Durham never entertained writing seriously. Early on, his desire was to fly. He "fooled around" writing short stories in college, and had a few published.

These minor authorial successes planted a genetic seed; which germinated. And inspired Matt to tunnel-focus his drive on creating communications from ideas and visions. Conveying in print what the mind's eye notices, the brain files, and on which humans act.

"After college, I'll go into advertising. Then later on, I'll write the 'Great American Novel,'" Matt told Karen as they walked in the woods. They regularly hiked the tree-filled ten acres that were part of the original Durham tract. "Meanwhile, you should follow in your father's footsteps. Become a brilliant and wealthy surgeon. Then I can afford to do what I choose. Which is man's destiny in life, right?"

"Wrong, buster," she responded, gently prodding his arm. "Surgeons put in long hours standing around operating tables. I'd probably end up with varicose veins. And my legs are too nice for that."

"Okay, I'll give you that point," he said, tugging her to stop. "Your legs are too nice for that. Seriously, what do you want to do?"

"I want my own career, Matt. There's something fulfilling about capturing on canvas what God made on this Earth. His works are transient. Momentary. Dandelion seeds in a breeze. Artists capture moments like these eternally. Hold them so others can see and appreciate God's wonders. I don't aspire to becoming the next Vincent Van Gogh. I do plan on involving myself with art. And by the way...you won't take care of me?"

It was then that their futures meshed; crystallized as one. Their dreams and goals, now defined in writing and art, overshadowed other likes and dislikes.

Mutual career interests in the creative disciplines further defined their partnership roles.

Uncovering this strong mutuality clarified thoughts the two had held since first meeting. And enabled them to recall, recognize and finally express what they unknowingly felt years ago in a leaf-carpeted October woods near Huntsdale.

"If love means needing someone so much it's painful...I love you, Karen," he whispered. His throat constricted with emotion, and nearly prevented him from mouthing the words. He pulled her tight against him. "More than anything or anyone else in the world."

She leaned her head slightly. Looked into his dark eyes. Her beautiful, youthful face reflected love's rapture. Karen felt indescribable excitement and exhilaration over Matt's words.

And her heart told her to reach and grasp the fleeting moment that arrived.

"I love you too, Matt," she breathed. She held him firmly, pressing her forehead against his shoulder. Her eyes brimmed.

Matt kissed her on the hair. She lifted her face, glistening tear trails on her cheeks. He kissed her fully on the mouth, and felt the danger point of passion rush past.

Today, all circumstances were right. The woods. The weather. And tender words, revealing heartfelt feelings; stripping away caution.

Karen leaned against a broad elm. He felt her soft firmness mold to him. His skin tingled, and absorbed her warmth where they touched. He knew she detected his readiness.

He lifted her slightly and they fit closer. Karen felt untold pleasure where he pressed. She parted her legs, and the couple embraced more snugly.

Her soft mouth opened wide and they breathed together, pulling air from each other's lungs in slow, steady gulps. She felt his tongue between her lips. And at the invitation, slid hers into his mouth.

Matt grasped her shoulders, gently eased her onto the cushion of leaves beneath the elm. Lowered himself on top. She locked her legs around him. And slowly they moved their bodies in unison.

He eased his right hand under her bulky sweater and cupped her left breast. Its nipple stood erect against her light silk brassiere.

"God, I want you," he said, kissing and tasting her ear.

"I know...I feel," she moaned. "I want you, too."

Warm sensations flooded Karen's lower body. Quick, pulsating, sensuous spasms that took her breath in short gasps. Left her cloaked in serenity.

Matt simultaneously savored the inexplicable pleasure as did Karen. And knew he could not hold passion's ebb. He thrust against her gently, between her parted legs.

"I love you...I love you...I love you," he gasped into her ear.

They lay together for several minutes. Nearly breathless. Entwined in each other.

Karen spoke first...studying his eyes: "Did we do wrong? Did we, Matt? Please tell me this won't spoil anything." Her face registered the quizzical look. Then concern.

"No, honey. It won't...at all. We didn't do anything wrong. Just something normal for two people in love. It was wonderful. We didn't go all the way."

"Yes, Matt. That's true, anyway." she rolled onto her side, leaning on her left elbow. Tears brimmed her eyes. "I really wanted to, though. More than anything."

"I did, too," he admitted. "As much as I love you, I can't stop myself."

"What will I do, Matt? Wanting you, and thinking about you all the time. Wishing to touch and hold you."

"It'll take both of us to resist, Karen. To deal with this. I love you, and hope we'll get married. Not as high school seniors, though. As we agreed...we want more from our lives than that. It would be terrible for us. Let alone our folks."

"My gosh!" she exclaimed. "I forgot about them!" Her face again flashed the puzzled look. "Matthew Durham. Do you really love me?"

"Yeah," he said. "I really do."

He kissed her forehead, stood and offered his hand. Easily pulled her to her feet.

Karen straightened her sweater while he brushed the leaves from their clothes. Then he grasped her hand and they walked slowly through the peaceful woods toward his home. Dust stirred from the layer of leaves where they walked. It wafted like smoke in the wide beams of mid-afternoon sunlight streaming through the trees from above.

That evening, neither Matt nor Karen slept well. Excited about the day's activities and discoveries. Already missing the other's company.

Matt finished his homework and was listening to the Jack Benny Show when the telephone rang. A moment later, Claire Durham rapped softly on his bedroom door, then opened it.

"Matt. It's Karen. She wants to talk with you."

He quickly slid the chair away from his desk and dashed past his mother.

"S'cuse me, mom," he said, bounding the stairs two at a time to the landing and wall telephone midway down.

"Thanks for such a wonderful day, Matt," he heard Karen whisper, her voice low and serene. "I just wanted to tell you again how much I love you."

"I love you too, Karen," he replied. "Good night, sweetheart. See you in school."

After they hung up, Matt started up the stairs, looked and saw his mother standing at the top. Claire wore a knowing smile.

"I should have realized when you nearly ran over me that things were serious between you two," she said. She stepped closer to him, put her hand gently against his cheek.

"I'm happy for you both, Matt." Then, almost as an afterthought. "Please think things through. That's all your father and I ask. I'm sure Damon and Evelyn feel the same."

"We will, mom," he hugged her softly, affectionately. "I promise."

Chapter 4

Suddenly Seniors

B EING HIGH SCHOOL SENIORS WAS to Karen and Matt like riding the crest of one of life's most enjoyable waves. Seniors achieved certain status at Huntington. And took advantage of the niceties that went with it.

Unlike sophomores who wore black and gold beanies until homecoming. During which time they burned them happily in a roaring bonfire. Or the juniors. Stranded somewhere between confusion and confidence. And not yet knowing which way to turn.

Seniors sat in the balcony of Huntington's auditorium. They had their own rousing cheer after singing the school fight song. They had their own parking section; closer to entrances. An all-night graduation party. A special area in the school cafeteria. And even more flexibility in selecting subjects.

Seniors could study beyond the usual range of required classes. Depending, of course, upon gradepoint and credits needed for graduation.

Connecticut, like most states in the late Forties, required students to complete successfully certain numbers of credits in English, history, mathematics and physical education. Proper planning and counseling, and a desire to achieve passing grades, enabled most students to amass required credits by their senior years.

Then they could consider elective classes, and improve skills in areas they enjoyed or intended pursuing in college.

Karen enrolled in a writing course Matt suggested. The instructor teaching it also served as advisor to the "Harbinger" staff. Matt reciprocated by joining her in a graphics design class.

A first-year art instructor taught that session. It was she who encouraged Karen to focus on the emerging field of interior design. Just then, Art Noveaux was making its splashy debut on the East Coast.

When senior year began, as planned, Karen and Matt shared every class but physical education. Their schedules opened with American History at eight-thirty in the morning, and closed with Solid Geometry at three-fifteen in the afternoon.

Matt enjoyed mathematics...except plane geometry. Which he considered: "Rote memory requiring little intelligence or reasoning powers."

In fact, he briefly considered following his father into engineering.

Karen also liked math, and had the more logical mind for solving problems. Matt often overlooked the obvious approach, favoring the creative.

He wisely banked what he earned during summers, and combined those savings with an advance against graduation money for a car. This financial maneuver enabled him to buy a used maroon 1940 Ford convertible, which he immediately set about "souping up." With the advice and aid of a friend whose father owned a garage.

The War effort slowed the need for auto repairs. And thousands of vehicles stood idle in garages awaiting their owners' returns. Mechanics spent more time tinkering with hot rods, and racing them, than fixing the diminished number of family cars.

As custom dictated, Matt presented Karen his class ring on receiving it his junior year. She wore it around her neck on a gold braided chain, signifying "hands off" to others.

At first, they were self-conscious displaying their feelings toward one another. Karen hid the ring in her dresser, taking it out and fondling it nightly as she completed homework.

Since summer, however, she boldly wore his ring in plain view. Damon and Evelyn Forsythe talked with her on first seeing it. They understood its significance. And wondered aloud if she weren't making a mistake restricting herself to one young man. Her parents were extremely fond of Matt. To the doctor, he was the son he never had.

"It's our problem, Evie," he told his wife after they discussed their concerns with Karen. "Not Karen's. Our suggestion about dating around upset her. You and I were too close to see their relationship mature."

"That's so, Damon," his wife concurred. "They've been two peas in a pod for nearly four years. What else can we expect? This is exactly what we've encouraged!"

"That's for certain," the doctor agreed, raising his hands palms up. "We've dreamed of these kids sharing their lives. Now we've got our wish. We should be thankful!"

After that, neither family mentioned the ring nor the increasing amount of time the two spent together.

Early on, Matt discussed with his father what he felt toward Karen. The two men built their strong relationship on respect and trust. After he first met Karen at The House, Matt kept thinking about her. And told his dad that.

"Especially in the fall," the young man had recently admitted. "When August's hot-and-humid dog days fade...and our woods changes colors. That's when I think of her. And The House. And hunting."

Walt and Claire did not compel Matt to think or behave in any particular fashion. They encouraged and motivated him. Asking only his genuine efforts on tasks undertaken. For these reasons, he was an exceptional student. He clowned occasionally, but most often acted mature beyond his age.

By his final year in high school, Matt envisioned a life to which he looked forward. One worth sharing. And enjoying. Although barring the unforeseen, unimagined circumstances which were to occur.

The young couple's closeness more than pleased Matt's parents. Claire and Walt often recalled the hard times they weathered in the early Thirties with her folks. Thankful having each other to count on for help, hope and encouragement.

October of his senior year was little more than halfway over. He turned 18 earlier in the month and the homecoming was only four days away. Matt and three of his teammates clustered in the high school hallway as he rummaged his wall locker for a book. Karen appeared at the opposite end of the long corridor.

"Hey Matt...here comes your steady," said Jerry Jouret, a Hornet halfback.

Matt turned and watched her approach. A tall and handsome figure, drifting effortlessly, gracefully toward them. Her ever present smile revealing sculpted white teeth and deep dimples.

Sunlight flooded through the windows down the hall. Outlining her trim figure, even beneath the loose black and gold cheerleader outfit.

Matt's mind reversed three months to the swimming party at Halen's Lake, west of New Haven. He lay on an old army blanket, drying off. She dove from the floating raft, waded onto the sandy beach. Then walked the clovered rise to their place among three other couples.

His mind replayed her approach, the sun to her back. She wore a stylish one-piece Esther William's bathing suit. He recalled his amazement over the youthful figure that matured over the summer.

Her breasts suddenly full and firm. Her legs, long and lithe, tapering from golden down-dusted thighs to wonderfully narrow ankles. Her soft, flowing curves carried from her shoulders to smoothly turned calves.

Matt yearned for her then. In earnest for the first time. As he had never. He wanted to possess her...entirely.

Karen discerned his desire, felt her body stir with longing. She flushed as she sat beside him. And wished they could reveal their love and wash away innocence right there, in front of everybody.

Instead, she teasingly kissed him on the cheek. Momentarily hoping the desire raging within would subside and bring the moment's promises to a less serious level.

Matt felt that same empty longing return as she moved nearer in the hallway, stopping a few feet away. She looked into his upturned face, her smile broadening.

"Good morning, Mr. Durham," she said. She shifted the load of school books under her right arm. Offered her left hand to help him up. "Care to walk your steady to class?"

"You bet!" he replied. He tugged a battered history book from the bottom of the pile of texts stacked in his locker. Grabbed a green spiral notebook off the top shelf. Matt closed the locker door and snapped shut the combination lock. He crooked his arm for Karen to take.

"See you guys at scrimmage," he said to the others as he and Karen walked down the hall toward their classroom.

Out of earshot he whispered, "Watching you walk down the hall, I couldn't believe you're mine. Sort of, anyway. Or at least you tolerate me after all these years. And might do so longer."

"No ifs, ands or buts about that, Matt," she replied softly, studying at his profile. Then, as he turned to face her: "I feel the same about you wanting just me. We do belong to each other."

He paused for a moment. Faced her fully.

"A minute ago, seeing you, I felt like I did this summer at Halen's Lake. Like last month. Wanting every part of you. Becoming one with you."

"Oh Matt, she said, tenderly touching his cheek. "I do love you. And I think this homecoming will be special for both of us."

"I guarantee it will," he said, holding the classroom door open. He felt so lightheaded he nearly let it slam in his face.

Huntington's Hornets took the field as odds-on favorites to win homecoming. They faced Stamford's top-rated Webster High School Wildcats.

By half-time, they led seventeen to three. Matt's dive up the middle into the end zone scored one TD. Jerry Jouret sprinted full field from kickoff for another. Points after touchdown and a field goal completed the tally.

Matt captained the offensive squad. And at half-time, escorted Huntington's Homecoming Queen to her "throne of honor." This year, the school's students elected Diane "Buttons" Simpson as their Queen. Hers and Karen's friendship spanned a dozen years. And Diane's father taught with Damon on Yale's medical faculty.

"Remember, buster," Karen playfully waved a tight fist under Matt's nose. "I'll watch from the sidelines. So no hanky-panky with Buttons! We cheerleaders kick pretty high. And I'll put your hanky pankier out of commission!"

Tradition cloaked high school homecomings then. Almost propagating a mystique of ceremonies. Boys toted large jugs of apple cider. Some of it hard, or cut with whisky snitched from some father's liquor cabinet. Coffee and hot dogs seldom tasted better than in the chilly night air.

Huntington's marching band seemed more in tune on homecoming turf. The school's precision drill team performed flawlessly. Its baton twirlers seldom missed a cue or toss.

In the second half, the Hornets devastated the Wildcats. They chalked three more touchdowns; off an end run and bullet pass by Matt. And another long yardage scramble by Jerry Jouret.

When the final whistle blew, bleachers on both sides of the stadium spewed spectators onto the field. Congratulating coaches and players. Stripping the crepe paper that encircled the goal posts to press as a souvenir in high school yearbooks.

The hapless Wildcats silently boarded their bright yellow school buses. Within minutes, the losers left on their quiet return to Stamford.

Karen and the other three cheerleaders disappeared into the girl's locker room. They changed into formals for the gala dance following the game.

In the boy's locker area, Matt and his teammates hit the showers. The steamy water and fragrant soap brought immediate relief after the hard-fought game. The combination helped ease the pain Matt felt in both knees. Jarring tackles took their toll this night.

In minutes, Matt scrubbed away the fatigue that ebbed during the final scrimmages. He toweled dry, and changed into his new grey suit. He examined himself approvingly in the full-length mirror.

"Behold," he announced ceremoniously to the other players in various stages of dress. "What stands before you is an escort worthy of guiding Buttons Simpson to her flowered throne."

Matt quickly fled the locker room amidst the splattering of soggy, wadded towels hitting the door behind him. Outside, he met Sid Blakemore, the defensive team captain. The two walked into the anteroom off the cafeteria and greeted the homecoming queen and her court.

Four players would escort the royalty onto the dance floor as the band played the school fight song. Matt took his place beside Buttons, and for the first time spied Karen in her formal. She was helping straighten the maids' rhinestone tiaras. He fought an impulse to rush and embrace her in the dim light.

Her skin radiated summer tan against the bright white tulle. Her eyes and teeth sparkled. And the ever-present smile broadened on seeing him.

She glided to where he stood.

"Hi," the smile beamed. She hugged his neck as he stooped and bussed her cheek. "You were wonderful, Matt. The whole team was. We're so proud."

"Either Stamford was down, or we're fair players after all," he said.

Nearby, the band struck the first chords of the school fight song. He turned from Karen, offered an arm to his escort. "That's our cue, Buttons. Now that I'm scrubbed, I don't feel self-conscious escorting you."

"That's okay, Matt," she replied. "There's something special about smelly football players that turns girls' heads."

She placed her hand on his arm, turned to Karen and winked. "May I keep him?"

"Sorry, Buttons. He's spoken for," Karen retorted.

"See you inside, hon," Matt smiled, putting his hand on top of Button's.

The couple trailed the other escorts and honorees into the makeshift ballroom. A huge revolving mirrored ball hung above the center of the dance floor. Black and gold crepe streamers looped beneath the ceiling and draped the walls. Folding wooden chairs lined all sides of the room.

The band launched into the school anthem. The throng of students parted, permitting the small procession's approach to the elevated paper mache court.

Karen and Matt danced every number. They stopped only for bottles of coke, or chatting with other couples crowding the compact lunchroom.

Matt couldn't take his eyes off her. Hated for the dances to end. Begrudged letting her go until the next song began.

During a break, while the band changed sheet music, he studied her as he had many times before. Admiring, and awestruck by her youthful beauty. He often called her "child woman;" a unique blend of innocence and maturity.

He flushed with pride when he noticed the class ring dangling on a fine gold chain. It nestled neatly in her cleavage, slightly exposed by the low-cut formal. He mused to himself the ring was the sun rising between two mountains. He squeezed her ribcage gently. Tugged her closer to his left side.

"I love you," he whispered. He kissed her soft hair, breathed the fresh scent of her shampoo.

Karen turned. The quizzical look flickered, fading into a sumptuous smile.

"I love you, too," she puckered and gave him a quick buss on the lips. Then turned into his arms as the band played "In The Mood."

The ten-piece orchestra consisted of top musicians from the marching band. They played loudly, but extremely well for high school bandsmen. They imitated the sounds of Glenn Miller, Benny Goodman and Tommy Dorsey. And the young man who played organ during assemblies mastered Duke Ellington's style.

Matt danced fair on slow songs. However, he couldn't negotiate the new jitterbug steps. No matter how much he and Karen practiced.

When the band blasted a fast number... "Stompin' At The Savoy" or "Take The A Train"...he and Karen retreated to the sidelines, clapped and watched the "boogey-woogiers" perform.

Huntington's principal came to the microphone at midnight. He paid tribute to the football team, the coach and the school's standing. And announced the last dance.

He then escorted Buttons Simpson to the floor. Surrounded by dozens of other couples, he twirled her to "String Of Pearls." Glaring cafeteria lights spelled the evening's end. Matt took Karen's arm and led her from the floor.

They stopped often to bid goodnight to friends. And chatted briefly with the coach and principal. These administrators standing and smoking at the exit, and shaking the hands of all leaving.

Matt opened the convertible's passenger door for Karen. Heard a shriek when the stiff formal lifted and her exposed thighs touched the cold leather seat.

Then he unlocked the door on the driver's side, slipped off his suit coat and settled behind the wheel. He inserted the ignition key, flipped the switch that unlocked the steering column, and pushed the starter button. The flathead engine cranked to life.

He let it rev for a moment, then shifted into reverse. Karen edged against him, shivering by his right shoulder. He lowered his head, kissed her softly on the mouth.

"Umm, tastes good," he said.

He backed onto the concrete driveway leading from the school parking lot and followed a parade of cars to the old highway that ran through western New Haven.

By the time Matt stopped at the padlocked gate, warm air circulated from the Ford's heater. He switched the headlights to parking lights. Karen, now warm and content, recognized the road leading through the woods a half mile behind the Durham's house.

He pulled on the emergency brake, keyed the lock and opened the gate. He steered the convertible through, pulled the gate shut, and reset the padlock.

"Does anyone ever come down here?" she asked, snuggling closer in the dark silence.

"No, hon," he said. He kissed lightly on top of her hair. "My folks are partying at your house. So we've got the woods to ourselves."

In bright moonlight, Matt steered the narrow path that ran alongside a creek bisecting the forest. He stopped at a clearing in a dense stand of cedars. He switched the lights off and pulled on the brake. Left the engine idling, and heater turned low.

He depressed the release, sliding the car's front seat fully back. He turned facing her. Slid his arms under hers and pulled her close. Karen's arms encircled his neck.

He felt her firm figure through the formal's stiff mesh. Lowered his hand to her waist. Karen rolled on her left side, and their bodies snugged.

He kissed her hungrily on the mouth. Her tongue explored his lips, eased into his mouth. They clutched together, sucking one another's breath.

Matt's hand located the zipper on the back of her formal. One fluid motion slid it open to her waist. He stroked the smooth, warm flesh of her back.

Using both hands, he pinched the catch on her brassiere. It unsnapped, and dangled loosely.

Soft moans undulated through Karen's lips. She breathed deeply, rapidly, exhaling through her nostrils. He lifted her gently, and she helped work the formal over her head. He placed it neatly in the back seat.

Karen's bra draped from her shoulders. He slipped it down her arms, exposing her firm breasts, nipples jutting with sensuous excitement.

He kissed her longingly on the lips. The side of her face. Her ear. And neck. He gently supported her left breast with his hand. Kissed it tenderly. His other hand eased between her legs.

Karen leaned against the seat. Lower torso forward. She parted her legs as Matt's hand explored her welcoming warmth. She unknotted his tie and opened his shirt. Her hands eagerly unfastened his belt and waistband catch. Slid the zipper over the firmness beneath her hand. Karen softly touched him. His breath caught.

She raised slightly, and he removed her garter belt, silk hose and panties. He added these to the clothes on the back seat. She delicately slid beneath him, while he slipped off his trousers. Then he was on his knees, poised between her legs.

"Please love me, Matt," she said in hushed, throaty tones.

"I do, darling," he said.

Afterwards, they lay for several minutes embracing. Bound together tightly. Legs entwined. Guy Lombardo music playing on the radio.

Matt whispered in her ear: "God, I love you Karen."

She lifted her head. Looked up at him. His face washed with pleasure and moonlight.

"Oh Matt, please say it always will be like this," she said. "We'll be together. Promise me."

"I promise, darling," he kissed her again lightly. Her warm body beneath him. Still encompassing him. Rekindling the longing. She sensed it, too. Clutched him to her again.

They made love twice more. At one-thirty Matt glanced at his wristwatch.

"I'd better get you home," he whispered.

She playfully pulled him tight in her arms.

"No, Matt Durham. Let's spend the night here in the woods."

"Believe me, Karen, I'd love to," he said, lifting away. "There's nothing I'd rather do. Our time's coming, though. Our future together isn't far away."

They dressed unhurriedly. He backed the car out of the clearing onto the crude road. The packed mud path gleamed silver in the moonlight.

"There aren't any lights on at our place," he said. He gestured toward the dark structures on the slight rise a half mile away. "My folks must still be at your house."

Cars lined the street outside the Forsythe's home.

"Good, they're still partying," Karen breathed relief. Matt switched the headlights off as he pulled into the long driveway beside the house. He stopped near the back door.

Karen leaned onto his shoulder. Snuggled against him. Took his arm in hers.

"This has been the most wonderful night of my life," she said over the lulling radio. "I never imagined anything could be so heavenly."

She sat abruptly upright. Matt turned toward her, surprised. Her face registered the quizzical look.

"You know, making love the first time combines good and bad... pain and pleasure. We're adults now, Matt. In some respects. Are we growing up too fast?"

"No honey," he cradled her face in his hands. "No more so than other kids. I'm sure our folks experienced the same emotions. The same doubts and desires."

"I want to spend the rest of my life with you," she said softly, her eyes tearing slightly. "And it's going by so quickly. We've already known each other for four years."

"Yeah...and I've loved you all that time!" He lifted her chin with his forefinger. Kissed her tenderly. "We've only got about eighty-five more years to go!"

"Oh, Matt. You know what I mean."

"Sure," he said, bussing her forehead. "C'mon, I'll walk you to the door."

They stood in the kitchen doorway, holding each other's hands. He stared into the upturned face. Again struck by the beauty reflected in the light streaming through the door.

"Goodnight, sweetheart," he kissed her once more and held her close. "Let's take in a matinee tomorrow. There's a 'Mr. Belvedere' movie at the Uptown."

"I'd love to," she said. She nuzzled his cheek, turned and opened the door and disappeared inside.

Matt climbed into the convertible, started it, pulled on the headlamps. He whistled happily as he backed up the drive.

"Matt Durham," he whispered aloud, "you're a lucky guy!"

He glanced back at the house as he pulled away and saw her waving from her upstairs bedroom window.

Two weeks later, another birthday and hunting season arrived for Matt. As a special present, his father, Damon and Judge Corley took him pheasant hunting near Hartford.

He sent Karen a postcard with a short note from the lodge where they stayed: "Write if you find work."

Karen and Matt grew closer after homecoming night. Now, with graduation six months away, they contemplated their college careers.

Matt won a scholarship to Connecticut State University in New Haven. Partly due to his football background. Mainly because of his academic abilities. Too, Conn State boasted an excellent journalism school.

"You know, son, Damon hoped you'd go into medicine," Walt told him after he'd voiced a career in journalism. "He'd like to see you at Yale. Says you'd be happier in surgery than perjury." Then Walt chuckled.

"It's your decision, Matt. Your life. Your mother and I know you'll make the best of it."

Karen earned an art scholarship to Hanley College; a private, expensive girls' school two blocks from Conn State. Hanley's art and design departments stood second to none. Karen's favorite high school instructor graduated from the college, and encouraged her to apply.

Conn State had nearly twenty fraternities. Matt received invitations from most before rush week. And attended several open-house parties.

He enjoyed meeting fraters at the various houses. In the end, Sigma Alpha Epsilon impressed him most and he accepted that house's pledge pin.

Understandably, it also was the fraternity to which his and Karen's fathers belonged at Yale.

"Like father like son," Walt kidded him. "Once a Sig Alph, always a Sig Alph. In fact, if it weren't a different chapter, I'd give you my old pin. If your mother kept it. You know, by the time I pinned her it was worn thin from being on so many girls!"

"Walter Durham, that's not true at all!" Claire objected from the kitchen where she prepared dinner. "You were too tall. And skinny. And boring! Always talking about engineering and airplanes. I was probably the only girl you dated. Now Damon, on the other hand..."

"Alright, Claire, you win!" he replied. Walt's eyes twinkled as he hung his arm around his son's shoulder.

The week before Thanksgiving, Huntington played its last football game against the Waterford Warriors. The Hornets held greedily to a perfect record. And ran to eighteen their string of consecutive wins over the past two years.

In the last minutes of the game, leading twenty-one to ten, stretching their standing to nineteen appeared eminent. Matt took the ball from his center on the Waterford thirty yard line, and dropped back to pass. One of his wide receivers scrambled along the right-hand sideline.

Suddenly, a large Warrior tackle lumbered through the left side of the offensive line and slammed Matt eight feet backwards. Then rode him to the ground.

When Matt collided with frozen earth, his shoulder blade cracked audibly. Within milliseconds, sharp pain twisted his upper body in agony. He watched through the instant blur of tears as the football bounced lazily off the tackle's back, then settled a few yards away where an alert Hornet recovered it.

Matt recalled that almost instantly Damon and his father were kneeling over him; dark silhouettes against the bright lights.

"Easy son, easy," Doctor Forsythe reassured him.

The physician pressed gently against Matt's chest to prevent movement. Matt raised his head slightly, and the pain shot through his upper body, drawing a moan from his lips.

Then Karen was beside him, sobbing heavily. Walt held and comforted her, and wiped the tears dribbling down her cheeks with his handkerchief.

"Don't worry, Karen, he'll be okay," Walt said, trying to conceal his own misgiving. "He's a tough kid. It's probably just a pulled muscle."

"I'm afraid it's more than that, Walt," whispered Damon. "His clavicle is splintered. It'll never heal completely."

The physician noticed the anguish watering his friend's eyes.

"We'll take x-rays to make sure, Walt. I'd bet on it, though. I'm sorry, Matt. It's going to lay you up for a while. And it'll probably keep you out of football."

The two men lifted and carried Matt to the sidelines. As an ambulance sped onto the field, Damon's words echoed in his mind, blocking the spectator's applause and obscuring a mumbled apology of the overzealous tackle.

Matt heard only Doctor Forsythe's voice repeating...he wouldn't play football again.

His concern was not for himself, however. From prone on the stretcher he looked at Karen, whose anguish surfaced in knitted brow and tear-streaked cheeks.

"Hey, I'm still alive," he smiled through the sharp jabs penetrating his chest with each word. Before he passed out, he squeezed her hand. "And I've still got an academic scholarship to Conn State."

The Hornet's relief quarterback, selected to head next year's lineup, finished the game for Matt. And led the team to another victory.

Matt wore a plaster cast for three months to keep the shoulder immobile. He and Karen frequently made love over the weeks that followed; even if clumsily. And a week before graduation he exchanged the heavy cast for an elastic and canvas halter that supported the crippled left arm.

The last day of their senior years culminated in the traditional all-night party held in the First Presbyterian Church basement. Karen and Matt joined ten other couples for an evening swim at a rock quarry outside of town.

They still sat around a small bonfire, listening to a car radio and yawning, as the late May sun poked its glistening face over the horizon.

In two weeks, Matt planned to be a college freshman, getting a summer's head start on his classmates. Still, he occasionally pondered, if only for a moment, about spending one last lazy summer with the girl asleep on his lap.

"Nah...there'll be lots more summers," he whispered into the peaceful face below.

Her eyes opened slightly. "Did you say something, Matt?"

"No," he kissed her eyelids closed again. "Get some sleep, honey. We'll drive out for breakfast soon."

Chapter 5

College Couple

COLLEGE IN JUNE 1947 WAS an education in itself. Without attending classes, preparing term papers or completing homework. Even though summer debuted on the Connecticut State University campus, the institution still bustled.

Students hurried to enroll or make last-minute class changes. Purchase texts and notebooks. Or grab a quick bite before the gymnasium opened its doors for registration.

Throughout the United States, thousands of ex-GIs descended on college campuses. Completing educations put on hold. Availing themselves of government money earmarked for veterans' educations. Or relaxing and raising hell in new roles as civilians.

The second "war to end all wars" had ended with Germany's surrender. Returning soldiers brought a devil-may-care flair to higher education that had not existed; nor probably will again.

Matt calculated he could graduate a year earlier by attending summer school. Over three years, he could collect eighteen hours during these sessions.

He still felt uncertain about graduate studies, so the one-year leeway would enable him to work. Then, if he felt he needed more schooling, he could re-enroll at the same level as his peers.

Through her high school art instructor, Karen landed a part-time job at Peck & Peck Interiors. Originally a New Haven interior design firm, it recently opened offices in New York and Boston.

She worked five days a week, and soon realized it would be her career niche. Charles Enright, Peck & Peck's owner, liked Karen immediately. And gave her increasingly challenging assignments.

By summer's end, and the beginning of Karen's freshman year, Peck & Peck noticed a surprising increase in interiors completed. Shortly before her fall term began, Enright called her at home.

"Karen, I'm frustrated and worried about finishing the work we've contracted," his voice registered panic. "Peck & Peck's reputation may be in the privy. Would you consider working part-time after classes and on Saturdays? You have such style, Karen. Please say you will. I'll make it worth your while."

She quickly acquiesced to his pleading.

"I can't promise every Saturday, Charles," she said. "I can work most of them, though. While Matt's hunting."

During their conversation, he complimented Karen repeatedly on her gift for interiors. He said she easily could become his top decorator.

Karen felt flattered.

What he said rang true. Several patrons already requested additional work because of her talented renderings. And asked for her by name.

"Bless you, Karen," he gushed, obviously relieved. "You're really saving my fat from the fire. Can you drop by for a while tomorrow?"

"Sure," she said. "I'm just enrolling. Matt says if Hanley operates like Conn State, there won't be full class periods."

"Good," he again sighed with relief. "I'll see you then."

"Good night, Charles."

Karen beamed as she went downstairs to tell her parents the good news.

The leaves had not yet begun turning. However, the early morning September air was crisp and fresh. Matt slumped comfortably in the convertible parked beside the curb in front of the Forsythes' home.

He drummed the steering wheel, anxious to collect Karen and help her enroll. Then they'd buy her supplies and books. And the next day, classes started at both universities.

Plus, he longed to see her again.

Matt weathered his maiden semester in college with flying colors. Earning top marks in sociology and composition. And already pre-enrolled for fall semester, opting a maximum load of eighteen credit hours.

His shoulder mended well over the summer. Still, Doctor Forsythe discouraged him from playing football for Conn State.

He decided early on to attack the more taxing required subjects by completing psychology, geology, biology, economics, American History and Spanish by the end of his sophomore year.

His high school standing enabled testing out of English and all but advanced math. This class he also decided to hold until the second year. There'd be more flexibility in his course schedule at that point, and he could pick more electives and lighten the load.

Since Hanley College catered strictly to women, Karen limited her extracurricular activities to tennis and painting. She retired her cheerleader's prowess and uniform to the Forsythes' attic, and like Matt, contented herself to be on the sidelines in sporting events.

"Hey, college girl, how 'bout a lift to campus?" he mused as she spotted him in front of her house.

She walked to where he parked. He climbed out, held open the door.

"Sorry," she put her arms around his neck, pecked him on the lips. "I only accept rides from seniors. Froshes have one thing on their little minds...and it isn't education!"

He chuckled, returned her buss, entered the car from his side.

"You're so right. And it's a darned good thing you have to register, or I'd attack you on your front lawn!"

"Promises, promises," she quipped, sliding beside him on the front seat. She hoisted his arm around her shoulders, nestled snug against him.

Evelyn and the doctor watched from the dining room window as they breakfasted. They smiled and waved to the handsome couple pulling away.

"I can't believe they're in college already," she said, grasping her husband's hand.

"Nor I, Evie," he replied. "One thing's for certain. They're getting older...not us."

A similar conversation had been held earlier at the Durham's house nearby.

Since the General's retirement in 1946 from the military, Connecticut Castings assigned him additional engineering research and development responsibilities.

In the latter part of the war, the company involved itself in designing, testing and producing airframes for fighters. Now, it tailored the same skills to commercial aircraft manufacture.

Walt traveled frequently to Washington, testifying before Congress on setting up a military branch called the "Air Force." This group would differ from existing air corps; its primary mission would be providing strategic air power.

Walt won the respect of the chiefs of staff. Overseas he got to know the Supreme Allied Commander of the Armed Forces, so the secretaries of the services listened to him. As did Harry S Truman, named President when Franklin Delano Roosevelt died in office.

With such prominent backing, Walt remained confident of Congress passing the proposal for a separate air service. The summer saw his hard work coming to fruition. The National Security Act created the U.S. Air Force from three different branches. Earlier in the month, it earned official recognition and approval.

Matt, meanwhile, enjoyed immensely the season, Karen, and the spellbinding, if sometimes morbid, tales told by warriors returning to civilian roles. Many of whom pledged his fraternity.

Then, the size of a frat's liquor cabinet underwrote its success. If well-stocked, the house flourished. While a skimpy supply implied lack of concern for those returning heroes who put their lives on the line.

Proximity loomed another key point. A brotherhood located near the women's dorms and sororities thrived.

Any within a quick walk of New Haven's major collegiate watering holes...The "Stables" and "Andy's Corner"... quickly filled pledge quotas.

Kappa Sigma stood atop a similar wooded hillside across from Sigma Alpha Epsilon. A small creek separated the arch rivals. Kappa Sig chartered its house at Connecticut State in 1883, two years after SAE built its house on a commanding promontory overlooking the western edge of the campus.

Gentlemen whose primary endeavors did not always focus on scholarly pursuits filled both houses. Open hostilities between the two groups raged for fifty years. Exacerbated in the early Twenties when Kappa Sigma bought the Tudor-style residence it now occupied.

Since 1900, a well-managed, fully staffed brothel existed at that location. A frequent stop-over spot for Sig Alphs lacking stamina to cross the creek and hike the steep hill to their residence.

Matt's and Karen's fathers pledged SAE at Yale. And they eagerly shared with the young man the tales of friendly inter-fraternity competition abounding on college campuses before World War I.

Their stories paled, however, stacked beside the rivalry thriving between the two houses claiming adjacent hills at Conn State. Midnight assaults prevailed. And retributions occurred swiftly.

Kappa Sigs engaged in early morning sorties, deprecating the SAE lion; a whitewashed cement statue standing vigil in front of the Colonial structure. Soon after, several Kappa Sig autos would "slip out of gear," and careen downhill into the trees.

Rival members regularly peppered each other's domiciles with B-B guns. Occasionally, well-aimed skyrockets, roman candles and aerial salutes added to the melee.

From the first, Matt cherished the camaraderie that flourished among the older fraters. Most served in the war. And regardless of military branch, stood loyal and ready to vindicate any wronged brother. At times, Matt wished he had been born earlier, and often felt he missed out on a crucially important event.

Other times, though, he reflected on his dad's letters. Written while the Allies battled for air superiority over England and France.

The general's writings outlined the death and destruction being wrought. And as a soldier, admitted deep remorse for a world settling its differences so inhumanely.

World War II whipped America's feelings to a froth. The public overlooked the atrocities. And instead, focused on the victorious events portrayed in the newsreels. On the screen, too, death seemed distant, unreal, and diluted by Hollywood hocus-pocus.

Matt recollected visiting a captured Japanese mini-sub that toured the U.S. It passed through New Haven. Crewed by paper-mache, uniformed, Japanese sailor mannequins.

He remembered their skin contrasting banana yellow against their black outfits. All displayed buck teeth and coarse mops of raven hair, and evilly slanted eyes rounded the effect.

Inside, on the vessel's bulkhead, hung photographs of the actual crew; slain when Marines captured the tiny vessel in a Philippine cove.

Throughout the sub's cramped interior, white circles pinpointed where machine-gun slugs dented or pierced the steel walls. Or ricocheted within the compact area, seeking and ripping flesh.

Matt recollected his uneasiness touring the enemy submersible. At the time, he reflected the hatred directed toward the midget craft.

It probably torpedoed American seamen. Therefore, it represented evil. Which in large measure accounted for its success as an allusive, stealthy, treacherous and destructive weapon.

Matt enjoyed the accounts of service life as embellished by his elder brothers. When occasionally he spent nights at the fraternity... after studying in its library...he laughed to tears over the pranks pulled. Typically, while the actives consumed a keg of beer before the huge living room fireplace.

In 1947, Sigma Alpha Epsilon at Conn State typified more than a conclave of forty men. It epitomized a gathering of blood brothers joined by a common incident; a close-knit family, beyond functioning as separate parts of a private club. Who instead, lived as sharing and caring comrades, daring the world or competing houses to cross them, their kith or kin.

Matt became quick and close friends with the man appointed his pledge father.

Spencer Ambrose "Jug" Hale, a junior five years his elder, found his schooling in Oklahoma interrupted by the war. He completed enough college to qualify as a Naval aviator, and successfully flew speedy fighter aircraft against German and Japanese pilots.

He earned his nickname flying the P-47 Thunderbolt, whose pilots affectionately shortened its designation from "Juggernaut" to "Jug."

When D-Day wrapped the war in Europe, Jug transferred to the Navy and kept flying. He became the Navy's top Ace, adding five Japanese Zeros to the four Messerschmitts collected over Germany.

Then he lost his right leg at the knee.

It happened during the invasion of Okinawa. A shrapnel-nicked oil line ruptured as he lined up for touch-down on the flight deck of the carrier, USS Bunker Hill.

Scalding oil gushed from the P-47's engine cowling and coated its bubble canopy. The sticky black film blinded Jug and he eased the control stick forward too quickly.

The aircraft's landing gears and propeller caught the leading edge of the flight deck, and its crippled fuselage tore apart in the grinding scream of metal scraping against metal. The twisting, crumpling metal instantly and cleanly severed Jug's leg.

Fortunately, shock set in and numbed the pain. He yanked open the oil-smeared canopy when the shattered aircraft ground to a stop amid tangled arresting cables. He unsnapped his parachute harness and seatbelts, and pulled himself out onto the P-47's left wing. Then wondered why he couldn't hold himself up...and looked down, at half a bloodstained pant-leg wetly flapping in the breeze that whipped the flight deck.

Jug clung to the edge of the plane's cockpit, praying against what he knew to be true. And passed out in the arms of his crew chief.

He had grown up a rawboned cowboy in the Oklahoma Panhandle, and shared Cherokee blood with thousands of other Sooners. Which showed in his narrow-slit, clear light blue, eyes and high, sharp cheek bones. Jug combed his thick, coarse black hair back from an inclined roach over his forehead, held firmly in place by Wildroot Cream Hair Oil.

At six-feet, three-inches, and two hundred and twenty-five pounds, he amassed All American halfback titles during his years at Oklahoma State University. The crack-up, besides taking half his leg, took his hopes of returning to the range life he loved.

"Goddamned if I'll ride sidesaddle," he grumbled, and often.

The Veterans Administration fitted Jug with an artificial limb. He still occasionally experienced sharp pains that doubled him, flooded his eyes and made him groan audibly.

When the VA released him in Boston, he migrated as far as New Haven and his favorite uncle; a lucky wildcatter who hit oil on his Oklahoma spread, and opted to trade it for whatever he wanted and the East Coast offered.

The uncle convinced Jug to enroll at Conn State, after letting the recuperating flyer drink his way through an entire summer, swimming in booze and self pity.

Spence Hale received nearly every decoration the United States could pin on him, and quickly and warmly welcomed and accepted the friendship and admiration Matt and Karen bestowed.

He selected Karen as his personal "Little Sister," and would focus lake blue eyes on Matt and menacingly growl:

"Kid, you better treat Little Sister right."

Matt would reply, "You can count on it, sir."

Sometimes wondering if Jug intended to sound so threatening.

"Hot rock Army Air Corps flyers...except your old man, Matt... brag the P-51 Mustang broke the backs of the Axis," Jug postulated one evening. "Well, that's bullshit!"

A red oak fire roared and crackled nearby as Jug tried washing down a Friday night steak dinner with four or five large tankards of beer. Which did little to ease the painful throb in his stub of a leg; just made his senses burn brighter through the mask of alcohol.

"The P-47 and F-4U Corsair were the most dependable aircraft ever," he continued, after hobbling for a refill.

"Hell, we'll use 'em long after Mustangs and P-38 Lightnings land in museums. Especially the P-47. I've slammed that snub-nosed gal smack into the deck of a carrier with half her undercarriage shot away...only control cables holding her together. We'd repack the ammo boxes and I'd take off again. The P-47 stood anything!"

"Now Jug, don't be so hard on the Mustang," Jody McClellan, also a junior and ex-Army pilot, defended his favorite machine. "After all, it saved Great Britain's ass when Me-109s and FW-190s infested the Empire, didn't it?"

Jody McClellan also had collected a chestful of medals during World War II, and with a dozen comrades flamed to earth over the Ploesti oil fields.

He commanded a P-51 fighter group that provided cover for B-24s making low-level bomb drops on the refinery. Screaming in, a hundred feet up at three hundred miles per hour, he realized too late that the bombers preceding his flight had fallen far behind schedule.

"Blue Danube," the first flight of twelve B-24s, dropped fifteen minutes late over the target. When their delayed-fuse charges detonated, the explosions nearly decimated the second group lining up for its run on the target.

When Jody's flight arrived over Ploesti minutes later, German anti-aircraft gunners waited; well-practiced and range adjustments honed on earlier groups. Their deadly accurate cannons cut his formation to pieces.

"Hell, Jug, even the smugged up Brits loved the Mustang," he added. "Modeled their planes after the P-51. Harriers and Spitfires and the like."

"Yeah...that may be true, Jody old pal," Jug retorted, momentarily forgoing brew for cigarettes. "Only because the Limeys couldn't copy the P-47, let alone fly her!"

Jug originally flew P-47s in a bomber-pursuit group under Walt Durham's command. In fact, met and drank with the general once. At a tiny airfield in England, where he received one of his many decorations, and a few days' rest and relaxation.

Spence respected and trusted General Durham. When the war had ended in Europe, it was Walt who helped arrange the flyer's transfer to the Navy. And who also sent several "buck up" telegrams as Jug lay recovering in Boston's VA hospital.

Walt visited Jug upon his own release from active duty, which probably influenced the Oklahoman's decision to be Matt's pledge father, good friend, and in occasional scraps, his guardian.

"Other than you flying it, what made the Thunderbolt so special?" Matt asked, stepping in the middle of the squabble between the veteran aviators.

"I'll tell you, young plebe," Jug retrieved the pewter mug, situated it against his lips and pulled long and deep. "There will never again be a more dependable aircraft put together and flown. Sure, you contended with her heavy nose taking off and landing."

He paused for another slug of beer.

"Airborne, she handled like a dream. Full throttle, she'd flatten you in the seat. Shove the stick forward or yank it back...she'd out-dive or out-climb anything. Screaming like a banshee all the while."

Jug paused briefly as his mind replayed a memory.

"I've dropped flaps and gears, throttled back and nearly stopped in midair. That's a trick we pulled when Krauts or Japs got on our tails. They'd zoom past, and we'd open throttle, catch up and bust their butts!"

The warm fire and beer conspired to float Jug's mind back to happier days of aerial adventure.

"In a dogfight, the P-47 really jinked. And on strafing runs, you'd kick your rudder side-to-side and she'd shimmy and spray lead over a fifty-yard area."

He put his huge hand gently on Matt's shoulder.

"On top of all that, Matt, you felt the P-47. Felt her vibrate. Felt her engine throb. If it ticked off a fraction, your asshole puckered. You flew and lived as one. And when a heart beats under your rear-end for eight hours straight, you get used to its rhythm."

Jug felt his point made, and settled comfortably into the easy chair. He stared into the fire, his mind's eye running spools of memories that highlighted life in the air.

"That's what made the P-47 special," he said softly to himself. "She almost killed me...but I loved that goddamned airplane."

Then he fell silent, succumbing to the effects of beer and the dancing hypnotic flames. The pain in his leg subsided at last.

Jody slouched in the easy chair beside him, also silent in slumber. Rough hewn heroes nodding before the blaze.

The other brothers had disappeared hours ago; off studying or on dates. Matt sat a few minutes...surrounded by the peaceful quiet... recognizing and understanding the sadness that tinged his comrades' voices and colored their recollections.

He felt no remorse.

Not for the crippled cowboy, living differently than he planned, whose pride battled daily against his handicap. Instead, he admired and respected Jug for bravely facing the challenges. For rearranging his future to fit reality's mold. And forgoing long-gone dreams of becoming a commercial pilot.

Matt rose slowly, walked to where the two slumped, and patted his pledge father lightly, affectionately, on the shoulder. Then he crossed the living room through the flickering shadows, walked out the front door to his car, and headed for Karen's house.

As he drove, he felt even closer to the sleeping pilots. Decided he'd like to fly, too, if he ever entered the military. Like Jug. Like his father.

For that compelling reason, Matt Durham enrolled as one of the first cadets in Conn State's Reserve Officers Training Corps for the newly named U.S. Air Force.

Throughout their freshman, sophomore and junior years, Karen and Matt studied together nightly. She, seeking his advice on fabrics, paintings, color schemes or favorite subjects. He, begging comments on his latest advertisement or article for class or <u>The Clarion</u>, Conn State's student newspaper.

Matt ranked as a "fair writer" according to Frank Duffy, his advisor and favorite journalism professor. For more than thirty-five years, Frank's bylines topped news articles on weeklies and dailies from Maine to Medford.

He wrote some of them sober; but not the three that garnered Pulitzer Prizes.

"Durham, words are the footprints of man's mind on paper," he espoused frequently. "Follow 'em closely. Pay attention to their direction. They'll lead you to wisdom and truth."

Frank's wizardry with a red editing pencil made surgeons envious. He deftly scalpeled verbiage from even the most parsimonious prose.

Hackneyed expressions; passive verbs; meaningless jargon; none left the operating table he called the copy desk.

"Don't grow up like me, Matt; at least in some respects," the copy editor told his protégé once when melancholy burned through the bourbon; which occasionally happened after proofing an edition and readying it for bed.

"And don't drink scotch...which tastes like owl piss and shoe polish. Or gin, which is English antiseptic. Drink sour mash...a man's elixir. Distilled for a person like me...a drinker with a writing problem."

Matt watched the editing pencil carve extraneous words.

"And another thing...don't waste your writing skills on advertising. Sure, the big money's in puffery; but, the world needs writers like you to cut through the crap."

Now the grizzled editor shook the pencil in his direction.

"Someone who can string facts together so anyone can read and understand 'em. Possibly even disagree with 'em...and start thinking for himself or herself!"

Since Matt edited the school newspaper, the J-School Dean collared him to help Professor Duffy assemble and polish the college yearbook. The pair collected, sorted and sized hundreds of photographs for cramming into one hundred-plus pages, and sketched rough layouts of the fraternity, sorority and local advertising sections.

When Karen's call came, Matt was praying for relief from tagging humorous captions under faculty photos. The professor snapped up the phone and answered in his best pressroom demeanor.

"Duffy here!"

Matt watched as the instructor immediately softened.

"Oh sure, honey...just a minute." He cupped the mouthpiece and turned facing him. "For you, Matt."

Then, so Karen could hear: "Must be that little redhead you raved about an hour ago."

"Gosh, thanks prof," Matt chided, snatching the handset. "Hi sweetheart, what's doing?"

"Little redhead, huh?" Karen feigned mock anger. "Listen, buster, keep in mind what I can do to a certain person's hanky-pankier!"

"Yes ma'am," he replied in snappy military tones. "We certainly don't want that!"

Frank smiled as he eavesdropped on the two needling one another.

"What time do you finish, Matt?" she asked. "My parents would like you and your folks for dinner tonight. After all, you leave for The House next weekend."

"Yeah, I know," he said, exasperated. "There's never enough time anymore."

Karen nodded as he ticked off activities.

"The autumn fraternity ball is next Friday night. And house officers and their pinned ladies must attend; it impresses the pledges. Then Homecoming's two weeks later...and Thanksgiving and Christmas."

"Plus, you left out an important birthday," she added. "Your days as a teenager are closing.

"Only physically," he replied. "Not in mind and spirit. Listen, if you want me out of here at a decent hour, let me get back to work. Duffy the slave driver punches my time card."

"This might be the perfect night for our announcement, Matt," Karen whispered. "Unless you're getting cold feet."

"Not a chance of that, sweetheart. Sure, I'll come for dinner and we'll throw the folks for a loop! Fall Festival is at hand...and there's lots of planning to do."

That evening, the three couples dined on Evelyn's succulent pot roast, prepared deep-dish fashion with onions, potatoes and carrots nestled around it. Broccoli, smothered in lemon-cream hollandaise sauce, complemented the main course, while pineapple upside-down cake and coffee topped it.

"Walt, what's this squabbling in northern East Asia?" the doctor asked the general later over dry sherry.

"Hard to tell, Damon. Intelligence says flare-ups between communists and anti-communists. Newspapers agree. Most of the military expect trouble where the 38th Parallel splits the country. That's what General MacArthur warned about...and the Chinese aren't lessening any fears, either."

"Will it flare up and involve the United States, Walt?"

"Could be, Damon. If the commies take up arms, we'll step in and help the people in the south. And it's a safe bet China and Russia will back the northern region."

"Lord, I pray that doesn't happen, Walt," Evelyn seemed stricken. "We've only begun recovering from the horrors of the last war."

For a few minutes, the group sat silent. Noticeably disturbed by discussing the slightest possibility of the United States involving itself in a skirmish in yet another corner of the world.

Matt stood, clinked his glass with the fraternity ring Karen gave as a stocking stuffer last Christmas. He reached down, took her hand, lifted her to her feet.

"Ladies and gentlemen," he said, suddenly, nervously serious. "We have an announcement."

The Forsythes and Durhams looked at each other, faces puzzled. Evelyn and Claire took each other's hands.

"With your permission and blessings...we're announcing our engagement." He paused for a moment, cleared his throat. "I've asked Karen to marry me after I graduate next summer. And she said 'yes'."

Walt sat his glass down, and in seeming slow motion rose and shook his son's hand. Then he hugged Karen, and enfolded them both in his arms. Damon did likewise.

"I take it we have your okay," Karen beamed.

The doctor spoke first.

"Yes, you certainly do, young lady. Congratulations, both of you. You're a handsome couple. I wish you the love Evie and I have known. Walt...Claire...we've shared our lifetimes; it's fitting we share our kids."

"We've got a good start toward the love you're talking about, sir," Matt said, clutching Karen close. "I've been crazy over this girl for eight years. Looks like some flaws would appear over that period."

He leaned down, kissed her forehead.

The doctor disappeared momentarily and reappeared with a bottle of champagne and six glasses tinkling against each other.

"I meant for us to toast the Fall Festival later," he said. "We'll put it to even better use."

The cork popped beneath a towel wrapped around the bottle's neck, and Damon poured everyone a full glass.

The others stood; Evelyn and Claire smiling broadly, arms still locked.

"Here's to you kids," the doctor said, lifting his glass in a salute to the couple. "And what you feel for each other. May those feelings comfort you. And grow even stronger over your years together."

"Thank you, daddy. And mom," Karen turned first from one to the other.

"You've made me happy throughout the years. Right now is the happiest I've ever been."

Her eyes filled, and Karen buried her face in Matt's shoulder. He cradled her tenderly.

Another fall melded quickly into autumn.

Then winter arrived decked in snow, painting Connecticut stark white from one end of the state to the other. And once again, Christmas holidays disappeared under heaps of wrapping paper, ribbon and tinsel.

Soon, spring erupted in a blaze of tulip trees, azaleas, magnolias, redbud and dogwood blossoms, touched here and there by canary flashes of forsythia.

Spring of 1950 ranked among the most breathtaking ever gracing the lawns, parks and woodlands of New Haven. It heralded Matt's final college semester, his plans for graduation, and, more important, his intent to make Karen his wife.

It also raised the curtain on Korea.

Chapter 6

Flight Training

I N MAY 1950, CONNECTICUT STATE University graduated its seventieth class of students. Matthew Ellston Durham stood twenty-first in the line of two hundred and ten students.

He graduated Summa Cum Laude with bachelors degrees in journalism and English literature. And earned gold bars as a second lieutenant in the U. S. Air Force. Matt was one of fifteen cadets commissioned through Conn State's Air Force ROTC program.

Walt and Claire Durham sat on one side of Karen. Damon and Evelyn Forsythe on the other. They applauded heartily when Matt strode across the elevated stage at one end of the basketball court. The gymnasium remained the only building on campus that seated several thousand people. As Matt clutched his degrees, sweat trickled down his spine under the black silk graduation gown.

Then graduation ended.

Nearly four years of untold hours, evenings and weekends... sacrificing and postponing personal wants and desires...fell twenty feet behind as he walked across a wooden stage, shook hands with the dean, and grasped the two parchment scrolls.

Matt's heart pounded proudly, clinging to his rolled and beribboned sheepskins. He descended three stairs and joined those preceding him. He threw a quick glance, broad smile and wink at Karen and the parents, then turned and watched the remainder of the ceremonies.

At eighteen, Matt registered with his local draft board like thousands of other young men. Now, with hostilities increasing in Korea, he applied for flight school.

In a month, he received orders to the U.S. Air Force Primary Flight Training School in Greenville, Mississippi.

Walt Durham donned his general's uniform for the official commissioning and armed forces swearing-in ceremonies. Twenty other young men joined Matt in taking oaths.

Walt never felt prouder than when he pinned gold bars on his son's blue uniform, and the two embraced briefly. Then General Durham stepped back, stood at attention, and snapped a salute to the junior officer...who returned it sharply.

"It's difficult turning your back on more pleasant and desirable things...to go serve your country," the general said on the drive home.

"Still, that's what some of us must do if our country means anything. We want her free and proud...or we help allies who want the same thing."

Both men fell silent for several minutes. Walt turned words in his mind, then spoke.

"I know how much you love Karen, son. How tough it is postponing the wedding until this is over. You've made the right decision, though."

Walt's eyes misted as he reflected on times past.

"I hurt a lot, being away from your mother through two wars. Hurt, hell! Separation came closer to killing me than flying! We lived through it, though. And it strengthened our relationship. We certainly realized how much the other person meant."

Walt reached over, slapped his son's knee.

"I've never said standing up for something is easy, Matt. It's just something a man has to do when he feels the time is right."

Matt turned, looked into his father's profile.

"What's it like, dad? You know, flying against the enemy? What's involved in becoming a good fighter pilot?"

"I'll tell you what I know, Matt," the general answered, pulling the car in front of the house and stopping. He turned and faced his son.

"Understand, a fighter pilot is a different breed. He's alone once he takes off. Even though twenty others are flying beside him...he's got his own little piece of air to protect. That's what he thinks about."

Walt stroked his chin thoughtfully.

"Fighter pilots are like Spencer Hale. Hell, he could have flown bombers. Still, he knew he could do a better job if he didn't have to worry about four men in the back of the plane."

The general ran his hands through his hair, and rubbed his eyes as if tired.

"Sure, you've got responsibilities to those you're flying with. Together, you perform like a precision team. When it comes down to it, though, you have to count on number one."

Walt turned to fully face the young man.

"A fighter pilot is a knight jousting another knight. You don't hate your opponent. Most of the time you don't know or think about him. There's just this driving desire to prove your machine and skills are better."

Walt switched off the ignition, clasped the keys, and pointed one toward Matt.

"Remember this...the Air Force will give you the best training and equipment available. It's your duty to reach down inside and find that special ingredient that makes the combination jell into a fighter pilot. Without that magic, you're better off on the ground."

"How do you know if you have that 'special ingredient,' dad?"

"You'll know, son. The first time you're head to head with the enemy. It'll surface if it's there."

"I think it's there, dad," Matt replied. "In fact...I'm certain it is."

"It is, Matthew," Walt squeezed his son's arm, opened the car door, and pulled himself out. "It runs in the Durham family. Now, come inside shavetail and I'll buy you a beer!"

June was extremely happy and hectic for Karen and Matt. They were together daily. Swimming; sightseeing up and down the coast; or going to The House with her parents. And, occasionally, the Durhams.

July arrived in a rash of hot, muggy days. Humidity reached highs that collected dew-like on the outsides of windows and instantly turned fresh clothes limp.

On the Fourth, the two families picnicked at Rock Park on New Haven's outskirts. They touched off firecrackers, sparklers, fountains and Roman candles, then watched the hour-long public fireworks display.

Matt and Karen made love frequently; often with carefree abandon. Carried away with passion, and paying little heed to precautions. Rather, striving to possess each other. Fully and completely. As many times as possible, before separating.

The general's string-pulling arranged a morning flight on a military transport headed for Greenville. The night before Matt left, he and

Karen returned to the quiet clearing near the creek in the private woods behind his house.

They first made love there, and returned many times since. And now lay naked together in the bright moonlight; fully touching, and welcoming cool evening breezes that rattled the trees.

The couple addressed the future.

"Dad and I talk for hours about Korea," said Matt, leaning against the car door with Karen stretched beside him.

"Why we're involved there, for example. I'm unconvinced about that. It's a political move, or we're rattling our sabers in front of the Chinese. Still, the U.S. is sacrificing American lives trying to settle conflicts in a country that's no threat to us. I just hope it's worth it."

"Darling...let's not discuss it any more," Karen put a finger on his lips, then kissed his bare shoulder. "I hear enough on the news...and read enough in the newspapers. I already despise Korea for taking you away."

"Only for a little while, honey."

Matt rolled onto his left side, slid his arm around Karen's waist, and pulled her warm waiting body tight against his. She felt his yearning, and kissed him hotly through his words.

"I'll come back...count on it. We'll build that house and family. And a lot of years together."

She rolled onto her back and pulled him on top. Once again, a single shape in the moonlight, in the cool, bright, quiet woods.

The general dedicated his remaining days with Matt to describing flight school, and soon found himself caught in the exhilaration of flying again. And hankering to climb into a jet fighter like those debuting in Korea.

"I've topped three hundred knots in a P-51 Mustang," he told Matt excitedly. "That's the fastest I've flown. These new jets fly nearly twice that. Hell, they break the sound barrier regularly!"

They discussed the basics of aerodynamics: lift, thrust and drag. And flying itself...involving yaw, pitch and roll. The subjects he'd studied as an AFROTC flight cadet.

Matt quickly grasped many of flying's basic components. Frat house discussions with returning "plane drivers" also filled blanks left by classroom lectures.

The relative ease with which his son caught onto new concepts pleased Walt, and Matt's keen interest convinced him the young man would be a quick, natural and skillful flyer.

A small group gathered at the East New Haven Airport to watch Matt board the olive drab DC-3 warming its engines. And pride twinkled the general's eyes as he inspected the young lieutenant standing before him, his arms encircling his fiancé and his mother.

"Matt, find a good top sergeant to latch onto, and you'll breeze through flight school," Damon quipped as the two shook hands.

The doctor momentarily clutched him close.

"Seriously...listen and pay attention, and you'll make out better than most. And don't volunteer for anything!"

Matt kissed his mother and Evelyn good-bye, when a young captain in flying khakis opened the side door of the aircraft. He nodded to the general.

Matt picked up the leather flight bag his father gave him, and with one arm, pulled Karen close for a final kiss. He looked into the beautiful face, etched with silvery tear trails, and felt his heart flip, realizing she was his.

"Good-bye, honey," he whispered. "I'll be home before you know it."

Then he turned to his father.

"Well, General, I'll remember what you've taught me." He clasped Walt's hand and firmly hugged him.

"You'll show 'em what flying is, son," Walt returned the squeeze. "Keep your eyes open and your head out of the cockpit!"

He boarded the DC-3, stowed his flight bag in a forward compartment, then settled into one of the firm seats that lined the transport.

Through the small rectangular window, he looked upon the cluster of loved ones seeing him off, returning their waves as vigorously as possible.

"Fasten your seat belt, lieutenant, and we'll try to get this thing off the ground," the captain shouted through the open cabin door over the roar of the airplane's engines.

Matt heart the pilot throttle up and the transport began rolling slowly.

The captain taxied to the turnabout loop at the runway's end, and amidst a deafening, vibrating, clattering drone the aircraft sped down the concrete strip.

Matt felt himself pushed backward against the cushioned seat, and soon the plane's tail lifted as the pilot eased back the control yoke, coaxing the DC-3 away from the ground.

Below, East New Haven Airport shrank to a cluster of six or seven buildings. The group of well-wishers appeared tiny dots on the white tarmac.

New Haven Julys ranked as scorchers.

Matt reckoned July in Greenville, at a rehabbed World War II flight training facility, came as close to Hades as he ever hoped to come.

The base sprawled over a hundred acres of flat Mississippi River delta land. Breezes stirring across this vast, bone dry cotton country singed where they touched.

Primary school consisted of four hours of basic military training daily, including marching in unit formation on concrete so hot it burned the feet bottoms through heavy-soled combat boots. Or on asphalt that bubbled and formed sticky pools which clung like discarded gum to footwear.

Greenville's flight school boasted sixty two-seater Piper Cubs, most of which logged countless hours as WWII artillery spotters. They flew slow and nose heavy, but the Piper was easy to maintain, extremely dependable and forgiving of pilot error. Plus, the little yellow aircraft withstood punishment well. And in lashing crosswind landings, dished it even better.

The young captain shepherding Matt's group flew fighters during the last two months of the War; then volunteered to stay in Greenville as an instructor, and complete his military obligation.

In the meantime, a Greenville girl charmed him into marriage. So he decided to "stay put" until his number came up for jet training.

His promotion to major seemed imminent, and remaining an aviator summed his career goals.

Like many other war-seasoned flyers Matt came across, the captain knew of his father, and readily recognized the general's role in establishing a separate air force. The admiration voiced by these veterans about Walt quickly transferred to the young man.

Matt amazed and impressed instructors and peers alike with his quick learning and natural ability to make aircraft perform as he wished; smoothly and swiftly.

By the middle of September, he had logged nearly twenty-five hours of dual instruction flights in the Piper. And suddenly, the time arrived for flying solo.

Soloing traditionally occurred on Fridays, and this one dawned crisp, bright and clear. The control tower reported visibility good enough to see twenty miles up the Mississippi.

Matt gave the little Piper a thorough pre-flight inspection under the watchful eye of his instructor. He checked the tires and engine intake. Worked the rudder, elevators and ailerons; checking the hinges for wear. He tested for water in the gas tank.

After completing the checklist...and satisfied with the soundness and operability of external surfaces...he opened the cabin door and swung up into the two-seater's cramped interior.

Matt slid open the Plexiglas passenger window and worked the rudder pedals. He watched as half the yellow vertical tail swung smoothly side to side.

Then he pulled and pushed the control stick, watching the left and right elevators raise and lower, and moved the stick from side to side, to see ailerons on each wing lift and drop.

One by one he went through the items on his takeoff checklist. And finally, he signaled thumbs up to his instructor, who slowly turned the propeller clockwise in a full circle.

"Switch off," the captain shouted to Matt.

"Switch off," Matt replied.

The other spun the propeller hard.

"Switch on," the captain barked, and again took hold of the wooden prop.

"Switch on," repeated Matt.

He flipped the toggle ignition switch as the captain let go the prop, and this time, the Piper's motor contacted and sputtered to life.

Matt eased the throttle forward a notch, and the light plane vibrated and strained against the chocks and hand-brake holding it back.

With his left hand, he throttled the engine to a loping idle as the captain yanked away the chocks, looked at him, smiled and motioned for him to take off.

Matt saluted, released the handbrake, and the Piper began rolling. He inched the throttle forward, braked to the right onto the taxiway and beamed as the captain returned the thumbs up gesture.

As he taxied, he tried to relax while keeping the nose pointed straight down the approachway, and watching for movement out the side windows. He eased back on the throttle to slow his speed as he entered the warm-up and takeoff circle. Then braked the machine to a halt.

"Okay, Durham," he whispered aloud. "Let's show them a smooth one."

He throttled the Piper, let off the brakes, and soon saw concrete zipping under the nose. A rushed takeoff loomed his greatest fear at this point; but then, amazingly, ground speed appeared adequate and the plane's tail lifted on its own.

"Damn...she's ready to fly!" he exclaimed aloud.

When Matt eased the stick back, he suddenly saw blue sky in place of brown cotton plants.

"I'm flying! I'm soloing!" he shouted over the engine's beat, and his heart pounded so hard he thought it would explode through his chest.

Within moments, he regained composure. Certain actions needed taking. Flight instructions crowded into his brain began surfacing in orderly fashion and, automatically, he became one with the airplane.

Matt checked his altimeter and leveled off at five thousand feet, then set a due West course as outlined in his flight plan.

"This is Heaven," he murmured, moving the control stick easily to the left against a light southwesterly wind.

The steady hum of the Piper's engine serenaded him into a feeling of reverie. The up and down tugs when he changed altitude compounded the sensation of floating. Effortlessly, he picked his way through puffy white cumulus clouds ahead.

Matt moved the control stick further to the left, and the wing on that side dipped. He could see the delta valley, a patchwork quilt of green and brown fields, all shapes and sizes. And the wide Mississippi, bisecting the land.

He shoved the stick to the right, and as that wing lowered, made out the town of Greenville. Feeling more at ease, he toed the right rudder pedal forward. The small machine slowly turned, and the flight school appeared out the passenger's window. Matt checked his watch. Already he'd been up nearly half an hour; practicing turns, climbs and dives, and all the time feeling more at home off the ground.

"Now, baby, let's see if I'll get us down in one piece," he finally uttered, patting away a slight film of dust clinging to the instrument panel. "And we will have licked this bugger!"

Matt swung the Piper's nose until the airfield disappeared beneath it, then began throttling back, banking for an East-to-West approach. His landing check-off list rested in his lap, and he began verbally going through the preparations.

When he completed final preparations, the Piper hovered at two thousand feet and a half mile from the end of the runway.

Matt saw the control tower flashing green to land, so he gave the Piper more power and aligned it on the airstrip. At a quarter mile out, and five hundred feet up, he judged the craft at the proper angle...and throttled back.

In seconds, the runway blurred beneath him, and he nudged the stick to the right to make up for a slight crosswind. Then the ground came to meet him.

A slight bump told Matt his wheels had touched, and as the Piper's nose lifted he cut the throttle completely. When the tail wheel contacted, he pumped the small brake pads above the rudder pedals.

Soon, the plane rolled slow enough for him to add throttle and turn toward the hangar area.

As he approached the tarmac outside the hangars, the group of candidates and instructors cheered and jumped up and down like school kids at a birthday party. Twenty feet from them, he spun the Piper around snappily, stopped and switched off the engine.

Matt unbelted and stepped out, and only then realized how much his legs were shaking. He supported himself on one of the airplane's wing struts until calmness returned, as his classmates pounded his back enthusiastically.

In October, Matt graduated from primary flight training. Along with twenty others in his class, he received orders directing him to basic flight training at Lacklin Air Force Base near San Antonio, Texas.

The government built Lacklin toward the end of World War II. It served as the major facility for B-29, B-25 and B-24 training, and rated as one of the newer U.S. bases.

Lacklin's runways stretched a half mile since its primary mission focused on bombers and heavy transport aircraft. The concrete strips intersected so planes took off and landed against the wind regardless of its direction.

Additionally, parallel taxiing roads made possible several aircraft lifting off simultaneously.

Matt enjoyed his tour outside San Antonio, and developed a fondness for Mexican food washed down with Tex-Mex beer. Most of all, he loved flying full throttle at treetop level over the flat scrub land surrounding the base for hundreds of miles in all directions.

Student pilots at Lacklin graduated to larger, heavier and more powerful T-6 and T-28 aircraft. He especially enjoyed flying the T-28, with its large sliding canopy, stiff hydraulic controls, retractable gears and a gutturally loud radial engine that roared to life with a touch of the ignition button. When a T-28 fired up, the ground shook.

Matt rapidly learned the intricacies of short takeoffs under full power, and soon felt comfortable dropping flaps to bleed air speed when landing, or to increase lift on take-offs.

He thought of Karen constantly, and sent her letters weekly. And when the longing and missing got to be too much, checked out a plane and flew low over the desert; clearing his mind, and scaring the wits out of jackrabbits, antelope, cattle and unsuspecting ranchers happening onto the prairie that day.

Walt wrote his son regularly, often penning a brief ending to letters his wife wrote. He kept Matt abreast of events occurring during the hunting season at The House, and recounted tales of his visits to Lacklin during the "Big War" when the bomber school first opened.

Matt relished one story in particular.

It occurred in the summer of 1945; when Lacklin turned out bomber crews almost daily...flying B-24 Liberators.

By sheer misfortune, a group of prominent nouveau riche Texans opened a nudist colony in the only wooded area for two hundred miles. Unfortunately, they located it just ten miles west of the base.

In no time, it became great sport for pilots to buzz the area at fifty feet, open bombay doors, and let crew members ogle and photograph the naked bodies that scampered for cover.

The base commander received frequent indignant letters from state officials, and finally proclaimed the area restricted. Further, he chopped flight plans approaching within ten miles of the site.

The day General Durham inspected the base, he listened as a flight crew received reprimands for flybys over the nudists. When the fliers denied the charges, the Security Officer Of The Day produced tree branches found hanging from the bombay doors.

Christmas in San Antonio found Matt homesick and lonely, even though he shared the holiday with several friends he'd made in primary flight school.

Houston "Hoot" Gibson...Matt's closest buddy and roommate... also hailed from Connecticut. His father published weekly newspapers and a magazine out of Middletown; halfway between New Haven and Hartford.

Like Matt, Hoot earned a bachelor's degree in journalism, although from New York University. He dreamed of helping his father run the chain of weeklies; eventually taking one over, or buying it outright.

"Look at it this way, Matthew," Hoot beamed Christmas Day as the two sat among wrappings and litter from presents received and opened. "I'll bet our folks are up to their kneecaps in snow, and it's colder than a well digger's ass!"

Hoot refilled their coffee cups from a bubbling pot they kept perking on a hot plate, and continued his patter.

"And here we are: warm, well-fed, flying as much as we want, and it's comfortable during the day in just a flight suit. Hell, my boy...what's to complain about?"

"I'm not really complaining, Hoot," Matt replied, wincing as he sipped the scalding coffee. "We're too busy to gripe. It's just...this is my first Christmas away from home. I didn't enjoy celebrating my twenty-first birthday by telephone, either. Hell, I couldn't have my first legal drink because we were up with the chickens and flying formations!"

"Yeah, partner...but we made up for it that weekend, didn't we!" Hoot exclaimed. "I've never seen a gringo pack away so much Mexican food and servesa!"

Earlier in the month, the two enjoyed a three-day goose hunt at a nearby private club. On the return trip, the radio announced that United Nations ground forces in Korea had suffered a setback.

Several units of MiG-15 jet fighters had advanced their area of operations to highlands between the Yalu and Chongchon Rivers. American long-range F-84E jet fighters in this region were escorting the B-29s that regularly pounded North Korea's industrial cities.

Later in the year, American pilots would refer to this air space as "MiG Alley."

Fresh spring blossoms burst through the arid Texas landscape shortly before Matt, Hoot and sixteen others received new orders.

Over the months, four of their comrades washed out for various reasons. And those remaining with the original group that formed in Greenville, Mississippi, suffered deep in their guts for each classmate who departed their ranks.

The students' next stop took them to advanced flight training at Luke Air Force Base near Phoenix. By this time, they had logged nearly two hundred hours apiece in heavier trainers, and formation flying and gunnery practice had become second nature.

Arizona's vivid red and orange soil, contrasting with its lush green cultivation, filled Matt's eyes. Underneath him, the DC-3 grabbed the Luke runway with howling tires and clouds of smoke.

When the olive drab transport taxied to the main hangar area, Matt craned over its port wing. Outside stood a quarter mile row of jet trainer aircraft; T-33s with occasional F-84s sprinkled here and there.

A group of five officers, led by a brigadier general, greeted the aviators as they stepped off the cramped DC-3. The one star singled out Matt, and shook his hand as he led him aside.

"Matt...hell of an honor having you at Luke," he said, raising his right hand to shade his eyes from the bright desert sun.

"Your old man and I go back a lot of years. Back to England during the last fracas. He was a keen flyer. Hell of a man. From what I hear, you're cut from the same cloth."

"Thank you, general," Matt replied, filing yet another glowing report on his father; but flushing slightly over the praise for him. "I think we're all excited about getting into jets."

"You'll have your chance, Matt, believe me. Incidentally, your dad's attending graduation, isn't he? I'd sure like to see the old fart."

"Yessir...he promised he'd be here."

"Well, we'll tidy the place by then," the general smiled warmly and clapped Matt's shoulder. "Let me know if there's anything that will improve training. Okay?"

"Yessir," Matt replied. He snapped to attention, saluted the senior officer. The general returned his honor, then about-faced to speak to the other student-pilots.

"Gentlemen, I'm General Keyton...Luke's Base Commander. I bid you welcome. You're about to undergo six months of intensive training, flying the newest jet-powered trainers. After that, you'll earn a month's leave before your next assignment."

The general walked between the three ranks of six pilots each, inspecting each man front and back, top to bottom. He continued his briefing as he walked.

"By the time you graduate from Luke, you'll act like part of the bird you're flying. Remember this above all else...you're highballing near the speed of sound. One little screw-up is all it takes. They'll pick you up out of three counties."

The general concluded his inspection and stood before the group, a riding crop in his left hand. He studied their faces, ensuring he had everyone's attention.

"One last word of advice...when you buckle in, make sure flying is all you have on your mind."

The general emphasized his words by whapping an open palm with the riding whip.

"Okay...enough said. Tell your instructor-pilots or me if we can improve your training...your chow...or your facilities. Enjoy your stay here; and feel free to use the privileges you're entitled to as Air Force officers. Good day, gentlemen. And good flying."

A colonel called the group to attention, then the general chatted briefly with each student, patted their shoulders, and disappeared into the flight headquarters building. Like the others, Matt retrieved his flight and duffel bags and boarded the bus awaiting them.

As he slid a window open, a tight group of four jets screamed overhead; barely a hundred feet off the ground. One by one, each did a snap roll and quickly climbed out of sight.

Matt's heart lurched and blood pulsed rapidly through his chest. He sensed tremendous excitement, tinged with fear of the unknown.

"Man alive, those things do scoot, don't they!" Hoot exclaimed from Matt's left side. He leaned to follow the disappearing dots through the open window. "Matthew, we've come to the place where it's time to learn what flying's really about!"

Matt nodded silent agreement.

Spring blossomed into summer, and Matt and Hoot acclimated to the dry desert heat. It danced off runways in shimmering waves, and reflected in the distance like pools of water.

Matt enjoyed flying the little T-33 trainer, and quickly became adept at recovering from spins and no-power stalls when his trainer flamed out during a day mission over the desert.

By the end of June, the Air Force beefed its fighter contingents in Korea. The 8th, 18th and 35th Wings moved to Kimpo, Pusan and Pohang; and the 49th and 51st set up bases at Taegu and Kimpo.

By mid-summer, the trainees flew the heavier, more powerful and faster F-84. In gunnery runs, its fifty caliber mounts spat a solid string of fiery steel with a single touch of the trigger button. Matt's instinctive eye for shooting held true in the air, as well, and he continually scored the highest percentage of hits on ground targets.

On September 28, he and thirty-eight other lieutenants graduated from advanced training; earning the designation Flight Officers.

For the second time in slightly over a year Walt and Claire Durham, and Damon and Evelyn Forsythe, flanked a beaming Karen, whose hands cupped her tear-streaked face.

Her heart pounded as excitedly as his when Matt received the official document and silver wings proclaiming him an aviator.

Shortly after their arrival at Luke, Matt introduced Karen and the parents to Hoot. He fit in immediately, and at once developed a kinship with the Durhams and Forsythes; and especially with Karen.

Nearly every pilot at Luke...except unfortunates pulling duty... turned out for the graduation ball at the officer's club. Matt kept Karen in sight since she stepped off the airliner, and now cradled her close as they danced to a Patti Page tune.

He rekindled the contentment he had lacked for more than a year. He wanted her passionately...yes. Right now, however, just to hold close and feel her warm cheek pressed against his, and breasts snug against his chest. He felt warm, and satisfied.

"I love you," he whispered in her ear, kissing the sweet smelling hair that hung over it. "I've missed you terribly."

"I love you, too, Matt," she bussed him on the cheek and pulled him even tighter. "Oh, so much."

Both families stayed at a new motel near the airport, and after the others turned in, Walt and his son enjoyed a nightcap.

"I talked at length with Bob Keyton, Matt. He and I flew together in Europe."

"Yessir, he told me."

"He puts you at the top of your class; which is one hell of an accomplishment. I'm proud of you pal. Your friend Hoot is no slouch either."

The general fetched a bottle of brandy, still in its brown bag, and poured another inch into their glasses.

"He also tells me you two have orders for Korea."

The general took a sip of the biting liquor and studied his shoes. "Have you told Karen, Matt?"

Matt rolled his answer in his mind.

"No dad, not yet. Guess I'm building up nerve. We don't report until November, and that gives me a month to figure out how to let her know."

Walt sat his drink on the coffee table, walked to where his son sat on the couch. He placed his hand on the young man's shoulder. Matt looked into his father's eyes.

"It's like we discussed before, son. Some things, a man feels he has to do. Karen understands that. She'll worry, and cry, and hate the decision. She'll understand, though."

Walt's hand rested on his son's shoulder, and now he sat beside him.

"When you get to Korea Matt, don't let anything muddle your mind. Like you heard time and again in basic...you can't fly and worry about home. Claire and I...and the Forsythes...we'll care for Karen. You remember that."

"I will, dad, thanks. Thanks for everything."

He hugged his father firmly.

"My pleasure, Burrhead," Walt replied, his eyes clouding. "My pleasure."

Chapter 7

Sabrejet Solo

DAMON FORSYTHE PAINTED THE HOUSE over the summer. Matt saw it for the first time in more than a year; shining like a white iceberg against a patchwork background of October woods.

"Stop here a minute...please dad," he said touching his father's arm.

The car rolled to a halt. Matt got out, and momentarily stood absorbing the tidy spread at the end of the white gravel road leading onto the Forsythe property.

Walt Durham also got out of the car. He walked to where his son stood and put his arm around the young man's shoulders.

"It is beautiful, isn't it son?" he said, making a statement more than seeking a reply. "Who knows...maybe you'll have a place like this... somewhere to take your son."

"That's the fascination of The House, dad," Matt turned to look into his father's grey-blue eyes.

"It's not so much the place; it's the fond memories locked inside. The hunts. The Fall Festivals. The funny and foolish tricks we played during the hunting seasons."

"And...Karen?"

Matt paused and reflected. A smile lit his face.

"Yeah, most of all. I still remember her peering through the banister railings. Seems like twenty years ago instead of nine."

"A lot has happened to and for us since, Matt. Certainly enough to fill those twenty years you're talking about!"

He nudged his son's elbow, walked around to the driver's side and slid in.

"C'mon. We've got preparations for this weekend's hunt. Old Damon is probably champing the bit!"

Matt swung back into the passenger's seat and the general eased the car down the road toward the semi-circular drive. His son watched, feeling The House loom larger in his heart.

Finally, he broke the silence.

"You're right, dad," he looked at Walt; patted him once on the knee. "Someday I'll have a place just like this."

When they pulled in front, Damon and Judge Corley greeted them. Matt noticed the judge carried a cane, and leaned on the doctor for support descending the six steps from the front porch.

He offered his hand to the elderly magistrate, who immediately clasped it fondly in his; then embraced him.

"Gosh, it's good to see you, sir," Matt said.

He looked into the old man's eyes, sparkling with pleasure.

"Sorry I missed last season, Judge. Dad kept me posted on everything that happened, though."

"Oh, did he now!" the judge leaned back at arm's length. "I'll tell you Matthew...without you here to protect me, these two birds took advantage of an old man! Made me scull the dinghy. Cook the meals. Clean The House. Even pluck the ducks."

The old man's eyes twinkled with each embellishment added.

"All the while I'd hear 'em bellowing: 'Don't leave fuzz in the wing-pits!' Well now, by God, they won't pull that crap!"

"You can be certain of that, Judge," Matt affirmed, stifling a chuckle.

The other two collected gun cases and overnight bags from the car as Judge Corley took Matt's arm, and cane whacking the stairs like a blind beggar, dragged the lieutenant up the stoop.

Inside, he steered Matt to the round oak table in the breakfast room, then lowered himself painfully into one of the straight-back chairs surrounding the table. He hung the curved duck's head cane over a rung on the chair next to his and looked solemnly across the table at his youthful comrade.

"You know Matt...I wondered if I'd ever see you again," the judge's voice was flat and low. "Lately, my old back poops out easily. Then the pain keeps me from sleeping. Hell, it's got so this is the only place I can get a decent night's rest!"

The judge pulled out a weathered meerschaum pipe and fired it with a stick match snapped ablaze with a thumbnail.

"Being here with you, your dad and Damon makes me feel better than I have in months. And if you'll help an old cripple to the blind tomorrow...I may feel chipper enough to shoot a greenhead or two."

"It'll be my pleasure, Judge; even if I carry you piggyback."

The old man reached out and tenderly patted his hand.

Heavy, late summer rains caused the Paginaw River to burst its banks and flood the woods on both sides. Bluebird days on Saturday and Sunday found the four men hunting flooded timber; pitching out a couple dozen decoys in a wide clearing and sitting atop small stepladder-type tree stands, their backs against the rough bark of cypress and pin oaks.

Temperatures both days hovered in the fifties, yet neither men nor ducks objected. The shooting was magnificent.

Matt towed a small flat-bottomed skiff through thigh-high submerged trees so Judge Corley could partake of the fun. The judge's protests for Matt to leave him... "and enjoy shooting without nurse-maiding a lame old fart"...touched him deeply.

At mid-morning, the sun shafted through the tall scraggly trees and a flight of fifty mallards settled on the water around the four men like cascading leaves.

Matt glanced at the judge...sitting on a stoop with his shotgun across his lap...and marveled that the eighty-one-year-old justice still quivered over the sights and sounds of graceful birds noisily splashing around him.

He felt a lifetime's contentment in towing the judge to that spot, and never forgot the enraptured look on the old man's face; hunkered atop the tree-stand and encircled by paddling, diving, and quacking mallards.

There are moments in life that freeze an event in one's mind; flashburn it forever into memory. This instant affected Matt in that fashion. He always would remember his dear friend, mentor and hunting comrade as he appeared then; spending life's last few months doing what he loved best, with those he loved most.

Matt told Karen about his orders to Korea soon after returning home on leave.

She had suspected; and spent several nights thinking...and crying... before he arrived and confronted her with what she already knew deep inside.

Claire and Evelyn, veterans of their own war-weary departures, comforted and grieved with her:

"It's a flaw in the blood of the men we marry, Karen," her mother said. "That makes them eager to spill it for some cause or another."

In a few days, the tears dried and the smile returned. Still, the haunting fears lingered...but suppressed.

After the two-day hunt, Matt and Karen spent every hour together. She had earned her bachelor of fine arts degree in May... majoring in interior design...and now worked full-time for Peck & Peck Interiors.

Her work so impressed Charles Enright he promoted her to Office Manager. Not only that, he dangled a partnership a few years down the road; with her heading one of the offices in New Haven, Boston or New York.

While Matt completed flight training, Karen donated her weekends and open evenings to completing interiors that needed revamping. Decorating firms on both coasts praised her abilities, and many of her elegant rooms appeared in national trade publications.

Owners of competing firms regularly told Charles they intended stealing her; although he knew he could depend on her loyalty. Just as Karen knew she could exercise her own creativity, and not check every decision through him.

Karen organized a surprise birthday party for Matt's twenty-second, complete with a German chocolate cake shaped like a large duck. He had decreed he wanted "his fill of duck" before leaving, and she granted his wishes.

As a special gift, she bought him a silver identification bracelet with his name engraved on front and "I Love You...Karen" on its underside. His parents gave him two heavy sweaters.

"It's colder'n hell over there, son," the general said, clutching his arms in mock chill.

Then he handed Matt a large and crudely wrapped box.

"This is something special. You open it later."

After taking Karen home, Matt delicately unwrapped the gift in his room. When he lifted the tissue folded inside, he saw his father's leather flying jacket; complete with aviator's wings and a new leather patch that read:

"1stLt. Matthew E. Durham, U.S. Air Force."

Two days later, he wore the flight jacket over his blue uniform as he walked to the transport. He and ten others...Hoot Gibson included...

carried orders directing them to the Air Force Training And Embarkation Center at Springfield, Massachusetts.

General Durham had commanded at Springfield during World War Two, and in those days the Army Air Corps base rumbled with P-51 and P-38 fighter aircraft.

Now, it housed a secondary jet training squadron, and served as an embarkation point for fighter wings and pilots bound for Korea.

For some reason, saying good-bye to his loved ones at New Haven's Airport didn't affect Matt as it had in the past. He felt remorse leaving Karen...and the parents. However, anticipation of what lay in store in the months ahead...and possibly years...overshadowed it.

He couldn't define or distinguish the feelings fluttering like moths in his guts: excitement; enthusiasm; fear; emptiness; and, somehow, an uneasy calmness and overriding sense that everything would work out right.

Neither Matt nor his father were deeply religious, yet they felt strongly that some divine power did exist; some inexplicable force that created from chaos something the magnitude of the universe. And they agreed that if man required a category for defining this all-powerful sovereignty, such indeed could be called God.

Actually, self-fulfillment emerged as Matt's strongest identifiable feeling. He trusted his abilities, and felt pride in challenging life and its commitments.

And he intended to continue doing so.

The departing serviceman looked out the window as the transport rumbled down the runway. Again, the cluster of people on the ground waved and blew kisses, then disappeared behind the transport's roar.

He returned the farewell gestures; although knowing they couldn't be seen.

Soon, fluffy cumulus wrapped the wing of the DC-3 and masked the earth below. The aircraft climbed to five thousand feet, then veered nearly due North for Springfield.

Twenty minutes later, he spied the air base through a break in the clouds. And soon, the aircraft dipped its left wing and dropped altitude to land.

From the letters his father had written while stationed here, Matt discerned several of the buildings. Some were new, and several had been remodeled. All wore Air Force grey paint, in place of the Army's olive drab.

Then Matt's eyes caught another sight; and widened in wonder.

Thirty-five F-86E Sabrejet fighters stood wingtip to wingtip along the flight-line, their burnished bodies gleaming shiny white in the sun.

Each brandished American insignias on its wings and fuselage, and a large red four intersected by four blue and white lightning bolts adorned its tail: the symbol of the Fourth Fighter-Interceptor Wing.

Matt attended several briefings at Luke on the "E" model; which represented the North American Company's latest venture in fielding an unbeatable daytime jet fighter.

The F-86E resembled its predecessor, except it boasted an all-flying tail; which enabled optimum control at supersonic speeds and deadly gun accuracy.

The new Sabre's rate of climb topped seven thousand feet per minute, and it reached point nine Mach -- over six hundred miles per hour -- at an altitude of thirty thousand feet.

"Beautiful birds aren't they, Matthew?" Hoot yelled across the aisle over the engine roar. At that moment, the DC-3 touched concrete and the pilot changed his propeller pitch and slowed. "I can't wait to get inside one!"

"Yeah...me neither, Hoot!" came the shouted answer.

The transport braked to a stop as the two discussed the heady thrill and excitement of flying one of the silver fighters.

Then the group of new pilots surrendered their orders and officially logged onboard with the duty watch officer. Check-in completed, they stowed their flight-bags at the bachelor officers quarters.

The pilots' orders directed them to report to the briefing room in Building 402, a block away from the BOQ and facing the East-to-West and Northeast-to-Southwest runways. There, they spent two days learning the controls, instrumentation and idiosyncrasies of the F-86.

On Wednesday, at zero-eight-hundred hours, Matt adopted aircraft number fifteen zero nine. The major in the briefing room looked at him and said, simply:

"Take her up. Get to know, love and trust her. She's your baby, now."

Matt gave the outside of fifteen-oh-nine a thorough pre-flight checkover, then a young sergeant helped settle him into the leather seat in the tight cockpit. The enlisted man tugged the shoulder harnesses as Matt leaned forward, then snapped him secure.

Over the months, Matt would accustom himself to the parachute pack snugged against the small of his back. He turned slightly, shifted its bulk evenly behind him, and readied for takeoff.

"Have a good flight, sir," the sergeant said, saluting.

"Thanks, sarge," Matt replied, returning the courtesy.

For a moment or two, he studied his shiny crash helmet; certainly more protective than the leather cap at primary, and lighter than Luke's head-gear.

The insignia of the Fourth dressed up its sides, and "Durham" graced its front; stenciled in black military block letters.

He slid the seat forward slightly so he could more comfortably reach the brake and rudder pedals. Instinctively, he tapped his inner thighs with the control stick; making sure of clearance.

Next he plugged in the helmet headset, flipped the power control switch, and instantly heard the crackle of static. He set the throttle at "start," looked to be sure no one was behind the aircraft, and pushed the ignition button.

The jet fired to life with a low whine that turned to a roar, making its airframe shudder. He kept the brake pedals firm as he performed a final pre-flight check of instruments, controls and engine.

Satisfied with his readings, he punched the intercom button beneath his oxygen mask.

"Springfield control...fifteen-zero-niner ready to taxi to take-off position."

"R-r-roger, fifteen-zero-niner," the clear, deep voice echoed in his helmet. "Proceed to runway tha-ree."

Matt signaled "chocks away" to the sergeant, who yanked the ropes holding the blocks in place. He returned a thumbs-up.

He raised his toes off the brake pedals as his left hand eased the throttle. The jet rolled forward slowly, and when it cleared aircraft on both sides he touched the left brake, turning toward runway three.

Once there, he checked his surroundings and eased onto the long concrete strip. He aligned the plane's nose with the center of the runway, locked his brakes and contacted the tower.

"Springfield control. Fifteen-zero-niner requesting permission to take off."

"R-r-roger, fifteen-zero-niner...you have clearance. There's a slight north-to-south crosswind at three knots...and your ceiling's between eight and ten thousand. No weather to speak of. Good flying lieutenant... Springfield control out."

"Roger, control...and thanks," Matt spoke into the mask.

He slid a small lever at his upper left and the Plexiglas canopy quietly closed and snapped shut. A last minute check of gauges and needles on the instrument panel indicated system readiness, so he flipped a toggle switch that lowered the plane's flaps.

Matt moved the throttle to maximum thrust and the noise and blast from the powerful turbojet rocked the aircraft from side to side. Finally, he released the brakes.

The F-86 lurched forward, its engine spitting a ten-foot-long tongue of blue flame as Matt alternately tapped his brake pedals to keep the nose centered. As ground speed approached one hundred miles per hour, he felt the aircraft's nose fighting to lift.

Still, he kept the control stick forward until the RPM indicator signaled it was safe to take off, and gently pulled the control stick toward his crotch.

The rate of climb indicator fixed at forty-five degrees, and over the Sabrejet's nose the horizon changed from concrete, to fence, to pasture and, finally, blue sky.

He lifted a wheel-shaped lever, and a red light on the instrument panel turned amber and then green as the craft's landing gears retracted with a thud. He flipped another lever and raised the flaps. And now, cleanly airborne...on his own...he savored the thrill of flight.

At ten thousand feet Matt moved the control stick midway, leveling, and eased back the throttle. He smoothed the jet's flight with trim tabs on the elevators and rudder. Inside, the tidy cockpit felt comfortable and cool and, as usual, he embraced the quiet and peacefulness of flying at altitude.

The pilot pushed the left rudder pedal forward and leaned the control stick toward his left knee, and the jet pointed its nose downward, disclosing Highway 90 leading to Boston. Through haze in the distance, he now recognized Quabbin Reservoir.

For the hell of it...and out of excitement and exuberance for again being in the air...Matt yanked back hard on the control stick and the Sabre nosed three hundred and sixty degrees in a tight snap roll.

"Yahoo...ride 'em cowboy!" he yelled, feeling his stomach lurch with the maneuver.

After twenty minutes, he banked hard left and returned to the airbase; comfortable with his new charger.

Over the next five days, Matt logged more than twenty hours in the Sabrejet; including night missions and gunnery practice. And at seven o'clock the following Monday morning, he and fifteen other pilots lifted off on their twelve-hour flight to Korea.

Chapter 8

Quonset In Quoseng

M ATT DIDN'T EXPECT HIS FIRST view of Korea.
Especially after flying two hours longer than planned, stopping briefly for fuel, food and stretching at Pearl Harbor, Guam and Okinawa.

For some reason, his mind pictured the country on a scale with pre-war Japan. Neatly terraced square rice paddies. Craggy, twisted cedar and persimmon trees clinging to rough coral bedrock. Coolies in conical hats. And pristine bamboo and rice paper homes.

Instead, as the four diamond formations of F-86s peeled off for landings, Quoseng Air Base appeared a concrete and Quonset hut island floating amidst dark green jungle and gooey red clay.

Rain misted and pattered against Matt's bubble canopy as he lowered wheels and flaps. The terrain reminded him of a high school film; a story of people living in the mining country squalor at the foot of the Appalachian Mountains.

Maybe the similarity to rust-colored Georgia mud, or perhaps the gloomy, blustery weather. Whatever...as the Sabrejet touched, turning water to steam and squealing rubber, he felt depression flood over him.

Ground crews staggered the sixteen new fighters along the apron beside the North-South runway. The pilots bunked in two large metal huts a hundred feet behind, near a cluster of shell-shattered palms.

The semi-cylindrically shaped, tin-roofed Quonsets afforded six rooms, each sleeping two officers. A centrally located structure contained the head, lavatory and showers.

Each hut boasted two oil-fired pot-bellied stoves, and screened windows that ran the length of the building for ventilation.

The pilots' personal belongings had arrived by transport a day earlier, so Matt and Hoot hung their uniforms, flight suits and civilian attire in wall lockers that divided their cubicles.

"God...what is that smell!" exclaimed Hoot, holding his nose against a pungent, acrid odor that filled the Quonset.

"It's these little bags of chemicals hanging in our lockers, Hoot," replied Matt. "They're supposed to absorb moisture and prevent rust."

"Between the chemicals, fuel oil, jungle smells and aviation fuel, I'd rather have the rust!" joked Hoot.

He turned to Matt, his big, warm, infectious smile momentarily cheering the clammy darkness of the hut.

"Reckon we should look at it this way, Matthew. We could be mud Marines on the ridge east of here; sleeping in the wet and cold in a smelly canvas tent. At least we've got warm racks and dry clothes. And unless I'm dreaming, that's the Officer's Club in the hut behind us."

"That's the only way to look at it, Hooter," Matt replied. He sat atop a lumpy rolled mattress at one end of his steel bed.

"I count on you for my glimmer of light in the darkness. Why don't we hustle over and see about chow?"

They closed their lockers, slipped on fleece-lined flight jackets, and walked the long corridor bisecting the other rooms. Outside, the blowing mist stung their faces.

Their watches read five o'clock, but the sullen sky, and little sleep, made it appear several hours later. The two walked through the group of sixty Quonset huts housing the Fourth Fighter-Interceptor and Eleventh Bomber Wings.

Light glowing from the rows of windows in the huts made them appear like elongated Jack-O-Lanterns. Occasionally, the pair stopped and talked with other flyers enroute to dinner.

A long, flat valley, thick with jungle vegetation, harbored the airfield, which actually nestled on the floor of an ancient volcano. Craggy mountains with snow-dusted peaks formed a mile-wide crater encircling the base. Peaks jutted to two thousand feet, and left little room for pilot error.

In the distance, day and night, they heard the hollow thump of artillery, and occasionally, flashes on a shadowy hillside underscored battle and death lurking close by.

The sixteen new arrivals helped bolster "Falcon Flight Eight."

Falcon Eight's nearness to the action...and frequent missions flying cover for bombers...made it the leader in casualties. The flight daily patrolled Sector Thirty-nine; a twenty-mile-wide strip containing the village of Quoseng and six others. A small windy river known as the Chungtzy crisscrossed the terrain and dumped into the Yalu.

The South Korean Army had constructed a training base and airfield several miles north of the American's camp; on the opposite side of Quoseng. Aside from these two military reservations, the area's only other target for North Korean pilots was a small petroleum refinery outside Quoseng.

North Korea considered Sector Thirty-nine important real estate, and especially the airspace above the cratered terrain.

It served as the primary avenue for the Eleventh's heavy bombers going after communist targets.

Flying patrol over Sector Thirty-nine involved less risk than flying the grids that made up MiG Alley; still, Quoseng Air Base suffered frequent strafings by enemy aircraft and occasional bomber attacks.

Major Warren Kellogg, a native of San Francisco, commanded Falcon Flight Eight. Like many others, he flew fighters in World War Two and stayed for career duty.

Warren piloted P-38 Lightnings against German pilots over the Libyan desert, so he transitioned easily to the faster, deadlier jet fighters.

At six o'clock their first morning, Matt and Hoot sat with a dozen others in the ready hut near the flight line. They listened and smoked as Major Kellogg unfolded their first mission.

A large map of Korea suddenly appeared on the screen before them, and the major took a collapsible pointer from his blouse pocket.

"We'll fly cover for the B-29s...heading two-six-zero at twenty-five thousand feet," he said, almost mechanically. "The bombers will trail us by half a minute."

He telescoped the pointer, transferred it to his right hand, and tapped an area near the center of the topographic blowup.

"Our heaviest opposition will be on the other side of the Yalu... roughly twenty minutes into the flight. If we spot bandits, and they pay us a visit, we'll drop external tanks and engage."

"What happens if we're outnumbered, major?" asked a lieutenant on the front row; one of the new pilots flying over in Matt's group.

"In all likelihood, we will be," the major replied flatly. He gripped the pointer at both ends.

"Remember this...we're better pilots, flying the best birds in the air. And we're used to being outnumbered. Americans thrive on being the underdogs."

The room hushed, and Warren studied the faces looking up at him. He shocked many by his light dismissal of the peril; and got the attention of all.

"Now then...the bombers' target is the Tiengsho railway yards. When we reach Shantso...about sixty miles away...we'll remain on station until we see the bombers. We'll lead them to the drop zone, then return to base."

He pointed to another area on the topo map.

"Falcon Four will rendezvous with the B-29s a half hour later at the Yalu...and cover them the rest of the way home."

With a quick snap the major retracted the pointer and tucked it back inside his coat. As if on cue, the screen went dark and overhead lights flashed on.

"Any questions?" he asked.

The room remained silent.

"Okay, gentlemen, suit up. We lift wheels at zero seven hundred."

The Korean rain that welcomed Matt the day before burned away in the steamy morning sun; resembling Easter more than Thanksgiving weather. Morning temperatures on the flight-line hovered in the mid-fifties.

Matt's scores in flight school earned him the slot as Group Two flight leader, and he picked Hoot as wing man to fly off his left wingtip.

At exactly seven o'clock, eight pairs of Sabres roared off the Quoseng runway, circled at five thousand feet until all pilots joined their respective groups, then headed due North to meet the B-29s of the Eleventh. The pilots locked onto their heading of two hundred and sixty degrees, flying at twenty thousand feet.

"Falcon Flight leader to Falcon groups," Major Kellogg rasped in monotone over the communications channel. "That's the Chungtzy River below. We'll reach the Yalu in five minutes. Keep your asses tightened up back there!"

The visibility at altitude was magnificent.

Matt spotted a silver ribbon of water a hundred miles ahead, sparkling like loose gems in the early sun. He glanced out the left side of his canopy at Hoot, motioned toward the Yalu and gave his wingman the thumbs up.

Hoot returned the gesture.

Matt felt content and eerily at ease flying combat formation with the others. He knew several only slightly, yet trusted them all. And knew he could count on them if the muck hit.

He also knew they felt the same about him.

He confirmed Group Three's formation to his right, and in the rearview mirror saw Group Four's flight leader and wingman.

Five minutes later his headset crackled again as Major Kellogg advised the fliers they were crossing the Yalu:

"Here we go, boys. Watch for enemy aircraft."

The major no sooner signed off than the voice of the flight leader for the Eleventh Bomber Group boomed in Matt's helmet.

"Falcon Flight, this is Eagle Flight leader. We have you visually two miles in front and below. Do you read?"

"Roger, Eagle Flight," the major responded.

Matt saw the flight leader twist his head, straining to spy the lumbering B-29s above and to the rear.

The bombers also flew combat formation, appearing as tiny specks that occasionally glistened in the now bright sun, their contrails ripping white streaks through the azure sky.

The headset crackled once more and the major spoke to both flights.

"Okay Falcon Flight, let's drop to fifteen thousand and troll for MiGs until the bombers get past. Give 'em hell, Eagle Flight."

"Roger, Falcon. You too. Good hunting."

At Major Kellogg's command, the four Falcon Flight groups nosed to fifteen thousand feet like a precision team.

Matt now distinguished villages through the haze as ground moisture evaporated in the hot sun sweeping the land. Thick banks of fog drifted across the cratered surface below.

"Skipper...company at six o'clock!" a pilot exclaimed.

Matt leaned forward and craned to the left to look under the Sabre's nose. Several white dots appeared a mile below, silhouetted against the emerald steam-shrouded landscape.

"Let's get the sun behind us, boys" Major Kellogg's terse words rattled from the radio; still in monotone.

The group of Sabres veered wide left, then circled toward the bogeys which remained at five thousand feet; concerned only with the ground area bordering the Yalu and paying little heed to aircraft that may be overhead.

Falcon Flight continued its semicircle approach, and at ten thousand feet, confirmed the bandits as North Korean aircraft. Major Kellogg came back on the air.

"Attack formation," he said tersely. "Drop tanks, arm and clear guns."

The sixteen jets jockeyed into a straight line...twenty feet apart... and pumped their remaining fuel onboard. Then they jettisoned wing tanks, the empty containers rolling lazily earthward, end over end, like large silver grains of rice.

Matt flipped the gun-arming toggle on the instrument panel... another on the arm console beside him...and with his right thumb pushed the serrated switch on top of the control stick.

The Sabre bucked slightly, and twenty rounds of fifty caliber ammunition streaked from the six guns located in its nose. Tracers were packed one-to-four, and Matt watched several white smoky trails disappear into the blue. On both sides, he heard his sister aircraft perform the same ritual.

"Let's get 'em boys!" barked the major, after checking the line of jets in both directions.

In unison, Group One's Sabres peeled and dove toward the flight of MiG-15s. The Korean pilots, alerted and panicking, dispersed in different directions; several nearly colliding as they sought escape.

Matt watched Group One launch into the attack.

Tracers looped toward the enemy, and a MiG burst into flames. The crippled machine spun cartwheel fashion into the green foliage on a hillside and erupted in a bright flash, as a roiling cloud of black oily smoke belched skyward.

"You got him, skipper. You got him!" he heard a Group One pilot shout to the major.

Matt's group dropped into the melee next, as he shoved the control stick and throttle forward.

The pass by Group One split the flight of North Korean planes. As he approached the area where the aerial battle raged, he spotted a Sabre with three MiGs in close pursuit on its tail.

He banked sharply to keep from overflying the foursome, and deftly brought his aircraft within fifty yards behind the MiGs.

The lone Sabrejet fishtailed a hundred yards in front of the Koreans, and they stuck with him, paying little attention to other activities filling the sky.

Matt worked his control stick and rudder pedals until the nearest MiG filled the circular sight in his windscreen; then slid the trigger switch forward in short jabs.

The Sabre's machine guns chattered in short bursts, buffeting it slightly, and tracers arched toward the MiG.

Matt tugged the stick slightly; raising his nose and the trajectory of the fifty caliber slugs.

Now his line of fire intercepted the enemy aircraft, and sparks danced as bullets penetrated the MiG's steel and aluminum fuselage and wings.

He pressed the switch for a long burst. Again, flashes stitched the MiG, this time accompanied by pieces of metal, black smoke and spewing fluid.

Seconds later, the MiG rolled lazily to one side and Matt released the gun switch. As he watched out the left side of his canopy, it spun, wing over wing, slowly and erratically, and erupted as a billowing, fiery cloud in a rice paddy.

When he looked forward again, the other two MiGs had parted. One accelerated away from the fray, while the other continued nipping at the Sabre's tail. He climbed toward the MiG shadowing his comrade, when another Sabre suddenly aligned behind it. It carried the tail number fifteen-ten: Hoot's aircraft.

He pressed the intercom to cheer his comrade and within seconds, another MiG appeared from nowhere and lined behind his friend.

Matt could see its twenty millimeter cannon spitting smoke and fiery projectiles.

"Hoot! Hoot!" he yelled into the facemask microphone. "One on your tail! Bank left! Bank left!"

Without hesitation, Hoot shoved his left rudder pedal and control stick. The Sabre stood on its left wingtip and the closing MiG streaked past.

As it climbed for altitude, Matt instinctively raised his plane's nose, fixed the attacker in his sight, and pressed the gun switch.

This time, sparks danced from the MiG's front-end and traveled tail-ward as round after round hit its mark. Matt tensed to fire another burst when the enemy craft exploded, and disappeared in a bright ball of white-orange flame, charcoal smoke and metal shards. Shattered fragments clinked his plane as he streaked through the explosion.

Matt lifted his Sabre into a steep climb and over its snout saw the plane the three MiGs had pursued. It abruptly lurched into a sharp dive, trailing smoke, hydraulic fluid and jet fuel.

He held his breath, waiting for the canopy to blow and a parachute to blossom, but instead, it maintained its steep descent, until it, too, smashed into the lush vegetation on the hillside below. A ball of flame touching, bouncing, touching and erupting in a fiery mushroom.

When he leveled, Matt swung left to the sector where the dogfight began.

Below, inky, billowing columns of smoke rose from flaming piles of wreckage; sophisticated combat machines reduced to strewn carcasses.

In the distance, the surviving communist jets fled north, climbing rapidly.

"Falcon Flight regroup," Major Kellogg's baritone voice rattled in Matt's earphones. "Let's head home. Sound off with name and damage report."

One by one, the pilots formed their original groups and responded as requested. Matt's flight remained intact, while a slot stood empty in Group One and only two aircraft comprised the group to his right. He turned to see only one Sabre missing from Group Four.

Back to his left, Hoot mimed the close call sign...wiping sweat from his brow...then flashed thumbs up.

The North Koreans had fared worse; losing eleven aircraft and nine pilots in the skirmish.

Major Kellogg posted three kills, while another pilot and Matt claimed two each. Four other Falcon Flight fliers scored singles.

The flight's twelve Sabrejets climbed to twenty-five thousand feet, heading South for Quoseng, and Matt experienced the strange, mixed emotions his father had mentioned: Overwhelming excitement, tinged with remorse for taking human life.

Yet beneath the facemask, he smiled broadly; anxious to land and discuss what occurred in the dogfight.

Once the pilots debriefed, they stowed their flight gear and walked to the officer's club. Hoot ordered the first round of drinks and proposed a toast.

"To Major Kellogg...and Lieutenants McNeal and Durham," he said, hoisting a mug of beer above his head.

"Falcon Flight's three hotshot pilots. Bravo!"

With that, all in the club stood and toasted, then cheered and applauded the three.

Matt flushed with embarrassment, then noticed the other two uneasy fliers. Major Kellogg set his drink on the table, raised his arms palms out for quiet, and spoke calmly and softly.

"Boys...you've tasted your first air combat. And fared well. Remember, however, we lost four buddies up there. Let's drink to them... and the Fighting Fourth."

The major lifted the glass to his lips and took a long pull. The others followed suit; this time in silence.

Later in the evening, Matt and Hoot sat at a table to the rear of the club, near a large trophy case containing mementos of the Fourth Fighter-Interceptor Wing. The latter placed his hand warmly on his friend's shoulder.

"Matthew, you saved my life today," he said. "Your warning kept that MiG from nailing me. I owe you a big one, amigo."

"Forget it, Hooter. Over here...doing what we do...I'll bet debts cancel out real fast."

"Well, anyway...thanks Matt. Buy you another brew?"

"Sure, partner. Why not? We owe it to ourselves."

Falcon Flight flew twelve sorties over the next three weeks, mostly covering bomber penetrations deep into communist territory.

However, the pilots also provided close air support to infantry units. Allied ground forces were finding it difficult to hold real estate they'd captured, and were paying premium prices in young lives.

Over the same period, Falcon Eight lost two more Sabres. Luckily, both pilots ejected and made their ways to friendly forces.

By Thanksgiving, the temperatures dipped into the low twenties. Several times, the ever-present humidity chilled and formed snow flakes.

By some windfall, Matt and Hoot avoided the duty roster flying cover or ground support, and on Thanksgiving Day, planned a respite to catch up on laundry and reading; topped by a turkey dinner in the officer's wardroom.

Walt Durham's letter arrived with two from Karen and one from the Forsythes. Matt tore into it first, anxious to hear hunting tales. As he read it, his eyes misted and a great emptiness claimed the pit of his stomach:

Sunday, November 11

Dear Son,

Your mother and I just got back from church. We thought we'd sit and drop you a quick note. I'll give you the bad news, and mom can provide the rest. Judge Corley passed away last Wednesday after suffering a severe heart attack. It happened without pain, Matt. He went into a coma and that was it.

The doctors did everything possible. They called Damon to lend a hand. He told me the Judge's heart was just worn out. He felt poorly a few days after you shipped out. Complained about sharp pains in his lower back and chest.

Damon checked him into the University Hospital Tuesday for tests. Guess it was too late to do anything but make him comfortable.

I know what he meant to you Matt. And I know you'll take it pretty hard. Remember he lived a good, full life. Did most of what he wanted. There are lots of us who will remember him fondly. You can't ask much more of life than that.

Take care, son. Write when you can. We miss and love you. Our best regards and warm wishes for Hoot.

Love, Dad

Matt read the short note his mother penned at the bottom of the page in her graceful flowing script, then reread his father's message; tears welling in his eyes. He remained in the lumpy easy chair by his bunk... letter in his lap...until Hoot entered the cubicle.

"Ready for chow, Matthew?" he asked.

He noticed his friend's doleful expression.

"What's wrong?"

Matt recounted to Hoot his favorite tales about the judge; about hunting, and the old man living season-to-season to see birds on the wing. Not caring about firing a shot; just being there seeing and experiencing.

A feeling the judge and Matt shared from the beginning.

Hoot sat on the edge of the steel bed-frame. He leaned over and touched his friend's shoulder.

"Weigh it like your dad said, Matthew. The judge lived to a ripe age and died peacefully among friends. Think of where we are; and kids dying on the slopes every day. Not really knowing why, and mostly in the arms of strangers."

Hoot patted him, and stood.

"When I die, I hope it's the judge's way. Closing out a fulfilling life, and leaving lots of good friends behind."

"Yeah, you're right, Hoot," Matt rose from the chair.

He folded the letter into its envelope and dropped it into the top drawer of the crude chest in his room. He wiped his eyes dry.

"I'll read the other letters after dinner. Right now, I could handle a good, stiff drink. How about you?"

As the two men walked into the dark evening from the Quonset hut, tiny particles of ice pelted them, driven by a howling, gusty wind. The crystals packed and sparkled like glitter under the large bare bulb that lit the board walkways through the muddy quagmire.

The pair downed two drinks apiece, then shared a carafe of white wine in washing down turkey prepared at noon and now slightly dry. They passed on the sage-seasoned bread-crumb dressing that had nearly solidified.

They talked about favorite Thanksgivings, and laughed over their previous one shared in Texas. And they compared their respective plans for "A.K."... or After Korea.

In the distance, artillery fire rumbled like faraway thunder and the ebony sky's horizon throbbed like an aurora borealis.

For Matt, this was an in-between Thanksgiving. Not a favorite, nor likely his worst.

It had stature, for he shared it warmly with Hoot; who daily became a closer friend. And obviously harbored the same feelings for him.

At nine o'clock, they returned to the BOQ and their respective rooms, thanking one another for enjoyable company. Matt read his letters, cheered by the Forsythe's recountings and fondest wishes, and warmed by the love reflected in Karen's writings.

Perhaps her words, the meal, the drinks and the wine conspired, but when he switched off the reading lamp he felt at peace and full of gratitude.

"After all," he wondered aloud, "Isn't this feeling what Thanksgiving is all about?"

He soon fell asleep. And that night, as Matt lay in deep slumber, his dreams skittered crazily from hunting, to Judge Corley, to Huntsdale and to The House.

Then Korea appeared, with its bamboo and steaming fish smells; thick sticky clay and verdant rice paddies; incessant rain, and bone-chilling humidity.

Then, floating through the misty half-sleep, the beautiful face of Karen. Loving Karen. His Karen.

In the dark early morning, his mind replayed their last walk in the woods. How she came to him in the front seat of the Ford convertible; stroking, touching, sucking his breath.

They lay there in his dreams; naked, warm, entwined, together as one. And even now...thousands of miles away...he sensed the pleasure known then.

And awoke with a start. And a groan. On discovering what occurred in his dreams.

"Shit!"

He murmured aloud as he swung from the warm bunk and felt icy concrete where his feet left the straw mat. In the darkness, he stripped the soiled underwear and stuffed it into his laundry bag.

He grabbed fresh skivvies from his foot locker, wrapped his wool kimono around him, and raced toward the showers.

Outside, snow plummeted harder than had sleet the night before, and several inches had collected on the wood planking between buildings, engulfing his feet and thongs, and making walking treacherous.

In the shower hut, his watch read three-thirty. He turned the faucets and a steamy torrent soon filled the room. Now, he remembered the dream that awakened him, and smiled happily.

"I really love that girl," he grinned, lathering his body. "Yessir...I really do."

Miles away, where men fought...shooting, bayoneting or bombarding each other...the battlefield grew mysteriously and completely quiet. Only plump snowflakes drifted silently downward from the black void, like bleached leaves blanketing the pitted ground.

Chapter 9

Korea Kills

MATT AND HOOT, DRESSED ONLY in skivvy shorts and kimonos, dashed outside to the latrine and showers. A dazzling white landscape welcomed them, above which appeared one of the bluest skies either remembered.

Wrapped in warm flannel, they stopped momentarily to breathe the crisp tingling air, and their breaths hung like thick puffs of white smoke. They felt immediately invigorated and frivolous.

"Nobody fights on a day like this," Hoot said minutes later.

Scalding streams of water washed away the soapy foam covering his body, leaving squeaky pink in its place. "It not only should be immoral... but illegal!"

As if on cue, the loud speaker attached to the telephone pole outside blared:

"All pilots to the ready room...pilots to the ready room."

"You said what, Hoot?" Matt grinned as he turned.

They quickly toweled semi-dry, donned their robes and raced through winter's bite to their hut. There, they changed into flight suits.

Shouts and men crunching through deep snow indicated the seriousness of the situation. From Quonsets on all sides, pilots scurried for the larger building near the flight-line.

Major Kellogg scampered past from his end of the hut.

"Better hustle it, guys."

Since early morning, Navy SeaBees had cleared the runways with huge caterpillar tractors equipped with snow blades. Flight line crews kept them company, clearing snow off the Sabres and checking fuel levels and starter batteries.

At the ready room, the Wing Commander personally conducted the briefing, outlining the day's mission with target slides and topographic maps.

"The Fourth Fighter-Interceptor and Eleventh Bomber wings received orders directly from Korean Allied Command," the commander reported sternly. "We're part of a major strike."

The colonel lit a cigarette, shook out the match, and walked to the front of the elevated briefing stage.

"You Sabre drivers will provide close air support for the Marines," he pointed randomly at several pilots in the Fourth. "The ground pounders are trying to capture a bloody piece of terrain called 'Porkchop Hill'."

The commander paced to the other side of the stage and addressed the pilots there.

"Your bombers are part of a large-scale raid on the Tchung Ko Airfield," the colonel tapped an enlarged map behind him that showed the cross-hatchings of runways.

"Intelligence says four squadrons of MiG-15s and 17s deployed there suddenly. Sabres from the Eighth and Eighteenth Fighter Wings will intercept you, and fly cover for your twenty-five B-29s."

The wing boss stubbed the cigarette in the base of a spent Howitzer shell and stood in the middle of the stage, arms folded across his chest.

"Rumor's out the commies are planning a major assault on several United States air bases."

He clasped his hands behind him and leaned forward from the waist up.

"Quoseng is one of those bases, and that pisses me off! Let's take the fighting to those bastards...before they try to bring it here!"

The commander strode to the blackboard and wrote the numbers as he spoke:

"Flight leaders...I want bombers off at zero-seven-thirty; fighters off at zero-eight-hundred. Good luck, gentlemen. Dismissed!"

The assemblage jumped to attention as the colonel tramped from the building followed by his aides.

An hour later, Matt looked out from the cockpit of his Sabrejet as he worked through his preflight checklist.

One by one, the lumbering eight-engined B-29s, queued in front of the fighters, roared down the runway; their powerful engines stirring thick swirls of powdery snow, behind which they disappeared, only to emerge a quarter mile away, rising above the horizon and droning for altitude.

With the bombers finally airborne, the jets began taxiing and taking off.

Matt rolled onto the runway, and felt winter crispness flood the open cockpit, the harsh cold stinging exposed skin around his tinted goggles. He slid the canopy lever back, and the Plexiglas bubble closed over him with a hiss and snap.

To the left, Hoot also buttoned up.

"Quoseng Control...Group Two leader ready for takeoff," Matt said to the tower.

He flicked Hoot a thumbs up and received the sign in reply.

"Group Two leader you have clearance for takeoff. Good hunting. Tower out."

"Roger Control," he flipped the switch for interplane communications. "Group Two leader...let's go boys."

Matt shoved the throttle forward, and as the RPMs reached the takeoff point the Sabre shuddered. He unlocked the brakes and rolled down the runway.

SeaBees had plowed the heavy snow and piled it on both sides of the concrete strip. And the bombers taking off packed any remaining snow into a solid and slippery surface.

Matt and Hoot steered their outer wingtips in relation to the snow banks and, as they had many times, the duo lifted in unison, raising landing gears and flaps as they climbed.

In his rearview mirror, Matt watched the other two Sabres of his group climb to join Hoot and he. They leveled at two thousand feet, heading for their rendezvous point.

Half an hour North, a Marine colonel in Sector Fourteen waited. He and his battalion of foot soldiers had orders to attack North Korean defenses on the peak of Porkchop Hill.

Matt looked out the cockpit at the mantle of white covering the ground below. The snowfall added a false sense of purity to the battle-scarred landscape.

As they approached the voice contact point, he noticed dark pockmarks in the chalky surface; incoming artillery and mortar rounds had punched and spewed red clay, leaving mounds that resembled festering pimples on a frail complexion.

"Falcon Flight, this is Mud Marine. Falcon Flight, this is Mud Marine. Do you read me...over?"

Matt received the Marine's transmission as they approached the target vector.

"Roger, Mud Marine. This is Falcon. Are target markers out?"

"Affirmative, Falcon. Five hundred yards due North of our position. Repeat...five hundred yards due North."

"Roger...I see them now," Matt answered.

He spotted the bright orange strips of cloth pointing the way toward a craggy, boulder-strewn hill. Dense copses of scraggly cedars splotched the steep terrain, providing ideal hideouts for the enemy.

"Okay Falcons...we'll hit a couple of times with guns and rockets, then lay napalm on the final pass. Form up single file."

The diamond formation melted into a diagonal line of four jets, each Sabre twenty-five yards from those leading and following it.

Matt aligned for the first strafing pass; followed by Hoot.

A mile out from the peak he dove steeply, and at a quarter mile could see enemy troops scattering like ants. Rifles and machine-guns flashed as the soldiers dropped to their knees and fired at the jets screaming around them.

Matt's eye detected artillery pieces hidden near a thicket of brush, and as his bulls-eye sight blanketed them, he punched a button on the control stick.

Four rockets ignited under the Sabre's wings, and streaked into the brushy outcroppings. Smoky trails outlined the missile's paths, and they exploded crimson bursts among the brush, cannons and soldiers.

Matt slid the machine gun switch forward and the Sabre shuddered as six firing ports spewed flame and bullets. Snow and mud danced around the tiny figures, and the hilltop erupted in sparks, pieces of rock, shards of wood and steamy craters.

He pulled back on the stick and the Sabre nosed upward toward clean, blue sky.

In his rearview mirror, Matt watched Hoot firing rockets, and the nose of Hoot's plane flash as his machine-guns spat blazing lead into the enemy position.

By the third pass, Matt saw cedars blazing, pieces of artillery strewn and smoldering, and black figures on the rugged peak denoting fallen soldiers.

This pass, he climbed sharply a hundred yards in front of the peak, flipped the bomb release switch on the instrument panel, and sent two one-hundred-pound canisters of napalm cart-wheeling into the entrenched communist stronghold.

As the four aircraft regrouped, Matt surveyed the flaming crest. Snow and burning fuel formed a steamy, greasy, black cloud rising two hundred feet into the blue sky.

He punched the intercom button on his facemask.

"Mud Marine, this is Falcon. We've softened 'em up, colonel. Now it's your turn. Good luck!"

"Swell job, Falcon. Hope to see you on the ground sometime. Drinks on us!"

Returning to Quoseng, Matt steered the foursome in a southwesterly direction, skirting the large port city of Nampo. From three thousand feet, they saw thatched huts nestled among oriental-influenced skyscrapers.

On streets below, people scurried like busy ants; a sharp contrast to the narrow mud roads in the rural areas where only occasional antiquated automobiles and ox carts trudged.

Farther down the southwestern coast, war's remodeling unveiled itself more clearly. At Haeju, black pockmarks, jagged walls and remains of buildings revealed recent shelling and bombing.

Out the bubble canopy to his left, Matt spotted a large cloud of brownish haze, stretching for miles and lingering above the refineries and oil fields near Seoul.

In all directions, the pilots discovered once radiant countryside ravaged by two years of turmoil: vegetation stripped; villages leveled; industries burned to the ground or hopelessly shattered.

Even the thick stands of wild bamboo showed scars, as if a gigantic scythe, haphazardly cutting large swathes, tossed splintered stalks in all directions.

Matt trimmed out, flying four hundred miles per hour above the war-torn terrain, and felt discomfort and depression over what he saw; anger for what led to such carnage.

He wondered if what others said could be right.

Perhaps Korea is strictly a political powder keg; ready for igniting by a premature commitment of American firepower.

'Why do we stop at the Yalu River?' he wondered to himself. 'Hell... day after day we chase MiGs back into China. Our guys can't follow and finish the job. The Chinese and Russians provide everything here but blood and guts. McArthur's right...we should give them a taste of what the Koreans are going through, or it won't stop here.'

Familiar terrain below brought his thoughts and frustration back into the cockpit.

'Oh, bullshit, Durham! Get your mind back on business! We'll do our jobs and get the hell out of here.'

Half an hour later they landed at Quoseng. The four pilots debriefed, then changed from their flight suits and beelined for the "O Club" to scrub away the foul taste of the day's activities.

Matt's first Christmas in Korea vividly locked itself in his memory. For nearly half the Fighting Fourth came down with dysentery; he included.

He lay in bed for two days; doubled with cramps. Not eating, and taking what little liquid he could. The bug...and incessant, hurried dashes to the latrine...caused him to drop nearly fifteen pounds.

The second Christmas came and went as unbearably.

A tremendous number of replacement fliers arrived during the holidays, fresh from abbreviated flight training. The '90-day Wonder' syndrome took its toll; many died through pilot error. And considerably more than from communist fire.

Korea's seasoned pilots suffered acute homesickness; tired of living amongst the squalid rubble of a foreign country. And now, even more depressed over the numbers of young men killed in what the papers labeled a 'police action.'

"If this is a police action Matthew," Hoot first exclaimed on seeing the term in Stars & Stripes. "Then let the goddamned Korean cops handle it...and send our asses back home!"

During their months in Korea, Matt and Hoot several times hitched cargo flights to Hong Kong. These forays afforded a few days' rest and relaxation, and always good times when they crossed paths with pilots from other wings. Especially those who loved recalling flying adventures as much as they did.

Over the summer, they shagged an airlift for ten days' leave on Guam.

They enjoyed hiking the jungled island; still littered with live rounds, bombs and military implements from World War Two. And occasionally, they stumbled upon war casualties.

One day near Talofofo Falls, they discovered several unburied and decomposed Japanese corpses laying in the thick jungle underbrush. They resisted close inspection, and reported their finding to the Judge Advocate's Office at Guam's Naval Air Station.

Using that volcanic atoll as home base, the two borrowed an Army Cessna and sky-hopped throughout the Marianas Islands, landing on WWII airstrips; both U.S. and Japanese.

They encountered war's remnants everywhere:

Guam's graveyard of gutted tanks atop a hill overlooking a peaceful green lagoon.

Japanese Zeros and American B-25 Mitchell bombers strewn like decomposing dinosaurs beside the runway on Tinian.

And several aircraft scuttled by fleeing Japanese; a few of which appeared in working condition, although vines, palms and breadplant entangled and enshrouded them from tail to propeller.

Throughout the atolls, skimming a hundred feet over the water, they spotted sunken vessels...ours and the enemy's...looming as rusty-black geometric shapes against the clean pink coral and vivid blue-green water.

They also toured local villages and towns, and awed over the healing war wounds in that tiny area of the Pacific, where trade and shipping again were regaining footholds; spurred by America's military presence.

Somehow the duo remained objective; oblivious to the facts of what transpired in that area less than a decade ago. They had toured the isles as historians, not warriors. Wishing to briefly ignore the horrors and existence of war.

Of military life...of shaving, showering, starched uniforms and impromptu inspections.

Of creaky bomb carts and rattling ammo boxes that contained long, glistening belts of destruction.

And especially of sickening sweet fumes permeating their hut in early light, and signaling napalm pods being loaded for the day's mission.

They spent their last two days of leave in a bamboo-thatched hotel on Ponape, then returned the Cessna and caught an air transport from Guam to Korea.

The Greenwich clock at the BOQ registered nineteen-hundred hours when they logged in at Quoseng; tanned, rested and slightly hungover, but primed to face what the final months of their combat tour dished out.

Matt and Hoot logged nearly a hundred missions apiece, and counted on returning Stateside in the spring. Their friend and commanding officer, Warren Kellogg, had received his orders in early November; he would be home in time for Christmas.

Fate, however, interceded to expedite the major's return.

The day after Thanksgiving, a dozen MiGs, hidden in the sun, jumped he and Lieutenant Craig Hart during morning patrol. Craig...a hometown acquaintance of Jug Hale's...had completed flight training and shipped out with Matt and Hoot.

Warren's aircraft took several cannon shots early on, and pieces of shrapnel ripped his legs. He escaped his pursuers by flying into cloud cover.

When finally he broke into a clearing...and returned to assist his comrade...he saw the other Sabre in the distance, out of control and spinning through the low ceiling toward the earth.

Major Kellogg succeeded in controlling his disabled aircraft, and landed at Quoseng before passing out.

Ground forces later recovered Lieutenant Hart's body from his shattered machine; he had died instantly in the barrage of cannon fire from the communist aircraft.

Matt, as ranking captain, assumed the position as Falcon Flight Commander; responsible for assigning fledgling pilots to their respective groups.

As his father had advised, he accustomed himself to discharging such duties from a detached and objective military standpoint; without feeling, emotion or remorse.

Korea had altered his outlook on life. He knew it, yet in the clouded recesses of his mind...hope glimmered. He believed he could revert to his former state of reason when this ended.

Even if actions compelled by his new post tarnished the glimmer, he prayed time eventually would erase memories of the turmoil occurring within and around him.

Matt and Hoot now resembled brothers: sharing thoughts, actions and ordeals. No secrets existed between them; and their closeness kept them sane in the midst of the insanity.

Hoot earned his captaincy soon after Matt, and became Falcon Eight's Group Two flight leader. Of the original sixteen pilots, seven had survived; counting Major Kellogg in San Francisco, convalescing and undergoing painful physical therapy.

Several times, Matt and Hoot limped to Quoseng with their machines heavily damaged. Once, Hoot bailed out; and luckily floated into Allied territory.

The mud, slush and ice of December melted quickly into spring, and fresh greenery punched through the torn red soil. The change of season heralded the arrival of orders Stateside for the two fliers.

Their names appeared at the top of the 1 May 1953 roster, which listed twenty men departing in the middle of the month for the United States.

Each wrote his parents the moment the orders clattered from the classified Teletype, and with only days to go, excitedly located, labeled and packed items collected over the tour of duty.

In the Quonset hut, Matt had begun briefing his replacement...a bright and extremely young captain....when the camp's public address system blared to life:

"Pilots to the ready hut! Pilots to the ready hut!"

Soon the large building filled with fliers, sitting or squatting two deep against its curved steel walls. Quoseng's Base Commander hurried to the front of the assemblage as one of his staff officers called the group to attention.

The Commander stood silent for an instant, then spoke:

"Take your seats, gentlemen. Smoke if you want to."

In unison, those who could took seats. Matt and the other flight leaders held the front row, and as the commander spoke, they jotted notes on their lap clipboards.

"G-1 says the commies are planning something...possibly another strong push in this direction."

With his pointer, the colonel traced a tiny circle in Sector Forty-two.

"We've blasted hell out of Tchung Ko airfield...and now Intelligence says squadrons of MiG-15s and 17s are basing at Wang Su...here."

He tapped another area on the large topographic map.

"These fighters are massing for a concentrated strike at bases near the Thirty-Eighth Parallel. In short, boys...we think the North Koreans plan on pushing ten miles inside our lines; possibly intent on capturing Seoul."

The colonel paced the platform silently for a moment, then placed his pointer in a tray on the briefing chart backboard. He crossed his arms and stared defiantly at the gathering.

"By God, we're going to stop that push! Our bombers from the Eleventh will join those of the Ninth and Fifteenth at a designated sector. They'll then proceed North to strike enemy production and supply points."

The colonel pulled a pack of cigarettes from his leather flight jacket and fired one.

"Like you...I wish to God we could fly past the Yalu and bomb the real targets...but our hands are tied."

He walked to the front of the platform, still looking out over the upturned faces.

"Fighters from the Fourth, Eighth, Thirty-Fifth and Fifty-First Wings will fly close ground support for our land forces; and cover our bomber missions. Flight commanders...hold tight for mission briefings to pass along. The rest of you can get your flying gear ready."

The crowded, smoke-hazy hut quickly emptied.

Matt and group leaders from the other two wings moved closer to where the colonel stood. Matt pulled a deck of Luckies from the side pocket of his flight jacket. Tapped one out and lit it. He took a deep pull, and listened as the colonel and two aides orchestrated the mission.

Using the topo maps, the trio outlined primary and secondary targets, as well as rendezvous and ditch points.

"This is the big show, gents," the colonel said rather matter-of-factly. "Let's really tear 'em a new one! Takeoff at zero-six-thirty hours. Good luck, and good hunting."

Matt jotted cryptic notes about Falcon Flight's mission, and when the colonel's strategy brief concluded, returned to his Quonset where Hoot and the other group leaders waited.

"Like the bird colonel said...this is big, boys," he stated flatly.

Matt sat on the edge of his bunk and lit another smoke. Then he pulled a terrain map from his foot locker, unrolled it, and outlined mission objectives and coordinates.

"All together, there'll be a hundred of us against twice that number of them. It's going to get plenty crowded up there!"

He detailed the air order of battle concisely and thoroughly, and when they wrapped, every pilot in the flight knew what to expect the next day. Then they adjourned to the officer's club for nonalcoholic "Flaming Fliers" until the evening meal; followed by an early lights out.

"Get through this one and we've got it made old buddy," Matt said to Hoot as they clinked mugs that brimmed with cherry red fruit punch. He took a large gulp of the liquid, then accentuated his statement with a billowing, puffy smoke ring that flattened against the tabletop, contorted slowly out of shape, and faded into nothingness.

"I'll drink to going Stateside...any day," replied Hoot. "How 'bout another?"

They joined the other airmen in another round, then walked to the mess hut in the middle of the barracks area. The base commander had anticipated the next day's ordeal, and arranged steak for the pilots.

Like the other aviators, Matt and Hoot ravaged their sirloins; the beef represented the pilots' first decent meat in months.

The fliers sacked out at eight o'clock, and arose at five. By six-thirty, Matt craned over his Sabrejet's nose as one by one, the gigantic B-29s clambered down the long runway.

When his flight's turn came, they received clearance, taxied and took off two abreast, joining the other fighter groups sharing the strike mission.

Airborne twenty minutes...cruising at fifteen thousand feet... Matt spotted ground flashes and massive clouds of smoke. They were approaching the target area where clusters of bombs turned earth, concrete and metal structures into huge smoky craters.

The wing commander radioed his instructions to the group leaders, and Matt's flight and those on either side shifted to combat formation. All airmen armed and cleared their machine guns, and awaited the enemy.

When the swarm of enemy fliers appeared, Matt never imagined such a melee.

For nearly half an hour, Sabres and MiGs skirmished across the smoke-laced skies, while below, Army and Marine Corps infantry battled hordes of North Korean soldiers; whose numbers multiplied by the minute.

Matt dove steeply on a MiG closing behind a Sabre from the Eighteenth. As the silvery shape filled his gun sight, he touched the firing switch and felt his aircraft bump as it spat rounds toward the enemy.

The MiG rolled onto its side, nearly colliding with the Sabre it pursued, then spun to Earth, impacting in an orange ball of flaming jet fuel.

Matt leveled, banked left, and was heading back to the fray when movement drew his peripheral vision to the right side of his canopy. There, wispy white smoke trails disclosed that twenty millimeter rounds were streaking past his right wing.

He immediately scanned his rearview mirror and spotted the MiG... less than a hundred yards away, and closing...its cannons flashing.

Instinctively, Matt tucked his chin tightly against his chest, grunted from the pit of his stomach as hard and as loud as he could, and yanked the control stick toward his crotch.

The Sabre stood on its tail, tucking into a steep roll, and for an instant, Matt felt he would black out as gravity restricted his blood flow and blurred his vision. He continued grunting as deeply as he could, joystick fully back, and the jet soon topped its loop.

As it did, he leveled behind the MiG, lifted his goggles, rubbed his eyes clear and tripped his guns in short, rapid bursts.

Again he felt the chatter as six gun barrels flamed orange, and fifty caliber projectiles sparked and pierced the MiG's metal skin. Almost at once, a fine trail of mist appeared beneath the enemy aircraft, signaling damaged hydraulic controls.

Matt slid the trigger switch forward again. This time, flames burst from the MiG's mid-section and it nosed downward. He followed the crippled aircraft in its plunge, and momentarily felt relief when its canopy blew at a thousand feet.

Unfortunately, the North Korean tangled in his seat belt or his ejector didn't fire. Whatever the cause, Matt watched incredulously as the craft belly-skidded across a pasture and exploded in the dense thicket of trees that bordered it.

He pulled the Sabre into a gentle climb and again headed toward the dogfight...now several miles away. Against the distant horizon, long billowing plumes of ebony smoke marked where flaming aircraft had plunged from the sky.

Smoldering wreckage lay strewn around charred areas where impact occurred; and he estimated at least a dozen shoot-downs.

By the time he reached the area where the MiG ambushed him, the conflict had ended. Twenty enemy aircraft, low and to the left, flew due North as hastily as possible.

Through his earphones, he overheard the excited, garbled conversations of fellow pilots.

"Falcon Flight...form on me," he said into his facemask intercom.

As flight leader, he breathed instant and gratifying relief when fifteen Sabres appeared from various directions and glided into formation behind him.

Hoot soon hung at his wingtip, flashing thumbs-up then drifting into his slot at the head of Group Two.

"Welcome back, boys," Matt chuckled.

He barely could contain his exuberance as the Sabres regrouped at twenty-five thousand feet and swung southward toward Quoseng. The pilots eavesdropped through their headphones as other flights reformed and headed for their respective bases.

"Glad everyone's accounted for," Matt said. "How'd we do?"

One by one, the Falcon Flight aviators recounted their victories. He listened intently; feeling proud of the team he helped form and train, and had fussed over like a mother hen.

All told, the sixteen destroyed twenty-one communist aircraft; nearly half of the combined air group's fifty-six. Only one U.S. jet fell in the process, and its pilot parachuted into the hands of friendly forces.

"You must have had a close one, skipper!" exclaimed the pilot flying behind Matt. "Something chewed your ass...you've got hits on your outside elevator, rudder and fuselage!"

"Yeah...I thought she flew a little sluggish," Matt replied. "I'm getting vibration, too. It's a wonder she didn't break apart when I snap-rolled!"

The sun glared off the dew-coated runway as Falcon Flight's Sabres touched down in pairs. They taxied to the flight line by the ready hut, raised canopies in the fresh spring air, then cut power.

Matt stretched for a moment, eyes closed. Then unbuckled, removed his helmet, goggles and facemask, and dropped them into the tiny storage area behind his seat.

He rubbed his eyes and face, and when he leaned forward a sergeant appeared to help lift him up and out of the jet.

He climbed down the metal ladder past 'CAPT. DURHAM,' stenciled in black military block letters beneath the cockpit. Under the name, he gently patted the three enameled red stars.

And this time, when his flight boots touched pavement, he knew he'd never again climb into a fighter.

Matt walked to the front of the Sabre...stood by its nose... and examined the black powder residue surrounding the machine gun ports.

Then he stepped to the rear of the aircraft to inspect the damage.

The middle of the elevator on his right wing boasted three baseball-sized holes, and his rudder displayed a ten-inch gash from a cannon round. Two large dents below the jagged opening revealed where shells impacted and ricocheted without exploding.

Matt patted the silvery fuselage the way others do horses and dogs, then walked to the ready hut for debriefing. He met Hoot halfway there, and the friends shook hands and hugged warmly; then continued to the building, arms around each other's shoulders.

On 15 May 1953, Matt and Hoot collected their orders.

The two were directed to report to the United States Air Force Base, Springfield, Massachusetts, "as expeditiously as possible," for processing and release from active duty.

A day later, they packed their belongings and said their good-byes. And the following day...slightly hungover from the farewell party of the night before...they boarded a U.S.-bound transport.

Five fuel stops and twenty-two hours later, Matt and Hoot prepared to again touch American soil.

As the four-motored passenger plane dropped through the clouds to five thousand feet, the duo craned out the rectangular window. Finally, they distinguished the dark coastline through the morning haze that hung below.

Matt stubbed his cigarette and turned to Hoot.

"I haven't formally asked, old pal...but would you honor me as my best man?"

"Matthew, I'd be proud to," the other beamed. "Let me know where and when, and I'll be there in tux and tails before you know it! Hey, look! It's the air base!"

The military airliner swung wide of the airfield and approached teardrop fashion from the low end of the runway. Soon, main landing gears squealed and smoked as they touched concrete, followed by a thump as the front wheel connected.

The pilot reversed the pitch of his props, and the sharp cut in ground speed sent Matt and Hoot sprawling against the seats in front of them.

Matt reached into the compartment above his head, and pulled on his flight jacket before the plane stopped rolling. The coat now carried insignias collected in Korea.

Hoot leaned over the row opposite their seats and peered outside. There, a cluster of welcomers waited patiently along the railing outside the flight operations building.

Matt hooked his arm around Hoot's shoulder and bent down so he, too, could look outside.

His parents stood there; waving and cheering excitedly.

As did Hoot's.

Beside them, he recognized the Forsythes and, most important, Karen.

Even forty feet away, standing slightly in front of the small group, he discerned her unmistakable beauty. She held her hands to her mouth; anticipating his deboarding.

And when she saw him stoop to pass through the transport's exit door, she squealed hysterically and ran toward him; arms open wide.

Matt dropped the flight bag he carried, swooped her into his grasp, and kissed her long and hard as her momentum swung them full circle.

Hoot exited immediately behind Matt, patted his friend's back, skirted the embracing couple and ran to clutch his parents.

Walt and Claire Durham approached Matt and Karen; the two still looking each other up and down, with tears trickling over their cheeks.

The general put his hand on his son's shoulder, and Matt turned and hugged him warmly.

"Welcome home, son. We've missed you. Your mother and Karen haven't breathed easily for a year and a half."

The Forsythes greeted Matt affectionately with additional embraces and kisses, and after collecting his gear, the six headed for the parking area.

There they met Ed and Mary Gibson...helping Hoot collect and stow his duffel bags.

"Hoot, remember Karen's and my folks?" asked Matt.

The young man instantly dropped his luggage, and took the hands offered by the general and the doctor.

"Certainly, Matthew," he said, shaking with the two, and returning warm hugs.

"And I want you to meet my folks...Mary and Ed," Hoot replied, his hand sweeping toward his parents, who greeted the other couples.

"Hoot...I wish you and your folks wouldn't hurry back to Middletown," said Walt, helping stow bags and boxes in his and the Gibson's cars. "We'd love for you and your folks to spend the day. Get reacquainted. And maybe celebrate a little this evening!"

"Oh Walt...for Heaven's sake!" Claire scolded. "Hoot and Matt are probably bone-tired, and want to get home. There'll be plenty of time for celebrating."

"Tell you what, general," said Hoot. "We'll take you up on breakfast. I'm starved!"

He slammed the trunk deck closed.

"Then, I'd like to get home and find out what's going on."

"I understand, son," said Walt. "Like Claire says...you're not that far away. We'll see lots of each other."

"I asked Hoot to be my best man, dad," Matt snaked his arm around Karen's waist and squeezed her softly. "We've got lots of planning to do...for the wedding and for jobs."

Matt held Karen at arm's length.

"Hoot and I are thinking about starting an advertising agency. We've been together quite a while now...and we'd like to keep it that way."

"Matt...that sounds swell!" Walt exclaimed. "You two are welcome to a shot at Conn Casting's promotional work. I don't know how much budget we've got for such activities...but I imagine it'll get you started."

"Listen you two...I've got newspapers down this way," Ed added. "They could use a couple of hotshot promotion men, too. And, we've got lots of accounts begging for the services you're talking about. Just say the word...and I'll be on the telephone!"

Hoot draped his arms over Matt's and Karen's shoulders.

"Well, partner...we've hit on something worth considering. Let's give it a go! 'Durham and Gibson Advertising'...sounds pretty impressive, doesn't it!"

"Mr. Gibson, you're on!" agreed Matt.

He pecked Karen on the lips, then firmly clasped his friend's hand.

"We need to firm plans for two partnerships," Matt yawned. "And I don't know about Hoot...but after breakfast, I could do with a hot shower and long nap."

"That sounds Heavenly to me, Matthew," Hoot replied, smiling broadly. "Just Heavenly!"

Chapter 10

Marriage-Minded

A COOL SPRING CARRIED INTO SUMMER, and by mid-June, the woods behind...and shrubbery nestled against...the Durham's two-story white frame house bloomed verdantly. Connecticut erupted in pastel wildflowers and pansies from one end of the state to the other, and Matt felt certain New Haven reigned as the spot most blessed with nature's beauty.

He and Hoot assiduously tried shutting from their minds the things they saw and did in Korea. Still, they abruptly halted whatever tasks they were performing when they heard the country mentioned in newscasts or conversations.

In late May, the two had tapped their savings...squirreled while overseas...and flew to the West Coast to visit Warren Kellogg. Therapy had helped the major regain most use in his legs, although a noticeable stiffness reflected in his gait; and shooting pain accompanied every step.

"They performed amazing feats on these old limbs," he had told his visitors. "The Navy doctors connected severed sinew and veins, and replaced shattered bone with stainless steel."

Warren hiked his pajama leg to reveal purple stitching running from knee to ankle.

"The only complication is poor circulation when I'm sleeping and my legs are level. I don't know if it's the metal or what...but sometimes, my legs feel like ice. Hell, if I marry and touch these icicles against my new bride...the honeymoon will end real quick!"

Matt and Hoot breathed easier discovering their friend still possessed a sense of humor. His positive mental attitude and outlook provided relief as well. After three days, they returned to Connecticut in brighter moods; anxious to continue their lives.

Hoot first returned to Middletown, then rejoined Matt in New Haven to help his comrade with wedding plans.

One Saturday morning, a week before the wedding, the two sat with Walt drinking coffee on the backyard patio, exulting in the sounds, smells and splendor of a quiet woods stirring to life.

"Well, Matthew...a week and a few hours and you'll be an old married man," Hoot quipped over the top of a steamy cup. "With 'Until death do you part...' staring you in the face; aren't you getting sorta nervous?"

"Nah...not in the least, Hoot," Matt replied. "In fact, I think you're saying that because you can't find a nice gal to settle with...or at least one who'd have you!"

"Darn it all, Matthew...you're right! I mean...Karen's a looker, and she cares about people. There may not be many others like her...but I'm looking!"

"Say, how are you two firming your business undertaking?" asked Walt, filling their cups with fresh coffee. "Like I said...let me know when you start making plans."

Walt returned the pot to a hotplate, then rejoined the two.

"Conn Castings is unveiling its first jetliner fuselage this fall," he continued. "We'll want a real blowout! In fact, the marketing folks are outlining their advertising and promotion budgets now; you two should plan on meeting with them in early August."

"Your dad's right, Matthew. We'll need at least a month to develop a presentation. When you return from honeymooning, we'd better bust our tails!"

"Tell you what, boys," Walt jotted a note to himself; "I'll bootleg you a copy of the jetliner's sales strategy. It'll provide background on the product and our customers."

"Sounds as if your people have done their marketing homework, dad," Matt said, detecting the enthusiasm that glowed on the general's face and crackled his voice.

"Frankly...we're excited over our plane! It's hard to keep from blabbing to everyone; but it's a first...and we're going to catch our competitors napping. 'Loose lips sink ships' has become our day-to-day philosophy."

"Don't worry, general...we'll keep everything under tight wraps," assured Hoot. "And between Matthew and me...we'll create a promotion that'll take your breath away!"

"I don't doubt it for a minute, Hoot. You two are going places; I'm certain of that. Now...how about some hotcakes and sausage?"

The three entered the house, talking excitedly about flying, business plans, the wedding, and the coming hunting season. Suddenly, Matt's emotions blindsided him; flooded his being with a realization of how neatly and correctly things were falling into place.

A happenstance he found incredulous...and for which he felt deeply grateful.

He pinpointed his sense of fulfillment beginning with the visit to Warren Kellogg. For some reason, that San Francisco jaunt lifted a veil; one that had clouded his future outlooks. And now, with such ambiguity removed, his plans were shaping.

He literally tingled with excitement as he walked into the kitchen, locked his arms around his mother's waist, kissed her cheek, and whispered in her ear in mock Humphrey Bogart:

"Look at it this way, sister...you're not losing a son, you're gaining someone else to pick up after!"

"Oh, you!" Claire shrieked.

She leaned back her head, looked toward the ceiling and laughed heartily.

"I hope poor Karen can survive a family of fliers and hunters!"

"She's done remarkably well so far, Claire," mused Walt, bussing her other cheek. "That's a fair inkling of her mettle."

Fittings for the bridal gown, bride's maid dresses and tuxedos crammed the following week. And in addition to selecting gifts for bridesmaids and ushers...and confirming honeymoon reservations at Cape Cod and Boston...Matt and Karen planned a quick stopover to see Jug; now a Reserve Officers Training Corps instructor at Boston University.

On Friday evening, the wedding rehearsal and dinner came off hitchless; although the Forsythes' champagne nightcap carried well into the early hours of Saturday.

Matt awakened at slightly past nine and tried focusing on his clock's dial; but to no avail. So he arose and stumbled to the bathroom for Bromo and aspirin to stifle a pounding head.

He lit a cigarette there, and through the haze between himself and his reflection in the mirror said: "Well, sport, this is it! Here's to us. We're getting one hell of a woman!"

He lifted the water glass of milky bubbly liquid in a toast and gulped it, then dashed icy water over his face to get the system pumping again.

As he shaved, he heard his parents talking at the breakfast table upstairs. In the guest room beside his, Hoot was singing in the shower.

His wedding day was under way; and he knew it would be superb!

A half mile away, Karen brushed her teeth then padded downstairs for coffee. The telephone rang as she entered the kitchen.

Matt chirped from the other end: "Just calling to see if you're still in town," he chuckled into the handset.

"Very funny, wisenheimer," she replied. "We're not supposed to see each other this side of the aisle; does that apply to talking, too?"

"Damned if I know, honey...or care. I'm not letting some silly superstition keep me from saying 'good morning' to my favorite gal!"

For a moment, only static hummed on the line; then she whispered softly. "I love you, Matt."

"I love you too, Karen. See you at three o'clock."

He whistled as he opened his bedroom door to walk upstairs for coffee, and nearly collided with Hoot; just exiting the guest room.

He grabbed Matt's hand and clutched it firmly in his.

"This is your day, Matthew. Enjoy it...and relive it the rest of your life. I hope you and Karen find it stuffed with the best of everything."

"Thanks, old buddy," Matt said, embracing his friend. "I appreciate those wishes, and I'm grateful you're standing with me. What a way to go...flanked by the two people who mean the most!"

"Roger that last transmission, Matthew. When I go down in nuptial flames...I'll expect it to be the same way!"

After breakfast, Matt packed his suitcase and flight bag, then he and Hoot washed the Durham's new Buick; loaned by the general for his son's honeymoon.

At first, Matt worried the day would drag and he'd become nervous. Instead, the hours sped like minutes and he barely completed his list of chores.

Suddenly, the time arrived to dress and leave for the church.

He donned his tuxedo and went upstairs, where Claire Durham immediately began fiddling with her son's bowtie. Hoot lit a cigarette for Matt, then mixed him a stiff bourbon and water; also pouring one for himself and the Durhams.

"Here folks," he said, cradling the glasses. "We need all the courage we can muster!"

A similar scene played at the Forsythe's.

Karen and her mother enjoyed glasses of Chablis as they fussed with makeup, hair and gowns.

"You'd think after fifty years my hair would behave!" Evelyn scolded, her voice tinged with mock exasperation.

"Mother...you always look beautiful," Karen said, slipping her arm around the woman's shoulders. She rested her chin atop her mother's head and studied the two reflections in the mirror.

"You look wonderful, darling," Evelyn sighed, reached to touch her daughter's face. "I hope Matt Durham realizes how lucky he is."

"I think we both are, mom; and we both do!"

Downstairs, Damon shouted they needed to leave soon.

The two women stood, took final glimpses, then embraced carefully to avoid mussing each other.

At three o'clock, Matt and Hoot waited in front of the altar at the First Presbyterian Church. Behind them, the cicada hum of whispers and organ music wafted through the packed chapel.

Matt sensed the bourbon losing its battle against nerves, as beads of perspiration trickled the small of his back.

Then the organ struck the wedding processional.

He turned instinctively and looked up the long aisle; and when Karen appeared, his heart trembled. He revered her graceful, wholesome beauty, and in the wedding gown, her comeliness dazzled. She lightly clasped her father's arm; whose golf tan and graying hair complemented the refinement imbued by the couple as they paced to the pulpit.

Karen's summer darkness heightened the flash of her pearly teeth, and her lacy white gown intensified even more her bridal loveliness. She clutched a corsage of tiny white rosebuds, and as she moved effortlessly and gracefully to the wedding march, Matt's chest pounded; a thumping he knew Hoot heard.

Karen's gaze fixed on his; following her pew to pew, ever closer, as familiar faces blurred before his eyes.

Damon escorted her to the groom, took her hand and gently placed it in Matt's, then kissed her softly on the cheek. He patted Matt's shoulder and smiled, then took his spot behind the young couple.

Matt looked down at Karen, and she turned, facing him; smiling broadly, and eyes glistening.

"I love you," he whispered.

"I love you, too."

Repeating vows seemed to require only scant minutes, and then rings quickly were exchanged in blurs of gold. Following that, a dash back up the aisle heralded another couple stepping into a new world.

At the reception, the newlyweds, wedding party and parents formed the traditional line. After which, champagne punch and an enticing seafood buffet sated the thirsts and appetites of the invited guests.

Later, Matt and Karen disappeared to their respective dressing rooms; furnished by the hotel hosting the reception so bride and groom could don more comfortable traveling clothes.

The couple then scampered to the crepe paper-adorned Buick through a gauntlet of well-wishers and rice tossers. And minutes later, Matt steered onto Highway Ninety-five.

Cape Cod beckoned; one hundred and seventy miles northeast.

The early evening drive along the coastal highway cooled and refreshed them; the heady fragrance of salt water and white pine wafting through the car's open windows.

Miles and hours sped past, as Long Island Sound melded into Block Island Sound and then Rhode Island Sound. Soon, the couple drove east out of Fall River, Massachusetts, and pulled into the New Harbor Lodge at Hyannisport on Nantucket Sound.

Cape Cod Bay glimmered at their backs.

They parked in front of the tidy lodge where they would spend the week, and the luminous dashboard clock topped eleven as Matt checked them in.

Minutes later, he opened the trunk and retrieved the suitcases.

"Matt, this is glorious!" exclaimed Karen, her hands stifling a gasp as she stepped out of the car and absorbed the panoramic view.

Salt white sand and glassy water beckoned less than a hundred feet away, and the full moon's bright image reflected in shimmering silver bands. In the distance, a lighthouse's rhythmic sweep painted the undersides of low clouds that hovered over the Atlantic.

She took his arm and leaned her head on his shoulder as they walked the driftwood lined path to their cottage. Matt opened the door and set the luggage inside, and with one smooth motion, lifted and transported her across the threshold.

Inside the beachfront bungalow, moonlight streamed through a glass-enclosed breakfast room; bathing objects within in silvered softness. Beyond the breakfast nook, a wooden patio jutted seaward atop pilings driven deep beneath the surf.

Karen switched on a desk lamp.

"Look, Matt," she said, her hand resting on an ice bucket in which stood a magnum of champagne.

She read the attached note that wished them luck and happiness in their lives together.

"It's from Hoot," she sighed. "He's so thoughtful."

Matt toted the suitcases to the bedroom, where they unpacked. Then Karen slipped into the bathroom...a lacy, wispy beige negligee in her hand...while Matt removed his clothes and donned pajama bottoms and his loose silk kimono from Korea.

He walked to the living room, uncorked the champagne, and poured two glasses. Then he switched off the desk lamp, and turned the radio low. While Karen readied, he reclined on the couch and stared out the picture window over the incandescent bay.

When she stepped from the bathroom, Matt discerned the light flowery fragrance of her favorite perfume. She glided in front of the picture window seeking the couch, and the moonlight silhouetted her beauty through the flimsy gown.

He instantly flushed with desire; then stood, holding the glasses of champagne. He handed her one.

"Here's to you, darling," he said. "This night will live with me forever."

They clinked glasses and drank the sparkling liquid. Without speaking, Karen put her arms around his neck, pressed tight against him, and kissed him passionately and deeply.

Beneath the bathrobe, he felt himself respond to her soft warmth and inquisitive tongue. He pulled her tighter, and her firmness strained against him.

Karen's right hand unhitched the belt fastening his garment. Then she slipped it open, and grasped him softly. Through their pressed mouths, he moaned with ecstasy.

"God, you feel wonderful," she gasped. "Let's make love, Matt... now and all night."

He set the empty glasses on the end table by the couch, lifted her effortlessly and carried her into the bedroom. He lightly placed her on the bed, then slipped off his kimono and pajamas.

Karen eased her nightgown over her head as he slid her soft silk underwear past her ankles and onto the floor with his garments.

Soon, she lay undressed and bathed in moonlight; her sculpted beauty capturing his breath. Her arms open, and beckoning.

For hours, the two merged with the silent darkness. Outside, fog horns moaned softly. And trawlers, a quarter mile offshore, putted by.

The incoming tide lapped rhythmically against the piers under the cabin while they kissed softly...and nibbled gently; their mouths cupped tightly, and breathing in and out in unison.

Matt and Karen wondered to themselves if anything ever could top the moment; that precise instant. With both exhaustively satisfied, yet still seeking further possession of each other; loving, touching and clinging tightly as one.

He awoke at ten o'clock; startled by a gull perched on an overturned skiff outside, screeching as a large soft-shelled crab skittered toward the water.

He glanced at Karen, sleeping; a half smile curving her lips.

She lay on her right side, facing him, with the sheet pushed to her waist; revealing firm round breasts and patches of freckles on her upper arms, and at the base of her slender neck. Without wishing to disturb her, he leaned on his left elbow and kissed her tenderly on the cheek; only to see the clear blue eyes sweep open.

She reached and pulled him to her, kissing him playfully at first.

Then deeply, as she felt his body respond.

She slid beneath him on the satiny sheets and with her hand, delicately directed him to her.

Outside, the gull had given up tormenting the crab, and a heady breeze wafted the salt water scent throughout the Sound. Overhead, puffy cumulus clouds tried blotting the sun; succeeding only occasionally.

Matt and Karen remained in each other's arms until nearly noon, then showered, dressed, and left the cottage in search of lunch.

From Plymouth to Provincetown, Cape Cod's landscape sparkled at midday. Clusters of clapboard and white brick cottages, villas and stately mansions snugged the hillocks, bogs and inlets.

On their left, Cape Cod Bay invited them to partake of pristine beaches and refreshing waters. To the right, Nantucket Island and Martha's Vineyard beckoned intriguingly.

They continued leisurely along the coast roadway, admiring the breathtaking views and beguiling New England fishing villages through which they passed. The couple stopped frequently, to poke through antique shops or admire works displayed by roadside artists.

It was nearly two when they pulled into Provincetown.

On the recommendation of Karen's boss, they stopped at Sailmender's Oyster Bar & Restaurant. There, they devoured a dozen fresh, baseball-sized, ice-chilled mollusks apiece, while Matt whimpered through watery eyes and burning nostrils after dipping too deeply into horseradish as he prepared his cocktail sauce.

All the same, he hungrily pried the mussels from their barnacled homes and slathered them in the fiery pink concoction.

When four one-pound lobsters arrived, the two hurriedly pulled on bibs and launched a shell-cracker assault. Bits of crimson and splashes of butter soon covered the red and white checked oilcloth.

Sailmender's served up fresh blackberry cheesecake as its dessert specialty, which they enjoyed outside on the deck. From this vantage point, they could look down onto the Provincetown market and into Cape Cod Bay, where a regatta of sailboats and yachts ghosted gracefully across the emerald waters, catching the late afternoon gusts.

They sat side by side...feet propped on the verandah's railing...and drank frosted mugs of beer; chatting about the antiques and paintings they'd seen, and what to take the folks.

Karen's hand clutched his; the late afternoon sun reflecting off her gold wedding band. Her head rested against his right shoulder; both enjoying every sight, sound, smell and minute together.

Below them, a radio came alive in one of the ivy-covered cottages that crowded the cobblestone street: the sumptuous voice of Peggy Lee, lilting a song about Cape Cod.

"I wonder what the poor folks are doing," he said, softly kissing the top of her head.

"Ummm," came her reply.

It was nearly six when they steered toward Hyannisport, opting to finish the night before's champagne and indulge in lovemaking before dinner.

Over the next four days, the two trekked every out-of-the-way spot they heard about; exploring both sides of the Cape's elbow-shaped peninsula. They immensely enjoyed the ferry crossing to Martha's Vineyard, and a day and night at its historic White Horse Inn.

They visited museums and galleries, and marveled at the juxtaposition of splendor and quaint beauty offered up by the tiny dot of land. Then from Martha's Vineyard, they ferried to Nantucket Island.

When Friday morning dawned, they returned to Hyannisport.

"This has been Paradise, Matt."

Her whisper came through steamy, freshly brewed coffee that accompanied a breakfast consisting of eggs Benedict and Sardot on the terrace behind the New Harbor Lodge restaurant.

"I can't believe we've been here a week."

"I can't either, sweetheart," he answered, quietly.

With his fork, he sopped a piece of English muffin and egg in the tart hollandaise sauce.

"It's been wonderful...busy, but relaxed and enjoyable. I'm certain we've done everything possible during the days."

"And nights...for that matter," she smiled mischievously.

Karen placed her hand on his upper thigh, and he felt desire well.

"Would it be rude if we mussed the bed for the second time today?" he whispered, tossing his napkin on the glass tabletop.

"Last one under the covers is a horse's rear!" she said. She hopped to her feet and dashed the path toward their bungalow.

"You're on," he shouted at her back.

He fumbled money for the check and tip, then jumped up himself; and caught her a hundred yards away at the front steps. He collected his wife in his arms and carried her inside.

Once again, he sat her down carefully in the bedroom and they hastily undressed each other. Unclothed, they fell back onto the bed and merged as one. And an hour later, the newlyweds collapsed in each other's arms; moist with perspiration and love, their bodies and senses spent.

That evening, the couple enjoyed a candlelight dinner at a steak house they discovered earlier in the week. Matt bought a fresh bottle of champagne, and they walked and sat on the beach until midnight; listening to breakers, seabirds and the familiar mournful notes of distant vessels.

They strolled the salt-laced darkness, arms about each other's waists; not talking, merely sensing what the other felt and thought.

When they approached the honeymoon cottage, he cast an undetected glance her way, and distinguished her sculpted features framed in moonlight.

He reflected on a day...seemingly not long ago...and two adolescents searching for walnuts. He had innately realized then; in fact, presupposed this outcome.

And now, filled with love so painfully strong, he vowed to do everything in his power to preserve it.

"Have I told you recently that I love you?" he asked, squeezing her hand.

"Not enough, Matt Durham," she replied. "Never enough."

They stepped into the dark bungalow to spend the last night at Cape Cod as they had the first; loving each other completely.

They loaded the car by nine o'clock Saturday morning, checked out, and drove northwest on Highway Six for Boston.

Behind them, Matt and Karen left beautiful memories...and a promise to return.

That promise they would fulfill many times in the years to come. And with each reappearance, manage to capture and outshine a large portion of the moments and feelings shared with this locale over their honeymoon.

They arrived at Boston at noon and telephoned Jug; who invited them to lunch at his apartment near Boston University.

"You don't know how great it is seeing you two," he said as he led the duo inside, following embraces at the doorway. "You're my favorite twosome; right up there with Roy and Dale. And I'm happy as hell you tied the knot."

Jug provided Matt and Karen with a brief tour that ended in the living room.

"Sorry I couldn't be there to see the Korean jet jockey go down in flames," Jug said as they sat. "You picked the one weekend in June when I had to wet-nose a bunch of ROTC brats!."

"He made it okay...even without 'Big Brother,'" Karen said, squeezing Matt's arm. The two sat on a large cushy sofa in the small but tidy apartment.

"Hoot kept him from fainting several times!"

"Hey...I'm proud of these two birds," Jug said, limping to the refrigerator.

He returned with three beers and frosted mugs and plopped into an easy chair across the coffee table from them.

"Yessir...he and Gibson are local heroes. Even made the papers up here! And to think, he was one of my little pledgies!"

"Enough of that malarkey, Jug," Matt protested. "If you ask me...the papers make too much out of little things. What the public should know is that hundreds are dying daily...without knowing why."

"Now you sound like your old man, Matt," said Jug.

He offered a cigarette, then torched it with a coffee table lighter bearing the U.S. Navy insignia.

"The general always said Americans would take on any foe if our country or freedom were in danger...or if one of our allies needed help. Trouble is, these things don't apply to that corner of the world."

Silence hung momentarily as they drank their beers. Then Jug continued.

"The boys coming home are saying talks have begun at a place called Panmunjon. Might mean an end to the conflict."

"I sure hope so, Jug," Matt brightened. "Sending kids up and never seeing them again ranks as the hardest chore I've ever had to do. That's what started me on these nasty things."

He held his cigarette at arm's length; looked disdainfully at it for a moment, then took a long drag.

"Goes with command territory, sport," said Jug. "You know that. It's never easy or forgivable to send young men to die. Someone has to, though; and it's better if it's someone who remembers them."

Jug lumbered to his feet and retrieved three more brews.

"By the way...I'm sorry to hear about Warren Kellogg and young Hart. He was a good kid; bright and well liked. And what a quarterback! I understand they mixed it with a dozen MiGs."

"Yeah...the major headed a patrol near the Thirty-Eighth. MiGs hit 'em on all sides. They tried hightailing it, but were just outnumbered. They swarmed on Hart. Warren shook two and went back for him, but it was too late. The major still got two before they splashed him."

"Warren got it in the legs, too?"

"Yeah...but he's doing great. A real soldier; and a lot like you, Jug. Says he doesn't mind the grounding...but sure hates giving up tap-dancing!"

"Hey, he **is** my kind of guy."

"You'll meet him one of these days. And you'll like him. By the way, you scoot around pretty good."

"Sure do, Pledgie," he said, punching vee openings in the tops of the new beers. "Got a new artificial leg. Must admit, the old stump doesn't hurt much any more. Only when it rains, or the humidity climbs."

Jug lifted his left leg, rapped the can against it.

"You probably don't know it...but your dad got it for me. He's been great; always calling or dropping by when he's up on business. Well sir, they developed a ball-joint kneecap at the Veteran's Hospital, and he heard about it. Darned if he didn't volunteer me as one of the first to try it out. I haven't had a problem since. How's the old man doing, Matt?"

"Fine, Jug, fine. Never more than a degree or two off heading. In fact, Hoot and I are meeting with he and Conn Casting's marketing people about doing some work for them."

"Oh, yeah...that's right. You and Gibson are going to be those guys who come up catchy slogans. Sounds like a real tough life! You ought to do good together; you made a swell team in the air!"

"Spence, these two already have clients through Mr. Gibson's newspapers," Karen jumped to Matt's defense. "They've even recruited me to help with layouts!"

"Well, they can't go too far astray if they involve you, Little Sister," the big man said, reaching and patting her knee. "How 'bout another beer?"

They stayed until six o'clock, reminiscing with their friend over enjoyable times shared in college; the fun and pranks of fraternity life... the sports events and dances.

Then they said farewell to Jug...amid hugs, kisses and handshakes... and soon were enroute to New Haven, and home.

Matt's parents had convinced the couple to stay with them until they could find a apartment. Now, driving from Boston to the Durham's front door, would roll another four hours of miles on the new Buick's odometer.

The moments and miles sped by, capping their honeymoon. Her head rested on his shoulder as he pulled into the driveway and eased to a stop; wishing not to awaken her, if she were napping.

She opened her eyes as he switched off the headlights.

"We're home, sweetheart," he said, kissing her forehead. She tenderly framed his face in her hands and kissed him warmly.

"These have been the most wonderful moments of my life, Matt," she murmured sleepily. "Please let it stay like this."

"It will, honey; I promise. This is just the appetizer."

Suddenly, light washed from the open front door as Walt and Claire hurried to welcome them...and help with luggage. And soon, the newlyweds cuddled inside; recounting their honeymoon adventures.

Now...the new Mr. and Mrs. Durham prepared to embark on the rest of their married lives.

Chapter 11

Open For Business

THE LAST WEEK OF JUNE clung tenaciously.

Matt and Karen tried packing it with more hours than would fit, searching out apartments, adjusting to the new routine of life together, and juggling two jobs that kept them apart during the days.

She, decorating houses she wished were hers. He, calling on businesses hawking advertising space in Ed Gibson's newspapers and magazine.

Hoot rented an efficiency apartment in downtown New Haven, and a friend of Damon Forsythe's provided the two veterans with an office above the bank. Cramped...but theirs; and free.

There they labored nights and weekends; developing their ad designs and copy behind two battered metal desks, a rickety layout table and clackety typewriter.

Matt and Hoot became even closer over the months. To the point of each knowing the other's thoughts intuitively. Many times, answering questions before they surfaced.

Between them, in a month's time, they established accounts throughout the state; from New London to Stamford, and as far north as Hartford.

Hoot sold a coastal real estate company several pages of space on a long-term contract, while Matt became adept at peddling ad space to grocers, clothiers and even mortuaries.

By the first of July, Hoot earned rent money without borrowing from his father. And Matt didn't need to tap Karen's earnings from her job at Peck & Peck.

Hoot startled his partner one Friday morning by lumbering into the office earlier than usual, causing the latter to slop coffee over a layout he'd prepared for a department store in Waterbury. Sniffing out the assignment had cost Matt two days of shoe-leather.

"Damnit, Hoot!" he howled. "You scared hell out of me crashing in like that!"

Matt hopped to his feet, futilely swabbing the steamy liquid that stained his lap and now dripped from the canted layout table.

"Now I've got to cut and paste another ad for the Jefferson Stores! Crap...I've been working on this one since seven!"

"Hey old buddy...don't fret," Hoot said calmly, helping sop the mess. "We've lived through worse. I'll give you a hand."

Hoot tossed a watercolor-smeared towel toward the sink, then hooked his arm around Matt and coaxed him to a chair behind one of the desks.

"I've just come from Hartford," Hoot beamed. "Triad Air Cargo wants space in our newspapers...and the magazine! They're inaugurating a commuter service into New York and Boston...and have lots of bucks to promote it. They want to see us Monday and get things rolling. What do you think of old Hooter now?"

"Damn, Hoot, that's wonderful. Wonderful! By God, it's tremendous!"

He pounded his friend's back enthusiastically.

"I read that four World War Two fliers launched Triad; started it as a mail and cargo line. And now it's a money-making operation!"

"You bet it is! When I called and mentioned we flew with the Fourth...the account just leapt into my pocket. Anyway, this calls for celebrating. I'll scare up a date, and let's go to Halen's Lake Saturday and celebrate the Fourth...enjoy some beers, dogs and firecrackers. And I'll even spring for the brew!"

"Sounds like fun, Hoot. Before we spend company funds, though... let's put some money in the bank. Now then...what did you say about helping salvage this ad?"

By mid-morning, the two finished clipping and pasting drawings of products the client store wished to promote.

The resulting page layout commanded reader attention; and placement of sales items subtly steered viewers' eyes into the display. Once there, the promotion's bold prices made its appeal nearly impossible to ignore.

Finally satisfied, the duo put the artwork away for fresh, more objective appraisals later. And began shaping plans for the holiday.

Halen's Lake bounded the western edge of New Haven.

Over the years, it had become the annual gathering place for dozens of families celebrating the Fourth of July with food and fireworks.

Late in the evening...when skyrockets flashed and glittered sonorously...the city would host its hour-long fireworks display. Preceding that, of course, traditional contests were held; watermelon and pie-eating; three-legged races; and, raw egg tosses.

With Matt's help, Hoot wheedled Karen into finding him a date.

"I'm still an out-of-towner," he had pleaded. "Unfamiliar with the guiles of New Haven females."

As Hoot's escort, Karen invited Barbara Lynn Halstead; a stunning young lady with whom she had shared several classes at Hanley College.

Bobby Halstead stood five and a half feet tall; thin, and elegant in appearance. An attractive woman on whom clothes hung flawlessly.

On first glancing at her, one presumed aloofness.

Just the opposite held true, however. For Bobby exercised a sparkling personality, keen wit and delightful sense of humor. And the city abounded with men pursuing her.

Since graduating Hanley, she taught art at New Haven Junior High where fellow faculty, administrators, parents and students alike spoke highly of her.

Hoot and Bobby responded to each other immediately; and appeared uncannily similar. Their personalities, slender athletic builds, and natural ability to talk with and instantly befriend strangers made them compatible at the outset.

On Independence Day, the foursome sat on army blankets spread over cushiony grass atop a hill overlooking Halen's Lake, and watched enthralled as violent bursts of silvered sparks bloomed overhead. They applauded the more spectacular displays, and gasped occasionally when aerial bombs flashed unexpectedly with ear-shattering retorts.

Matt fished four long-necked bottles of beer from a galvanized washtub filled with chipped ice, and flipped off the cork-lined tops with his opener. He passed them around.

"Ummm, Matthew...this hits the spot!" Hoot exclaimed, tipping his bottle for a long pull. "Nothing like cold brew on a hot evening."

"I'll roger that," Matt said, clinking his bottle against Hoot's as a whooshing skyrocket exploded high above and stretched twinkling orange fingers in all directions.

"Hey...amigo," Matt asked. "What about those hotdogs?"

"Coming right up, guys," Karen said, hopping to her feet and retrieving a paper-wrapped package from the ice tub. "Give me a hand, Bobby," she said, helping her friend up. "And I'll teach you the finer arts of haute cuisine that men rave over; especially when their tastes run to beanies and wienies!"

"I take that as a slur upon my gentlemanly attributes," Matt retorted, feigning offense and slapping her rump playfully. "My palate focuses on legumes and franks because that's all you can cook!"

Matt winked at Hoot thinking he effectively had countered the verbal jab.

"Oh? Well...here's something else I can cook!" Karen quipped, pulling the neck of his sweatshirt out and dropping a handful of ice inside.

Matt moaned as the frozen bits touched his bare back, then jumped to his feet and shook them from the loose garment.

"Now you've had it, lady," he growled menacingly as Karen ran squealing into the darkness toward the lake with him in close pursuit.

As the two disappeared, Hoot arose and went to Bobby who stood near the stone barbecue pit turning hotdogs with tongs. From below, Karen's shrieks merged with the splash of bodies hitting the water.

The visually brilliant panorama above reflected in a chorus of appreciative sounds as spectators clustered around the lake murmured their approvals with each lacy burst.

Hoot casually slipped his arm around Bobby's trim waist and tugged her gently beside him. She as comfortably slipped her arm behind his back. He looked into the lovely upturned face.

"You think those two will ever grow up and start acting like old married folks?" he asked.

"I hope not...for their sakes," she replied. "This is how marriage should be."

"Maybe I'll find that out too, some day."

"Perhaps you will, Mr. Gibson," she chuckled, then unexpectedly kissed him lightly on the lips. "You'd better round up the Durhams or the franks will be cinders."

Bobby watched as Hoot sprinted into the darkness toward the lake, which now reflected shimmering moonlight and the floral pyrotechnics.

Suddenly, she felt lighthearted and radiant, and knew deep within she wanted to see Hoot again; soon, and often.

Loping toward the lake, Hoot shared the feeling. In the distant darkness, he heard Matt and Karen splashing and talking softly.

He stopped thirty feet away, cupped his hands around his mouth and yelled:

"Hey guys...the wieners are ready."

Matt and Karen stood waist deep in the tepid lake water, arms entwined around each other. He clutched her tight, and firmly kissed her soft open mouth. Passion instantly swept his loins, and she pressed closer, her body warming his wet trunks and molding snugly to him.

She detected his arousal.

"Feels like someone else's wiener is ready," she joked, then chuckled over the humor.

"Well...you blew that moment to hell," he said, swatting her firm buttocks. "We might as well eat now...but just wait 'til I get you home."

"Promises, promises," she breathed, kissing him quickly on the lips, then grabbing his hand and leading him from the water up the dark slope to where the others waited.

The fireworks ended an hour later.

Matt and Hoot shook grass from the blankets, then folded and stowed them in the convertible's trunk. While Matt held the door for Karen, Hoot and Bobby climbed into the back seat on the other side. Karen slid past the steering wheel and waited midway across the seat for her husband to enter.

Soon, cars pulling onto the gravel road leading from the lake formed a caravan of headlights that blazed through swirling dust kicked up by tires.

Matt pulled his sweatshirt on as he waited to back out of his parking spot. He turned to his passengers in the back.

"You two warm enough...or should I put up the top?"

"We're fine, Matt," Bobby replied, taking Hoot's hand and leaning her head on his shoulder. He slid his arm behind her neck as the car pulled onto the roadway and joined the traffic streaming toward New Haven.

By seven-thirty Monday morning, Matt and Hoot sped down Highway 91; destination Hartford, and their first pitch to the owners of Triad airlines.

They arrived shortly before eight thirty. A secretary ushered them into a small conference room and provided cups of coffee.

In minutes, Triad's principals arrived.

Bob Griffith and Sid Masters flew in the Marine Corps, while Don Stein and Larry Harst earned wings as Naval aviators.

Through fate, the four were thrown together flying Corsairs off the U.S. Carrier Yorktown during the battle of Midway.

They became fast friends, and nurtured that relationship after VJ Day.

Their corporate seal...the Triad...featured three elongated prisms, joined at their tops and enclosed by an equilateral triangle. During World War Two, the Third Marine Division earned a similar insignia by proving that Leathernecks could fight valiantly on land and sea, and in the air.

The four veteran fliers admired the camaraderie displayed by Third Division Marines, and adopted a similar symbol to depict their own.

"Even before the war ended, we talked of forming a cargo service," said Bob Griffith, who headed the company, as he explained its origins to the two newcomers.

"We knew there'd be plenty of DC-2s and DC-3s left over...and figured we could collect two or three for peanuts; which we did."

The president fetched the coffee pot to refill their cups and kept the commentary going as he crossed the room.

"The Triad describes our organization beautifully...three flight locations and three arrival times. And one day, we'll fly to three continents. Of course, that's a few years off."

"That's where we're headed, boys," Don Stein picked up the patter.

Don served as marketing director because his background included the only college studies that focused on the sales activity.

"We started by finagling government contracts and mail flights," he continued. "And the next thing we knew, the operation hit the black!"

"Sid dreamed up the daily commuter flights to New York and Boston," added Bob. "Like I said, our luck runs in threes."

"We want to promote the hell out of our new service," Don stated emphatically. "We're the first offering East Coast business flights, and we're certain they'll turn profits."

He scooted his chair closer to the pair.

"If you two can develop a promotion strategy...then handle the scheduling and advertisements...we can get this venture started."

"Don isn't kidding about the urgency of the situation," chimed Larry Harst, the company's attorney. "We plan to offer commuter service by mid-August. By then, we'll have certification from the Federal Aviation Authority, our airliners will be shipshape, and the schedules locked in."

"Of course, the four of us already hold commercial licenses to fly passengers," commented Sid Masters.

"Incidentally, Hoot," Bob smiled from his position beside Larry. "If you and Matt want to sign on for one or two flights weekly, you could handle this promotion 'in-house!'"

"We appreciate the offer, Bob," Hoot snickered. "However, I'm afraid we're stuck flying typewriters for the time being!"

"Fair enough, gents," Bob replied, leaning to shake their hands. "The offer stands if you ever want back into the air."

The four men escorted Matt and Hoot from the meeting room. At the door, Bob put his arms around their shoulders.

"What do you think...will you have something for us to review by month's end?"

"You bet," affirmed Matt, taking the president's hand. "And you'll be pleased...I guarantee."

"I'm sure we will," Bob answered. "We'll see you boys soon."

The duo shook farewells with the other partners, then stopped at the company's sales office.

There, they collected biographical sheets on Triad's principals, the organization's history, and samples of sales literature produced to date.

Presently, they left for New Haven.

"Like I promised, Matthew," Hoot chortled, smacking his comrade's arm as they accelerated onto Highway 91 West. "We've got our first major account. It's downhill from here!"

"Whoa...hold on, Hooter. Keep in mind that we're presenting to Conn Castings in mid-August; or had you forgotten?"

"Nope...it hasn't slipped my mind, old buddy. I'm just excited over the prospects of us being successful; you know, like the Triad guys."

"We've got tons of work between now and then, pal. I agree, though... providing the creative for Triad will be something special!"

They stopped briefly at Middletown and paid respects to Hoot's parents, then Matt dropped by Jefferson Furniture for approvals on several ads. The owners praised the work done by the agency, which meant they now could produce asbestos repro mats for their full-page promotions.

After lunch, the two continued to New Haven, arriving slightly before two o'clock. Once there, each ran errands and visited accounts. And at five, they rendezvoused in their cramped office to discuss the day's activities.

"You know Matthew...I've got a good slant for a Triad campaign."

"Well, c'mon pal...give!"

"What's hot and heavy right now; and will fizzle about the time Triad introduces its commuter flights?"

"I haven't the foggiest, Hoot!" Matt spun his chair to face the other.

"Baseball, partner, baseball!" Hoot exclaimed adamantly.

He plopped on the edge of Matt's desk and sat with one leg dangling.

"I'd bet the most profitable commuter flights would be those to New York...hauling Yankee and Dodger fans. It's a cinch New York and Brooklyn will slug it out in this year's World Series."

"Hey, I've got it!" Matt yelled, clapping his hands together. "We tie the introductory campaign to the World Series."

"Roger, wilco...over and out," nodded Hoot. "I see a headline like: 'Triad Airlines makes your home runs easy.'"

He held his hands in front of him as if sizing a photo.

"Sales copy would describe tagging the three East Coast bases... New York, Hartford and Boston...and getting commuters home for dinner. Maybe even in time to listen to the game."

"Yeah," Matt stood, stroking his chin and feeling his creative current flowing. "I'll bet Triad could schedule business and family flights for people wanting to see the series."

"Sure...and for radio spots, we could get the managers and players from East Coast teams to provide the voices."

"Right...with ballpark sounds in the background."

The two stood quiet for a moment.

"Well, Matthew...what do you think?"

Matt draped his arm around Hoot's shoulders.

"I think it's a dandy idea, Hoot. Triad will love it. Let's call it quits... and start polishing tomorrow."

"I'll roger that, too. It's been a long one."

Matt switched the lights as they walked out of the office into the narrow hallway.

"Any plans for dinner? I think Karen's fixing a roast."

"Thanks, Matt; but I promised Bobby we'd do something if we finished at a decent hour."

"Well...bring her with you. Later on, we'll play Monopoly and listen to the ball game. Probably a good idea to stay on top of the standings."

"You're on, Matthew. I'll call her from the apartment after I've changed. See you around seven thirty."

Driving to his and Karen's apartment, Matt grew even more excited over Hoot's idea for Triad's campaign. He stopped at a liquor store for wine, then spun wheels pulling from the curb, anxious to lay Hoot's concepts before her.

Karen met him at the door with a warm kiss and hug, and he led her across the small living room to the sofa. She sat, while he kneeled at her feet, looking up. He recounted the meeting and Hoot's thinking, and that he and Bobby were coming for dinner.

"Matt, what a tremendous idea for promoting the new service!" she smiled broadly, teeth glistening.

She slid off the couch and settled by him on the floor.

"Like I said...you two make a winning combination."

He looked into the beautiful face, lifted her chin with one finger, and kissed her gently on the lips.

"Thanks, honey. That means a lot."

He kissed her again. This time more firmly. And felt her respond; rolling onto her side so their bodies touched.

He craved her...there and then. Instead, she pulled from his clutch:

"Hey...we have company coming, don't we?" she said, standing and brushing wrinkles from her cotton skirt.

He arose also; his passion conspicuous.

"Right...I'll go splash in cold water," he said, kissing her forehead. "We'll postpone this until later."

"That's a deal," she said, giving him a quick buss. "I love you."

"I love you too, honey," he replied.

He pecked her cheek, then walked to the bedroom to change while she tended the roast.

The other couple arrived at half past seven.

After a leisurely dinner of beef, parsleyed potatoes and fresh asparagus...capped by homemade peach cobbler...they clustered at the card table in the living room and played Monopoly.

Later, the foursome listened to the mammoth Philco radio and munched popcorn; Matt and Hoot drinking beer, while Karen and Bobby stayed with the sparkling rose served with the meal.

At nearly nine, the telephone rang. Karen excused herself and walked to the serving table in the hallway where the instrument stood. She answered it, cupped her hand over the mouthpiece, and called Matt:

"It's your dad...excited about something!"

Matt leapt to his feet, ran to her side and snatched the handset.

"Dad...what's up?"

"Not up, son...over! The conflict in Korea has ended."

"What! Really! My God!"

He listened for a minute, then turned to the others; who came to their feet in unison.

"They've stopped fighting, and brass from both sides are meeting at Panmunjon."

Each stared at the others in amazement until the general's voice booming through the telephone cracked their reverie.

"Son, I want to give a party this weekend. You and Hoot round up some buddies and we'll really celebrate! What do you say?"

"We're snowed with work, dad," Matt replied. "Still, it's a cause for commotion. Sure! Why not! We'll get on the horn to everyone tomorrow. Thanks calling, dad."

He returned the handset to its cradle, bussed his wife quickly on the cheek and ushered her into the living room.

Hoot and Bobby stood...also embracing...and at that moment, the radio announced the conflict's end. Fans enjoying baseball at Brooklyn Stadium sent a reverberating uproar over the airwaves.

"My ticker can't take this much excitement in one day!" Matt said, reclaiming his seat at the table. He lifted his beer bottle in a toast.

"To peace again," he said.

Around the table the foursome clinked bottles and glasses.

"Here, here," agreed Hoot. "Let's pray it lasts."

On the radio, Brooklyn fans again went berserk as Roy Campanella slammed a homer and led the bums to a five-to-two victory over Chicago.

In one week's time, Matt and Hoot roughed layouts and copy for Triad Airlines that promoted the "Homerun" concept. Then the former compiled a list of closing dates by which major newspapers and magazines in the tri-state area would require finished materials.

Once Matt outlined placement schedules, Hoot estimated the costs of running the ads in the magazines recommended.

As the two critiqued the campaign they were shaping, the only apparent weak spot surfacing was the artwork. Commanding photographs or drawings would be needed to capture reader attention;

and Matt's stick figure sketches failed miserably at symbolizing the excitement conveyed by the writing.

Karen...who provided ad designs in the past...already had her hands full completing Peck & Peck's summer remodeling assignments. Plus, she lagged in submitting her projections for the firm's fall schedule.

"I know someone you could call," Karen volunteered over Matt's telephoned plea for artistic assistance. "Mary Bauer...our commercial design instructor at Hanley. Her son, Eddie, is back from Korea. From what she says, he suffered severe wounds. He's really good, Matt. Mary brought his sketches to class and they were marvelous. Why not call Mary...and see if he's interested?"

"Thanks, honey," his voice sounded desperate. "I'll do just that."

He hung up and instantly thumbed the telephone directory for the woman's number. Finding it, he dialed. After the fourth ring, a young man's voice came on the other end.

"Hello?"

"Hello...is this the Bauer residence?" Matt asked.

"Yes," the voice responded flatly.

"Could I speak with either Mary or Eddie?"

After a short pause, the reply came.

"This is Eddie."

"Eddie, my name is Matt Durham. I'm a partner in an advertising agency here, and we need someone to provide us with artwork. My wife knows your mom from Hanley...and saw your work...and suggested I call. Think you could help us?"

Another moment of hesitation preceded the answer.

"Gee, I'm not sure, Mr. Durham. I'm just out of the army hospital. Got shot up pretty bad. Thought I'd take things easy awhile."

"I understand, Eddie...believe me. My partner and I came back recently. We know the shithole well; and how it affects you."

Matt's mind groped for the right words.

"I think the best medicine for all of us is forgetting what we've been through. And, one of the most effective ways to do that is to stay busy as hell. We're offering an opportunity to do just that!"

Again, a moment of silence. Then: "I don't know, Mr. Durham. Let me sleep on it."

"Okay, Eddie...square enough. We're making a major pitch in two weeks and we need first-class artwork. My guess is it'll take the better part of two weeks to do the job."

Matt paused so Eddie could ponder the deadline.

"Tell you what...if we don't hear by Monday, we'll assume you're not interested and look elsewhere. Okay?"

"Yessir," the young man responded blandly...and hung up.

Matt turned to Hoot, still clutching the telephone.

"If he doesn't call us, I'll call him again, Hoot. He needs help...and friends...and probably a kick in the ass to get him going."

"You're probably right, Matthew. I've seen lots of Eddies these past few months."

Between business calls, the two contacted several comrades from Korea about Walt's party, and received RSVPs from Major Kellogg in San Francisco and Spence Hale in Boston.

Walt took a week's vacation and busied himself buying liquor and snacks for the affair, then helped Claire with house work and, in general, made her life miserable.

"Walt...if you don't get out from underfoot I'll lambaste you with this broom!" she scolded as he bent to pick minuscule specks of lint off the living room carpet.

"Sorry, Claire. I'm just fidgety...anxious to see Jug and meet Major Kellogg and the others. By the way, have you put fresh towels in the guest rooms?"

"Yes, Walt, yes! For the third time! Now go away!"

He paced to where his wife stood; kissed her on the lips and held her tightly.

"How have you endured me all these years?"

"Actually, quite easily," she responded. Then, looking up at him: "You were gone for most of them!"

A smile crinkled his wife's face and the two laughed amiably at her retort.

"Still, after all those years, you're the same apple-cheeked, high-spirited coed who stole my heart. I find that remarkable...and love you dearly for it."

"I love you too, Walt," she replied, returning his buss. She clutched his hand in hers. "Let's have breakfast."

By late afternoon, guests began arriving for the general's soiree. The caterers had dug a shallow pit in the backyard, and were barbecuing half a side of beef secured to a revolving spit. The Texas-style cookout commemorated the months Matt and Hoot spent in the Lone Star State during flight training; and also sated their love for zesty meat.

Walt promised Claire the catering service would fill the cavity after the party; then cover it with mulch, so it would be unnoticeable.

Several washtubs of beer lined the brick patio, and three red cedar picnic tables groaned under hors d'oeuvres, sandwich meats and cheeses.

Myriad bottles of liquor stood in rows by the kitchen sink, while bottles of Burgundy, Rose and Chablis wines protruded from ice buckets scattered about.

Walt had done himself proud by following up on every detail; including napkins and placemats printed with names and insignias that reflected the military units that would be represented.

He also rented a speaker system so music could be played in the living room and piped to the backyard. As he bustled about handling last minute chores, Les Paul and Mary Ford sang "Mockingbird Hill" in the background, and the melody reverberated across the spacious back lawn to disappear in the woods.

Claire and Evelyn Forsythe provided final touches to eats that covered every available serving location, then sat to relax momentarily. The doctor was tending bar for early comers, and passed stingers to the two women.

"Thanks, darling," Evelyn smiled. "This will bring back some spark!"

Jug arrived by train shortly past five o'clock, so Matt and Karen picked him up and drove him to the Durham's. Warren Kellogg flew from San Francisco, and Hoot and Bobby collected he and two others who arrived on the same flight.

Triad's Bob Griffith and Don Stein motored from Hartford, and parked in front of the house just as Ed and Mary Gibson pulled in from Middletown. The Gibsons were nearly as excited over meeting Bobby Halstead as seeing their New Haven friends.

At six thirty, the chef slathering the beef with barbecue sauce declared it cooked to perfection, and the group of thirty lined with plates and received thick, succulent and steamy slices of spicy meat.

Jug clutched Matt's Sig Alph beer tankard...filled it to the lip...and joined Warren and the two Triad pilots at a glass-topped table near the rose garden.

The four struck an immediate friendship, and guffawed over Jug and the major joking about not squatting on the grass with most of the others:

"The only time a one-legged, pot-bellied pilot hits the grass is when he falls on his backside!" cracked Jug.

"I'll lift one to that, Jug," agreed Warren, clanking mugs and sloshing his beer.

Since returning Stateside, the major headed operations for his father's prospering seafood company; helping his aging parent oversee a fleet of shrimp boats moored in San Francisco's West Bay area near Fisherman's Wharf. The Kelloggs' thirty vessels worked the deep Pacific channels on the opposite side of the peninsula.

Walt felt in his element overhearing the various groups describing World War II and Korean flying adventures. Never before had he witnessed such camaraderie as with this group. He knew...or knew of... most of those attending. Plus, his aviator's background created instant rapport.

The temperatures remained cool for a Connecticut July, and by nine o'clock cicadas hummed in the woods and a light breeze cooled the evening even more.

The entourage devoured most of the roast cow, and the food servers trimmed what remained from the bones and packaged it for the Durhams.

Then, the caterers left as stealthily as they arrived; taking with them trash, bottles and carcass, and refilling the depression with dirt.

Matt and Karen teamed with Hoot and Bobby in collecting plates, napkins and silverware, while the rest of the group helped stow leftover snacks and liquor.

When he and Hoot began emptying ice tubs down the woodsy slope at the rear of their property, Matt's mother called him to the telephone.

"A young man for you, dear," said Claire, passing him the handset.

"Hello?" answered Matt.

"Mr. Durham...hi. Eddie Bauer. Sorry if I'm interrupting anything."

"Not at all, Eddie. We're straightening up after a dinner party. I'm glad you called."

"I've talked with mom about your offer, and we agree it's a good opportunity for me. I can't sit around feeling sorry for myself forever. Besides...there are plenty worse off than me."

He listened to the young man, and unconsciously watched Jug and Warren carrying on an animated conversation; obviously about flying, since the two made sweeping loops with their hands, like birds trailing each other.

A sudden sadness flooded him...then disappeared. His mind jumped back to the conversation at hand.

"I can't tell you how glad I am, Eddie," he enthused. "You're making the right decision. When can you start?"

"Would Monday suit?"

"Sure, Monday would be swell. We're above the bank on Garth Street, and we get there around eight or eight-thirty. Come by around then and we'll explain what's needed. Okay?"

"Yessir, Mr. Durham."

"Incidentally, Eddie...it's Matt. Please."

"Okay, Matt. See you Monday. Thanks."

"Thank you, Eddie. And your mom, too."

Matt sensed warm and positive feelings about the young man after hanging up. He walked to where Hoot was helping his mother scrub glasses and silverware.

"Guess what partner," he smiled broadly. "We've got a layout artist. Eddie wants the job."

"Oh, Matt, that's wonderful," Karen overheard, and responded from where she stood drying dishes.

"Boy, it sure is, Matthew!" exclaimed Hoot. "When can he start?"

"I asked him to drop by Monday morning."

"Hey amigo," Hoot clasped his arm around the other's shoulder. "We're rolling now!"

"You said it, Hooter. You said it."

It was past eleven before most guests departed; and the evening air turned cool, making sitting outside uncomfortable. The elder and younger couples...accompanied by Jug and Warren... retreated to the living room.

"You know, dad...you, mom, the Forsythes and Gibsons performed an outstanding feat tonight," Matt said.

He and Karen sprawled on the floor near the sliding glass patio doors; the others sat on various pieces of furniture around the space.

"That was a top-drawer observance...everyone had a great time."

"Speaking for us...we certainly did," confirmed Mary Gibson.

The others seconded her approval.

"Thanks, one and all," Walt replied, draping an arm over his wife's shoulders as they sat on a large couch opposite the others.

"I enjoyed it more than I can express...mainly because our sons and their friends are here to celebrate with us. Lots of parents were not so fortunate."

"Maybe Korea will be the last conflict, dad," Matt stated, wishfully.

"Perhaps, son," said the general, his tone unconvinced. "They sign the armistice soon. Still, I have a gnawing in my guts that says the communists aren't through stirring trouble."

For a moment, the group fell silent. Each wondering in her or his heart if, indeed, another Korea might arise.

On the radio, turned almost inaudibly low, Judy Garland sang, "Somewhere...over the rainbow."

Chapter 12

The Cometliner Account

M ONDAY CAME ON THE HEELS of thunderstorms and constant drizzle, and nasty weather socked New Haven by mid-afternoon Sunday; just as Warren Kellogg and Jug Hale began their respective returns to San Francisco and Boston.

They became comrades overnight, and spent most of their time together reminiscing about days as army pilots in "The Big War"... World War Two.

Jug also impressed Bob Griffith and Don Stein from Triad, who spent hours with him discussing opportunities in the airline industry.

Matt, as usual, arrived first at the small offices of Durham & Gibson. He perked a pot of coffee and placed it on the hotplate in the supply room; then raised a window to bring in fresh air since the office had remained shut over the weekend.

Below him, rain-glazed streets reflected ominous dark clouds clustered low over the city. While the coffee burbled, he descended the narrow back stairs to the bank's mailroom where the postman delivered D&G's letters and parcels.

A young woman sorting the bank's correspondence greeted him, and handed over a stack of letters, several large manila envelopes, and a half dozen magazines.

He thanked her, then climbed the stairs to the office where he poured a steaming cup of coffee and picked through the mail.

The most important envelopes featured clear acetate windows; for these contained commission checks. He uncovered several in the stack; one mailed a week ago by Hoot's father, and earnings from three other accounts. He would deposit D&G's windfall when the bank opened.

Hoot entered the office as Matt tore into the last letter; an invoice from a printer who produced repro mats for them. At the same moment, the office clock struck half past eight. Raindrops beaded Hoot's light jacket and dripped from his umbrella.

"Nice weather for quackers, huh pal?" Hoot joked, shaking droplets from the umbrella and hooking it on the wooden coat-rack inside the door. "Looks like it may hang around a while."

He poured himself a cup of coffee and brought the pot to refill Matt's. He continued: "Bobby and I soaked ourselves running from the theater to the car last night."

"Oh yeah? What'd you see?"

"'From Here To Eternity'...that new movie with Frank Sinatra, Burt Lancaster and Lana Turner. Jees...wait'll you see the beach scene! Turner and Lancaster rolling around in the sand! It gets you hot!"

"I'd better not take Karen if that's so," Matt replied, frowning. "I've been really pooped lately; flamed out and in the sack before ten o'clock. Don't even know if I can perform my husbandly duty anymore!"

"Matthew, you better hit the vitamins if you're that bad off! You're sounding like my grandpa!"

At that moment, someone rapped the glass door and both turned to see Walt Durham standing there. He held a dripping umbrella in one hand, and in the other clutched a large brown folder.

"Morning men," hailed the general.

He hung his umbrella next to Hoot's on the coat rack, shook moisture off his raincoat, then carried the pouch to where the two sat.

"I collected these at Conn Castings."

He opened the container and handed each of them a thick sheath of papers.

"These are marketing plans for our new jetliner," revealed Walt. He pointed to Matt's cup of coffee. "You mind?"

"No, dad...sorry. Have a seat. I'll fire up a cup."

Matt returned to the supply room.

Walt stripped off his slicker and caught it over his umbrella. Then he accepted the mug that Matt offered.

"We call it the Series 440 'Cometliner.' It features four turbojet engines for power, and will carry forty passengers and crew. It cruises at four hundred miles per hour at twenty-five thousand feet."

The general tapped one of the hefty stacks of papers in front of them with an index finger.

"You can read the details in here, and look at engineering drawings and artist mockups."

The two young men hurriedly thumbed to the plastic-coated pages that contained color sketches of the aircraft.

"Whooeee...she's beautiful, general!" Hoot exclaimed.

"Boy, she sure is, dad!" Matt echoed the other's zeal. "No wonder Conn Castings is excited about introducing her."

"We are, Matt...we are," Walt beamed as he clapped his son on the back. "Please keep the drawings and technical specs under tight wraps. We don't want anyone to find out what we're up to."

"Sure dad," confirmed Matt. "We'll lock 'em up."

Walt sipped his coffee momentarily, then snapped his fingers as if remembering something.

"Almost forgot, Matt...an agency out of New York is also shooting for our business. I couldn't do anything about it; someone on the board recommended letting them propose. Anyway, I'm confident you two will submit the winning package."

Matt felt more than slight disappointment learning another group would compete; but kept the feeling to himself.

"What company is it, dad?" he asked flatly.

"Bradley Agency," answered Walt. "Do you know of them?"

"Yes...I do," Matt displayed relief. "I went to school with Lyle Bradley. He's not the creative type. His dad started the firm about twenty years ago, specializing in publicity and promotions."

"Hey, aren't they also involved in political campaigns?" queried Hoot. "In school, I read about a Bradley Agency in New York that handled Dewey's campaign."

"That's them, Hoot," answered Matt. "A sterling lesson in political flackery. If you back the wrong person or party, you end up a case history of what not to do. And people won't let you forget about it, either."

"How'd they learn about Conn Castings?" asked Hoot.

"We're not sure. Several people outside know we're developing a new airplane; they just don't know what kind."

The general lifted from his chair.

"Could be Bradley heard a rumor...imagine they're just checking things out."

Matt fetched his father's umbrella and coat, and handed him the items.

"We'll give this our best shot, dad," emphasized Matt. "You can count on that."

"I'm sure you will, boys. You two have more clicking than most New York outfits. And, I know you won't shy from hard work!"

"Thanks for the plans, Walt," said Hoot, offering his hand as the other turned to leave.

"You know...when you land Conn Castings, it may interfere with your hunting!" the general chuckled as he shook their hands.

"Don't worry, dad. If we get the account, we'll package and wrap it on schedule; before the duck season. Or at least by the time you're ready for full-scale production."

"That's the ticket, son. I'm confident you two will do a crackerjack job on the Cometliner."

The general walked through the office door into the outside corridor.

"See you, boys," he barked from the hallway.

After Walt's departure, the two returned to their respective desks.

"Matthew...we have to dream up something terrific for the Cometliner," said Hoot, swallowing the remainder of his cold cup of coffee with a gulp and grimace. "This will be D&G's maiden voyage!"

"Yeah...I agree. You know, for some reason Lyle Bradley certainly doesn't concern me at all. I just want to knock Conn Castings' socks off for dad's benefit."

Matt handed one of the company's sales blueprints to his partner.

"Tell you what...let's digest these marketing plans individually, and see what each of us comes up with by Thursday. We'll both be on the road...which is a good time for noodling. What do you say?"

"Makes sense, amigo. Speaking of being on the road, I'm delivering ads in Milford today. Bet the weather has traffic balled all along the coast."

"Probably so, Hooter; you better highball it!"

"What time is Eddie Bauer coming?"

"He didn't say for sure. Nine-thirty or ten, I think. Anything to tell him?"

"Yes...impress upon him the importance of Triad Airlines. If they like our copy...and his artwork...maybe later we can afford him full-time."

"I'll relay that, Hoot. Hey, get shoving!"

"Roger, pal. See you around noon."

Hoot grabbed his umbrella and dashed out the door while Matt walked to the supply room to brew a fresh pot of coffee. That chore completed, he returned to his desk and leafed through his copy of Conn Castings' selling strategy.

He didn't notice his visitor until the young man rapped the door frame.

Matt looked up, then stood and walked with outstretched hand.

"Eddie?" he asked.

His mind's eye had pictured the stranger differently; for some reason...perhaps the name...he expected red hair, a boyish face and tall lanky frame.

Eddie Bauer possessed none such characteristics: He stood shorter than medium height; his dark hair rippled with waves; and, a heavy beard and bushy eyebrows bestowed upon him a swarthy complexion.

The young man clutched a large artist's portfolio under his arm, and as he approached to clasp Matt's hand, he limped noticeably on his left leg.

Matt immediately detected a twinge of remorse.

Only momentarily, however. For beneath the thick brows, startlingly clear blue eyes sparked with resolution.

Matt took his hand, shook it firmly, and ushered him to a chair beside his desk.

"Cup of coffee, Eddie?"

"Sure, Mr. Durham...ah, Matt. Black, please."

Matt returned with another misting cup, handed it over, then sat down and turned his chair so he faced his visitor.

"My wife says you're quite an illustrator, Eddie," he accentuated his statement with a swallow of coffee. "Where'd you get so much experience? School...or home?"

"Home, mostly. I went to college two years before Korea broke. Then dropped out and enlisted like a lot of other guys. Actually, I got kind of tired of school, anyhow."

"Think you'll go back?"

"Oh, maybe. Some day. Right now, I want to work and forget about what's happened."

The contrast of Eddie's pale blue eyes surrounded by his grainy features struck Matt again; yet now, looking into his stare from across the desk, he detected the pain.

"I'd enjoy seeing your work, Eddie," he said, clearing papers, magazines, books and letters from the side of the desk closest to the artist; and placing Conn Casting's folder in his top desk drawer.

Eddie unzipped the leather portfolio and placed a weighty stack of drawings in front of Matt. Then he painfully pulled himself to his feet, wincing as he did so.

Matt started to help; then thought better of it. He had learned about pride from Jug and Warren.

He sorted through the drawings as the young man explained the reasoning behind each; and at once ranked Eddie's layouts among the most unique he had seen...topping even those prepared by the big New York studios that dominated the trade publications.

Matt savored the elation he felt; knowing straight-away that Eddie's artistic flair and conceptual grasp epitomized the qualities sought by D&G.

"These are good, Eddie," he said. Then, unleashing his exuberance: "In fact...outstanding!"

"Thank you, Matt," came the embarrassed reply; however, through a broad smile. "Maybe my mom's artistic talent is taking root after all."

The young designer sat; again, grimacing as he stretched out his leg.

"Plus, I enjoy creating ads; taking products and services and portraying their best qualities."

"That's music to this huckster's ears, Eddie. And what we're looking for. Up to a point, that is. This agency will never produce a misleading ad; regardless of the client."

"I'd never do that intentionally, Matt."

"I know, Eddie. People complain about advertising being dishonest; and say ad men are con artists. I admit there are a few bad apples in the barrel; but they're decreasing in number. And D&G is not going to be among them."

"I understand, Matt. And I agree. If my artwork ever promises more than can be delivered...just let me know."

"I'm not too worried about that, Eddie. The blame for dishonesty should be shared by advertisers, agencies, media and consumers. Each group plays a part when misleading ads appear."

Matt stopped abruptly; embarrassed by his tirade over deceptive practices.

"Enough of that...let me explain what Triad Airlines is looking for."

He pulled a fat Manila folder from the file cabinet, and handed Eddie the rough sketches, copy and headlines he and Hoot had developed.

"Excuse the stick figures...neither Hoot nor I can draw worth a damn," he said. "Still, these should give you an idea of our thinking."

Matt paused while the illustrator studied the sketches.

"The campaign theme is tied to baseball, and especially the World Series; which will be played in New York. New York also serves as the final destination for Triad's commuter flights."

Matt shuffled through the drawings roughed by he and Hoot. "We need action artwork or photos that will highlight the baseball approach; designs that will focus reader attention on the 'home run' concept."

"Why not spin the whole campaign off the home run idea?" Eddie asked. "You know...feature old photos or sketches of Babe Ruth belting one out of the ballpark. The copy could say: 'Like the Babe...we're making the New York home run popular.'"

"Hey...that's the idea, Eddie! How much time will you need for layouts? We'd like to present a preliminary campaign outline to Triad in two weeks."

"I'll have pencil sketches this Friday, Matt," the other replied. "That's enough time. If you guys like my ideas, I'll polish 'em. If not, I'll start over."

"You're on, pal," said Matt, shaking his hand.

He helped Eddie return the artwork to its leather holder, then provided him carbon copies of preliminary copy and headlines written by Hoot and he.

"Keep a log of your hours, Eddie, so we'll know how much to pay you...and how much to bill Triad," Matt added. "By the way, what's your hourly or daily rate?"

"I don't need money right now, Matt. The government pays disability for my legs. I'll just work for the experience...and to get out of the house."

"I couldn't live with that, Eddie. How about two-fifty an hour to start? We'll pay more later."

"I appreciate your wanting to pay, Matt; but that's way too much."

The young man tucked the leather case under his arm.

"That's a reasonable price for work this good," Matt countered, leading him to the door. "One day soon...there'll be more where that comes from. We'll see you Friday, Eddie."

"You bet, Matt. And thanks."

He watched as Eddie limped down the hall toward the stairway; and felt incredibly good about the meeting's outcome.

Outside, rain gave way to puffy cumulus clouds; still tinged with dark somber outlines, but gradually melting in the hazy sun.

Hoot returned from Milford shortly after twelve, and Matt recounted the details of the meeting with Eddie.

"Sounds like we've got an illustrator onboard, Matthew," Hoot said afterwards. "Or certainly the makings of one."

"He's good alright, partner. You're right on both counts! He snagged the baseball theme instantly; even suggested conveying our home run concept through drawings or photos of hitters like Ruth, Ott and Gehrig!"

"When do I see his work?"

"Friday. That allows time for him to polish layouts we like, and for us to sharpen our headlines and message."

"Sounds swell, Matthew. You had lunch?"

"Nope...been waiting on you. Want to grab a burger?"

"Yes, indeed! I'm starving. We can talk at the diner."

They walked into the fresh, moist air as sunlight punched through overcast skies and mist-laden rainbow beams mirrored in the wet streets.

After an unhurried lunch, Matt visited New Haven accounts while Hoot returned to the office and began crafting the Conn Castings presentation.

Like his partner, Hoot voiced confidence in D&G winning the account. For some reason, however, he felt skitterish over competing with the Bradleys. After a moment's thought, he filed the concern in his subconscious and pored over the marketing plan provided by Walt.

Matt spent the next two days with clients along the Coast. Hoot, meanwhile, drove to Middletown, carrying layouts and copy that required Ed Gibson's approval. Plus, he wanted to see his dad's new printing press; purchased recently for a quarter million dollars.

On Thursday morning, Hoot beat Matt to the office by a half hour. Donuts and coffee awaited the latter's arrival.

"This is hard to believe!" Matt quipped, laying his attaché case on top of his desk. "Miracle of miracles, Hoot...you got to the office before me!"

"Not only that, Matthew...I brought donuts and made decent coffee for a change!"

"What's the occasion, partner?" Matt queried, opening the briefcase and extracting a clipful of scribbled notes.

"Well, I've got an idea for your dad's company...one that'll make 'em take notice!"

"C'mon Hoot, out with it," Matt begged. "Don't leave your pal hanging."

He walked to the supply room for a roll and coffee, with Hoot following closely behind.

"What's more and more valuable every day?"

Matt paused a moment, puzzled.

He took a sip of steamy coffee as he thought.

Finally: "I don't know...could be anything. War's over. No more rationing. Lots of rubber and metal. And you probably don't want me saying something obvious like uranium, gold and silver. So...what's on your mind?"

"Time!" Hoot exclaimed excitedly, then fell silent, awaiting Matt's reaction.

Which, when it came, depicted puzzlement.

"How do you mean, Hoot?"

"Old Ben Franklin said it first, Matthew. 'Time is money.' Even more so today. People are hungry for ways to make better use of time; methods for coming up with more leisure hours. Especially in business."

Hoot pulled his chair close to Matt, who had stopped at mid-bite on a donut.

"Granted...lots of folks take trains. Still, wasting a week traveling to a meeting on the West Coast doesn't make good economic sense. More and more, the airlines are flying newer and longer routes."

Hoot snatched an airline schedule off his desk.

"Look here...by flying, a trip from New York to Los Angeles takes one day instead of a week."

Hoot remained silent for a moment; leaning on his elbows and letting his words penetrate Matt's skull.

"Flying costs a lot less, too. By the time you consider meals, booze, rooms and extras needed to travel by rail."

"Okay...Hoot! I get your point. Where are we heading?"

"My bright idea is this...we sell airlines and business passengers on the Cometliner being a 'time machine': A way to conduct coast-to-coast commerce between breakfast and dinner...in quiet luxury. Unlike the old slow and noisy prop jobs. And think of the spinoff angles we can develop, Matthew!"

"I gotcha...something like: 'Successful companies can count on the time machine to bring business meetings closer.'"

"Yeah, that's it, that's it! What do you think?"

"You've done it again, Hooter. Let's gnaw on it, and see what else develops. Any thoughts for illustrations?"

"I'm wondering about a Buck Rogers approach...you know, real science fictionish. Space movies are popular now."

"Sure...the benefit to industry would be time saved by flying in hours rather than riding for days. What would you think about bouncing our concept off the boys at Triad?"

"I think they'll love it," Hoot instantly affirmed. "If their airline flies between major cities in less time, they can schedule more flights, carry more passengers and probably make more money. Plus, they'll cut fuel costs because jet engines are more efficient. Triad could reduce its per-passenger costs significantly by flying Cometliners."

"Jees, Hoot! That's impressive! You've done your homework. I wonder if Triad would give us pointers?"

"I bet they'd be glad to...and we can trust them to keep any discussions confidential."

"I agree. Let's inquire about picking their brains when we outline their campaign."

"That's my thinking, Matthew...ask the buyer what he wants before we sell it to him!"

Matt paused, put his hand on Hoot's shoulder, and looked him face on.

"Honestly...I think it's a swell idea, Hoot. You've given us another winner to work with."

"Thanks, partner. Warm your java?"

Hoot fetched the pot, poured fresh coffee into their cups, and the two brainstormed for the remainder of the morning; jotting ideas and scribbling graphic concepts while discussing the Cometliner campaign.

Minute by minute, the promotion unfolded as fresh ideas surfaced and took hold.

They met until noon...then hurried lunch at the cafeteria across the street...and by early evening, had roughed a campaign for Conn Castings. It would run in magazines, newspapers and on radio. And even included commercials for television; the up and coming medium.

Shortly before seven, Matt called Karen while Hoot telephoned Bobby, and the foursome dined at a steakhouse near Hoot's apartment. There, they excitedly unfolded their ideas for Conn Castings.

"I think it's a terrific concept for the Cometliner," said Bobby, delicately carving a thin slice from the pinkish sirloin on her platter. "Especially the time machine approach...it fits the outer space craze that's sweeping the country."

"Bobby's right, guys," affirmed Karen. "Consider the past two years' movies."

"Like Bobby's favorite," interjected Hoot, contorting his hands like lobster claws and screwing his face into a grotesque mask: "'The Thing'...you know, with James Arness."

"You better cool the creativity, Hoot!" exclaimed Matt, gripping his friend's arm. "If we get too carried away with that space concept, we'll scare customers away!"

The four chuckled for a moment over the thought. Then Matt continued:

"I hope dad and the board like Hoot's idea as much as we do," he dug into the sour cream-laden potato on his plate. "If we can carry it off, our campaign will position the Cometliner as the leader in commercial aviation."

Hoot refilled their wine glasses with dry burgundy, and set the bottle in the middle of the table.

"I wonder what the Bradleys will present?" asked Karen.

"Please, honey...let's not spoil a good dinner," Matt grumbled. "Although I'd enjoy being a mouse in their office. No, I take that back. We've got the winner without knowing what tricks they're up to."

"Everyone agrees with you, Matt," beamed Karen. "You two creative geniuses must be heading down the right path."

"We'd better get Eddie started on Conn Castings when he brings Triad's materials," Matt said tersely, jotting himself a mental note. "Smashing artwork can sell this idea; and he'll need time to discover the right approach."

"I'm really looking forward to meeting him, Matt," Hoot said, buttering a breadstick. "We'll know if he's as good as you think when we see the Triad layouts."

"I'm confident you'll be pleased, Hooter," responded Matt. "In fact, you'll love his work."

"I'll second that," added Karen. "He inherited a flair for graphic design. We've all heard the saying: 'Behind every successful man there's a woman.' Well, Eddie's mom is that woman! She'll make sure you get his best effort."

"He'll probably provide it without her encouragement," replied Matt, dabbing his mouth with a napkin. "I think Eddie has his future under control; and, our agency may play a bigger part in his plans than any of us know."

"Well, then...here's to our extremely successful agency," blurted Hoot, hoisting high his glass of wine as the others followed suit.

After dinner, the two couples returned to Hoot's apartment for nightcaps, and to continue piecing together the large jigsaw puzzle he kept scattered over the card table.

They chatted past ten o'clock, when Matt turned to Karen and suggested calling it a night.

"I am a little tired, honey," she agreed, suddenly yawning. "Charlie Enright and I check fall colors at the materials warehouse tomorrow; and that's always exhausting."

"Well, Bobby my dear...you and I are lone rangers again," said Hoot. He slipped his arms around her waist from behind and rested his chin on top of her head.

"I hope if we get hitched, we keep our spunk...unlike these old fogeys!"

"That's not nice, Hoot," pouted Karen. "Matt can't help it if he can't function without eight hours' sleep."

"Hey, wait a minute!" Matt protested. "I don't deserve all the blame! After all, folks...this is a week night. We've got lots to do tomorrow."

"Some of us do, for sure," nodded Bobby. "Next weekend is August, and school opens three weeks later. Seems I just paroled my last class yesterday, and already it's time to face the little pointy-headed monsters again!"

"Boy...how you carry on about the future generation of American artists!" scolded Hoot, bussing the top of her head.

"Really...we've got to scoot," chided Matt. "Eddie will be in first thing, and we've got lots to talk over."

"Okay, okay! Goodnight you two," said Hoot, kissing Karen lightly on the cheek and shaking Matt's hand. "We had fun and the steaks were broiled to perfection. What else could you ask?"

"Good night, Bobby. Good night, Hoot," said Karen.

She turned and walked through the door Matt held, and he followed her into the muggy July evening.

At eight thirty the next morning, Eddie rapped the frosted glass of D&G's door. Matt was pouring his first cup of coffee, so Hoot yelled to the young man:

"C'mon in, it's open!"

Eddie entered, toting the large leather portfolio from the previous Monday. Hoot reached out his hand, which the other took and shook vigorously.

"I'm Hoot Gibson, Eddie. Matt's partner. Sorry I missed you earlier."

"That's okay, Hoot. You guys stay busy."

"How about coffee out there?" Matt shouted from the supply room.

"Love some, partner," Hoot replied. "Eddie?"

"You bet, Matt," came the reply. "Please."

Matt brought three cups of coffee into the central part of the office, and set them on a large walnut conference table off to one side. It represented the only new furniture in sight; a reject from the bank boardroom downstairs.

Matt and Hoot sat on one side of the table while Eddie slid behind the other. He opened the large case...removed several poster boards... and laid them face down.

"I did this one when I got home after talking with you, Matt," Eddie said, flipping a piece of artwork face up. "It follows the theme you two developed."

The pencil sketch represented one of many photos of Babe Ruth pounding a homer out of Yankee Stadium. The headline above the illustration read: "You'll cheer for our home run, too!"

A reader's eyes would naturally flow across the headline, be directed down the Babe's bat, and end up in the sales message. Immediately below the copy block, Eddie had incorporated the company's symbol. An extremely effective format.

Matt and Hoot nodded mutual approval, impressed at how well the headline, message and drawing worked together.

"This one plays on the same theme," Eddie said, turning over another poster.

This one boasted: "Triad Airlines makes the home run a hit!"

A pencil outline revealed the interior of Yankee Stadium and a baseball zooming off the page toward the reader; making the graphic connection.

"This one's great, too!" enthused Hoot.

Eddie displayed three more layouts, and explained the concepts behind each. When he finished, he leaned back in his chair and sipped the half-cooled coffee at his elbow.

Matt and Hoot switched looks from one layout to the other; nodding their heads all the while.

Finally, the latter spoke:

"Eddie, these are exceptional. And effective. You've done a hell of a job portraying the benefits we'll weave into words. Don't you agree, Matt?"

"I certainly do, Hoot. Let's write copy for all of them; and show the boys at Triad the whole works! They'll love 'em!"

"I agree," affirmed Hoot. "Eddie, I can't wait to see these in final. You did a swell job!"

"Thanks, guys," the young man replied, flushing slightly. He looked first at the layouts; then at the two partners. Abruptly, his look grew serious; the clear blue eyes sparkled.

"I want you to know how grateful I am for this opportunity," he began. "For the chance to do something for myself. Korea's all I've thought about since I came back. For the past week, however, I've gotten my mind off the place; thanks to you two."

"Eddie...Korea is yesterday's bad dream," Matt said softly. He leaned across the table and looked directly into the young man's eyes.

"They'll sign the armistice agreements Tuesday, and the ordeal will fade into the history books. From here on, we'll provide you as much work as you can handle; and that's a promise!"

Matt turned when he felt Hoot's hand on his arm.

"Speaking of which, Matthew...better tell Eddie our Conn Castings brainstorm before we forget." Hoot stood to fetch the coffee pot. "That'll keep him employed a while!"

"Right, thanks Hoot," Matt replied, then turned back to Eddie:

"What I mean is...you've got a future with us if you want it. And let's not dwell on the past. Agreed?"

Eddie sat silent for a moment, thinking.

"You're right, Matt," he grinned. "Onward and upward!"

For the next several hours...including a diner lunch...the three discussed the Cometliner presentation; and the role of Eddie's artwork in presenting the time machine concept.

"It shouldn't be difficult making the plane seem like it's out of the Twenty-first Century," the young man said as he studied a portrait of the aircraft flying. "We'll show the heavens as a backdrop...stars and all...which presents an impression of outer space; which is where you'd find a comet!"

Eddie stood and walked around the office; still gazing at the Conn Castings depiction.

"We'll reverse the type...turn it stark white against the dark background. The effect will be eerie...and attention getting!"

"It sure would!" Hoot exclaimed. "Eddie...we make our pitch on the twentieth; which means rough layouts in a week to ten days. Is that enough time?"

"Plenty, Hoot," he replied, zipping the portfolio. He walked to each and shook hands. "I'll see you two pronto."

After he left, Matt and Hoot leaned over the table and studied the drawings.

"Has the touch, doesn't he," Matt cracked.

"Sure does...with plenty to spare! Like you said, Matthew; his future's with D&G."

"Tell you what, Hooter...if we land dad's account, I'd like him onboard full-time. There's plenty to do, and it could save a lot of running around."

"I agree, partner. Hey, it's nearly three! Why not close shop early, gather the ladies and picnic in the woods?"

"You smooth talker, Hoot Gibson! Let's get out of here!"

Matt gathered the layouts and carefully stowed them in the credenza behind his desk. Meanwhile, Hoot rinsed the coffee pot and cups. Minutes later, the two walked the hallway to the stairs.

"Matt...we're actually making a go of it!" exclaimed Hoot, clutching the handrail that ran down the steep stairway. "For the first time, it hit me in the face like ice water."

He turned to look at his friend on the step behind.

"What we've fantasized these last several months is now reality...it's here! With even more promising prospects looming in the near future."

"You surprise me, Hoot," chided Matt. "We've been in the black for two months. I'd call that moderately successful. And you've had doubts?"

"No...not doubts, Matt. Reservations, perhaps. Now, I'm more confident of our abilities...and with Eddie's swell artwork, our chances of landing fat accounts."

"I'm anxious too, partner," agreed Matt, holding the door as they stepped into the street that ran alongside the bank.

He put his hand on his buddy's shoulder and looked into his face.

"Fear and anxiety are what make this crazy business so much fun!"

As the two walked to their respective automobiles, a light breeze whistled across Garth Street; feeling remarkably cool for late July, and suggesting the rain that paid a visit earlier in the week planned on returning.

Chapter 13

Trying For Triad

MONDAY, AUGUST 1953, DAWNED SPECTACULARLY bright and clear. For the last week in July heralded signing of the Armistice agreement; and an end to the Korean conflict.

The week had been fraught with intermittent thunderstorms and torrential downpours that cooled temperatures significantly and washed the coat of summer dust off New Haven.

Matt awoke at six o'clock to the clattering of his trusty alarm clock, bought in Greenville, Mississippi, at the start of flight training, and kept by his bed ever since.

In the early darkness of shades drawn over the apartment's windows, he noticed Karen's slumbering outline. She lay on her left side...sheet pushed to her waist...and her long shapely legs exposed where the flimsy nightgown had ridden up slightly.

On seeing her, he sensed stirrings within and wrapped his right arm over her waist; pulling her close and touching and caressing her to consciousness.

He kissed the nape of her slender neck, moistening a trace of perfume that further aroused his senses.

Karen moaned softly, awakening, and felt him pressing tightly against her; his hand gently caressing and her body responding. The hand moved swifter, and lower, and her desire welled within, erupting in successive, delightful spasms.

Matt nimbly coaxed her silken bedclothes to the floor, lifted her gently and settled her on top of him. And now, the wonderful warmth encircled him, and pulled him closer and tighter.

Karen entwined her legs under his and swayed softly, and when they peaked, their breaths ripped deep from within.

They lay silent in each other's arms; spent, yet wonderfully revitalized.

"God, I love you," he whispered in her ear.

He darted the tip of his tongue along her neck, and savored the searing body stretched atop his, legs still entwined.

"And I love you, Matt." She hugged him even tighter. "Oh...so much."

They stayed together in the silent darkness for nearly half an hour, then he helped her ease to one side and pulled himself from bed.

"Much as I'd like to stay here all morning...Hoot will be by at eight. I'd better clean up."

"Let me in the bathroom just a minute, please," Karen urged, rolling off the bed clutching her garments. She playfully slapped his bare backside as she dashed past and closed the door.

Matt strode from the bedroom to the kitchen, plugged in the coffee pot, then returned and sat on the edge of the bed. He lit a cigarette and switched on the radio.

In the bathroom, he heard Karen using the toilet and then brushing her teeth.

Soon, the door opened and she stepped out.

The bathroom light silhouetted her trim figure through the flimsy nightgown, and Matt sensed morning yearnings building again.

He walked to his wife, wrapped his arms around her, and pulled her close against him. He tasted and smelled her peppermint toothpaste as he pressed his passion against her softness.

"Matt...I thought Hoot was going to be here," she whispered, hooking her arms behind his head and detecting warm sensations deep within herself.

"I'll shave faster than usual," he said, covering her mouth with his.

He led her to the mussed bed and lowered her gently on top of the covers as she again slipped off her night clothes. Karen pulled him on top and guided him to her.

The two lingered in bed until almost seven thirty; bodies molded, as they embraced, kissed, sensed and experienced each other.

Too quickly, the time arrived for him to shave, shower and dress.

Again, Karen raced to the bathroom, then to the kitchen, and brought him coffee. She scrambled several eggs in a large bowl, and popped four pieces of bread into the toaster.

When she returned to the bathroom to refill his cup, she paused at the door, admiring his slender muscular body. A towel wrapped his waist as he scraped the coarse stubble with his safety razor.

She padded to him stealthily, and gently kissed his shoulder. Then set the coffee pot on the bathroom vanity, wrapped her arms around his chest, and hugged close against him.

Matt felt her firm breasts press his back, and winked at her over his right shoulder.

"We keep this up and I won't be dressed when Hoot arrives!" he said.

Karen noticed the towel began rising, and playfully, eased her hand into its folds and softly clutched him.

Matt placed the razor on the sink, wiped off the shave cream with a towel, then slipped Karen's nightgown over her head.

He led her into the shower...his longing apparent...turned on the water and adjusted its flow.

She leaned against the tile wall...her right leg on the side of the tub... and he snugged close against her, the warm water hitting the small of his back.

The couple moved slowly back and forth in the cramped space, each clutching the other tightly as passion engulfed them, then almost collapsing against one another.

With only minutes before Hoot's arrival, they soaped, rinsed and toweled each other dry.

Karen hurriedly slipped into her nightgown, wrapped a terrycloth robe around her, and stepped into a pair of fuzzy houseshoes as the doorbell chimed.

Matt heard their voices in the living room as he knotted his tie. He took a brown suit off its hanger, pulled on the pants and joined them.

Hoot sat at the breakfast table, enjoying his first sips of coffee, when Matt entered. The partner looked up and smiled knowingly at Matt's hair glistening with dampness.

"I didn't mean to interrupt you two newlyweds," he joked. "We should have scheduled for an afternoon presentation...rather than morning!"

Karen opened the drapes inviting brilliant sunlight, then turned and joined them at the table, reddening slightly over Hoot's correct assumption.

"Wait'll you get hitched, Hooter," Matt scolded, rising to fetch the coffee pot. He bussed his wife's head as he passed behind her.

"You'll also enjoy the luxury of discovering that once in a while, pleasure takes precedent over business."

"You're probably right, Matthew," Hoot said, intent on making her blush again. "Who wants to go to work and leave someone like Karen behind?"

The new flush surpassed her first effort.

"Speaking of work...Hoot and I must make tracks, honey," Matt said.

He gulped another swallow of hot coffee, collected his coat off the chair's back and bent to kiss his wife on the forehead.

"We've got an hour's drive...and a hectic morning of rehearsing the Triad presentation."

"Understand," she replied, returning his kiss.

"Bye beautiful," Hoot smiled, also pecking her cheek.

"Bye you two. Knock 'em dead in Hartford."

"We will, babe," Matt said, holding the door for Hoot. "See you sometime this evening."

Karen listened to the two men walking down the flights of stairs, jabbering over the details that needed completion prior their presentation.

Clearing the table, Karen unconsciously whistled to herself and contemplated the morning's lovemaking; reveling in the deep sense of satisfaction that permeated her being.

She smiled broadly with the immense love felt for Matt, that at times like this filled her soul to a point of exploding.

"It must be sinful to be so happy," she said to the beaming face in the bathroom mirror as she readied for work.

She hummed as she brushed the long, silken, honey-colored hair.

"Mrs. Durham...you're a lucky gal."

Outside the apartment, rush hour traffic weaved through the narrow streets, carrying people to work, kids to school and mingling with cars of students and professors headed for the Yale campus.

On Highway 91, enroute to Hartford, Matt lowered the sunvisor and shielded his eyes from golden sunlight streaming from his right.

"What a swell morning, Hooter," he said, lighting two cigarettes and handing one to his companion.

"This is the day Uncle Remus sang about in that kids' movie."

He whistled a few notes to himself, then burst into an off-key chorus of "Zippety doo da."

Hoot laughed and caught his breath with smoke, then coughed, wheezed and agreed.

"Sure is, Matt. I feel everything's going as planned. Hey, what about that ball game last night? Yankees trounced the White Sox!"

"Yeah...looks like they'll face the Dodgers in the World Series. What we've written for the Triad campaign is actually happening. Bet Stengel's Yankees win the Series, too."

"Probably so; they've got powerful hitters and the most talented pitchers around."

"Hope Triad buys our idea of special World Series fares to New York. Bet anything they'd make a bundle flying people to the games."

"I'm sure you're right, Matthew. Now that Korea's in the past, folks need something to free their minds of the last three years."

"Ike looked good on television...explaining the Armistice conditions. Think he'll amount to much as President?"

"Don't know, Matthew. If he leads the nation like he led troops, he'll do okay. Still, he's not as political or aggressive as Truman."

"Or soft spoken," Matt added facetiously, tapping another cigarette from a fresh pack of Luckies. "Another smoke?"

"Sure. We'll be there in a minute. It'll calm me some." Hoot took the lighted cigarette and sucked a long draw that made the tobacco crackle. He exhaled through his nose, looked at Matt, and flashed a wide grin.

"Our first real presentation, partner. You know, even though these guys are pals...I'm nervous as a Baptist deacon in a cathouse."

"No reason to be, old buddy," Matt patted the other's knee. "We've got outstanding artwork and copy, and I'm certain Bob and Don will love our approach."

"Well sir...we'll find out in a few minutes," replied Hoot.

He pulled the Chevrolet sedan through a tight turn and onto a blacktop road. A mile in the distance, the path dead-ended at Triad's hangar and office building east of Hartford.

Triad Airlines, in addition to purchasing World War II military DC-3s, leased a small airport from the government. Artillery spotter pilots trained there, and it provided facilities for the local Civilian Air Patrol.

Early on, Triad extended its northwest-to-southwest runway, and added a second half-mile-long concrete band that intersected the first.

This strip made landings possible for larger aircraft, and enabled smaller planes to lift off in shifting winds.

Hoot centered on the asphalt drive that lead to the executive building.

Triad had converted a hangar to work spaces, and located its corporate offices there. As the two approached the corrugated steel structure, Matt noticed a windsock hanging limp on a tall metal pole in a grassy island between the two runways.

On the tarmac near three larger hangars, a half dozen DC-3s displayed the three-bladed Triad Airlines logo.

Hoot followed the semicircle drive to a parking spot near the middle of the structure. There, a small foyer built midway down the side of the hangar housed the front door.

He shifted the Chevy into reverse, turned off the ignition and eased out the clutch.

"Well, skipper, let's give 'em a show," he said.

He shook his partner's hand firmly for good luck, then opened the car door and lifted out.

"Indeed, let's!" Matt replied enthusiastically, exiting from the passenger's side.

The two retrieved briefcases and the leather folder containing Eddie Bauer's artwork from the back seat; then shut the car's doors, and walked through the glass entrance into Triad's waiting area.

"Hoot Gibson and Matt Durham to see Bob Griffith and Don Stein," Matt said to the receptionist who asked to help them.

She buzzed the men on the intercom.

Bob was the first emerging from the doorway leading to inner offices. He flashed a friendly smile and stretched to shake the newcomers' hands.

"Welcome, guys."

He patted each on the back, then ushered them through the doorway from which he appeared. There they met Don Stein, waiting halfway down a long corridor that ran the length of the metal building.

Don also shook their hands warmly.

As the four entered the conference room, Sid Masters turned from pouring a cup of coffee and greeted them.

"How about java?" Sid asked, clasping their hands. "Brewed fresh on your behalf."

"Yeah...you guys get royal treatment!" admonished Bob, clasping the back of Sid's neck. "If it were just us, he'd add grounds for a week. By Friday, we need jackhammers to crack the shit that collects in the bottom of the strainer!"

"Thanks, Sid," Matt smiled. "It's what I need to get the old pump going."

He turned the plastic tap and filled his cup. The other four did likewise, then seated themselves around the oval table.

Around the conference room, shattered propellers and other fighter aircraft memorabilia stood in corners or adorned tables, bookcases and shelves.

Insignias of various nations...many on canvas or metal sections of wings and fuselages...hung on the walls.

The walnut-paneled enclosure still reeked of aviation fuel; a heady fragrance for the five flyers meeting within its confines.

Matt and Hoot pulled copy sheets and artboards from their cases. The former stood at the head of the table, facing the group.

"The campaign theme we've developed focuses on two key events occurring on the East Coast," he said, looking one at a time at the bystanders.

"Those two events are the World Series and...most important...your offering of commuter flights between New York, Boston and Hartford."

"These three cities serve as major East Coast business centers," added Hoot, standing on cue and holding an artboard that depicted Triad's flight routes.

"We figured...why not unite the two events!" Matt said emphatically. "Tie the introduction of your commuter service with the World Series."

He flashed Eddie's layout with a sepia photo of Babe Ruth hitting a homer. Its banner headline read: "If you like cheering for home runs... fly ours!"

"Here's an ad linking the World Series to Triad Airlines," Matt continued. "It identifies your service offering as a 'home run'...meaning your two-way flights between these cities."

Hoot kept the pace.

"The copy reads: 'In 20 years of baseball, The Babe accounted for 714 home runs. In 20 working days, Triad Airlines accounts for 414. On Monday, August 16, Triad inaugurates the first ever commuter air service between Hartford, Boston and New York. Three morning flights leave Hartford at 6, 7 and 8 a.m. They arrive at Boston at 6:30, 7:30 and 8:30 a.m. And land in New York at 7:30, 8:30 and 9:30 a.m. Return flights from New York to Boston and Hartford leave at 6, 7 and 8 p.m. Whether you're commuting for business or baseball...fly Triad Airlines today.'"

"There'll be room at the bottoms of ads so you can offer telephone numbers for local travel offices," concluded Matt.

He picked up Eddie's other four layouts and handed them around the table.

"Here are variations on the World Series theme."

Triad's executives studied the ads in silence for fifteen minutes. For Matt and Hoot, it seemed as if hours passed before Bob spoke.

"The concept is excellent, guys," he grinned. "I love it! Attracts attention and touts Triad's services. As you know, though...what we want is the business commuter. Does this tie us too much to just flying folks to baseball games?"

"No...not at all, Bob," replied Matt. "We're just adopting the baseball motif to drive home a point; that Triad is introducing a home run commuter service for East Coast business travelers. Timeliness... economy...convenience...these items will become our major selling points once we introduce the service."

"By the time the World Series ends...and we're betting it'll be played in New York...businessmen on the Coast definitely will know about Triad's flights," added Hoot.

"We also recommend radio commercials featuring well-known Yankee and Dodger players," continued Matt. "We'd schedule these during hours businessmen drive to work. These spots also would promote easy, inexpensive and worry-free commuting."

When Matt finished, he sat, sipped his lukewarm coffee, and lit a cigarette. He passed another to Hoot, who also fired up. For another ten minutes, the Triad partners remained hushed; exchanging the layout boards without comment.

Finally, Bob Griffith again broke the silence; which had hung the room like morning breath for the two from D&G.

"I'm speaking for all when I say: 'Congratulations, boys.' These are superb!" the president leaned in his chair and also lit a cigarette.

"Your campaign will catch their fancy; and certainly let 'em know what the hell Triad is! I think it's top-drawer all the way."

"Bob's right, gents," Don agreed. "There's something addictive about New York baseball. My God, they built Yankee Stadium to honor one player! Anyway, baseball gives people warm fuzzies. And that's how we want customers feeling about our airline. Gotta admit...the name 'Babe Ruth' conjures good memories for New Yorkers."

"Whoa, Don, hold on!" interjected Sid, putting a hand on his friend's shoulder and voicing his opinion. "I'm a Dodgers fan, remember? Agreed...our flights will make it easier to see 'The Bums.' Still, we have to focus on economics. I catch the commuter express to New York regularly for twenty bucks. Our flights are nearly double that."

"True, Sid," acknowledged Matt. "However, you're overlooking the time factor. A businessman making fifteen grand averages twenty or thirty bucks an hour. If he has to spend three to four of those hours riding rails, then the economy of flying becomes apparent."

Matt passed around research data on the numbers of people who lived outside New York, but worked in the city.

"There are thousands of others who don't commute daily, but would fly regularly for special meetings or appointments; maybe maintain an apartment in the Big Apple."

"Okay, okay...enough said, Matt," Sid held his palms up in submission. "You're right. I hadn't thought in that vein. What you two say makes sense. I agree...this is a damned fine effort."

"Well, boys...how do we get things rolling?" asked Don.

"First, our art director will prepare final drawings and repro mats for the media," said Hoot, again digging into his leather briefcase. He handed them several papers.

"These are the placement schedules we recommend. They hit major dailies and weeklies throughout the three-state area."

Hoot provided each with another page containing statistical data and graphs.

"Over the next month and a half, your ads will appear in thirty-three publications and reach 20 million readers. All for an estimated thirty-five thousand dollars; including space and production costs."

None of the Triad partners seemed stunned by the media costs, so Matt pushed on with the presentation.

"If you'd like radio spots later...say, when the Series begins...they would cost about fifteen thousand more. That includes talent fees for the players who would read the announcements."

The three Triad men looked at each other, then back to Matt and Hoot.

"So everyone understands...if Triad goes first cabin, the campaign costs about fifty thousand...right?" Don Stein stated the question rather than asking it.

He turned to Bob: "That's a quarter of monthly net. What do you say, Mister President?"

"There won't be monthly net without advertising our wares, Don," came the answer. "I vote D&G gets started on our campaign, pronto. In fact, round up coaches and players who'd like doing radio commercials for us!"

"Can do, Bob," said Matt, smiling.

Then he addressed the trio in serious tones: "Thanks for your friendship...and the business, gentlemen. I promise...if you ever need us for anything...we'll get here as quick as we can."

"We're sure you will, Matt," replied Bob. "If you two have a contract for us to sign...and need cash upfront... let's settle, and then grab a bite of lunch. Triad will collect the tab to celebrate the occasion! Right, Don?"

"Hell, Bob...you just spent fifty big ones," the other replied jokingly. "What's another lousy thirty bucks?"

"Lunch sounds good, Bob," said Hoot, rising from the table and handing the contractual forms to Triad's president.

"There's another matter we'd like to discuss...perhaps after lunch? We would value your opinions on an idea for another prospect; it concerns the time element Matt mentioned a few minutes ago."

"Sure, Hoot," said Bob. "We'll help any way we can. Remember though; we're just old hack pilots...not Madison Avenue, jet jockey, whizz-bang types like you guys!"

"Ah, c'mon, Bob," said Matt, ushering him through the door. "Jet jockeys...yes. However, not Madison Avenue whizz-bangs. Perhaps someday...who knows?"

"Matt..." replied Bob, stopping abruptly and looking squarely into the other's eyes. "I feel that's a certainty."

The five first stopped at the men's room outside the conference spaces, then went to the office area where Don asked Triad's bookkeeper to draw a corporate check for ten thousand dollars; payable to Durham & Gibson Advertising.

Minutes later, Larry Harst, the fourth partner, returned from a meeting, and fell in with the quintet as they walked out the front door.

"Here's D&G's advertising contract, Larry," said Bob, handing him a folder of papers. "You're our legal eagle...what's your opinion?"

He paused a minute...studied the papers...and handed them back to Bob.

"Looks kosher to me. Sure sorry I missed the presentation."

"Okay, gentlemen," said Bob.

He scrawled his name at the bottom of the cover sheet, removed the carbon paper and Triad's copy, and handed these to his secretary.

He gave the top copy and a company check to Matt, shaking the latter's hand.

"It's official...D&G is now Triad's agency of record."

"Again guys, thanks," added Hoot.

After a leisurely lunch of roast beef sandwiches, Cole slaw, and icy bottles of beer, the six returned to Triad's conference room. There, Matt and Hoot unveiled Connecticut Casting's plans for the Cometliner 440, and their tentative "time machine" concept.

Sid volunteered a first opinion of the idea.

"Listen you two...you've convinced me about businessmen paying more to save valuable time. This is a humdinger of a sales message; especially for us in the airline business."

"I agree completely," echoed Bob. "Time is our biggest enemy. Think how much we'd save if we could log a round trip from Hartford to Boston and New York in half the amount! In pilot and crew hours, as well as passenger minutes."

"And that doesn't take fuel savings into account, Bob," added Don Stein, who then turned to Hoot. "I hear these new jet engines are plenty energy efficient."

"That's right, Bob," confirmed Hoot. "According to General Durham's per-seat-mile estimates...considering passenger load sizes... jetliners fly for about ten bucks versus twice that for prop jobs like your DC-2s and 3s."

"Over the long haul, I see where jets would be more efficient," agreed Don. "And time savings are phenomenal."

"Matt...it's unanimous," Bob concluded. "You've hit on a dandy approach to selling your dad's plane. Tell him for us it's a beauty, and if our commuter succeeds half as well as we think it will, we'll buy a few of those babies soon."

Bob stood behind his partners, and placed his hands on Don's and Sid's shoulders.

"The four of us have it in the backs of our minds that someday, Triad will offer international flights."

"I'll affirm what the president says," added Sid. "Flying to other countries has been part of our dream from the beginning. And we're off to a good start introducing a commuter airline."

"We'll learn soon enough, Sid," responded Don. "When ads start appearing in East Coast newspapers, we'll find out quickly if our hunch is going to pay."

Over the next couple of hours, the six pilots chatted about the Cometliner, flying and jets in general.

At five o'clock, Hoot glanced at his watch and suggested to Matt they'd better return to New Haven. He turned to Bob Griffith:

"We're stopping through Middletown on the way," he explained. "Dropping off ads for my father. When we reach New Haven, we'll call our art director and let him know the outcome of our meeting. And give him the go-ahead."

"We understand," answered Bob.

He stood, as did the other Triad officers, and they walked Matt and Hoot to the front entrance. There, they shook hands and waved as the two drove away.

When the Chevy edged onto Highway 91 south, Matt and Hoot loosened their ties for the return trip. The former fired two cigarettes, and passed one to his comrade.

Matt reached into the backseat, retrieved the check from his briefcase, and waved it, tantalizingly, under Hoot's nose.

"Hooter...our first full-fledged account. What do you think about that?"

"Well, Matthew," the other turned to face his partner, smiling broadly. "Triad will be one of many. However, it'll always own a spot in my heart, and can count on D&G's best.

"I feel the same, amigo," said Matt, studying the check. "I can't wait to see Eddie's face when we give him the good news!"

"Yeah...it'll tickle him, okay. You know, if we get your dad's work, we'll need him full-time. What say we hire him after the new year...if things go as planned?"

"Gee, that'd be swell, Hoot! Here we are, in business three months and suffering growing pains!"

"Yes, but healthy pains, Matt," beamed Hoot.

For the remainder of the journey...including the Middletown pause to drop off ads and tell Hoot's parents about Triad...the two talked excitedly: Reviewing the day's happenings; the work needing doing tomorrow; and the future that brightened almost daily.

Then they were in New Haven.

Hoot pulled in front of Matt's apartment building.

"Come in for a drink, Hoot?"

"No thanks, Matthew. Dying to tell Bobby the good news!"

"Understand, pal," Matt replied.

He snatched his briefcase, coat and tie from the back seat.

"See you tomorrow morning. I'll call Eddie tonight and ask him to come in. We'll pay him for his work so far. He probably could use a few bucks."

"Sounds fair. Goodnight, Matthew. See you in the morning. Love to Karen."

"Sure thing...same to Bobby."

Hoot drove away, and Matt took the stairs to his apartment two at a time.

Karen heard, and met him at the doorway.

"Hi honey," he said, pecking her lips.

Without a word, he led her into the living room. When they settled on the couch, he held her at arm's length.

"Great news, sweetheart...we got the account! They loved our campaign!"

"Oh Matt, that's wonderful! Of course...it's what I expected. You and Hoot are unstoppable."

She hugged him close and looked into his eyes.

"Was Hoot excited?"

"Oh God yes!" he exclaimed. "Couldn't stay for a drink. Had to rush and tell Bobby."

"Sounds like they're serious."

"Could be," he teased.

He stood and walked to the bedroom to change.

"We're almost to the point where he can afford a wife."

"What!" shrieked Karen, running to where he stood with his pants half off.

"Listen Mr. Potato Head, Bobby's holding down a job, too. And as for affording a wife...my salary from Peck & Peck comes in handy, doesn't it?"

"Whoa. At ease! Brother...did I say the wrong thing!"

He turned to face her, smiling sheepishly.

"Only kidding, babe."

He walked to her, slipped his arms around her waist, drew her close and kissed her lightly on the lips.

"Forgive a stupid remark?"

"Sure," she returned his kiss, and playfully nipped his nose. "You hungry? I've got chicken frying."

"Famished," he answered, buttoning a favorite knock-around oxford cloth shirt. "While you're setting the table, I'll call Eddie with the news."

"Great. It'll surprise him. Perk him up."

"Hope so. Although, I'm convinced he knew they'd go ape over the layouts we presented."

Karen disappeared into the kitchen as Matt walked to the telephone in the living room. He lit a cigarette and dialed the Bauers' number.

Mary answered...briefly exchanged pleasantries with Matt...then called her son to the phone.

"Hello?"

"Hi, Eddie. It's Matt."

"Oh, hi Matt. How did it go?"

"Swell, pal. They loved your stuff. We can produce and place it by the middle of the month. That enough time?"

"Oh, Yessiree, Matt! I'll have final art ready by this Friday. And repro mats pulled the following Monday."

"Excellent! Hoot and I will prepare insertion orders by then, and contact the major dailies...make sure they're holding space. If you'd stop by the office tomorrow, we'd like to pay for your time, Eddie."

"Okay, Matt. Like I said, it's not necessary. The government pays me, and I'm doing what I enjoy."

"We still want to pay you, Eddie. And if things keep perking like they are, we'd like you to join us full-time."

"You mean that, Matt?"

"You bet. It makes sense having you in the office with us; handling the art director's duties and helping brainstorm ideas. You've got a creative mind, Eddie. We'd like you onboard."

"Gee, Matt. I appreciate your wanting me to join you and Hoot. Means a lot."

"We'll make good team, Eddie. See you tomorrow?"

"Sure. I've got artwork to show you anyway."

"Fine," said Matt, stubbing his cigarette in the ashtray near the telephone. "Goodnight."

"Goodnight, Matt. And thanks again."

The two hung up, and Matt walked to the dining room where Karen spooned fresh broccoli beside the fried chicken breast on his plate.

He sat down, took a long swallow of icy milk, and watched appreciatively as his attractive wife bustled around the kitchen. Finally, she removed the lacy apron she wore and joined him at the table.

He reached across and took her hand.

"I love you, Mrs. Durham."

"And I, you, Mr. Durham," she replied.

"What an exhilarating way to start a month! And if we get the Conn Castings account...what a tremendous way to end it!"

"I'm sure you'll win that account, too. Like I keep saying, you and Hoot are going to succeed in a big way."

"You honestly think so?"

"I'm certain of it, Matt. This is only the beginning."

"Yeah...I think so too," then switching to a James Cagney impression: "Stick by me, doll...we'll have a hell of a life together."

"Consider me glue," Karen replied, smiling and squeezing his hand firmly. "Consider me glue."

Chapter 14

Conn Castings Contest

A S PROMISED, AT MID-MORNING EDDIE Bauer rapped the door of
Durham and Gibson. Tucked under his arm was the familiar
bulging leather case.

Hoot opened the door, asked him in, and offered coffee.

"Oh, no. Thanks, Hoot," Eddie answered. "Too much already.
Feeling twitchy!"

Matt appeared from the supply room with a brimming coffee cup
in hand.

"Gee, had I known...I'd have brought you one," he said to the
newcomer, nodding toward his container.

"That's okay, Matt," said Hoot, pointing Eddie to a chair. "He passes
on the java. Guess last time he found our brew a notch above river mud."

"Oh? You must have made it that day, Hoot!" Matt responded.

Then, to Eddie:

"Well, Mr. Art Director...anything for us?"

Eddie unzipped the folder and removed several poster size artboards.

"See if these communicate outer space!"

Matt glanced at the boards, and whistled softly. Eddie's watercolor
sketches had captured perfectly the concepts the three discussed earlier.

The layout contrasted the Cometliner against a dramatic telescopic
photo of the Milky Way. The technique...highlighted with shading and
blurring...stylized the jetliner as if it were speeding through the galaxy.

The headline stated, simply:

"The Cometliner 440...tomorrow's time machine."

Eddie had hand-lettered a typeface that complemented the
photograph, and imparted additional movement and three-dimensional
effects to the in-flight aircraft.

Matt glanced sideways at Hoot and detected his partner's Cheshire
grin.

"You've done it again, Eddie," the other stated matter of factly.

He exchanged renderings with Matt.

"A swell job capturing the futuristic aura. Don't you agree, Matthew?"

"Yeah...I sure do. If we can write copy as well as Eddie illustrates, we'll clinch this presentation!"

He studied the board Hoot held, which depicted the Cometliner taking off. Its nose pointed toward the reader, and a clock's face had been superimposed over the artwork.

"Wow! We've hit on how to sell the Cometliner!"

Eddie tugged several more boards from his valise.

"I roughed four more thumbnail sketches that pursue the same thinking," the young man said. "If any of these interest you, I can have 'em by Friday."

"You'll have time, Eddie?" asked Hoot...amazed. "Even while you're producing Triad's materials?"

"Sure...it's a cake walk now," Eddie replied. "Hardest part is getting the conceptual format on paper. We've got that. Now, I'll spruce these a little, prepare full-size layouts, and we're ready! It won't take much time."

"That's outstanding, Eddie," said Matt, patting his shoulder. "By the way..."

He lifted his suit coat off the rack, retrieved a cashier's check, and handed it to the young man.

"Does this seem fair enough for your time so far?"

"More than fair, Matt. Thanks...loads."

"Our pleasure, Eddie," chimed Hoot. "Like we said...Triad loved your work and gave us partial payment for space, materials and time. That's where we got the dough, and you've earned a share of it."

Eddie tucked the check into his shirt pocket, collected his layouts, and stowed them in the leather case.

"I gotta go if we want Triad's ads produced," he said, fixing Matt with the crystalline blue eyes, which now twinkled happiness.

"I called the typesetter, who can get on our job pronto. Plus, I pulled baseball photos from the morgue files at the newspaper office. We're set, guys."

"Let me know if you need additional baseball shots," urged Hoot. "Dad's papers have anything we need."

"Will do, Hoot," said Eddie, clutching the doorknob. "I'll touch base later this week."

"Swell, Eddie," said Matt, placing his hand on the artist's back and helping him with the door. "If you need us, we'll be here writing copy for Conn Castings."

"Okay. Bye Matt. Bye Hoot." Eddie waved as he walked out the office door.

Matt paced to his desk, sat and turned to Hoot:

"It'll simplify things getting Eddie onboard."

"Boy...for certain!" Hoot exclaimed. "He seems excited about joining us, too."

"He is...but not like I am about getting him on our team. Gotta hand it to Karen...he's sensational!"

"Tell you what, old buddy," said Hoot, standing and ambling to where the other sat. "Let's get a bite of lunch, then come back and write sparkling sales copy to match Eddie's layouts."

"You're on, Houston," Matt said rising. "By the way, it's your turn to buy the burgers."

"Why? You're the guy who pocketed ten grand!"

"Okay, amigo," Matt relented, grabbing the door for his friend. "I'll spring today...even though I've got a wife to support."

"I swear I heard Jack Benny's violin screeching sad music," Hoot chuckled, walking into the hallway as Matt closed and locked the door.

Connecticut Casting's extensive manufacturing facilities enveloped ten acres of land northwest of New Haven. A converted pre-World War Two dirigible hangar housed the casting plant, which rose nearly as high as it was long. Inside roared five coal-fired smelting furnaces.

A ceiling-mounted, oval-shaped monorail automatically shuttled huge melting pots to the pouring areas. There, dozens of coal-stained, sweat-drenched workers toiled year-round in temperatures topping ninety degrees.

Since he could remember, Matt awed over the brute strength and sheer force of the smelting and manufacturing operations.

As a youngster, he thrilled to white hot steel spilling from the pots, splashing fiery sparks of molten metal everywhere...and fantasized it was gold.

The furnace smell...the noisy machinery and workers...the hiss of streaming steel lava...and the intense heat; all bestowed in him an appreciation and respect for the crude industry.

Conn Castings fabricated its assembly area fifty feet to the rear of the smelting plant, contained in a corrugated steel building the size of a football field.

Inside this facility hummed immense conveyor belts, forming a ceaseless assembly line that ran the structure's entire length.

A hollow fuselage took shape at one end of the belt, and twenty days later emerged from the opposite end as a nearly flyable aircraft.

Conn Castings began designing, developing, testing and manufacturing fighter aircraft at the outbreak of World War Two. Only recently had the company retooled and remachined to accommodate larger airframes such as the Cometliner's.

More than five hundred workers scurried throughout the assembly area, each performing a specific task in piecing together the stainless steel giants that soon would emanate from the enormous building.

On both sides of the assembly building, vast warehouses contained tons of various-sized gleaming metal panels. Stacked inside, twenty feet high, they suggested sheets of plywood.

Cranes positioned these burnished pieces on a conveyor belt to one side of the building's interior. There, they crept slowly into a gigantic gear and pulley-laden piece of equipment which resembled a crude printing press.

Amongst hissing, grinding and screeching sounds the metal disappeared, only to emerge from the other end of the machinery as a perfectly formed and graceful portion of gleaming fuselage.

Sections fit one another like jigsaw pieces, and when riveted, formed a jumbo shiny cigar, ready for final machining.

A ten-foot-high chain-link fence cordoned the periphery of Conn Castings, and security guards manned booths at the front gate by the highway, and back gate behind the manufacturing area.

A railroad siding entered the property through the rear entrance, and continued as an oval track around and through the smelting and assembling areas. The spur enabled diesel engines to haul loads to any point in the work-yard.

Conn Castings erected its headquarters building several hundred yards north of the manufacturing and assembling areas. The glass and brick structure stretched a city block, and stood three stories high over a wide circular drive.

In the turnaround's center reigned a marble water fountain, sculpted in the Romanesque style of the late 1920s. The monument sprayed daily until December's chill froze it solid, compelling the company to shut it off until spring.

A ribbon of asphalt ran from Conn Casting's sweeping approachway and linked with Highway 63, opening to points North and South.

The headquarters building contained sixty offices, most located on the first and second floors. The main floor boasted four large conference rooms, an auditorium and employee cafeteria.

Conn Castings situated its executive offices on the third floor when it erected the building in the early nineteen hundreds. The elevation provided key managers with visible vantage points overlooking the production areas.

The company also constructed a preview theater in the middle of third; which seated thirty spectators and functioned primarily for screening flight tests, engine and wind tunnel trials, and company presentations.

Here, Matt, Hoot and Eddie...and their competitors, the Bradleys... would present proposals to Conn Casting's officers. The D&G team members felt as if two weeks had been compressed into one. For no sooner had they written copy...and Eddie completed four more layouts... then presentation day arrived.

On that Thursday morning, Walt met his son and the two others in the parking lot shortly before nine, and escorted them to the third floor presentation center.

There, the three busied themselves arranging proposal binders and leave-behind materials, and placing agendas and outlines on the seats so all officers could follow their performance.

"You'll show your ideas first, Matt," explained Walt on the elevator. "The Bradley Agency presents this afternoon. We're shooting for a decision tomorrow...after we've heard both pitches, read the summaries, and conferred."

"I don't mind telling you, General...I'm nervous as all get out," said Hoot, lighting a smoke.

"I can understand, Hoot," replied Walt. "Many's the time I've stood before groups. I've never felt comfortable; large gathering or small. Just remember...the men you're addressing are friendly and fair. I've knocked around with most of them for more than thirty years. They'll listen hard... then recommend what's best for Conn Castings. You can bet on that."

Matt earlier introduced Eddie to his father, and now, the general focused on the young man.

"These birds tell me you're quite an art director, Eddie," Walt said affably. "And Karen says your mom taught her at Hanley."

"Yessir, general," Eddie stammered, exhibiting an enlisted soldier's nervousness in addressing a senior officer. Plus, his legs throbbed from standing and compounded his fear of presenting his artwork.

Walt noticed and placed his hand on the other's shoulder.

"Have a seat, Eddie, please. The rest of our people won't be here for another fifteen minutes, so relax while you can. I'll have the cafeteria bring coffee and rolls."

Walt went to the telephone, punched the intercom button, dialed a number and spoke into the mouthpiece. In minutes, a restaurant worker wheeled in a large stainless steel cart.

On it stood silver coffee carafes, water pitchers, cups and glasses. Next to the drinks rested a tray stacked high with sweet rolls.

The four served themselves.

By twenty minutes past, the other executives arrived for the nine-thirty talk.

They collected coffee and rolls, then gathered near the front of the room facing Walt, Matt, Hoot and Eddie; who still sat on the right-hand side in the front row.

The general opened the meeting:

"Good morning, gentlemen. Today, we're looking at proposed campaigns for the Cometliner. We'll listen to a presentation this morning, and another at two this afternoon."

Walt stepped back, put his arm behind Matt's back.

"The first group presenting is the Durham and Gibson agency. So without further ado, here's my son, Matt, and his two partners: Hoot Gibson and Eddie Bauer. I'll let them explain what's in store for us."

Matt shook his father's hand and stepped behind the podium, nodding to those in the audience whom he knew. Hoot moved to his spot beside the easel, ready to display Eddie's artboards.

"Thank you, general. Good morning, and thanks for this opportunity to present our promotional ideas for the Cometliner. It's an exciting aircraft...and I think you'll find our suggested approaches heighten its excitement."

Matt walked from behind the lectern, crossed his arms, and addressed the audience from only feet away.

"Being ex-fliers, Hoot and I are convinced you've developed a swell plane. Regardless of who merchandises the Cometliner for you...it will succeed."

He paced from one side of the room to the other.

"The market and time are ideal for faster and more enjoyable air travel. Turbojet technology has arisen to replace older, slower and less efficient propeller-driven machines. And I'm proud that Conn Castings will be the first to unveil such technical advances."

Matt surprised himself over the ease of words shaping in his mind and rolling from his tongue. Earlier, he jotted only sparse notes and a few ideas on a sheet of paper.

Now, his brain retrieved and indexed those thoughts in orderly fashion, and he merely opened his mouth to let them escape vocally.

For ten minutes, he highlighted the criticality of saving time which, by modern standards, meant increased productivity; a subject to which the audience responded positively.

He then turned to the promotional platform that outlined D&G's time machine approach. At this point, he asked the Conn Castings officers to review with him the presentation folders the three had prepared and distributed.

When Matt and Hoot felt confident the company's executives grasped the theme, they switched to artwork and copy. And in an hour's time, they finished presenting and fielded questions.

One of the first focused on where and when to place their advertising. Hoot answered:

"Airline industry and flying magazines merit the bulk of your advertising monies, although we also recommend radio commercials in our media mix; for attention-getters, more than anything else."

Hoot referred the listeners to sections in the hand-out that illustrated media expenditures and projected revenues.

"Right now, we don't see television as a medium for Conn Castings," he concluded. "Later on, however, when Cometliner sales start booming, we have some thoughts for TV commercials."

Matt thumbed his presentation binder and directed the attendees to the budgeting section:

"We estimate space and time costs at around three-quarters of a million dollars," he said, pausing to glance around the room. "Production will run about a quarter million."

When he tossed the figures, several of the businessmen whistled amazement over the anticipated campaign costs.

Matt raised his hands.

"Granted...that's a lot of money; but it's also what it costs to pioneer a product like yours. This approach can gain national and international recognition for the Cometliner...as the first of its kind."

Again, Matt strode in front of the assemblage and looked into their faces.

"When we succeed...Conn Castings' lead will prohibit competitors from catching up. To act as swiftly and boldly as possible means a heavy investment upfront. In the long run, though, it'll pay back tenfold."

When hushed whispers died, Matt and Hoot invited other questions, then thanked each man for his time and, again, for the privilege of presenting.

Afterwards, most of the Conn Castings businessmen approached the three, congratulating them on their ideas and verbal and visual performances; which made the trio feel even more positive about the proceedings.

"You boys did fine," commented Walt as he helped collect the presentation materials. "Your performance reflected a lot of time, effort and solid thinking; and everyone recognized that."

"They seemed to, dad," agreed Matt. "Although...our projected costs rattled a few cages!"

"Well hell yes, son!" the general exclaimed. "Remember, we're mostly engineers...used to working with known quantities or things we can calculate on a slide-rule. Conn Castings has never marketed a commercial product; we've just dealt with the military. Which means you put your best and final offer forward and that's that. Most often, you win based on price."

Walt hooked his arm around his son's shoulder.

"I know that doesn't hold true in the commercial arena. A product has to have sex appeal and all sorts of thingamajigs. That's a new ball game for us, Matt, and you guys need to help us with our hard-sell naiveté."

Hoot had lit two cigarettes and now handed one to Matt.

"I hope we stressed the importance of being first with a new product like yours, general," he said. "The Cometliner needs to take the industry by storm; and that takes money."

"I know you're right, Hoot," Walt replied. "I also know our marketing boys will find the bucks. We're convinced the Cometliner means the difference between piecemeal work and long-term, big dollar contracts; the kind that keep us manufacturing at full capacity and employed for decades. Who am I kidding...the Cometliner is this company's future!"

"With that much at stake, dad...a million bucks isn't a lot, is it?"

"No, son. Not really. Here's hoping we spend it with the three of you."

Walt ushered them to the elevator, then accompanied them on the ride down and walk to Hoot's car.

"We'll give you the outcome tomorrow, boys. Again, you did a fine job. If your thoughts impressed the others as much as me...you're home free."

"Thanks, general," said Hoot. "We appreciate your backing."

Hoot pulled the car from its space and steered onto the drive toward the front gate and Highway 63. Behind them, Walt waved as he crossed the parking lot and returned the building.

On Highway 63, Matt passed around his pack of Luckies and the three lit up.

"Well...a damned good shot," declared Hoot, taking a long drag off his cigarette. "I think they liked our stuff."

"I've got the same feeling, Hoot," agreed Matt. "Lyle Bradley and his dad are following a tough act."

The telephone danced in its cradle when the three returned to the office. Matt hurriedly unlocked the door, dashed to his desk.

"Hello...Durham and Gibson," he said, panting for breath.

"Matt? Hi darling," Karen said excitedly. "How did it go? I couldn't stand not knowing."

"We think well, honey," he replied. "Several officers came up afterwards and said it was an outstanding effort. Dad really seemed positive."

"Well, that's comforting! When will you know?"

"Tomorrow...dad said he'd call tomorrow."

"God, I'll be on edge until then."

"You'll have company sweetheart. Hey, I have to run. Ads to show some grocery people, and I need approvals from several others. Should be home at a decent hour, though. And I'm looking forward to relaxing."

"I'll bet. Okay, Matt. See you then. Bye."

"Bye babe."

He loosened his tie, then collected the items needed for calling on his accounts.

"You and Bobby have plans tonight?" he asked Hoot.

"Nah, nothing special. Thought we'd get a burger, then hit my place. Maybe pop corn and watch television. Goodyear Playhouse is presenting 'Marty'."

"Sounds perfect to me, pal. Karen and I'll do the same. How about you, Eddie?"

"I'm the Third Musketeer, boys! I'm hitting the sack early."

"What gay blades we are!" Matt replied, chuckling.

The three picked up their briefcases and walked from the office, and in the street below, each wished the others a good day, climbed into his respective car, and pulled away.

That night, a thunderstorm drifted into New Haven from the coast, bringing with it heavy downpours that began at sunrise and continued through the traffic rush hour.

Matt pulled into his parking slot behind the bank, snatched his briefcase from the passenger's seat and held it over his head as he jumped from the car and dashed the rain-slicked alleyway to the side door.

He flicked rain from his shoulders as he reached the top of the stairs and noticed the office light on. He entered, and nearly collided with Hoot, rushing in the opposite direction.

"Oops...sorry Matt! Left my damned headlights on!"

"That's okay, pal. Why are you here so early?"

"Couldn't sleep. Nerves I guess. Coffee's ready. Be right back," Hoot hollered over his shoulder, skipping steps two at a time.

Matt removed his suit coat, hung it, then poured a cup of coffee. He went to the window and looked over the glistening streets below, flickering with the head and taillights of the stream of rush hour automobiles.

Hoot returned and fetched his cup, then joined Matt at the window. He clutched his friend's shoulder.

"Well, partner...big day," he dabbed his rain-soaked hair with a silk handkerchief. "Should know this afternoon if Conn Castings is ours. And, if we'll hack it as an agency."

"Hey, hold on, Hooter! One account...an agency doesn't make. Don't sell us down the river so quickly if this one falls through. At last tally, we had more than ten...not counting Triad. Our monthly billings have been averaging three thousand bucks a month...after taxes. That's a fair salary for you and me. And lets us pass more work to Eddie."

"Sure...you're right, Matthew. I shouldn't squawk. Besides, Karen and Bobby could help if things got really tough for the two of us."

"Bobby? Gosh, Hoot...sounds like you two are already hitched. By the way...Karen thinks you're serious over each other. You are, aren't you? C'mon...give!"

Hoot's face flashed concern. He stood, walked into the office area, and fired a cigarette.

"That probably compounded my actions last night, Matt," he said, sheepishly. "I had one beer too many and we landed on the couch. Anyway, I made a damned ass of myself trying to get into Bobby's panties. She flew in a huff, and probably won't speak to me again...ever!"

"Oh, c'mon Hoot. Give her credit! Hell, Bobby's a smart gal. She knows guys get carried away once in a while."

"That's no out, Matt. I feel like shit warmed over. Maybe I'll call her later and apologize...if she'll talk with me."

"This definitely sounds like love to me, partner," Matt concluded aloud, and clapped the other smartly on the shoulder.

He took their cups for refills.

"Want me to have Karen call her?"

"No, pal...thanks. I dug this pit and stumbled in."

Hoot followed Matt to the supply room, dug a pack of cigarettes from his damp jacket.

"I'll pull myself out. And to think...I was gonna pop the question this Christmas if business takes off."

"Well, I'll be go to hell!" Matt said, grasping his cohort's hand and shaking it vigorously. "That's swell, Hoot. When do you figure on tying the noose?"

"This summer...if she'll have me."

"Your sin's not that bad...believe me. Great! You two make a neat couple."

"Here's hoping we're still a couple, Matthew. She's the finest girl I've ever met."

"You're not a real bad sort yourself, Houston. She'll forgive you about this. You'll see."

The two moved from the window to their desks, then sat working various ads and carrying the conversation. At nine-thirty, Eddie appeared.

Matt brewed another pot of coffee while Hoot called Bobby to apologize.

Hoot talked in hushed tones...his conversation blending with the steady drumming of rain against the window...and Matt couldn't make out his comrade's words.

However, relief flooded his chest when Hoot broke into a wide grin, nodding affirmatively. Moments later, Hoot hung the phone and returned to the others.

He winked at Matt, and slapped his own wrist in penance.

"It's okay," he said. "All is forgiven...and forgotten. I've been granted a reprieve."

At ten o'clock, the telephone rang. The three stared absently at each other through two more rings, then Hoot snatched it from its stand.

"Durham and Gibson," he answered.

Hoot paused and turned to Matt, his hand covering the mouthpiece.

"It's your dad, Matthew."

Matt took the handset passed to him, and caught his breath.

"Hello, dad?"

"Hello, son," Walt replied, his voice sounding higher pitched than usual.

Matt recognized his father's nervousness and at that instant, for some inexplicable reason, relaxed inwardly. After a few seconds' pause, Walt continued:

"We met last night...and again early this morning. In fact, our discussions concluded just a few minutes ago. I won't keep you in suspense, Matt. The board asked me to inform you that D&G can handle Conn Castings' account...if you want it."

"Want it!" Matt yelled into the handset, raising up from his chair. "Want it! Want it! My God, dad...of course we want it! That's wonderful!"

He muffled the mouthpiece with his palm.

"We got it, guys! Holy shit...we got the account!"

On the telephone, Walt asked what was happening.

"Matt? Matt?"

"Right here, dad. Just telling the guys."

"Hoot and Eddie?"

"Yes...they're both here. Pacing the floor, like me."

"Well, tell them to stop. I'd like to meet with you three for lunch. Discuss a few things. Can you join me at McKenzie's Steak House at noon?"

"Hell yes, dad. We'll be there. I'll even pick up the tab."

"No dice, son. This treat is mine."

An interminable amount of time passed for the three until eleven-thirty. Finally, they piled into Matt's car and drove to the restaurant. At five minutes til, they found a parking space in front of the steak house. Matt pulled in and they went inside.

The general, seated at a table, waved them over and rose to greet them, shaking hands with each. On the table in front of him lay a loose-leaf folder brimming with papers.

"Congratulations, boys," he said, gesturing for them to sit.

A waitress immediately appeared.

"You deserve a cocktail or two," said Walt. "Eddie, what'll it be?"

They ordered around the table, then Walt briefed the trio on the high points of the previous afternoon's happenings.

"After you left, nearly everyone commented on how well you presented your ideas. To a man, they thought your concepts were on target."

Matt gave his comrades a thumbs up sign.

"In fact," Walt's voice quavered, "most questioned why we would consider another agency. They're keen on you three. And Matt, I've never been prouder."

Matt exchanged pleased looks with his two partners as the general continued.

"Lyle Bradley and his father showed up around one o'clock. They put up a few promotional pieces and talked about themselves. My God, it was awful! They clearly didn't do their homework on aircraft...the airlines...or even the benefits of jet engines!"

He flushed, obviously upset, and took a long pull of scotch and soda; then continued, somewhat calmer.

"They talked snob appeal: High income folks preferring jet travel as if it's the 'avant-garde' thing to do! They didn't touch on time savings or seat-per-mile economies. And to think...they received the same materials you did!"

Matt laid a hand on his father's arm.

"Dad, our backgrounds differ considerably from theirs," he rationalized. "I'm not defending them; it's just Lyle never hungered for anything. And I know he didn't go into the military, so you couldn't expect he or his father to know much about something new like jets."

"I'll give you that, Matt," Walt shrugged, poising his glass for another sip of scotch. "There's something else about those two, however. Something treacherous. I just can't put my finger on what."

"Treacherous, Walt?" queried Hoot. "In what way?"

The general turned in the question's direction.

"When our marketing vice president asked the Bradleys why they exaggerated facts about fuel consumption and travel time, the old man told him: 'Advertising sells generalities...not facts!' Now...that doesn't sound cricket to me, Hoot!"

"I don't know, dad," Matt countered. "Lyle's a huckster, sure. I doubt he's a crook, though."

The general fixed on his son's eyes and his voice ebbed to monotone:

"Matt...I've pulled duty with lots of men in my lifetime. Most good, but some bad. My guts can gauge 'em...know which will hack it and which will run. You can pick men by how they talk into your eyes. Which Lyle couldn't do, son. He'd look down, or off to one side."

Walt took another swallow.

"Matt...you boys...don't trust that man. Enough said."

He turned a serious expression on the trio.

"I don't know if you'll cross paths with those two in your crazy business...but if you do, watch your backsides!"

Silence hung over the table as the three looked inquisitively at each other. Finally, Matt spoke: "We will dad. That's a promise."

He patted his father affectionately on the back, then took a gulp of bourbon and water to quash uneasy feelings over the delivered warning.

Hoot quickly switched the conversation's flow to the large folder in front of Walt.

For two hours the foursome discussed Conn Castings' promotional needs, until creating ads and radio spots meshed with the company's manufacturing schedules.

"As I explained earlier, Cometliner flight testing is completed," Walt tapped a flow-chart with his index finger. "We intend rolling out the first production model in October."

He paused and looked into the faces around the table.

"You boys think our campaign will be ready to unveil by early November?"

"Sure, dad," Matt replied instantly.

Then, turning to the other two:

"You guys see problems with that?"

"Nope," they chimed, almost in unison.

As part of their presentation, Matt and Hoot had proposed media schedules for national magazines and radio stations. Now, they suggested local coverage through newspapers and billboards.

The general asked the pair to gather prices and schedules, then turned his attention to Eddie's artwork and minor questions that arose after D&G's pitch.

"One other thing," he added. "We're inviting executives from several airlines to visit Conn Castings in November. We plan on showing them Cometliner test results, and maybe giving them a short ride."

Walt tucked the charts he'd shown the three back into the folder.

"Of course, we'll also take them on the town. Make it a real gala affair. Could you guys suggest some mementos and plan some special ceremony for us?"

"We'd be honored to, Walt," Hoot answered. "Perhaps we could work with Triad and arrange special flights into your airfield."

"Hey...that's a dandy thought, Hoot!" exclaimed Walt. "Start working on that angle."

They conferred on remaining aspects of Conn Casting's campaign, then the informal meeting adjourned. Walt paid the check, left a hefty tip for the waitress and walked to his car with the three men.

"Congratulations again, boys," he said, embracing each and patting their shoulders warmly. He slid behind the steering wheel and looked up at them.

"The best group won; I want you gentlemen to understand that. See you this weekend, Matt?"

"Sure, dad. Karen and I will stop by tomorrow night after the movies."

"Good. So long, Hoot...Eddie."

He closed the door, started the automobile and backed out of the parking slot.

"So long, Walt," said Hoot, waving. "And thanks again."

The three rode to the office in Matt's drafty convertible, talking excitedly about the luncheon discussion, and the work needing doing over the next few months.

When they arrived at the office, Matt and Hoot raced to call Karen and Bobby. Before either lifted a handset, however, the outer office instrument jangled noisily.

Matt answered the demanding telephone.

"Hello...Durham and Gibson."

"Matt?" a tense voice came from the other end. "Lyle Bradley here."

A moment passed in silence. After which Matt spoke:

"Oh...hello Lyle. Been some time."

He looked at Hoot and Eddie and rolled his eyes.

"Congratulations, Matt. Understand you and Hoot Gibson formed a small agency and landed the Conn Castings account."

"That's right, Lyle. Just found out ourselves. I hear you and your dad pitched it, too."

"Oh...sure. However, we figured we didn't stand the chance of a fart in a whirlwind; what with your dad a corporate officer and all."

"That didn't factor in, Lyle. In fact, dad backed out of the decision-making for that reason. And they let your agency propose, didn't they?"

"Well, whatever, Matt. No big deal. That's not why I'm calling, anyway. You and Gibson have some choice accounts in New England. So how'd you like to join the Bradley Agency? It's a chance to make lots more money."

"No Lyle, I don't think so. I'm not interested, and doubt Hoot is either. We plan to make a go with our own shop. We do appreciate the offer though."

"Okay, Matt. Have it your way. You're making a doozy of a mistake, though. We're big in New York."

"So I hear, Lyle. Funny thing...we intend to be so, too."

Matt heard his heart pound excitedly against the silence from the other end of the telephone line. His temples felt they were bursting outward.

Finally: "You figure on coming to New York someday, Matt?"

The voice, miles away, frosted over.

"Perhaps one day we'll have to," he answered. "It's a big town; a major advertising center. I'll bet there's room for another agency."

"Durham...I'll tell you," Lyle hissed with anger. "It's one thing competing over nickel and dime accounts like Conn Castings. Here, however, we play tough. New York groups like ours will eat you alive... faster than a gnat can fart!"

"Could be, Lyle. Like I said, though...we're not worrying about that right now. One of these days...but not now."

Matt stood, pulled a pack of cigarettes from his shirt pocket, and shook one onto the desk. Soon, it dangled from his lips as he talked.

"Listen, Lyle, I've got to hang up. Haven't called my wife with the news yet. So, if you'll excuse me..."

"Sure, Matt. Just keep what I've said in mind. Call me if you two want a shot at real dough. The offer's open."

"Okay, Lyle. Good talking with you."

Matt hung up the telephone and slouched into the chair behind his desk.

"Guess you know who that was!" he said to the others.

Both nodded affirmatively.

"I know we'll lock horns with the Bradley Agency again, Matthew," said Hoot.

"Yeah...smells that way to me, too, Hooter," Matt answered flatly. "You better call Bobby while I try Karen."

"Right," Hoot replied.

Matt took a long pull of smoke and dialed Karen's work number. As he exhaled, he felt exhilaration over the new life he had begun shaping. And hoped it would not be overpowering.

Chapter 15

Fall Festival

B Y FALL FESTIVAL IN LATE September, Matt, Hoot and Eddie introduced the Triad Airlines campaign, placing ads in major East Coast weeklies and dailies, and even developing, scheduling and airing radio commercials that featured the Yankee's Casey Stengel.

The three also completed artwork and copy for Conn Casting's ads and commercials, and maintained a comfortable lead over the deadline of introducing the campaign by mid-October.

Matt and Hoot joined in the traditional squirrel hunt with Walt, Damon, and a dozen Huntsdale men, and in four days collected sixty squirrels for the Festival dinner.

Karen and Bobby accompanied their men to The House, and helped Claire and Evelyn with fall cleaning and cooking for the gala. In general, the two girls merely craved an outing in the fresh country air.

Evenings already wrapped a chill around the hillock on which The House set, and the doctor enjoyed building roaring fires in the fireplace off the living room.

Then he would sit for hours reading, or survey Huntsdale valley and the Paginaw River with binoculars from his commanding bay window view.

Matt and Hoot, meanwhile, busied themselves chopping, hauling and stacking cords of wood. Over the annual rite, they cut, lugged and stockpiled enough lumber to last a hunting season.

On the day of the Festival the two arose before dawn, and under a crisp pink September sky drove down the hill to the river's flood plain. Matt steered onto a smooth undulating dirt road across a soybean field, that every other year Damon had planted in corn.

He soon stopped at a boat put-in point on an oxbow of the Paginaw. There, rust-colored rows of soybeans grew to within feet of Damon's tobacco barn boathouse.

The two inspected the structure...relieved to find it withstood summer's squalls in good shape...and hoisted a square-nosed skiff from its resting place in the rafters.

They gingerly slid it off the dock into the swirling waters, and while Hoot held the vessel at bay, Matt attached a ten horsepower outboard motor. Then he fetched a pair of oars from the building, and placed them in the boat.

Both men donned cork lifejackets and climbed aboard, Hoot clinging to the pier as Matt jerked the starter cord.

The small engine fired immediately, and after popping and sputtering blue smoke a few seconds, soon ran with a steady razz. Hoot shoved them off as Matt slipped the machine into reverse, and the craft churned slowly backwards through the roiling waters. Twenty feet into the current, Matt shifted into forward gear and applied full throttle. The snub-nosed skiff veered toward the center of the Paginaw, planing for the duck blind in the shallow pool downriver.

Hoot hunkered his back toward the front of the boat, cupped his hands and lit two cigarettes. He offered one to Matt.

"Mite nippy on the water, amigo," he said, taking a deep pull and watching the smoke stream from his mouth in a long contrail.

"I can imagine how it'll feel when it gets colder."

"I wear a ski mask running the boat," Matt yelled over the purring motor. "Two years ago, got so cold my eyes watered and nearly froze shut. You'll soon learn firsthand about our frosty, early morning downriver runs!"

Matt steered the boat through a gradual bend in the river toward two willow-lined fingers of sand and rock that jutted into the channel. Their destination...a hideout on stilts standing in a quiet, shallow pool... appeared between the twin pilings.

As the craft approached, rafted puddle ducks flared from their resting place, wings beating furiously and webbed feet tapping circular tracks on the water's surface. In seconds, the waterfowl dispersed in all directions.

"What kind were those?" Hoot asked, as the johnboat nestled alongside the blind.

"Wood ducks and teal, Hooter. They stay around most of the year, living on the tributaries that feed the Paginaw. You'll hear 'em whistling over early in the morning as they dart among the flooded trees. Beautiful little birds...I'd never shoot one."

Matt fastened the boat to one of the round posts on which the blind set, then stepped up and out, taking a helping hand from Hoot. He unlatched the hut's door, crouched and went inside.

Most of the structure's willow, Johnson grass and smart weed camouflage had blown away, or been whipped bare by hard rains. Its construction remained sound, however.

In some places, the interior tarpaper lining had cracked or torn slightly. Still, minor patching easily could ready the hut for the season.

As he inspected the inside, Matt's foot trod something beneath the floor's straw covering. He reached and picked up a spent twelve gauge shotgun shell; a purple Canadian Monarch in shot size six.

"One of Judge Corley's shells," he said pensively, pocketing the casing as remorse bit the hollow of his stomach.

Hoot's excitement instantly displaced the anguish.

"This is more than swell, Matthew!" the other exclaimed. "Wow... what a view of the river! Hey, look there!"

Matt's eyes followed Hoot's pointing finger to where a large vee of big ducks pumped rapidly downriver.

"Mallards, Hoot," he said, thrilling as the quacking waterfowl whistled past.

"Come back in a month, boys," he yelled at the disappearing formation. Then, to Hoot: "We'd better head back for chow."

Now that he'd seen birds winging, Matt was even more anxious for the season to open. On the return trip to the boathouse, he scanned the sky for telltale black dots in the distance.

Fall Festival actually served a dual purpose: It wrapped melancholy farewells to another year in autumn gaiety; and, gave Huntsdale's menfolk an excuse to shed their wives when the trees changed colors.

For nearly two hundred years, outdoorsmen like these succumbed to the call of October's woods. And spent twinkling cold nights in rustic cabins, sipping Tennessee bourbon and swapping tales before crackling oak fires.

Falls hit Matt hard; and affected him as they always had his dad.

When trees behind his home blazed orange, gold and maroon...and leaves crunched like eggshells beneath his feet...his heart yearned so to join the outdoors it nearly burst within his chest.

And Karen felt the same.

Her Augusts also dragged by; muggy, dusty and wrapped in burnt ocher. Each seemed to last sixty days; not thirty-one.

Yet September first, something miraculous happened. Like maple sap stirring, her internal system coursed with life and her mind, body and heart...like Matt's...pulsated anew.

Sure, Fall Festival meant patching blinds and inspecting quail and pheasant hatches. Beyond that, however, it served to rekindle acquaintances with Huntsdale's townsfolk; all of whom knew Damon and his kin.

Many Huntsdalians planted and harvested crops specifically to keep wildlife abundant in the vicinity. In return, Damon provided them several hundred acres to farm...free of charge; the only stipulation being ample grain spillage during harvest to feed the birds, deer and smaller varmints.

Farmers around Huntsdale respected the doctor, as they had his father and grandfather; dating well before the Civil War.

From the onset, generations of Forsythes earned the villagers' praises as the first to comfort their neighbors: With food, medicine, healing or money; and, occasionally, all four.

When Damon and Evelyn stayed at The House, they attended Sunday services at Huntsdale's First Presbyterian Church. Over the years, trust cemented the mutual respect linking the Forsythes and villagers, and it hung tighter than tree bark.

By noon, folding tables bisected the quiet meadow beside The House. Most of the furniture had been borrowed from the Church, and carted up the steep grade by a horse-drawn wagon. Later in the day, the same wagon would provide hayrides to dozens of squealing kids.

Shortly after noon, participants arrived in cars, trucks and wagons from all directions; toting varied cuts of beef, fish and poultry, as well as vegetables and rich desserts in large spatterware containers, or glass chafing and casserole dishes covered with tinfoil.

Zetta Noble's iced tea sloshed in a huge stainless steel pot, and a dipper or two in a glass rendered elixir so potent it nearly dissolved fillings...yet refreshed like no other brew.

Uncle Billy Noble...who turned one hundred and two this year... would help Zetta lug the metal container in which she concocted her potion, then disappear into the copse of hardwoods with the other men; to talk, smoke and spike homemade cider with whiskey.

Food-covered tables eventually formed a serving line thirty feet long, groaning under the weight. The diners lined and filed by... collecting whatever they wanted on plates...with kids helping themselves first, followed by adults.

Pies, cakes and pastries covered at least half the tables, and to cap the feast, Uncle Billy's Vermont ice cream makers would churn gallons of fresh peach, maple and pecan ice cream.

Typically, the Festival wound down with sunset's golden streaks pulling the last ray of warmth from a darkening sky, and October's chill settling for the evening. The revelers would help clean the yard and stow trash, then gather youngsters and journey home. And another Festival would be filed among fond memories.

After rising early, Matt and Hoot compounded their long, strenuous day by setting up tables, carrying chairs, spreading tablecloths, and stacking plates, glasses and silverware. And other make-ready chores with which the women lassoed them.

For recompense, the two topped their fatigue with too much squirrel and homemade ice cream, and now lay stretched before the living room fireplace, their backs against Karen's and Bobby's legs, and half dozing in the warmth radiating from the hearth.

"We've got a couple of live ones here!" Karen wisecracked to Bobby.

She reached and patted Matt's head.

"Oh God," he groaned, rubbing his stomach; rock hard from the abundant feast. "Please...let me die in peace."

"It's your own fault...both of you," scolded Bobby, joining Karen's harangue. "Two grown men...gorging themselves like they're eating a last meal. Then complaining because their tummies are so full they can't buckle their belts!"

"Don't blame Hoot, Bobby," Karen interjected. "Matt knows better... he does the same thing every Festival!"

Walt and Claire entered the room, followed closely by the Forsythes.

"Now Karen...these are growing boys," countered the general, smiling. "They need to stockpile fat for the winter hunting season."

He eased into an easy chair beside the fireplace.

"After all...they'll be working so your dad and I can enjoy shooting. And from what I read, it's a positive outlook for ducks...a record hatch in Canada."

"I read that same <u>Ducks Unlimited</u> report, Walt," Damon remarked from the couch where he and Evelyn sat opposite the younger ladies. "Should be a boomer of a season."

Damon lifted a meerschaum and can of tobacco from the pipe stand beside him.

"By the way, boys...a little brandy might speed your recovery. Feel like a nightcap?"

"If that's your prognosis, Doctor...it sounds good to me," Matt replied, boosting onto one elbow and winking and smiling at the Forsythes.

The immense meal, fiery brandy, lapping flames and crisp air stroked the group's seasonal biological systems, and one by one they drifted to bed.

Karen and Bobby shared a second floor bedroom at the northeastern corner of The House, while Matt and Hoot bunked in a room at the opposite end.

The two kissed the women goodnight at the top of the stairs, and that was the last any of them remembered until midmorning.

Then, they tidied The House, packed their respective cars, and journeyed to New Haven.

Conn Casting's first Cometliner emerged on-schedule from the assembly line in mid-October.

Matt, Hoot and Eddie quickly roughed the jetliner's campaign materials, and confidently presented them to the board; which approved the entire package.

Soon, the three had created the required promotional elements, and the entire campaign...scheduled for a November first kickoff...occupied several shelves in D&G's storeroom.

The trio even crafted presentation materials for Conn Castings to use when hosting executives from the major airlines. They scheduled the tour for the week before Thanksgiving, then printed and mailed formal invitations.

The fifteen businessmen invited returned positive responses, and D&G scored another coup.

During October, Matt, Hoot, Walt and Damon logged return trips to Huntsdale, recamouflaging and wind-proofing the blind, and repairing broken decoys as well as those gnawed by varmints.

Although they described such repair work as essential, the four actually enjoyed playing hooky from work, city life and the hustle with which they contended for ten months of the year.

During the first week in October, Casey Stengel's New York Yankees beat the Brooklyn Dodgers four games to two; nabbing their fifth straight World Series Championship as Matt and Hoot predicted.

Triad Airlines' campaign gained a tremendous amount of credibility with the flying public. And most gratifying of all, the company's commuter business outdid its expectations.

D&G conservatively projected bookings would fall by a third when the Series ended. Such did not occur, however, as numbers of passengers increased steadily, and flights from Boston to New York filled to capacity; as well as return flights from New York, to Boston and Hartford.

Triad, operating in the black on its new venture, now seriously considered offering additional early and late afternoon air travel. Hiring and training additional pilots appeared its only impediments.

With hostilities in Korea settled, however, the Triad partners sought interviews with any military jet jockeys seeking jobs. In fact, Hoot and Matt recommended several comrades from Quoseng Air Base.

Wednesday, October 28, ushered Matt's twenty-fourth birthday, and he and Hoot labored over final preparations for opening day of the duck season on Saturday.

Each hunter listed items to buy, pack or check to ensure working order, and both jittered so with anticipation their ladies couldn't wait for them to leave.

The two drove to Huntsdale in Matt's convertible on Thursday morning, with General Durham and Doctor Forsythe planning to arrive in early afternoon:

"After the boys build a nice fire, and The House is more hospitable for older bones," Walt informed Karen and Bobby. The two elder gentlemen played their age advantage to the hilt, and already, the two younger men pondered if they weren't serious after all.

Soon after arriving, Matt journeyed outdoors to retrieve a day's supply of firewood. Already, the sky spat dry, puffy flakes of snow and a grey blanket of roiling clouds promised more before the next dawn.

He stood by the woodpile, paused a moment to light a smoke, and looked toward the northeast and the Paginaw River. The fine snowfall created a hazy barrier between he and the dark, craggy outlines of towering sycamores, elms and cottonwoods lining the distant stream's banks.

He took a deep drag, and his exhaled smoke blended with the flakes dusting his face, causing tiny drops of moisture to form on the warm flesh.

Through the snowstorm's dark veil, Matt spotted a bright twinkling navigation light a mile downriver, and recognized it as the beacon on which he focused while guiding the johnboat from the main channel into the slough toward the duck blind.

He dropped the cigarette onto the pebble path leading to the shed, behind which he and Hoot had stacked the woodpile. Then crushed the butt, donned his leather work gloves, and filled the log carrier with split chunks of hickory, red oak and walnut.

Half an hour later, as Matt placed a final log atop the neatly stacked cord on the iron log stand, Hoot opened the French doors leading from the parlor. His hands clutched two steamy cups; one of which he passed to Matt.

From within the room behind wafted the heady blend of burning hardwood and freshly brewed coffee. Matt hung his arm affectionately around his friend's shoulders, and ushered him back inside.

"What say we carve that ham and roast beef the ladies fixed...and make sandwiches for the old-timers," he suggested. "You know, they'll be along soon; and bitching like hell if we don't have something for them to eat!"

"Damned smart idea, Matthew," agreed Hoot, sliding the bolt tightly shut on the doors to the porch. "I have a feeling this duck season brims with servitude for you and me, so we may as well start cooking now for the old coots."

They both chuckled, and no sooner sliced quarter-inch portions of meat onto platters when tires crunched on gravel in front of The House. Two quick honks of Damon's horn announced the elders' arrival.

Matt turned, and down the gleaming hallway leading to the front he saw the door open. Soon, his father and the doctor appeared, brushing powdery snow from their shoulders.

"Hey boys," Walt shouted, entering the foyer. "We need someone to unload bags and guns. Any lunch ready for two starving white hunters?"

Matt looked at Hoot and smiled.

"Any questions about which 'someones' unload and which 'white hunters' eat?"

They helped the new arrivals with their gear, then the four clustered around the oak table in the warm kitchen, drinking frosty beer, stacking slices of ham, roast beef, Swiss and Cheddar cheese on Russian rye, and slathering their culinary creations with brown horseradish mustard.

"Much snow on the way up, Walt?" Hoot asked.

"Nah, not much...until about five miles south of Huntsdale. Mostly blowing. Doubt it'll amount to much."

"We thought about going out later for a couple hours' fresh air," piped Damon. "Maybe collect a few quail and a pheasant or two. Might even shag a rabbit."

The doctor took a healthy slug of brew.

"Raymond Daley has a new pointer named 'Romeo,'" he continued. "Said we could use him if we wanted. Can't shoot rabbits over him, so I figured we'd shoot a few birds then drop off the dog and head back here. Probably kick up three or four bunnies on the way back. You boys interested?"

"Give us twenty seconds to collect boots and shotguns, and we're ready," Matt replied, grabbing Hoot by the arm and tugging him from his chair, nearly causing him to guzzle half his beer unexpectedly.

Walt and Damon laughed as the duo dashed up the stairs, taking risers two at a time. In minutes, they returned carrying boots, jackets and caps, which they pulled on before the fireplace in the living room.

The two seniors cleared the table, covered the platters of meat with waxed paper, and refrigerated them. Then they joined in preparing for the hunt.

The howling wind of three hours earlier now hung silent, with only occasional bits of snow zigzagging to the ground. Not quite an inch had fallen, but enough to make tracking birds easier for the dog.

They walked the circular drive leading to the south side of The House, then onto the main gravel road that snaked through the woods to farmlands below.

Raymond's farm was a half mile down the trail, tucked at the base of another hillock and barely visible during summer because of tall corn planted on the acreage that bordered the gravel pathway.

Raymond already had harvested his corn crop, and where the horse-drawn picking rig traveled, broken brown stalks looped a foot off the ground, their parchment leaves rustling dryly.

Like other Huntsdale farmers, Raymond made sure a fair amount of loose yellow grain spilled during picking, as well as hundreds of full cobs so the valley's wildlife could find ample food to last the winter.

The four crunched the gravel route, shotguns unloaded and cradled, and muzzles pointing downward. Time and again, rabbits alarmed them by exploding from the brush and multiflora rose that lined both sides of the thoroughfare.

"Looks like a bumper crop of rabbits this year," Walt said aloud to the others. "I doubt we'll have problems collecting hares for dinner this weekend."

They hiked the rutted mud path that led to the Daley farm, and spotted Raymond laboring near the barn, pouring alcohol into his tractor's radiator.

He waved when he spotted the group, set the can on the ground beside the tractor's front wheels, and walked toward them, pulling a blue bandanna from his back pocket.

He swiped at his cherry nose, made drippy by the frigid afternoon.

"Howdy boys," he said. "Doc...General...always nice to see you up here."

He offered a hamhock of an arm...a pieplate-sized palm attached... to the two younger men first; then shook firmly all around.

Although the four others stood six feet on average, Raymond dwarfed them, reaching six foot four, and weighing two seventy-five. Yet even for his size, he rated as the most congenial farmer in Huntsdale.

He and his wife, Ruth, were first to endorse helping kin, townsfolk and even strangers out of jams.

Like all the area's farmers, Raymond took work seriously and proudly. He rose at four every morning, and tucked in by nine each night; after the news ended on the television Ruth bought with her egg money.

The couple birthed four children...three boys and a girl...all grown and married. And with hunting season at hand, Raymond missed the boys. Especially missed them two months earlier when he hired outsiders to harvest beans and corn.

On Saturday afternoons, Raymond and his wife drove fifteen miles to Centerbrook. There, he played banjo, guitar and mandolin with a group of old-timers.

The band had picked, sung and whooped together on local radio station KFRU since it began broadcasting in the early Thirties.

When two Huntsdalians got together, a fair wager would be they'd end up singing country songs.

Raymond had been born in 1890 in a coal miner's shack in Flat Lick, Kentucky, at the foot of Pine Mountain. From childhood he remembered hunger, cold and his dad coming home black from head to toe; save for wipe-smudged white circles around the eyes.

Every night his father scoured himself, then played with his children in the flickering orange glow of a kerosene lantern. Then he'd go to bed, to awake and again eke a living from a filthy hole.

Black lung claimed Raymond's dad at thirty-one. The boy was only nine at the time. And he, his mother and two older sisters fended as best they could.

They fared better than most, however. His mother's sister married a prosperous farmer near Hartford, Connecticut, and took the four in.

Which is where Raymond learned farming, music and to respect and love the soil. And where he recognized how kind fate had been, and vowed to pass along what he could to others less fortunate.

He wed Ruth McBaine in 1915, and the two moved in with her folks in Huntsdale. Her parents died in the mid-Thirties, within a year of each other, and the Daleys inherited the farm. Over the course of the last twenty years, Raymond tripled the amount of acreage worked.

He planted soybeans, corn, winter wheat and tobacco, and like the four other farms edging Damon's property, tilled twenty of the doctor's acres for pocket money...and to provide food for area wildlife.

"Halloo, doctor," Ruth Daley yelled.

She lumbered down the gully washed road, hand outstretched and face beet red from exertion.

"Afternoon, Ruth," Damon replied, wrapping his arms around the stout woman. "Why are you outside on a day like this?"

"We've got a mama cow having trouble calving, doctor," she answered. "I've been in the barn with her...while old Raymond readies the tractor for cold weather. Hey, do I know these two good-looking gents?"

"Hi Missus Daley," Matt beamed, taking the offered hand. "Any way we can help?"

"Oh, lawsy no, Matt. Thanks. She just wants female company, soft words and maybe a pat or two. She'll be fine, believe me."

Ruth turned to Hoot.

"Hey, I remember you from Fall Festival."

"Yes ma'am," Hoot smiled. "Hoot. Hoot Gibson."

"Well, sure, Hoot. You did my scalloped potatoes proud." She clapped his hand between her two.

"Always a pleasure having you boys here."

"Doc...got time for coffee before you hit the fields?" asked Raymond. "Ruthie keeps a pot bubbling on the iron stove."

"Sure, Raymond," Damon replied. "We'll sit a spell. Be walking soon enough, and these two long-leggedy characters can wear us older gentlemen down fast."

The six walked the steep path to the grey painted front porch, to one side of which lay Romeo, chained to a clothesline pole. The pointer fixed a haughty stare on a big orange cat that recently mothered kittens. Four now kneaded and pulled on her teats.

Matt's nose detected chicken cooking as the group entered the dwelling, and his stomach ignored the thick sandwich consumed a half hour ago. The savory aroma wafted from a spatterware roasting pan simmering on Ruth's enormous cast iron, corncob-fired stove.

They chatted for fifteen minutes, then Raymond took them outside and introduced them to Romeo.

"Come with us, Raymond," urged Walt. "Conditions are right for fine shooting."

"No, thanky, general. Wisht I could, but need to get the old tractor ready for winter. And I better hang close case that cow needs help delivering. 'Sides...I snuck off by myself this morning. Put a couple of cock pheasants in the larder. Got a hog and half a deer hanging in the smokehouse now, and I don't know what we'd do with more game."

The farmer unfolded the corduroy earflaps on his cap then snugged it back on his head.

"That's 'nuther reason I miss those boys," he again dabbed his nose with the bandanna. "Those rascals ate us out of house and home for twenty some odd years. Now, Ruth'n me have more'n we can eat."

They bid good-bye to Raymond, who turned the dog loose and ambled back toward the tractor. Damon smacked the back of his leg and Romeo quickly fell in behind.

The foursome departed for thirty acres of soybeans planted at the rear of the Daleys' property. And when they'd crossed the barbed-wire fence enclosing the field, they loaded their shotguns.

Romeo sprayed a tree, and soon ranged zig-zag fashion among the thick patches of weeds bordering the field. He hadn't covered fifty feet when he jerked to a sudden stop, head swiveled toward the brush, right front leg lifted, and quivering tail frozen parallel to the earth.

Slowly, Romeo crept toward a thick cluster of orchard grass and foxweed. Then fixed...his nose pointing the quarry.

The hunters spread several arms' lengths between them, and Damon whispered:

"Hoot...walk in front of Romeo and kick up the birds."

Hoot held his shotgun chest level and approached from Romeo's left for a clear shot. As he did so, the dog flinched slightly, then stealthily eased a step closer.

Hoot kicked the clump of weeds in front of the pointer, and the ground exploded as twenty small, blurry brown projectiles flew in all directions, wings chirring as they sped for cover.

Quail enjoy scaring hunters senseless, even when the stalkers know their exact location. And this time was no different.

Hoot leveled his double-barreled sixteen gauge at an easy straightaway shot and missed the tiny image cleanly as it put a tree between itself and him.

He then swung on a late riser zooming to his left and dropped it in a puff of feathers. Behind him, Damon's and Walt's four-tens popped, and Matt's twenty gauge created a slightly louder smack.

It ended as quickly as it began.

Hoot watched the birds reform into a group and pitch into a tangled growth of overgrown brush a hundred yards away.

"Hunt dead, Romeo," commanded Damon.

The dog immediately crisscrossed in front of them, his nose inches above the frosty ground.

Matt and Hoot collected a bird out of two shots apiece, while Walt and Damon scored doubles. Romeo triumphantly retrieved all six, and received his reward of heads...which he swallowed whole, beaks and all.

Matt dropped his bird into the game pocket of his hunting jacket, then fumbled open a pack of gum with cold hands still trembling with excitement.

"Piece of gum anyone?" he asked, stepping closer to the other three.

"Yes, thanks," came the replies.

Matt reached to hand over the pack when a huge cock pheasant jumped from under his left foot and beelined toward the woods, its pounding wings whistling like empty tin cans.

The men bunched too close to chance shooting, and as Matt rotated following the pheasant, he strung sticks of gum in a wide semicircle on top of the weeds.

"Damnation!" he yelled, startled, as the big bird disappeared into the dark trees. "I stepped on that bird's tail!"

"Well Matthew, why didn't you just whack him with your gun butt?" chided Hoot as he bent to help collect the scattered pieces of gum.

"Yeah, Matt," added Walt. "You're more deadly with the wooden end of that shotgun...no question about that!"

The four shared a laugh, then reloaded. Romeo ranged fifty yards away, and already scented fresh birds. Before they moved twenty yards the dog assumed another firm point.

This time they bagged two birds apiece, which Romeo retrieved promptly; even finding a cripple that had crawled under a brushpile.

By four o'clock, the sky spat snow again, and they each had collected a cock pheasant and eight quail. Swishing through thorn bushes, cockleburs, weeds and corn shocks left the tip of Romeo's tail bloody, but he still wanted to hunt. And when Damon whistled and slapped the back of his thigh to return, Romeo's eyes flashed disappointment over quitting.

Damon cradled the dog's big head in his healer's hands.

"Don't fret, old pal. We'll come by and hunt with you again, soon."

He reached into an inside pocket and retrieved several dog biscuits, and held them in his palm while the animal gobbled happily.

They returned Romeo to the Daleys'...stopping briefly for a small glass of Raymond's bitingly sweet, soul-warming homemade concord grape wine...then headed for The House to clean birds, enjoy tall bourbons and waters, and prepare dinner.

On the return trip, a dozen kamikaze rabbits made easy targets of themselves. However, the men felt they had game enough to clean and eat...and almost too much to carry...and none felt like loading his shotgun.

That night, they supped on Damon's delectable pan-fried round steak, biscuits and cream gravy, with baby peas and onions on the side. And after the rib-sticking meal...capping a day in the field...the brandy and crackling fire muted everyone.

By nine o'clock, Walt stood, yawned deeply, and announced he was "hitting the sack." The others followed suit without commenting on the early hour.

Friday morning broke fresh, crisp and gleaming. Four inches of powdery snow fell during the night, and outside temperatures hovered in the mid-twenties; warm enough that by noon, the snow would settle from the moisture of melting.

Hoot and Matt awoke at six thirty, scrambled eggs with bits of ham and Cheddar cheese, then prepared sausage, hot cakes and grits...which they'd become fond of during flight training in Mississippi and Texas.

Steamy coffee also awaited the two elders who hobbled downstairs, drawn by breakfast's perfume, their growling stomachs and the warmth of kitchen and hearth. And forgetting the stiffness in their bones from unaccustomed hiking over rough terrain.

Except for thick comforters piled deep on beds, the upstairs afforded little heat. Although two of the bedrooms contained fireplaces and both second floor bathrooms featured gas wall heaters.

Master craftsmen constructed The House of excellent materials, and layered ten inches of asbestos batting between the attic rafters. The thick cushion provided efficient insulation, but when outside temperatures plunged well below zero, warmth on the second floor could only be found beneath the cozy quilts adorning the massive four-poster oak beds.

The two young men ate quickly, donned their hunting clothes, excused themselves and walked outside. As they pushed through the white drifts blanketing everything, the grandfather's clock near the stairway chimed seven.

The trackers walked the weedy growth bordering both sides of Magusett Creek, now flowing under an inch of snow-covered ice. Not more than thirty feet from The House the first rabbit jumped from under Hoot's feet, dashing for the woods and zigzagging in a series of five-foot bounds.

Hoot leveled his sixteen gauge on the speeding bunny, snow erupted and it cart-wheeled to a silent stop.

Half an hour later, they reached the tangle of ground ivy, sweet pea and honeysuckle vines where an artesian spring fed the stream.

Four more rabbits bulged their game pouches.

"This ought to provide outstanding dinners this weekend, Hoot," said Matt, shucking live shells out of his twenty-gauge pump. He pulled a pack of Luckies, lit two, and handed one to Hoot. Then they trudged the undergrowth back to The House.

That afternoon, the four drove to the boathouse. There, they lowered the johnboat and small skiff packed with duck decoys from their nesting places suspended from the ceiling. Then they climbed aboard and motored down the Paginaw River to arrange their decoy spread.

As had happened earlier, when the lead boat pulling the skiff rounded the bend above the blind, the shallow pool between the two willow barriers erupted with ducks. They had rafted out of the wind whistling down the river, until boats and hunters flushed them from their resting place.

The noise of startled ducks taking wing and quacking alarm at the approaching boats flooded the acoustic hollow in the willow-lined inlet.

"Look there, boys!" Damon shouted over the motor's roar. "That's a sight to behold."

Matt rolled the Johnson outboard's throttle handle counterclockwise, and the square bow of the johnboat dropped as it slowed.

Around and over the shoulders of the three seated in front, he saw dozens of ducks lifting in all directions, darting along the water's surface and leaving splashy tracks as they pumped for speed and altitude.

Matt let the boat coast with the current and watched the swarm of waterfowl disappear into tiny specks, then he motored into the shallow sandy area where the blind stood.

As the craft approached the stilted structure he shifted into reverse, slowing forward motion, then into neutral. Finally, he switched the outboard off, lifted its lower unit out of the water, and joined Hoot in tugging on rubber chest waders.

The vessel gently nudged against the blind, and the two young men climbed overboard into the cold, waist high water. They tied the johnboat to one of the blind's pilings while Walt and Damon shifted into the smaller dory. This they towed in front of the blind, and pitched out decoys as the two elders untangled strings and weights.

In forty minutes, nearly two hundred pressed board blocks bobbed and weaved in the current in front of the duck blind, held securely by ten foot lengths of brown nylon parachute cord and bell-shaped lead weights that clung to the sandy bottom.

Matt and Hoot steadied the empty scow against the johnboat as the other two scrambled back into the larger craft. Then they tied the small boat behind, hefted up and in, and peeled their chest waders.

Soon, Matt yanked the Johnson's starter cord. It caught immediately, and Walt untied the rope securing them to the blind. The foursome backed away, and swung upriver in a wide arc. Already, ducks that earlier rested in the shallow pool were returning, attracted by their lifeless friends on the water and wanting out of the nippy northern breezes.

By the time they rounded the bend and the blind faded from view behind the willows, birds splashed among the floating decoys. Other ducks, with wings cupped or circling low, prepared to join the gathering.

"Tomorrow ought to be one heck of a day!" Matt shouted, mouth cupped with his hand.

Hoot turned from his seat beside Damon, nodded, and passed back a lighted cigarette.

"Don't know about you, Matthew...but I'm excited. It's gonna be tough sleeping tonight."

"I think that applies to all of us, Hoot," the doctor said, patting the young man's back. "Remember, though... you guys still have dinner to cook. Quail and gravy sure will hit the spot."

"And you thought hunting here would be fun...huh Hoot?" Matt quipped from the back of the boat.

The last day of October traditionally marked Connecticut's opening of the duck season. Icy winds blew into the Huntsdale area just as routinely, and hung around through April. Around tax time, foot-high accumulations of snow were common.

Matt's dependable military alarm clanged to life at four-thirty, and he and Hoot rolled out of feather beds to the shock of bare feet on cold oak flooring. They headed for the two bathrooms on second floor, and minutes later Matt rapped the others' bedrooms then returned to his room to dress.

They wore long underwear to bed, and as Matt opened the door he found Hoot so attired, leaning against a bedpost and tugging canvas pants over two pairs of heavy wool socks.

"Wind's out of the northeast, Hooter," he said.

He took a chair by the bed and pulled on his share of wool socks.

"We'll have it to our backs going downriver. Count on it being frosty, though. That also means ducks will land into it from our side."

The two quickly dressed...save for heavy wool shirts worn beneath their hunting coats. These they donned last, for fear of getting too warm and perspiring.

The pair went downstairs to tend their kitchen chores.

Hoot started coffee perking while Matt stirred the usual scrambled eggs with bits of ham and cheese. Minutes later, Walt and Damon entered the kitchen wearing wool lumberjack shirts, canvas trousers with bloused pants legs, and canvas, wool-lined hunting caps.

"You're turning into a fine camp cook, Matt," the doctor said, taking the steamy cup of coffee Hoot offered. "I love the smell of bacon sizzling in the morning."

"I didn't think I could face breakfast after last night's quail feast," confided Walt. "Man alive...I'm famished again!"

Hoot had popped homemade biscuits into the oven, and now retrieved them and the crisp bacon. Matt ladled eggs on all four plates, refilled coffee cups, then sat with the others to eat.

They heard the faint howl of the wind outside, and standing near the kitchen sink, felt its icy whisper through the window panes.

The four took their time over breakfast, then Matt and Hoot enjoyed smokes over a last cup of coffee while the two seniors rinsed cups and dishes. Then they gathered waders, hunting jackets, caps, guns, knapsacks, thermos bottles and sandwiches, and trooped through the front door to Damon's stationwagon.

In the inky darkness, the air swirled fresh and frigidly crisp, laced with tiny beads of stinging moisture that threatened to mature into adult snowflakes by day's end.

The doctor fumbled the ignition key with gloved hands and finally started the car. As they pulled up the semicircle drive in front of The House, Matt looked overhead through the window at a thick bank of low hanging clouds blanketing an ashen sky.

"Ceiling's about twenty five hundred," he said to the group. "Ought to keep the birds low and stirred through the day."

"Probably right, Matt," his father agreed.

Matt forgot to listen to the farm weather report when he awakened, but Walt hadn't.

"They'll move ahead of the snow coming our way."

In five minutes, Damon steered off the gravel road running along the bluffs and turned onto the tractor path leading through the soybeans in his bottomland acreage. They soon pulled to the jetty stretching to the boathouse.

Wind knifing down the river cut considerably keener than that on the hilltop, and Matt shivered as he stepped from the car.

"Listen!" said Hoot, and the four craned to dog-yipping sounds emanating from fields across the river.

"Are those geese?" he asked.

"You bet, Hoot," replied Damon. "We get a heavy concentration around here. They don't stay long, though. By Thanksgiving, they'll move to warmer temperatures down the coast."

The foursome loaded guns and knapsacks into the johnboat at the boathouse dock, then hoisted themselves in; donning cork life vests stowed in the bow under an olive drab tarpaulin.

While Matt primed the outboard, his passengers made themselves comfortable for the frigid trip down the Paginaw.

Straw and burlap bags filled the bottom of the craft, and served as camouflage and cushions, totes for decoys, and covers against the breeze.

Matt jerked the outboard's starter cord, and on the second pull it fired, spewing a plume of white oily smoke that shrouded them in the blackness. He rolled the throttle handle a quarter turn, let the engine warm momentarily, then pulled the gear lever forward and steered into the river's current.

Up forward, Damon sat on the left side of the front seat, hunkered beneath burlap bags and flicking a large six-cell flashlight from side to side as he watched for logs, buoys or debris floating in the current.

Matt cranked the outboard wide open, and now the johnboat lifted its blunted nose. The healthy, study hum of the motor carried them quickly down the two mile stretch to the willow fingers marking their pool.

When they rounded the bend, Damon caught the blind in the flashlight beam and waterfowl danced in all directions, skimming like ballerinas across the top of the water and flapping for the heavens.

By the time the boat nestled against the blind, only floating feathers offered proof that minutes ago ducks coated the shallow basin.

As they had the day before, Matt and Hoot eased over the side into the water. The doctor kept them outlined in the flashlight's beam as they straightened decoys tangled by wind and current, and spaced those that had drifted close together.

"Hey...there's a crust of ice out here!" exclaimed Matt.

He felt it push and crunch against the thick insulated waders. Soon, they satisfied themselves with the spread and towed the skiff under the blind; first covering it with smartweed, willows and Johnson grass.

Matt trailed the others up the three-step ladder submerged at the rear of the blind, then stepped onto the foot-wide platform bordering the hut. While he and Hoot stripped their chest waders, Walt fired the two kerosene heaters inside and Damon organized knapsacks and folding chairs so all could move and shoot.

Once settled, the doctor retrieved the ceremonial flask of blackberry brandy from his knapsack. He held the container in a toast and said:

"Judge, here's to you...wherever you are. I hope you're opening the season, too."

He took a full swallow of the sweet, cutting liquor and passed the decanter along. Each man, in turn, performed the ritual, and Hoot handed back the bottle.

"Matt told me about the judge, Damon," he said. "I'm sorry I never met him."

"He was one of a kind, Hoot," said Walt. "A true sportsman and gentleman. He loved duck hunting and the law. And served both well."

Inside the blind, the heaters glowed a sunset orange and warmth roiling from their vented bottoms penetrated rubber hunting boots, making feet tingle as they thawed.

Matt lit a cigarette, checked his watch in the lighter's flame, then snapped its lid closed.

"Six o'clock!" he exhaled a cloud of smoke that sucked up through the open top. "Anything straying close is legal."

They loaded their shotguns and propped them in gun notches cut into the horizontal two-by-fours running the front of the blind. Matt stood and stooped to peer out under weed coverings that hung in front of the shooting opening.

As he poked his head through damp Johnson grass, he winced slightly against the wind slapping the left side of his face, and instantly watering his eyes.

The sunrise, masked by dingy clouds, soaked through in pink and orange. Over dark skeletal cottonwoods lining the opposite bank, he saw vees of ducks and geese crossing beneath the clouds, flying to feed in fields that bordered the Paginaw. Movement caught his peripheral vision, and slowly he turned his head rightward. A large flight of bluebills, wind nipping their tails, highballed downriver, passing less than thirty feet out front and too quickly for shooting.

He sat as the ducks whistled by, and began blowing his duck call. Walt and Damon heard the bluebills, pulled their instruments and warmed up with Matt. Hoot soon joined, and the blind sounded like a floating refuge.

Suddenly, Walt thought he heard a response to their calling. He eased up gently and looked through the willows. Out front hung thirty mallards, wings cupped, webbed feet reaching, talking to their floating look-alikes, and hovering inches off the surface. Noisily, they skidded in.

Each man slowly and carefully reached for his shotgun, and when all were ready to rise and shoot, Damon urged: "Now!"

They lifted the hinged front of the blind's roof as startled ducks flared all around them.

Matt picked a drake to his far left, folded it with the first thump of his twelve gauge, then swung on another greenhead skimming the surface toward the finger of willows.

His first shot kicked up water well behind it, but his second cart-wheeled the bird into the ice crested pool.

Hoot needed two shots to drop a huge drake climbing vertically, and his third round scored another male going straight toward the far side of the quiet water.

Walt and Damon fielded double-barreled twelve gauges, and by the time the two younger men finished firing, each accounted for two drakes floating in the outer fringe of decoys. Overhead, scattered ducks from the flight winged furiously in all directions.

"Now that's a beautiful sight," said Walt, referring to the clean kills bobbing in the water. "Hey, look here!"

At that instant, ten mallards swung from the right and fluttered into the decoys. Behind them came a tremendous flight of forty, followed by an even larger bunch of pintails.

The four quickly reloaded, then stood in unison as waterfowl filled the air.

Matt covered a straight-away drake with his shotgun barrel and as he touched off, a male pintail criss-crossed behind the mallard at an inopportune time; and both tumbled into the pool. Beside him, he heard the steady bark of the others' weapons.

Hoot spotted a fat greenhead lifting slightly later than the others and scored the bird cleanly with one shot. He then swung on another grabbing for sky, and repeated.

Damon touched off the last round, dropping a banded male at the edge of the decoy spread. The fresh tally revealed another eight drakes had joined the earlier eight.

As the hunters watched the remaining waterfowl flee, Damon broke open his double barrel and ejected two empty number six casings onto the floor.

"Good shooting, boys," he said. "A quick limit if I've ever seen one!"

Matt glanced at his watch, now visible in daylight's bright orange glow. It read six twenty-one.

He shucked the remaining shells from his shotgun, rested it against the gun rack, then reached and retrieved a thermos from his knapsack.

"Coffee, anyone?"

Counting himself, four takers filled their cups.

The quartet sat in the blind until eleven o'clock. Guns empty and in their cases.

Talking. Drinking coffee. Eating cold sandwiches, apples and candy bars. And admiring flights of mallards, canvasbacks, bluebills, pintails, wood ducks and teal heading up and downriver, and appearing as long vees of tiny dots everywhere they looked.

Earlier, they collected the downed birds. Now, a hundred live ducks meshed with the decoys, swimming, diving, preening and, in general, causing a ruckus in which the hunters reveled.

The foursome enjoyed live duck calling instructions from professionals carousing out front, and kept their calls warmed practicing highball and feeding tones.

When quitting time arrived, they stood...and the shallow pool exploded with squawking, flapping and splashing waterfowl. In minutes, only downy tufts remained...drifting earthward like large, elongated snow flakes.

Matt and Hoot refastened their chest waders and retrieved the boat from under the blind. The two elders climbed in, and loaded the encased guns and knapsacks in the front. Then the younger men pulled the skiff to the three steps behind the blind, and used these to hoist into the boat.

For the second time, Matt yanked the outboard to life, steered slowly around the decoys and into the open channel. Overhead, the blanket of clouds gave way to a bright bluebird day, and seeing sunlight made the trip upriver warmer...if only psychologically.

Matt cranked the throttle to three-quarter speed and the johnboat planed level. The heavily-laden craft carved a smooth wake past the willow finger and into the main current, pitching lazily from side to side as it sliced into the Paginaw. Overhead, ducks still strung endlessly across the horizon.

When they rounded the bend the four were awestruck by the concentrations of Canada, blue, snow and whitefront geese milling above corn and wheat fields across the river. They resembled flights of locusts Matt remembered seeing in National Recovery Act films.

Over the motor's razz, Walt pointed to the thousands of birds in the air...swirling like dead leaves as they landed to feed...then turned to Matt and slapped his knee.

"How would you like a flight like that decoying over your head, son?" he chuckled.

Matt stared at the thick, black swirling tornado of waterfowl, mouth gaped in amazement and cigarette dangling.

For a moment, he imagined being in a goose pit with such a conflagration of geese hovering above; which loomed too much to comprehend.

He took a long pull on the cigarette and exhaled slowly, grinning at his dad.

"It would be like dying and going to Heaven, dad," he replied. "A lot like it!"

Chapter 16

Christmas At The House

IN MID-NOVEMBER, CONNECTICUT CASTINGS CORPORATION held a two-day meeting. Fifteen executives from four major airlines toured the company's headquarters outside New Haven, and stayed at a contemporary Holiday Inn that had opened the past fall.

Conn Castings' officers joined their guests in hours of discussions, covering the ramifications and benefits of jet air travel. As a side benefit to the seminars, the callers also enjoyed marvelous dining and any luxury desired.

Matt, Hoot and Eddie spent two hours on Friday afternoon previewing current publicity, and then briefing the visitors on Conn Casting's generous approach to cooperative advertising. For airlines participating in its co-op program, the company would pay two-thirds the costs of print and TV sponsorship.

In return, of course, promotions would feature Cometliners sporting the carriers' colors and insignias.

The airline managers accepted the business proposition even more enthusiastically than D&G and Conn Castings had hoped, and signed agreements on-the-spot to feature Cometliners decked in their companies' markings.

Most of the airline representatives resided in New York, so Hoot arranged with Triad to fly the group directly to Conn Casting's field, landing on the test runways west of the main building. This way, the transport could taxi to within thirty feet of the meeting facilities.

When the dignitaries boarded Triad's DC-3 for the return flight to New York, Walt and the other corporate leaders waved them off. By that time, signed orders for thirty Cometliners rested in his in-box; including allowances for spare engines and parts, and maintenance and repair training for ground crews.

Triad's transport rumbled down the runway past the group, then lifted and banked southwest heading for New York.

And instantly, Conn Castings' president invited the gathering for champagne in the third floor conference room. Additionally, he sent several cases to the employees' cafeteria so they, too, could enjoy the celebration.

Over the public address system, he then announced the company had landed an extremely lucrative Cometliner contract. Even on the third floor, Matt could hear cheers and thunderous applause emanating from below.

It was nearly seven o'clock when he eased the Ford into his parking space behind the bank. He and Hoot invited Eddie into their office for a quick, private celebration, so the young man stowed his leather art case in his car and followed the others up the stairs.

Inside, Matt opened the supply cabinet that doubled as storage for several bottles of liquor, and poured a couple fingers' of bourbon in three glasses. He splashed a small amount of fountain water into the containers, and passed them to the other two.

"So ends a great day gents," he toasted, lifting his glass high and taking a sip. "Conn Castings closed some sweet deals today, and that should mean excellent tidings for us."

"Did you hear Conn Castings' guys rave over our campaign?" asked Hoot. "Several said the deals closed mainly because our stuff excited the airlines."

"I heard 'em too, Hoot," chimed Eddie. "And I never imagined it would be so easy to convince the airlines to pick up a third of the ad costs!"

"Well, guys," Matt added, suddenly serious. "We've landed two choice accounts. I'm convinced we're going to succeed."

"I'll tip one to that, partner," added Hoot, clinking the others' glasses.

Matt turned to Eddie and smiled into the clear blue eyes.

"With that in mind, Eddie, how about coming on-board as our full-time creative director?" The young man had not sensed the proposal, and flushed visibly over the impromptu offer. He caught his breath, leaned against a desk, shifted his weight and stuttered:

"Short of leaving Korea alive, nothing has meant more...or been more fulfilling...than working with you. You guys make me feel appreciated and worth something."

Matt watched the eyes sparkle with moisture.

"I'm not Madison Avenue caliber, but I'll work my butt off trying to be. And I'll make it with a little luck. Sure, if you birds will have me...I'd love working for you full-time."

Matt placed his hand on Eddie's shoulder.

"Not for, Eddie...with," he interjected. "And I'll tell you this...we've eyeballed the efforts of graphic illustrators and designers up and down the Coast; including New York. Most lack your knack for exciting layouts."

Hoot set his drink glass down and put his hand on Eddie's free shoulder.

"We're glad as hell you're with us," he said. "And we'd be honored to have you as a partner in a new agency...Durham, Gibson and Bauer, or DG&B."

"Think about it, Eddie, please," Matt said softly. "Also, how does six thousand sound as a starting salary?"

Eddie's face reflected wonderment.

"Too much, Matt...way too much," he blurted, aghast at the figure. "I never dreamed of making such money."

"You deserve it, pal," Hoot replied. "And believe me, you'll earn it."

He took the artist's hand in his and shook it warmly.

"Next week, we'll shop bigger offices," Matt announced, tossing papers into his briefcase. "Tomorrow, Karen and I are buying a new car. The tax people say our traveling justifies company autos; and we're all entitled. Right on time, too. The old Ford's ready to die! Plus, I need to check something I have in mind for Karen's Christmas present."

Matt tossed back the remainder of the drink, and placed the empty glass on the table for sorting mail, clipping ads and storing extra mats in a box. Then he pulled on his overcoat, shook with the others, and joined them leaving the office, descending the stairs and walking to their respective cars.

"Guys...have a wonderful weekend," Matt yelled. "See you Monday."

The overcast sky spat snow again, but for Eddie, the sun shone as he whistled the way to his mother's house.

Matt nabbed a parking space in front of the building in which he and Karen lived, and as he got out of the car, squinted against puffy snowflakes drifting to earth like goose down.

He entered the enclosed staircase and hopped the steps two at a time. Above, Karen opened the apartment door.

"I thought you pulled in," she said. "I looked from the window but couldn't see through the snow. The folks asked us over for dinner...you up to it?"

"Sure, honey," he said, pecking her lips as he brushed by. "I'll change and be ready in a jiff."

She followed him into the bedroom and sat on the edge of the bed as he removed the suit and tugged on a pair of corduroy slacks, a sweater and penny loafers.

"Well...Matt! How did it go? I'm dying to know, goshdarnit!"

"I'm sorry, babe. Swell. Better than swell! Everything went perfectly. We got the airlines' nods on co-op advertising, and Conn Castings nailed thirty orders for Cometliners!"

"Bet your dad's happy about that."

"Ecstatic! You should have seen it! Conn Castings went berserk after the meeting. Popped champagne and everything."

He tucked his shirt and walked around the bed to her side. Karen stood, draped her arms around his neck, and kissed him softly on the lips.

"Matt, I'm so proud of you. In just six months, you and Hoot have built a successful agency."

"We have been lucky...haven't we? By the way, there are three of us now. We asked Eddie to become a partner."

"That's wonderful, Matt. What did he say...as if I have to ask?"

"For a minute...not much. He choked a bit. Hell, we all did! Then he said he'd be happy to hitch with us. So, DG&B is launched!"

They joined hands walking from the bedroom, and he helped her with her overcoat. Then the two descended the stairs to the car.

Snow, piled two inches deep, squeaked under their feet as they dashed to the convertible. Ten minutes later, Matt steered the cul-de-sac in front of the Forsythe's, and Karen's mother opened the door as they dashed through the snowfall.

"Hello, kids. Come in, come in," Evelyn said, stepping out of the way behind the door.

The two entered and Karen took their coats, shook them in the entry hall, and hung them in the closet beneath the stairway.

"How about an eye opener?" asked Damon from the wet bar in the adjoining family room.

Karen clutched her mother's arm and Matt followed the two into the other room.

"Scotch and soda for me, dad," said Karen, bussing her father on the cheek as he stooped over the bar.

"Coming up. Bourbon and water, Matt?"

"Sounds tempting," he replied, patting the physician on the back. "Thanks Damon."

"How about you, mother?" the doctor asked his wife.

"A glass of sherry...please Damon."

Drinks in hand, the four walked to the living room and sat on couches facing each other across a large glass-covered walnut coffee table.

"Well, Matt, how'd things go at Walt's company today?"

"Extremely well. Dad's group sold thirty Cometliners."

"They did? That old coot! Bet he's happy as a fat pig in the sun. I expect he'll call tonight."

"I don't know, Damon," joked Matt. "When we left the company, champagne bottles still were popping. Dad may be out celebrating with the other managers by now. Or else snowed in at the plant."

"I'm sure you're right, son," the doctor said. "Well, here's to Walt and Conn Castings."

He hefted his glass in a toast, took a swallow, and the others followed suit.

"Now that we're gathered...I've got big news, too," piped Karen.

The others looked her way.

"As of December first, I'm in charge of Peck & Peck's New Haven office!"

"What!" Matt sputtered, snapping his head around so suddenly he nearly tipped his glass.

"Honey...you didn't tell me! C'mon, out with it. What's the story?"

She took his hand, smiling broadly; her pearly teeth glistening in the overhead light.

"Charlie Enright called me into his office first thing and announced the Peck brothers wanted him to head the New York branch. Which is like being in charge of the entire firm."

She sipped her drink, hand trembling as she relived the excitement of the morning.

"Anyway...the Pecks are semi-retiring. They've opened an office in Beverly Hills. They'll run that, and let Charlie manage the rest of the operation. Which is why they're calling him to New York. He loves the big city...and is flying high, believe me!"

She turned facing Matt, still beaming.

"I thought we'd get a new boss. Instead, Charlie touted me for the vice president and general manager's slot. And the Pecks agreed with him!"

"Darling, that's wonderful," said Matt, clutching her and bussing her cheek. He clinked his glass with her's, and in his best Bogart tones lisped: "Here's looking at you, kid."

Damon lifted from the couch and walked to the kitchen.

"Offhand, folks, this merits champagne," he said over his shoulder. "I'll chill a couple of bottles. Evelyn...maybe Walt and Claire could join us for dinner."

"That would be fine, darling," his wife replied. "We certainly have enough meat and potatoes to go around."

"Want me to call and see, Damon?" Matt asked.

At the doctor's approval, Matt arose, walked to the telephone, and dialed his parents' number. Only moments earlier Walt had arrived from the Conn Castings' celebration. He said they'd be there within the hour.

"Goodness me," said Evelyn, jumping to her feet. "Speaking of dinner...I'd better tend the roast! It'll be dry as corn flakes!"

Karen and her mother disappeared into the kitchen, while her father and Matt freshened drinks. Soon, the Durhams rapped at the front door.

The six dined on tender sirloin, potatoes Au gratin, spinach soufflé and chocolate mousse. And afterwards, Karen recounted her day's blessings over champagne.

"By the way, kids," the doctor announced as he passed among the group refilling glasses. "We four are going to Florida for the holidays. The medical faculty are meeting there after Christmas...and Walt has vacation to take...so he and Claire are joining us."

"Gee, dad, that's the first time you two will miss Christmas at The House," said Karen, feeling the bubbly's warmth spread through her body.

"I know dear," Damon gave her arm a gentle squeeze. "Our first green Christmas in twenty-seven years!"

"Cheer up, Damon," admonished Walt, draping his arm over his friend's shoulders. "You'll love it for a change."

Walt's hands framed an imaginary picture.

"Just think...lolling in the sun on a white beach. Drinking sweet rum drinks with fruit and little umbrellas. Yachting off the coast. And eating marvelous seafood!"

"You don't have to sell either of us, Walt Durham," scolded Evelyn. "We've packed our suitcases full of lightweight clothes, and we're running from cold weather for a change."

Damon stood in front of the younger couple.

"Anyway, kids," he continued. "You're welcome to spend your Christmas at The House. There's plenty of food and firewood. And maybe you could ask Hoot and Bobby to join you."

"Sounds like a swell idea to me, Damon," agreed Matt, putting his arm around Karen and squeezing her affectionately. "What say you... Vice President Durham?"

"It does sound dreamy...doesn't it?" she replied. "You won't run off hunting and leave me, will you?"

"Not a chance...I promise. The duck season will poop out by then, and most birds will have flown south. Plus, our pool will be frozen solid."

Damon fetched another bottle and topped their glasses.

"You'll do it then?" he asked.

The two nodded affirmatively.

"Good! Now Matt, when we quit hunting before Christmas, we'd better check supplies. It wouldn't do to be snowed in, and Huntsdale a good distance away."

"It sounds wonderful, Damon," Matt beamed. "Thanks a lot."

At eleven o'clock, Matt and Karen excused themselves, thanked her parents and darted from the front door to the car; she using Matt's parka to keep wet flakes out of her hair.

When they awakened Saturday, another four inches of snow covered the earlier three, hiding city grime that collected on its crest.

Matt looked over at Karen, sleeping on her left side, and whacked her rump with a throw pillow.

"Hey, you, wake up!" he urged. "Let's go buy a new car! I'll brush my teeth and the bathroom's yours while coffee brews. Okay?"

"Uh-huh," she said through a stretching yawn. "Hurry, though...the champagne calls!"

He jumped from bed, opened the drapes and exclaimed over the beauty of the fresh layer of snow. Then he went to the bathroom, emerging minutes later to yell to Karen, and padded to the kitchen to perk coffee.

An hour found the two dressed warmly and walking downtown car lots; shopping models that arrived in showrooms two months earlier.

Matt loved his convertible, and considered buying another Ford or a Chevy. His dad, however, swore by Buicks. And when he spotted the glistening Navy blue Roadmaster sedan, he suddenly knew why.

The shiny marvel boasted sporty chrome portholes along its hood, and the powder blue interior featured plush and alluring crushed velvet seats. A newly developed V-8 overhead engine equipped the machine with passing power to spare.

Matt immediately recognized the model he wanted, and Karen soon shared his excitement as they drove it off the showroom floor for a test spin.

Buicks now featured air conditioning, power steering and power brakes, and when Karen switched on the radio, Patty Page's new song, "Tennessee Waltz," wafted from speakers near the back window! The two delighted over the spectacular advances made in modern automobiles with comfort and relaxation in mind.

Karen particularly enjoyed the heavier auto as it moved soundlessly along cobblestone streets, delivering a gentle, forward pitching motion. Its quiet ride suggested traveling in a silent vacuum, save for stereo emitting from in-dash and rear deck speakers.

"This baby's got power, honey!" Matt exclaimed, easing onto Highway 95 and driving the eastern edge of the city. "Look...the speedometer goes to one hundred!"

Karen leaned across her seat and looked.

"Not with me in it, Matt," she replied calmly.

When finally he asked if she liked the car...and could they buy this particular one...she nodded approval with a broad smile.

"It is beautiful, Matt," she agreed. "And it's almost like floating on a cloud."

Their decision made, the couple returned to the dealership where Matt and the salesman briefly discussed the trade-in value of his car. Half an hour later, they signed and notarized the title papers, and completed the purchase.

"Monday, I'll visit the bank downstairs and arrange the loan," Matt said as the two walked from the showroom. Over his shoulder Karen watched the sales rep carefully steer their new car into the service area.

"Then I'll call our accountant and let him know about our purchase."

When they climbed back into the Ford, he looked at Karen and noticed her watering eyes. He recognized, too, he'd miss this first car, and the wonderful memories it carried.

As anticipated, when Monday arrived and strangers drove his convertible into the dealer's garage...and Matt watched it disappear in the rearview mirror...remorse reared in his chest. The sadness disappeared, however, in the thrill of a virgin auto responding to his commands.

Thanksgiving arrived and passed quickly in a smorgasbord of roast duck, turkey, cornbread dressing with oysters, casseroles, pumpkin and pecan pies; and overindulgency by all concerned.

This year, the Forsythes hosted the meal and invited Hoot and Bobby to join the festivities. The two declined, however, promising the Gibsons they'd spend Turkey Day in Hartford.

November's final weekend dragged December onto the scene, and only two hunting weekends remained. Then Christmas week arrived suddenly behind winter's breath.

The Durhams and Forsythes packed and left by rail early Monday morning, and on Wednesday, Matt and Karen arose to pack their belongings and drive to The House.

Christmas would fall on Friday, so Thursday they planned to walk the woods and cut a tree. And decorate it with ornaments and lights stored in The House's attic.

They only packed several winter sweaters and slacks for her, since Matt kept plenty of warm clothes at The House during the hunting season. Then the couple walked to the parking lot, he carrying her large suitcase and his shave kit, with gaily wrapped boxes wedged under his arms and overcoats slung over.

Behind him, Karen toted several more gift boxes in her arms, and a brown bag full of cookies for consuming at The House. As they crunched through the snow to the Buick, he put his arm around her waist and whispered into his wife's ear:

"Want to take my car...or yours?"

Karen stopped abruptly, and fixed him with the funny, quizzical look. "What do you mean, my car?"

Without a word, Matt gently turned her full around and pointed her toward a fire-engine red MG-TD roadster, gleaming in its parking slot and contrasting with the snow and large cedars on each side.

"Merry Christmas, darling," he smiled.

Karen shrieked with excitement, dropping the presents and bag of groceries in the snow. She raced to the little roadster, and without opening the door, bent over, cupped her hands and peered through the removable glass window on the driver's side.

Inside, she studied the highly polished oak dashboard, the thick red pile carpeting and tan leather seats. Her excited breath made foggy circles on the cold glass, and when Matt appeared beside her, she wrapped her arms around his neck and kissed him repeatedly, as tears tracked her cheeks.

"Matt, it's wonderful! I don't know what to say. What a surprise. You shouldn't have. I know it was expensive."

"Not really, sweetheart. I saw it at a dealer's last week. Someone ordered it, then decided on a larger car. I got a real swell deal. You needed transportation, so I bought it. And, it fits you...well built and racy as hell!"

"Oh, you!" she said, faking a rap to the chin then kissing him again.

He handed her the keys and she unlocked the door, and sat in the low slung sports car. Matt entered from the other side, stowing gifts, suitcase, coats and bag in the area where the top folded behind the seats.

Over a few minutes' dry run, he showed her how to shift gears; although she had become proficient with the convertible's floor-shift. Then he explained the various gauges, toggle switches, lights and dials on the gleaming wooden instrument panel.

Finally, Karen inserted the ignition key, clicked it counterclockwise, and pulled the starter knob. Instantly, the little four cylinder engine snapped to life with a throaty purr.

She adapted to the TD quickly and comfortably, and soon coordinated her hands and feet after only a few lurching starts and engine stalls.

By the halfway mark to Huntsdale, she downshifted curves like a seasoned pro and watched the tachometer to ensure she didn't lug the engine too low or red-line it going through the gears.

Karen coveted the little machine at once, and he felt immense satisfaction over her initial surprise and obvious delight with his gift.

Driving to Huntsdale they passed thick groves of trees, bushes and wild hedgerows that glowed vivid green, contrasting with an overcast sky and the white mantle that blanketed the countryside.

They encountered only sparse traffic, and made excellent time over the snow-crested roads and ice-glazed bridges and overpasses. Only occasional flurries of powder gusted against the MG's small windscreen.

After an hour's ride, Karen steered onto the main road that bisected Huntsdale. The two chuckled over the aging Christmas decorations: faded candy canes that revealed yellow plastic beneath and four strings of huge multicolored bulbs that every year hung from the same light standards that bordered the asphalt trail.

They also recalled, though, how even these scant ornaments thrilled them as youngsters.

Soon, the tidy sports car maneuvered the sharp right turn across from Arch's store, and they droned along the snow-packed gravel road leading into the river bluffs and up to The House.

At last, The House appeared over the sparkling chrome radiator cap: a white square framed by dark, verdant foliage, as if snow had blown against a wall and frozen.

Karen steered the semicircle drive covered by deep, untouched snow, and stopped at the front steps. Matt opened his door forward, noticed it skimmed the snow's surface, then stepped out, yelling as the white stuff packed into his low-cut loafers.

He asked Karen to wait while he opened the front door and changed into rubber knee boots. And then, armed with a broom, swept a path from the MG up the stairs to the front door.

Next he helped her lift out, and swept a clearing around the car. Then he collected the presents, coats and suitcase and entered The House, stopping first to tromp snow from his boots on the front porch.

Karen waited inside the front door, and when he walked through the entranceway pressed close against him. She draped her arms around his neck, kissing him fully and hotly on the mouth, her tongue darting and probing.

Matt felt inner forces controlling his emotions, stirring him and creating warmth and longing at once. He responded to her embrace.

Without speaking, they walked hand in hand up the stairs to the master bedroom, undressed in half-light seeping through curtained windows, and slid beneath the thick comforters piled atop the wide brass bed.

For nearly an hour they made love; their bodies locked tightly and barely moving, yet intensely feeling. Mouths pressed and tongues exploring, and the warmth of flesh on flesh helping them discover passion's peaks over and again.

"I craved you on the way here," she said, looking up at him, and feeling deeply satisfied and spent.

Her legs wrapped his and as she spoke she felt him within, and throbbing.

"I barely kept the car on the road. I love you, Matt. And my little MG, too. You'll never know how much."

"Maybe...but keep showing me like you just did," he said through traded kisses. "I may buy you a new car daily! I love you, too, Missus Durham."

They made love again. Slowly. Sensuously. Wonderfully.

Then arose, dressed, and walked outdoors to stretch the weather cover over the TD.

Matt retrieved it from the storage boot, unfolded it, and they draped it across the sports car. That done, they returned to The House.

While he laid logs in the fireplaces in the study, living room and bedroom where they slept, she sliced ham and scrambled several eggs for brunch.

After dining, they lit a fire in the study fireplace, and relaxed on the large couch, drinking coffee and looking out the bay window over the river valley below, her head resting on his right shoulder and left arm entwining his right.

They sat for nearly two hours.

Chatting occasionally, and listening to the red oak logs sizzle and snap. Scanning with Damon's binoculars the virgin whiteness that coated the outdoors. And, enjoying the comfort and peace of being together.

Finally, Karen arose, retrieved the coffee pot from the kitchen, and filled their cups. He caught her waist playfully and pressed his face against her stomach, feeling the athletic firmness of her figure.

"Tell you what," he breathed into the sweater she wore. "Let's bundle up, grab a sled and cut a tree today. Tomorrow we'll decorate it over hot buttered rums. Deal?"

"Sounds nifty. The fire and cozy couch are making me sleepy."

She kissed him on the top of the head, strolled to the kitchen then returned and sat beside him. After they finished coffee, she went upstairs and changed into bluejeans while he poked the fire dead. It crumbled in a heap of glowing embers at the rear of the firebox.

Matt secured the fireplace screen, then climbed the stairs himself to change into insulated coveralls.

Twenty minutes later, the two crunched the snowy woods north of The House, towing her old Western Flyer sled and carrying a u-shaped band saw and length of rope. They traced the same path they had trod beside Magusett Creek eleven years earlier.

A large patch of cedar and fir trees nestled in a flat area near the peak of the hill on which The House set. They entered it, breaths hanging in the stillness of the glade like floating puffs of smoke.

Matt led the way to a cluster of pine and balsam, encircled by hardwoods.

"Hoot and I discovered these last September when we chopped firewood," he said, dropping the sled's tow rope and picking up the bandsaw. "Now I'm glad we did. Never figured needing one for a Christmas tree."

They walked the clump of evergreens, finally settling on a six-foot, well-shaped and bushy balsam. Matt touched the saw to its base, and minutes later they hefted the tree aboard the sled, secured it with rope, and started back.

They emerged slightly above The House at a clearing near the edge of the woods. They could see their footprints, and the sled trail leading from the structure. The picturesqueness of the setting dazzled them; as if on an antique postcard, or perhaps a Currier and Ives landscape.

The House stood like a Christmas present swathed in ermine. And stretching into the snow-hazed distance, the Paginaw River Valley added a master's touch to the wintertime panorama.

When the two returned, Matt leaned the tree against the back porch off the kitchen and rustled around the attic until he found a Christmas tree stand. He brought it and several boxes of bulbs and ornaments to the living room.

The tree fit snugly in the stand, and Karen filled its base with water while he fussed with adjusting bolts until it stood straight. They had placed it in the northwest corner of the room, far from the fireplace and visible outside from the road.

He next untangled the strings of lights, and plugged them in to locate burned-out bulbs. In the meantime, Karen went to the kitchen to fix highballs and begin preparing supper.

She bought a small package of chicken thighs and breasts the day before, and put these in a deep iron skillet; covering them with thick mushroom soup. She set the burner on simmer, mixed the drinks and joined her husband in the living room.

Matt had stretched the light strings across a large oriental rug...in preparation for hanging...and unpacked and placed ornaments and metal candy canes beside the tree; ready to assume their appointed places among the balsam's branches.

When she entered the room, he stood in front of the window, hands jammed into the pockets of his favorite cable-knit cardigan sweater, watching the sinking sun paint the glistening snow crest pastel pink.

"Penny for your thoughts," she said, handing him a glass.

"Oh...they're worth considerably more than that," he said taking the drink. He slid his arm around her waist and nestled her beside him.

"Just thinking what a beautiful, peaceful sight this is. December sun going down over snow-covered hills. All's quiet. You can smell the Christmas tree. And we're here enjoying ourselves. What more could you want?"

"Matt Durham...you're a hopeless romantic," she said, and bussed him on the cheek.

They stood silently watching the sunset, then she left to finish dinner while he turned on the living room table lamps. He switched on the large wooden Philco radio occupying its stand between two easy chairs, and sat back to enjoy his drink and listen to the news.

Already, succulent dinner smells emulated through The House, and the drink made his gut rumble after eating only a slight brunch during the whole day.

Karen discovered a bottle of white wine tucked back in the refrigerator...chilled since the men began the duck season...and opened it to cant. Then she placed plates, napkins and silverware on the table.

In the living room, she heard Matt chuckling over the radio adventures of the "Great Gildersleeve," and busied herself spooning portions, making coffee and pouring wine. When the show ended, she called him to eat.

Both were famished, plus favoring chicken prepared in mushroom soup. They devoured the fowl, plus two helpings of green beans apiece and several buttermilk biscuits with honey.

After washing dishes, the two enjoyed coffee and brandy in the living room; until Karen announced through a stretching yawn that the day's excitement had worn her down. And at nine o'clock, they turned off the lights and radio and walked upstairs to bed.

Christmas Eve day, Matt awakened and dressed by seven o'clock. He went downstairs, pleasantly surprised by the strong, pungent scent of the Christmas tree perfuming the rooms.

He fixed a pot of coffee, plugged it in to perk, and switched on the radio. He listened to the morning news and farm reports while starting his day. Upstairs, a flushing toilet and running water told him Karen was awake and dressing.

He put on his overcoat, picked her car keys off the kitchen counter, and walked outdoors to where she'd parked the MG. Its canvas cover, dusted with crisp snowflakes, hung stiff from the cold.

He drew it back, folded it crudely and placed it on the front porch swing; making a mental note to thaw it inside before returning to New Haven.

Matt stooped and entered the squat sports car. Inside, he pumped the accelerator twice, eased the choke out two clicks, switched on the ignition and pulled the starter knob.

The motor caught on the second turn, its raspy exhaust humming steadily as the tachometer needle fixed at twelve hundred revolutions.

He warmed the TD for five minutes...listening to the news...then switched it off and returned to The House. He shivered off the cold as he glanced over his shoulder to admire the crimson vehicle that glistened in stark contrast to the surrounding snow.

Karen met him in the entry hall with a steaming cup of coffee.

"I didn't know where you were," she said, clutching his arm and leaning her head on his shoulder as they walked to the kitchen. "I heard the MG start and figured you'd deserted me for her."

"Belay your fears, me lady," he joked, patting a chair for her to sit and dropping into one himself. "She may be cute...but she takes a lot longer to warm up!"

"Oh you!" she cried, and smacked him on the arm.

Matt lit a cigarette, and volunteered to fix breakfast while she kindled a fire in the living room hearth. By the time the two finished his fried eggs, hash browns, sausage and toast...and put dishes to soak...a healthy blaze roared over the oak logs.

They carried their refilled coffee cups into the living room and began decorating the tree.

"Stringing bulbs is dad's job," he said from the top rung of a step stool brought from the kitchen. He looped a long strand of colored bulbs around the branches and secured it with green twine.

"Same with my dad," she confirmed. "He'd spend hours fiddling with the lights while mom and I cooled our heels; waiting for him to finish before we hung candy canes and ornaments. In our family, heresy meant two bulbs of the same color next to each other!"

Matt wound the last coil of wire and lights around the lower half of the tree, and Karen began hooking glass, metal, wood and cloth ornaments on the balsam's limbs.

As she worked, he fetched the coffee pot from the kitchen, along with two large boxes of tinsel. Karen climbed the ladder and capped the tree with a satiny angel that had witnessed more Christmases than even her dad could remember.

After they hung the tinsel, Karen spread a red, green and white patchwork quilt around the base of the tree. Then they collected the presents brought along for each other and placed them on the cover.

Finally, Matt plugged in the extension cord and the two admired the radiant tree glowing in the corner of the room.

"It's beautiful, isn't it," she said, looking into his face and flashing the quizzical look he loved.

"Sure is, honey," he replied, kissing her lightly on the lips. "Nearly as pretty as you."

Only occasional vehicles moved along the road that ran by The House: Farmers passing by on tractors or in old trucks, or sometimes, behind teams pulling large wagons or harrows.

This day, however, boasted frequent passersby; mostly neighbors driving from house to house, exchanging greetings, gifts and something to take the chill off the weather.

Raymond and Ruth Daley stopped and wished the couple a Merry Christmas.

"Saw that pretty little red buggy out there and thought we'd stop and see who was about," said Raymond. "Glad we did, 'cause now we can wish you folks happy Christmas."

Raymond's cheeks and nose glowed red as Karen's car. From the wind's nip, possibly; and from a little cheer stopping at the Suther's farm down the road...probably.

"You'all coming to church tonight, Karen?" inquired Ruth.

"Yes, certainly. We wouldn't miss it," came the reply.

"Welp...see you there," said Raymond.

He ushered his wife toward the door and daubed his nose with a bandanna.

"We best mosey, mom," he urged. "You folks have a real good 'un, hear?"

"Thanks Raymond...thanks Ruth," Matt responded. "And merry Christmas to you."

They waved as the couple scurried off the porch and into a Studebaker pickup.

"Nice of them to stop by," Karen said as they stepped back into the entry hall.

"Yeah...folks down here are really swell. They care about you, and watch out for you. Raymond would give anything he owned if you asked for it."

After lunch, they fired the MG and toured the snow-covered countryside, admiring the wholesomeness of outdoors sparkling so fresh it hurt their eyes. And when they came to the road leading along the river, Matt took it.

Minutes later he slowed to point out the boathouse in the distance. Eight inches of virgin snow layered the soybean field, so they stayed on the main path for fear the little roadster would drag its bottom on the tractor path through the tract.

"Three miles downriver from that boathouse is the best duck shooting in the territory," he said, downshifting to second and coaxing the peppy engine to thirty miles per hour.

When they reached the junction of Highway 9, he steered back toward the river valley and Huntsdale seven miles away.

Until two years ago, the swath of blacktop linking Huntsdale to Highway 95 consisted of a rough and winding rock-covered road. Matt remembered traveling that route dozens of times, listening as stones kicked up and clanked around the metal linings of the fenders.

He would watch for rabbits graveling along the road in early dusk, and sometimes he and his father potshot them with a .22 caliber rifle; being watchful for oncoming cars.

Now, the state called the asphalt ribbon Highway 9. And teenagers who drove the stretch to Huntsdale...returning along the river road... called it Seven Hills; for the number of sheer inclines and declines it contained. These, the kids raced over at breakneck speeds, making stomachs slam pelvises on steep climbs, and float to their throats cresting the peaks' summits.

From time to time, teen drivers careened too zealously over the Seven Hills course, and their cars' front tires would leave the pavement.

Before Matt entered high school, one young man lost control, rolled his father's car five times, and killed himself and three friends.

Still, Seven Hills drew challengers almost nightly.

Road graders were working Highway 9 the day before when Matt and Karen arrived from New Haven, and managed to plow and scrape the snow into a deadly coating of glare ice.

Now, as Matt pulled out onto the road, he felt the back wheels lose traction. He immediately let off the accelerator, and the TD's tires bit as they slowed. Soon, the dainty car purred steadily toward Huntsdale.

When the two reached the quaint village, Matt pulled alongside Arch Jacob's combination grocery store, gas stop, pool hall and beer joint, and they went inside.

Arch, as usual, divided duties between bartending, making cold-cut sandwiches and swapping gossip.

A short, balding, seventy-plus-year-old man, he enjoyed hunkering behind his bar...leaning against wood shelves brimming with sardines, Vienna sausages, pork and beans, and boxes of Saltine crackers.

When he saw Matt and Karen, his face lit and blue eyes sparkled. He immediately sashayed from behind the bar to shake hands.

"Well, howdy do, Matt Durham!" the barkeep bellowed, his hand-rolled cigarette dribbling hot ashes and sparks with every word.

"Now the duck season's winding down, didn't figure seeing you 'til spring. Whatcha up to here?"

"We're spending Christmas at The House, Arch," Matt answered. "Say...you remember Karen, don't you? We're married now."

"Well, hornswaggle me! Sure I do! Doc Forsythe's little girl. Not so little nowadays. Hi honey," he said, taking her hand warmly in his. "I remember you wasn't much more than a whisper, Karen. You've sure growed into a beauty. You're a lucky feller, Matt."

"I think so, Arch," he said, hugging his wife tighter with his right arm. "You want a beer, sweetheart?"

"Sure, why not?" she replied.

They sat on red plastic-covered stools that lined the low-slung wooden counter and discussed the cramped market. So near the holidays, the place bustled with activity.

Arch's wife Ethel came to help from their house next door, and after saying hello to Matt and Karen, pulled six bottles of Pepsi from coolers beneath the bar. These she arranged in an empty motor oil box that doubled for a grocery bag and handed to a woman who lived across the road.

The rear of the structure housed a haggard pool table that lost its level during the crash of '29, and boasted enough roll-off that a ball placed on center circled before finding a pocket. Still, it provided a free game of eight-ball and amused shooters, onlookers, kibitzers and beer drinkers from sunup to sundown.

Twenty farmers and their lanky offspring packed the parlor, drinking, smoking, shooting pool and, in general, killing a day too cold for plowing; and too close to Christmas for sitting.

Matt recognized several of the farmers and their sons, nodded to them, and called them by name from where he and Karen sat. From around the pool table, several cat whistles emerged as Karen took her seat; followed by low murmurs and chuckles...all in good fun.

The attention flattered, but also embarrassed her.

"They're just spoofin' with young Matt, honey," said Arch, patting the back of her hand as he sat two long-necked bottles of beer in front of them.

"They don't mean nothin' by it. Most of these country boys seldom see pretty city gals like you, and act sort of foolhardy when they do. Don't pay 'em no mind."

They stayed at Arch's for an hour, drinking two beers and listening attentively as the storekeeper reminisced about Huntsdale. He recounted the village's citizenry, hunting, fishing and even Karen's ancestry over the seventy-odd years he toiled as stockboy, apprentice blacksmith, mechanic, partner and business owner.

Finally, Matt suggested they head for The House.

"I'm starving, honey," he pleaded.

The two excused themselves, wishing Arch, Ethel and other inhabitants happy Christmases, then piled back into the MG; this time with her behind the wheel.

Karen again felt the excitement of the previous day when she started the MG, shifted into first gear and pulled from beside the store. She steered the road climbing toward the bluffs, and minutes later, the auto topped the snow-covered grade leading to The House.

As always, it stood in front of them, beckoning.

She guided the small vehicle into the previous day's tire ruts, and as the pair climbed out, they noticed the sun smothered by grey clouds that threatened additional snow.

She had left a wax paper-wrapped package of quail thawing while they drove, and now rolled the birds in flour and began pan-frying them.

Matt, meanwhile, laid another fire in the living room hearth and switched on the radio. He adjusted the volume so they could hear from the kitchen, then joined her near the stove.

He slipped behind and slid his arms around her waist. She craned her head back and kissed him, turning the quail in the hot, snapping cooking oil.

Green beans with bacon and onion rings bubbled on another burner, while cottage fries turned golden brown in a pie tin in the oven below.

"Dinner smells delicious," he said, nibbling the back of her neck. "So do you, I might add. How about a spiked eggnog?"

"I'd love one, Matt. Please, not too stiff, though. You know me and bourbon. And I'm already feeling giddy from the beers."

"That giddiness is Christmas, honey," he said, this time kissing her cheek.

He took two drink glasses from the liquor cabinet and poured a finger of Kentucky bourbon in each.

"You'd best not fall asleep, either. I've got big plans for the couch in front of the fireplace."

"Oh, listen to you," Karen scolded. "You obviously have more on your mind than waiting up for Saint Nicholas! And I don't wonder; you've been a bad boy and deserve only coal."

The quail simmered to perfection as the beans sputtered delicious aromas through the downstairs, and the cottage fries boasted honeyed hues by the time the couple finished their nogs.

Matt rinsed the glasses and set them in the sink while Karen turned off the range and oven. Then he lit the Yule candles in the center of the table and retrieved the bottle of white wine opened the night before; happily humming Christmas carols as he poured the amber liquid.

In the background, KFRU played an Irving Berlin tune: "White Christmas," sung by Bing Crosby. "Der Bingle" had just wrapped a movie by the same name, co-starring with Rosemary Clooney, Vera Miles and Danny Kaye.

"I love that song," Karen murmured as she spooned stringbeans onto his plate, making sure to include a strip of bacon in his portion. He especially liked it cooked this way. "It really brings home the meaning of Christmas."

"I know," he replied, topping their wine glasses. "I've never been more homesick than when it played in Korea. And the Armed Forces Network spun it often."

"Those days are past, darling," she smiled, lifting her glass and clinking it against his. "From now on...nothing but happy times."

"I'll second that, babe," he returned her toast.

Matt devoured three quail and two helpings of beans and fries. Karen did well, too. Polishing off two birds herself. Unlike Matt...who lived to eat...she ate only to live. That and her high energy level...always at doubletime...kept her tall, slender frame in perfect athletic pitch; firm and lithe.

Matt, conversely, worked to stay fit.

During the January-to-April period when outdoor activity slowed considerably, he tended to a paunch amidships. And love handles occasionally challenged his belt at the waist.

After clearing the table and washing dishes, the two took her car to Huntsdale's Presbyterian Church for Christmas Eve services. Many of the people they'd seen during the day attended, and all wished them a happy season and prosperous new year.

Around ten o'clock, they returned to The House, mittened her roadster, and went inside for the night.

Matt fetched brandy and two snifters from the kitchen and tossed two more logs on the fire while Karen went upstairs and slipped into her flannel nightgown, bathrobe and slippers. When she returned, he changed into his night clothes and returned to the living room.

The soft, flickering orange light and warmth radiating from the hearth competed with the tree's delicate glow of muted pastel bulbs, bathing the room in peaceful shades.

The pair sat quietly on the couch, listening to carols on the radio. Matt's legs propped on a leather hassock, and Karen sat with legs tucked behind and her head on his shoulder.

Over the radio, they chuckled with the exploits of Jack Benny, and Fibber McGee and Molly's Christmas broadcasts, and thrilled delightfully when Phil Harris and Alice Faye spotted Santa Claus at their fireplace. And they savored the warmth of the feisty cognac burning its way to their toes.

That first Christmas consumed them.

Its combined elements painted their memories and desires from that point onward. The fire. Christmas music. Solitude in a wonderland setting. And, especially, the pure passion of love felt for each other; manifested on the couch.

They lay naked on its velvet surface in the dim firelight, his bathrobe wrapping them together, until midnight. Then, with the fire burned to glowing red coals, they walked arm in arm to their bedroom and sleep.

At half past eight, Matt awoke. He studied Karen sleeping... comforters pulled around her face and only the pert nose protruding... and gently nudged her.

"Hey, sleepyhead. Let's get up and tear into presents!"

He rolled out of bed, yawned and stretched his way to the bathroom to brush his teeth. When he finished, she followed suit as he went to make coffee.

Matt peered out the bay window in the study and exclaimed over three additional inches of powder that had fallen during the night. He switched on the radio.

By the time Karen came down, he had perked coffee and poured each a cup. They went into the living room where another fire lapped at the fresh logs he'd dropped into the firebox.

"Merry Christmas, honey," he said, leaning to kiss her.

"Merry Christmas to you, too," she said, returning the buss.

He handed over presents the parents and he had got her; then tore into those bought for him.

Karen gave him a leather briefcase with his initials emblazoned in gold lettering. He also collected a beautiful bulky green cardigan sweater he had admired a month ago; which she immediately bought for him.

Additional loot included several dress shirts, a pair of gold cufflinks, and a framed color print of mallards landing in dark, icy, wind-swept water.

In addition to a gold monogrammed key ring that featured an MG crest...and extra set of keys...Karen received a pair of expensive leather driving gloves, a nightgown, bottles of her favorite cologne, perfume and bath powder, and a jade and gold Egyptian bracelet with matching earrings and necklace.

"Matt, you shouldn't have," she protested. "Especially after buying me the car!"

She held the necklace and admired the jade teardrop capped in gold, then leaned and kissed him firmly on the lips.

"God made you to spoil, honey," he said. "Hey...I made out damned good too!"

The card enclosed with the parents' combined present revealed they had purchased enough china, silver and crystal goblets to furnish the couple with ten place settings.

Inside the greeting the two found a paid receipt redeemable for dinnerware at their neighborhood gift shop.

Also hidden in the parents' box were various tins of cheese, crackers, sardines, smoked oysters, sausages and a small baked ham.

"This 'care package' is in case you don't feel like cooking during the holidays," read the note above their folks' signatures.

The couple sat on the floor talking, joking and recounting Christmases past for several minutes, then Matt arose to fetch fresh coffee while Karen collected shredded wrapping paper in a grocery bag for burning in the incinerator out back.

On returning to the living room, he barely sat when the wall telephone in the kitchen jangled three short and one long rings. Recognizing the party line signal for The House, he arose and answered.

Damon Forsythe's voice came from far away on the other end: "Hello...is that you, Matt?"

"Doctor Forsythe?"

"Yes, son...Merry Christmas to you two!"

"Thanks, Damon. Same to you and the folks. Hang on...let me get Karen."

He cupped his hand over the black, hard rubber, funnel-shaped mouthpiece on the wallphone and called to her:

"It's our parents, honey."

She joined him immediately.

"Karen's right here, Damon," he said. "How's Florida?"

"Superb, Matt, superb! Having the times of our lives!"

The two giggled at the doctor's enthusiasm.

"In fact, yesterday Evelyn and Claire sunburned. Walt and I went out after sailfish, and the girls stayed too long in the sun! What's it like your way?"

"Beautiful, but chilly," Matt replied. "Three degrees outside, and ten inches of snow on the ground. Perfect Christmas weather."

On the other end they heard loud whispers, then Evelyn came on to wish them Christmas greetings. Matt handed the phone to Karen, who talked a few minutes then placed the handset between their ears as his folks joined the conversation.

"You missed one hell of a day, son!" Walt exclaimed. "Old Damon landed a marlin that topped a hundred pounds! Fought the blasted thing for nearly an hour. He's having it mounted for his office."

"Yes...because Evelyn doesn't want the stinky thing cluttering the family room!" chimed Claire.

They talked another ten minutes, describing gifts received and Karen bubbling over the MG, and thanked their folks for the china, silver and crystal.

Then it was time to hang up. Miami Beach temperatures hovered in the eighties, and the parents were brunching with two other doctor-couples attending the medical soiree.

After saying good-byes, Matt and Karen ventured upstairs, changed into comfortable pants and sweaters, then returned to fix their own food.

Matt cracked the eggs and began preparing his Cheddar scramblers when they heard jingling sounds out front, and a deep voice yelling: "Ho! Ho! Ho!"

They looked at each other quizzically as the last egg splopped into the bowl, then rushed to the front door to see what was outside.

When Matt opened wide the portal, the two burst out in raucous laughter; Karen's hand to her mouth and hysterical tears welling in her eyes.

There sat Hoot and Bobby in a horse drawn four-seater sleigh, swathed in a heavy comforter, mufflers around their necks, stocking caps on their heads, and cheeks glistening red as Jonathan apples.

"Where did you get this outfit?" yelled Matt from the porch.

He leaned forward in amusement, hands on his kneecaps. "And what are you doing down here?"

"Well, partner, I remembered this sleigh down at Raymond Daley's," Hoot replied, crawling from beneath the comforter and stepping down. He helped Bobby do the same. "I asked if we could rent it a couple of hours. He said to just take it, because he planned on taking you riding anyway. Already had the horse hitched. He's quite a guy."

"Most these river folks are, Hooter," said Matt.

He shook the offered hand, and put his arm around his friend's shoulder. They tied the horse to one of the front porch columns then went inside.

When Hoot and Bobby stripped their coats and gloves, she held her hand in Karen's and Matt's faces and displayed a one carat diamond nestled in an antique gold setting that glistened on her ring finger.

"Look what Hoot gave me!" she said excitedly.

Karen immediately snatched her hand close and examined the sparkling gem.

"Oh, Bobby, it's glamorous!" she said, hugging her friend. "I felt you two getting serious."

"Yeah, me too," confirmed Matt, again taking Hoot's hand in his. "Congratulations, old pal. You found that winner you talked about last June."

"Sure did, Matthew. And speaking of that...how about returning the favor and standing for me when we get hitched?"

"Proud to, Hoot," Matt clapped him on the back. "Thanks for asking. Say...when is the happy event?"

"Believe it or not...Sunday, July Fourth!" said Bobby, accepting the cup of coffee offered by Karen. "Dumbo thought it would be nice if we married on the anniversary of our meeting. Remember Halen's Lake?"

"At least I figured on remembering anniversaries this way," quipped Hoot.

"Karen...would you be my matron of honor?"

"I'd be happy to, Bobby," she said, hugging her again. "I'm thrilled for both of you."

Matt added four eggs to the bowlful he scrambled while Karen dropped six more sausage links into the frying pan. Then everyone filled her and his coffee cups, and the foursome sat talking around the kitchen table.

In the living room, the radio continued its selection of Christmas carols.

Afterwards, they bundled up, climbed into the sleigh, and traveled the snow-covered roads networking Huntsdale valley; ending at the Daley's hours later.

They helped unhitch the sled...and wished Raymond and Helen Merry Christmases over cordial glasses of homemade wine...then the four piled into Hoot's car and returned to The House.

At Karen's insistence, the newcomers agreed to stay until Sunday. They had brought overnight bags...counting on being invited...so Bobby called her parents and relayed their plans.

That evening, they prepared spaghetti and meatballs with cheese garlic bread on the side. Matt tossed a Caesar salad while Hoot uncorked two bottles of dry Chianti. Then the couples sat around the kitchen table and played Monopoly until two in the morning.

On Saturday, they hiked the snowy bluffs that bordered the Paginaw River; and packed hotdogs and marshmallows which they roasted and ate in a huge limestone cave the river carved thousands of years ago.

Sunday followed quickly.

Matt and Hoot straightened The House and made beds while Karen and Bobby washed and put away dishes and glasses. Then, after inspecting to ensure fireplaces felt cold to the touch, they boarded their respective cars for the drive to New Haven; Karen leading the way in her tidy MG.

New Years Eve, 1954, arrived four days later.

It fell on a Thursday, creating a short week and long weekend for the two couples to celebrate; which they did with champagne, quail and sirloin at the Forsythe's.

Matt's parents attended, of course, and when midnight chimed, and Guy Lombardo's band struck the traditional "Auld Lange Syne," they toasted the coming year...each other...and the good, nearly unbelievable happenings of 1953. And, especially, the bright prospects of the years ahead.

The past year meant to Matt and Karen the end of Korea and beginning of their life together; the joys of finding his and her ways professionally in advertising and interior decorating.

The outlook also shone bright for Hoot and Bobby, whom seven months hence would vow marriage forever.

And for the Durhams and Forsythes, another mellow year passed, enjoyed with close friends, good fortune and excellent health. They recounted nearly half a century behind them, and the beginnings of a new and exciting era.

They had raised their kids proudly, and well. And now grown, those offspring mirrored happiness, success and a commitment to full and rewarding married lives. And, probably, to soon making grandparents of them.

Walt and Damon were winding down what they'd planned early in the new century. And now, retirement looming close, would be able to intersperse work with more leisure.

The four couples viewed on television the excitement of Times Square, and Matt and Hoot recalled toasting each other a year ago that night with pilot's punch; since they flew missions the next morning. Now, however, the two delighted in repeating the ceremony with the real thing.

Chapter 17

New York Calls

IN JUNE, ELVIS PRESLEY RELEASED his latest hit, "Don't Be Cruel." It followed on the heels of "Hound Dog." Destined to be Number One on hit charts across the United States.

The saucy novel "Peyton Place" sold out at book stores across the country. Especially in New England...its setting.

Matt, enroute to Hartford to catch the 7 a.m. Triad flight to New York, tapped his right hand on the steering wheel in rhythm with the song. Rock and roll they called it. The new rage. And he enjoyed the faster, livelier sounds being recorded and aired.

Last night, Karen and he double-dated with Bobby and Hoot. Screened a new Glenn Ford movie: "Rock Around The Clock."

Matt embraced the speed at which things were changing. Music. Clothes. Everyone exhibiting feelings of greater personal freedom. Expressions.

The sense of better controlling one's decisions. A more serious air of independence emanated. As opposed to acting on rote assimilation of what peers and parents wished.

Everywhere, reflected by all age groups. He surmised this new wave of self-confidence reflected positively for people in general. And the country in particular. Pop music conveyed this high-spirited message. And embodied the thinking it carried along with it.

President Eisenhower, making a determined bid for a second term in office, campaigned intensely against Adlai Stevenson. He eventually would defeat the latter, capturing fifty-eight percent of the vote.

During July, Ike's stumping tour included a whirlwind sweep of the East Coast. He barnstormed through New Haven. A high point in Walt Durham's life. The two generals served in Europe during World War Two. Knew of each other, but never met.

Finally, the chance meeting occurred. Nearly ten years later when the President called on his fellow ex-general at Conn Castings.

For New Haven, it ranked an historic event. Before continuing to New York, Ike spent half a day with executives, officers and employees at Connecticut Castings. Matt, Hoot and Eddie raced to the company at Walt's invitation to come meet The General.

Hoot and Bobby no longer classified as newlyweds. The couple tied the nuptial knot two Julys ago. As planned, Karen and Matt stood with them. Now, the two rented an apartment two blocks from DG&B's offices.

Business increased steadily for Matt, Hoot and Eddie. The agency serviced regular clients involved in soft goods, grocery and farm implements. Beyond their Cometliner and Conn Castings duties.

Existing clients ranged from New Haven to Rhode Island...and included Boston and upstate New York.

In the past year alone, they added two account executives. Who also doubled as space salesmen. These in addition to two hired soon after that first year in business. Coupled with two secretaries, a bookkeeper and market research and media managers...and Durham, Gibson & Bauer boasted twelve employees.

Triad Airlines and Conn Castings still ranked as the bread and butter accounts. Lumped together, however, the others accounted for nearly half the agency's net billings.

DG&B mirrored other businesses feeling growing pains. The economy started perking midway through the Korean conflict. Now, it readied to burst the Fifties at the seams. America climbed headfirst past other nations. And enjoyed the view from her *nouveau riche* perch.

Employment escalated. Inflation deflated. And a Republican President cajoled Big Business into expanding, diversifying, employing and increasing productivity.

Triad Airlines recently moved its corporate headquarters to New York. And asked Matt and Hoot to fly over and spend a day discussing the account.

Hoot finally arranged meetings with a large grocery chain he'd been wooing. Its owners intended building several giant stores called supermarkets along the Coast. It meant major account billings. And Hoot opted to keep his appointments. So Matt made this Monday morning trip alone.

He drove into a filling station enroute to the Hartford Airport. Knowing there wouldn't be time to gas up if he caught the late return flight. He filled the Buick's tank with ethyl, and collected change from his five dollar bill. Then continued to the airline terminal.

His watch read six thirty, so he took time checking in. He carried only the leather briefcase Karen gave him two Christmases ago. He glanced to the southwest, saw the sky sullen and ominously dark. Figured they'd fly into August thunderstorms. The ones that rumbled into New York off the Atlantic, and hung for days at a stretch.

At six forty-five, he boarded the red, white and blue Triad airliner. Inside, Triad's stylized triangle logo adorned everything. Matt no sooner settled into the cushy seat than the pilot fired the four engines. They exploded to life in bursts of flame and inky diesel smoke.

Once airborne, he lit a cigarette. Looked out over familiar highways leading to Boston. In minutes, the plane touched down at that city. And twenty minutes later...most seats filled...it took off again. This time, the aircraft landed at La Guardia in New York.

He glanced at his watch again. Triad met its schedule. At twenty before nine he hailed a cab in front of the airport. Half an hour later he arrived at the airline's new Broadway offices.

Triad's managers foresaw numerous advantages in jet travel. Which is why the company rated first among airlines ordering these new aircraft when they became available. Only recently had the Federal Aviation Authority granted Triad approval to offer flights between New York and Los Angeles, San Francisco, Phoenix, Dallas, Chicago, and Honolulu. They also planned special routes to Nassau, the Bahamas and Jamaica.

The baseball campaign heralding the company's first flights between Hartford, Boston and New York succeeded beyond all expectations. At Triad's insistence, DG&B dusted it off and applied it even more fruitfully the previous summer and fall.

Matt's New York trip this time would allow him to suggest expanding the sports theme. Triad could promote activities taking place year-round. And in the most enjoyable locations. Tennis in the Bahamas during the dead of winter. Golfing in Jamaica or Hawaii. Baseball spring training in Florida. Football at any number of locations forming professional teams. And, of course, water sports and fishing in the warmer North American climates.

Bob Griffith and Don Stein reacted positively to rudimentary proposals offered by Matt and Hoot earlier that summer. And asked for a more detailed presentation by September first.

With the new campaign commencing in mid-October. In time for people making winter and spring travel plans.

Matt tucked Eddie's leather portfolio under his arm. It contained watercolor layouts of four ads they'd developed. He took an express elevator to Triad's offices on the fifteenth floor. Walked off facing a receptionist's desk...behind which sat the young lady he'd met when first calling on Triad with Hoot three years earlier.

She smiled broadly and greeted him by name. Buzzed Bob Griffith to announce Matt's arrival.

Bob and Don appeared almost immediately, pumped Matt's arm, and led him from the paneled waiting room to the inside offices.

Bob's office overlooked Broadway and Central Park. The three sat talking and drinking coffee at a circular conference table in front of a large picture window.

The squall moving from the Atlantic down the Coast arrived in full fury. Outside, rain violently pounded the glass, streaming sinewy torrents. Lightning crackled spasmodically, bleaching the tall, dark, dank granite office buildings lining the city's major corridor.

"After coffee and a chat, we'll take you on a half-dollar tour of our offices," said Bob. "First, however, there's something we need to discuss."

"What's that, Bob?" Matt asked. He accepted a refill from the coffee pot Don held.

"Well, pal...we seem to be growing leaps and bounds. Whether by accident...or because what we're doing is right. Regardless. We're making more goddamned money than we thought possible! Growing all the time. And needing more promotion and publicity."

Don returned to the group. Picked up the conversation. "What Bob means is we depend on you and Hoot to provide what we need as quickly as we need it."

Bob rose from his chair, paced to the window. He stood quiet for a moment...examining the weather and city, above and below.

He turned, facing the others.

"What it shakes down to is the action will pick up even more when we roll out nationally. Right now, we're dealing with Conn Castings to buy five more Cometliners and spare parts. We'll soon be at the point where we'll need our agency closer at hand. So we can convert instant decisions into ads, news stories, special promotions and publicity."

He returned to the table. Sat down, and placed his hand on Matt's arm. His expression solemn.

"I'll stop pussyfooting, Matt. What if you opened a DG&B branch here in New York? I know other businesses that love your work. I'll gladly refer them to you. That way...you can afford to spread out. What do you say?"

Matt contemplated imaginary grounds in the bottom of his cup for several seconds. He knew and halfway feared the shoe that finally dropped. He straightened himself with a sigh. Looked first at Don, then fixed on Bob's questioning eyes.

"Over the past two years...watching Triad's growth and plans for New York...I surmised it would come to this," he said. "You guys mean more to us than clients. You're true friends. Hell...family! You got us rolling as an agency. We'll always remember that."

Matt pulled a cigarette from his pack. Offered smokes to the others.

"Since Triad announced its move, we've discussed doing the same. Like you say, Bob. There's no other way to provide the services you require. And maybe now's the best time to start making arrangements."

The other two stood, walked to Matt and took his hand.

"You know, Matt...Triad will be with you from here on," said Don, excitedly. "We wouldn't drag you to New York and leave you dry."

"What Don says is true, Matt," Bob enjoined. "We're using half the sixteenth floor. The rest is offices and several small businesses. We'll rent you space directly above us for peanuts."

Matt flushed from their generosity.

"Like I said...Hoot, Eddie and I discussed this. And, of course, I've aired it with Karen. It looks like I'm the one who'll commute here regularly. Hoot's dad began two more magazines for the banking and insurance industries. Lately, he hasn't felt up to snuff. So, Hoot could stay in New Haven and handle the shop there."

Matt pulled the cigarette to its end. Stubbed it out in the ashtray on the table.

"I wouldn't have problems hiring staff. There are plenty of creative types available. Couple of copywriters. Art director. Media buyer. And secretaries."

"Matt...you commit to be here when we need you, and we'll all benefit. And don't worry about paying for leased space the first year. We'll let you have what you need for free. To get you up here."

"I appreciate that, guys. Really," Matt replied. "Guess I'll become a three-quarter resident of New York. My gosh! Speaking of that...where can I find an apartment?"

"You're in luck there, too," Don said. He placed his hand warmly on the other's shoulder. "A supervisor transferring to our Los Angeles operations lives in a nice one bedroom on Fifth Avenue and Fifty-Seventh Street. We'll have him hold it...and make the rental arrangements. He leaves in three weeks. Could you clear the decks and commute here by then?"

"I don't see why not," answered Matt. "I could fly over Sundays, and back on Thursday evenings. That way, I could spend Fridays at the New Haven shop and weekends with Karen. Of course, I'd stay there for holidays. And maybe some hunting?"

"Sure, Matt. It's a deal," said Bob, pumping his hand and patting him on the shoulder. "Welcome to our New York family. How about more coffee and a tour? Then we can talk about Triad's new stuff. Don thinks with us going national we should make a big splash. We're upping our budget half a million. Television is catching hold. And a lot of other airlines running commercials. We should, too. And it's expensive as hell!"

"That it is, Bob," said Matt. He accepted a fresh cup of coffee. "Still, think of the travelers you reach via Ed Sullivan's 'The Talk Of The Town.' Or 'Lawrence Welk' and that new game show, 'Sixty-Four Thousand Dollar Question.' We've roughed storyboards for new Triad commercials. I think you'll like them."

"I'm certain we will, Matt," said Don. "Television's the coming thing. My kids park in front of the set all weekend watching 'Howdy Doody,' 'Flash Gordon' and 'Mr. Wizard.' I'm sure we grown-ups have favorites, too. We need to find those that reach our market."

"We've researched television shows for those reasons, Don," said Matt. "And several hit the travel segment we're looking for. They offer the right demographics. We'll price those if you like what we recommend. Then we'll know exactly what it'll cost to reach them."

"Sounds like you're on top of it, Matt," Bob added, giving his shoulder a squeeze. "Let's see what you've got."

By four o'clock, Sid Masters and Larry Harst returned to the office. Their meeting in New York proper with the FAA concluded successfully. They greeted Matt warmly.

The five sat and chatted for an hour. Then took Matt to dinner before he caught the returning seven o'clock flight. The rain stopped briefly so they went to Floriellos Restaurant, three blocks away on Broadway. And regarded the best Italian food in the city. Verified by people lined and awaiting seating that early in the evening.

They topped their superb meal of linguini with clam sauce, veal parmisiano and thick cheesy lasagna with three bottles of aged biting Chianti. Then rushed Matt to the airport. He clambered aboard the return flight as the engines began turning over.

Once settled in his seat, he loosened his tie. The plane made altitude, the lights flashed off, and he lit a cigarette. He took a long pull, excited over coming to The Big City...Mecca of advertising...regularly. Then thought about Karen.

Already he dreaded being without her four days a week. Still, he thought: "I lived through Korea. Completely without her! And nobody's shooting at me here. She'll understand. For right now, we don't have a choice."

He stubbed the first smoke. Instantly lit another.

When the stewardess offered a snack, he opted for a double sour mash instead. He felt better when the DC-8 squealed wheels at Hartford. And he stepped into the evening cool.

Morning showers lashing through Connecticut into New York returned temperatures to the bearable range. Everything reflected a slick coat of wetness.

Matt found his car. Unlocked it, and tossed the briefcase and portfolio into the back seat with his jacket. He fired another cigarette, and wheeled toward the highway to New Haven. Hoping the ride home would provide time to figure how he'd break the news to Karen.

He wedged the Buick into a parking slot on the lot outside their building. Left the cases inside, and locked the car doors. Then trudged tiredly up the stairs. As always, she met him at the top of the flight. Holding the door open...flashing the twinkling grin that adorned her beautiful face on seeing him.

When she encountered his exhausted look...a mixture of fatigue, tension and anxiety about telling her the outcome of the trip...the smile gave way to concern. Replaced instantly by the quizzical look to which he had become accustomed after thirteen years of knowing...living with...and loving each other.

"Hi honey," she said. And the original intended perkiness flattened, detecting his dour, pained expression. Then, "What's the matter!"

"Hi sweetheart," he replied. He kissed her on the cheek, led her into the apartment. He closed the door behind them. Tossed his suitcoat onto the couch. Slid off his tie and hooked it over the bedroom doorknob. "I need a drink...join me?" he asked.

"No...not me, Matt. But go ahead."

She followed him into the kitchen.

"Didn't the meeting with Triad go well?" Her voice edged higher than usual. Strained. Worried.

"Yes, I guess so," he said over his shoulder. He poured two inches of bourbon into a glass. Filled it with tap water. He hung his arm around her shoulder...headed her into the living room. They sat on the loveseat.

"The Triad folks want their creative people closer. And I tend to agree with them. They're good people. And represent a lucrative account."

He took a swig of the drink. Grimaced against the bite. "Anyway... the long and short of it is I've agreed to stay in New York four days a week. Monday through Thursday. And provide whatever they need."

She stared at his profile for a full minute. Eyes blank. Without a word. Then spoke, calmly.

"Couldn't you and Hoot hire someone there to handle the work?" She bit the words quickly. Already anticipating the answer. Trying to mask the unpleasant feeling of emptiness suddenly gnawing her stomach.

She scooted off the couch, snuggled his leg.

"Or...what if you commuted back and forth?" Then, detecting the burden asked...three hours both ways by train. One and a half flying. She rested her head on his knee...discouraged.

He detected her discomfort. Slid off the couch onto the floor beside her. Kissed her forehead.

"It won't be bad, honey. Honest. And, won't last long, I promise. Once we've assembled a creative group to handle New York, I'll come back and stay here. Believe me, I'm topsy over that crazy city."

Deep down...once the words surfaced...he knew he deluded himself. And mouthing them only fine-tuned the knowledge that some day he'd be part of New York. Its hustle. Bustle. Mystique. Romanticism. And... in his guts, compelling fear.

Yet The City held him in some inexplicable grasp. And until now, with a bubbly tingle in the pit of his stomach, he didn't know how strongly.

He'd experienced the provocative sensation before. The first time in New York with his Conn State advertising class. They'd toured a major agency. And he'd learned, advertising held court in New York.

Other cities: Philadelphia. Detroit. Chicago. Indianapolis. St. Louis. Los Angeles. Masqueraded as creative hotbeds. In reality, they represented minor rungs on the creative ladder...eventually leading to Madison Avenue.

He knew he'd end up in New York. With a hot shop of his own. Now, opportunity dangled its hook.

Not many years ago he imagined they'd both wind up there. Things changed since. Karen excelled in working for Peck & Peck. And he believed it unfair to pull her from her job. Unless, of course, Peck & Peck wanted her in New York. Which loomed unlikely. Charlie Enright nailed that position.

Conflicting thoughts flashed through his brain like streams of light. So he shut them off. To worry over later.

He picked up the conversation.

"Triad will refer other accounts to us. And Bob and Don made an extremely fair offer on work space and an apartment. I think we can afford to run a small New York office."

Karen shifted uncomfortably when he mentioned an apartment. Her knotted eyebrows signaled the unspoken question.

"It's a small efficiency. Belonged to a Triad supervisor transferring to the West Coast," he volunteered. "On Fifty-Seventh and Fifth Avenues. A good location...and not far from the office. Probably smaller than a matchbox, though. Still, it's a place to hang my coat overnight."

By now, his announcement struck home in her heart and mind. When she lowered her forehead into her palm..leaned an elbow on the arm of the chair...he saw a large teardrop plop onto her wrist. It rolled downward, leaving a silvery trail sparkling in the light of the nearby table lamp. He turned and lifted her chin with his right hand.

"C'mon sweetheart," he said softly. "It's not worth your shedding tears. Lots of men and women commute to New York for the whole week. I'll only be gone three nights. At least it's not like Korea."

After several minutes of silence...thinking...remembering the intense loneliness felt as he boarded the transport for overseas...she looked up at him. Tearfully.

He rose to his knees. Held her in his arms. Felt her shudder one last sob. Then kissed her on top of her head again. She looked up, half smiling, and wiped tear tracks with a curved index finger.

"I'm sorry Matt. You're right. Lots of married partners work in New York. If they can make it, so can we. I love you so much. I don't want anything causing us to drift apart."

"That won't happen, Karen. I promise. I love you more than anything else. Even my work...and the agency."

"What about Hoot?" she asked. Her momentary serious look melted into the warm, wide smile.

"Not even a close second, believe me! Your legs are much, much better!"

He kissed her on the lips. Pulled her firmly against him. Then held her at arms' length.

"It's going to work, darling. You'll see. Nothing will come between us."

"I believe you, Matt." This time she put her arms around his neck, kissed his lips.

Karen fetched a platter of cheese, summer sausage and French bread from the kitchen. He fixed her a drink, freshened his, and they went onto the balcony through sliding glass doors at the far end of the living room. They sat in the wrought iron and glass furniture, feeling its coolness against their bodies. The humid stillness of August enveloped them.

The rain squall that whipped through New Haven during the day washed the stars. Now they twinkled brightly overhead with new vigor.

The two sat and talked in low, hushed voices until midnight. Watching glimmering dots of headlights in the distance in the downtown area. Listening to the droning, comforting sound of cicadas humming in the giant elms and oaks that surrounded the apartment building. Then went inside to bed.

As they lay in the dark...only a wisp of outside air stirred the curtains. He unfolded the plans for Triad's television commercials. Relating how the four hosting him that day went berserk over storyboards roughed out by he, Hoot and Eddie.

Finally, they pecked each other goodnight. Closed their eyes in silence. Her, feeling worrisome gnawing return. He, half dreading and anticipating the promises of New York. Restlessly, each succumbed to sleep.

The next morning, the two ate a light, uneasy breakfast of toast, orange juice and coffee. Kissed each other, and departed for their respective offices. He watched her MG pull from the parking lot onto the street. And felt a pang of remorse. Soon replaced, however, by the excitement of briefing Hoot and Eddie on the Triad meeting.

Durham, Gibson & Bauer's offices now overlooked Newport Avenue. Situated four blocks from New Haven's downtown area, and prosperous financial district. East of DG&B's four-story office building stood First Connecticut Trust Company.

It sprawled over a third of the block. The New England headquarters of Tushness, Bocok, Herald and Mayhew, investment brokers, occupied the other third of the square on their west side.

Beside the building in which DG&B leased the top floor, another older structure housed law firms, assorted financial consultants and minor enterprises.

Directly behind, nudging against the cement and asphalt downtown area, spread Tilly Park. It stretched ten acres in all directions.

Matt's and Hoot's offices were at the rear of Thirty-Two East Newport. They faced east, overlooking the park's trees and small lake. On which dozens of waterfowl nested year-round. The two joked that if the city closed the park to make room for construction, they'd hire the building full of lawyers next door and sue for "violation of Mother Nature." Then, trap the ducks and turn them loose at Huntsdale for breeding stock.

Between their offices rested a cozy niche with the same breathtaking view. In it sat Olivia Park, their secretary of two years. "Ollie" walked into their lives two weeks before they moved from above the bank. She had a newspaper under her arm and pointed out their classified ad. It described the secretarial position needed filling. And she convinced them she could handle it.

Ollie previously worked twenty years for two doctors up the street. She turned forty-eight just before they retired. And she had outlived her husband. So she opted to leave the medical profession and find a more exciting field.

Hoot and Matt instantly appreciated and respected her candor and no tomfoolery abruptness. They hired her after interviewing one other applicant. Since, she became the mother hen of the office. Tidying up. Making sure coffee was hot and fresh. Cups either filled or scrubbed spotless.

The three men, accustomed to coffee buildups inside their cups, amazed over how different coffee tasted.

No one matched Ollie for typing, dictation or proofreading ad copy. She was the complete professional secretary. Heading off intruders in person or over the telephone. Ensuring appointments were kept, and meetings arranged. And letting everyone in the organization know she was fourth in the chain of command. Which she most certainly was.

In front of Mrs. Park's domain opened a reception area with chairs on both sides.

Eddie located his office beyond that, with a panoramic view of New Haven's countryside over the low roof of the investment brokerage firm on the left.

A large conference and creative meeting room was found to Ollie's right. Beyond that were six smaller offices with secretarial desks and filing cabinets lining outside walls.

A legal firm earlier leased the offices, but needed more space and moved to the building next door. Consequently, DG&B's spaces featured exquisite solid walnut paneling and rich, plush deep pile carpeting. Walls requiring painting boasted autumn beiges, oranges and yellows.

Numbered and signed lithographs of waterfowling scenes adorned the offices. And nearly half the west wall featured various ads produced and awards received.

"What did Karen say, Matthew?"

Hoot's question surfaced as Matt sat across from him, drinking coffee with he and Eddie.

"Actually...she took it pretty well, Hoot. She recognizes that keeping Triad happy means bending a little. She knew you couldn't commute back and forth. Your dad needs you. So, it was my decision."

"Bobby would have hit the ceiling!" Hoot rolled his eyes upward, emphasizing his point. "It upset her when we attended the national advertising convention last spring. That just ran three days!"

"What schedule will you follow, Matt?" asked Eddie.

"Looks like New York Sunday evenings, and back on Thursdays, Eddie. Triad will lease us space on the floor above. In fact, they're giving it to us the first year. I may need to rent or buy furniture. Probably hire a couple of people."

He lit a cigarette before continuing.

"The guys from Triad are referring accounts to us. We may get busy real fast. Anyway, I'll work here on Fridays and keep abreast of what you two birds are doing!"

"Tell us...old buddy. How did they like our suggestions for television commercials?" Hoot picked up the coffee pot, refilled cups around.

"They thought they were swell, Hoot. Bob especially liked the 'Flying With The Finest' tag line. He caught the reference to the airline, employees and equipment...and the passengers themselves.

"Felt the idea of interviewing tourists and businessmen on why they selected Triad was keen. And employees talking about pride in doing jobs well lends even more credibility. Overall, it was a smash!"

"Do we have the go-ahead?" asked Eddie.

"Not officially," Matt replied. "We probably will when I return in two weeks to move into the apartment and furnish the office. They raved over the concepts you sketched. We've got a better than average shot at our ideas being accepted."

"Tell you what, Matt," added Eddie. "I know a heck of an illustrator from school. He's in New York now. Works for a mail order house. Bet he'd be happy to sign with us. I also know a film-maker who's leading the pack in commercial production. You may want to talk to these guys pronto about helping produce our commercials."

"Sounds promising, Eddie. Give me names and phone numbers. I'll meet with them soon as I can."

"I'll go you one better, Matt. Soon as we're finished here, I'll call and handle details from this end."

"Well partner," said Hoot, now serious. "It won't be the same without you during the week. Who'll keep us on our toes and entertained?"

"That's your new hat to wear, Hooter," replied Matt. "While I'm wowing 'em on Broadway!"

All morning, Karen paced her office. Trying to select swatches of materials, wallpaper and carpeting. Searching the right combinations for Harold Sappington...her father's close friend and young associate at Yale.

Doctor Sappington recently established his private practice. And, at Damon's suggestion, asked Peck & Peck for interior decorating.

The previous night's conversation with Matt upset her. And now, that took its toll on her concentration and color coordination abilities.

Hal was nearly two years older than Karen. Extremely bright, with an excellent wit and sense of humor. He had been a protégé of Damon's through med school.

She liked him as a friend from the start. Primarily because of his outgoing personality and affability. And gift for putting people at ease.

Which, she learned so well over the years, ranked an uncommon trait for doctors. And not to be confused with so-called "bedside manner."

This young doctor differed from the many other medical practitioners she knew. Plus, he made her laugh and feel good. She also recognized his fondness for her.

At eleven o'clock, Karen tossed her hands in frustration. She telephoned Bobby to see if her good friend could meet for lunch at the Crest House...midway between their two locations.

Bobby had been developing her teaching plans and class schedules for the coming year. She had strewn papers throughout the apartment... more balanced precariously on the kitchen table...and she leapt at the opportunity to meet and chat up her friend.

They arrived within five minutes of each other. The maitre d seated them in a small dining room off the main eating area. A cozier, quieter location. They both ordered wine spritzers.

"What have you been up to, Bobby?" asked Karen. "We haven't seen you two for a couple of weeks. Mad at us?"

"Oh, heavens no, Karen!" came the reply. "I'm sequestered during the day getting classwork prepared. And poor Hoot's pooped between worrying over his dad and handling his own work. I know they've hired more people. Still, when they hire someone, they land more accounts. Sorry, Karen, didn't mean to be so bitchy. Maybe it's the prospects of facing the little no-neck monsters again. Why can't summers last six months?"

"Wait until you have kids of your own, Bobby. Then you'll wish they lasted only six days!"

Karen sipped from the fat goblet of bubbling white wine in front of her.

"I know how you feel. Whether it's August heat...summer ending... too much work or what. I can't concentrate on what I'm doing, either. Hoot hasn't mentioned Matt's decision, has he?"

"No, hon...what's up?"

"Triad Airlines wants its agency closer at hand. They've asked Matt to form a small group in New York. He agreed. So, he'll be staying there Sundays through Thursdays. Then returning and working Fridays downtown."

"Oh, Karen, no. I didn't know! How do you feel about Matt being gone so much? I'd be pissed at Hoot."

"I was, too...at first. More hurt than anything else. As if I had done something wrong. Driven him from me. The more I thought about it, the more I realized it's just his work. What he loves doing. What he thinks needs doing. I won't stand between him and his career, Bobby. I just won't!"

"Karen...Matt probably decided to commute so Hoot wouldn't have to. Not because of anything you did or didn't do. Those two have faced a lot together. They love each other...would die for each other. I guarantee...if Hoot's dad hadn't been so ill, he'd be making the trip. At least going every other week and splitting it up."

"I know you're right, Bobby. I just felt sorry for myself. Either one of them would do what it takes to keep Triad happy."

"You bet. Remember, they're ex-fliers, Karen. Those guys stick together, believe me!"

"How well I know, Bobby. How well I know." Karen sighed, drained her glass. "Let's have another spritzer and see a menu."

The two ordered tomato and crabmeat appetizers. Followed by mushroom quiche. And washed their light lunch with third glasses of wine and soda. When Karen returned to her office at one-thirty...and Bobby resumed paper shuffling in her apartment...both experienced giddiness.

Karen felt better airing misgivings with her friend. And now concentrated on selecting complementary and tasteful accouterments for the doctor's offices. She even whistled a meaningless tune as she coordinated colors, fabrics and materials.

After meeting with Hoot and Eddie, Matt spent the rest of the morning in the conference room. Approving copy and layouts prepared for full-page grocery ads for the Sampson Supermarket chain.

Repro mats needed pulling on the ads the next day. Then they would be delivered to newspapers around the state for printing in Friday and Saturday editions.

When he arrived home that evening, Matt found Karen in a happy mood. He suggested seafood at a nearby restaurant. She agreed, and they called Hoot and Bobby to make it a foursome.

As in the past, Matt and Karen turned to their friends for advice, understanding and comfort. Hoot and Bobby returned the trust...always doing the same.

This night, they discussed the impending New York move at length. The four explaining openly how they felt. By the end of the evening, the quartet agreed. However taxing, commuting seemed necessary to hold this important client. Sticking together as a team, they could pull through the ordeal.

Two weeks later, Karen waved Matt off as he pulled from the parking lot below. He turned right, headed for the airport. And in an hour and a half, he steered into a slot in front of the Hartford Airport terminal. Another twenty minutes found him seated in a Triad airliner, enroute to New York via Boston.

The plane banked hard left and dipped its wing toward Boston Harbor. Early morning sun streamed through the round porthole to Matt's left. Catching wispy strands of others' cigarette smoke in its beam.

He lit up, clutched the waxed cup of coffee the stewardess offered, then leaned on the cushion behind his head. Below, the coastline fell away as the plane churned inland. He thought to himself how many more times he'd relive this exact moment.

Soon, New York's craggy outlines appeared on the horizon through the window to his right. He matched a final smoke. Through the open cabin door he saw gauges, dials and switches packed into the aircraft's instrument panel.

Listening closely, he heard La Guardia's tower passing landing instructions and approach clearance in broken, staticky sounds.

This time, Matt lugged two suitcases besides his leather briefcase.

Bob Griffith waited at the gate.

They collected his luggage. Then walked to the reserve parking spaces nearby.

Stacking it in the trunk of Bob's Cadillac.

"This parking space will be yours, Matt," the other said as they wheeled from the lower level garage. "We've got a couple of company cars. You may as well use one while you're in New York. We'll park it here from now on. You pick it up on Sundays, and drop off on Thursdays. That'll save us lots of time and money, believe me. Taxis charge too damned much in this burg!"

"I hadn't considered transportation, Bob," Matt replied. "Figured I'd walk where I needed to go. However, I'm sure a car will be handy."

"Handy, hell. It's a necessity. Even though it'll be a clunker stationwagon. At least it runs good, and will get where you're going. Most of the time it's easier to hail a cab downtown. Rather than fight for parking, or hock your soul for garage space. You'll only be about ten minutes from some of the hottest spots in New York."

Matt paid particular attention to landmarks and other details on the drive to the Triad offices on Broadway. Knowing he'd need to find his way around the city.

When they arrived, Bob pulled in front of the building. He held a rear door open for another man to step down from the curb and slide into the back seat. The man reached out his hand to Matt.

"Hi, Matt. I'm Pete Selby. Understand you're taking my apartment."

"Nice to meet you, Pete. Yeah...looks like I'll spend quite a bit of time in the big city."

"Well, it's not much inside. However, it's furnished with decent stuff. I'll miss that. When I get to Los Angeles I'll have to buy my own furniture.

Matt inquired if Pete had begun packing.

"I've already shipped most everything to the Coast They'll pick up the rest today. I'll be out of your hair in no time."

Minutes later, Bob eased the Cadillac into a garage entrance for one of the tall buildings lining Fifty-Seventh Avenue. The dark entranceway inclined slightly. They pulled to a guard's booth.

Pete flashed a plastic card with the number sixteen twenty-four on it. A black and white-striped barrier gate in front of the car raised for them to pass.

The Caddy corkscrewed to the second garage level.

Then Bob nosed into a parking spot by the elevators. The threesome climbed out and retrieved the luggage from the trunk. Pete pushed the "up" button, and they stepped aboard the lift when it arrived.

Bob nudged the twenty-fourth floor button, and the car lurched upward with a low electric hum. When they reached the designated floor, the elevator bumped again. And when its door opened, Matt's face registered incredulity.

The building exuded a Victorian plushness. Probably Thirties vintage. Built with luxury at the forefront. The long, wide corridor carpeted in a plum-colored deep pile. Accented by yellow-gold diamond-shaped designs every ten feet.

At both ends and in the middle of the hallway rested couches and chairs. Serving as casual conversation areas for residents. Dotted along the corridor stood potted plants and large brass cigarette receptacles... even spittoons.

Pete led the way leftward. They walked the plush carpeting. Matt squinted against sunlight streaming through three large windows in a semicircular vestibule at the end of the hall.

They had paralleled a park on the right side of Fifty-Seventh street before Bob steered into the garage. Matt estimated if his navigation held true, the park should be directly ahead. Indeed, he saw tops of trees in the hazy distance as they approached the last door on the right-hand side of the hallway. The three stood before room 2412. Pete inserted his key and opened it.

The first thing Matt remembered seeing was bright white sunlight flooding the apartment. To his left opened a huge semipentagonal bay window. Even with its white silken inner liner drawn, the impressive glass opening permitted the blinding rays to penetrate.

It stretched along the east wall of the living room. And Matt's mouth gaped in surprise and wonderment. The other two, knowing, turned and chuckled.

"The view was why I took the apartment, Matt," said Pete. "I'd have paid a king's ransom. Come here...it's even better from the bedroom."

The trio walked past four gigantic cardboard boxes stacked neatly along the wall. A short hallway passed a bathroom on the right, and floor to ceiling closets on the left. And led into a bedroom nearly as large as the room they'd just left.

This room featured wide picture windows that opened into the sun on the left, and the murky skyline of Manhattan on the right.

"You're right, Pete. This is magnificent! I know why you hate leaving."

"Guess that's the breaks, Matt. However, don't worry. I'll gladly trade this for warmer temperatures and my view of the Pacific Ocean."

A massive oak roll-top desk and banker's chair dominated one corner of the bedroom. In the other squatted a console television. Between the two, directly in front of the window, stood a small round table and two chairs. Strategically placed to absorb the breathtaking views.

Matt crossed to the window and looked. Nose nearly pressed against the glass. He saw Central Park, and traced blacktop paths crisscrossing it like a maze.

The park's center housed a small lake, on which swam several swans and various waterfowl. It reminded him of the view from their New Haven offices.

To the left, the Hudson River snaked into the distance. Several ships and barges plying its swirling, muddy current. Panning to the far right, Matt's eyes skipped along the outlines of Manhattan's office buildings. Crouched beside and peering down on Park Avenue. Which also appeared, and bumper to bumper with traffic.

Walking toward the living room, Pete opened the closet doors to reveal their roominess. Then switched on the bathroom lights. A sweep of his hand took in the toilet, and an antique pedestal sink with a large medicine cabinet above. A combination bathtub and shower completed the ensemble.

The bathroom floor boasted hexagonal ceramic tile. White, with black border. Matt reckoned a coat of paint could perk the little room.

"It's not much...but serves its purposes well," Pete said. He flipped the switch and returned the two to the living room. Matt now spotted two fat, comfy, cushioned couches facing each other. Between them reposed a rectangular brass and glass coffee table. Flanking them stood two matching easy chairs.

A refurbished antique wooden icebox anchored the northeast corner of the living room. Its brass hardware gleamed in the morning sun. Perpendicular to it ran a serving bar with three stools clustered in front.

The corner opposite housed a marble-topped serving table. And built-in bookshelves framed the wall butting against the large linen closet opposite the bathroom.

"You'll have to supply your own books, Matt," Pete said, slapping his shoulder. "Most of these are reference books from college and training courses I've attended for Triad. I'll need them. And they'll go today with the remaining boxes."

"No problem, Pete," he replied. He already envisioned wooden duck decoys sprinkled among his marketing and advertising volumes, novels and encyclopedias.

The three went into the kitchen, which barely fit them at one time. Still, it contained the essentials: stove, refrigerator, broom closet, and large double porcelain sink containing garbage disposer and dishwasher.

"Have some coffee, boss?" Pete asked.

"Sure," came the answer. And the three sat at the dining table along the wall opposite the entrance to the kitchen. Pete had brewed coffee since he knew they'd tour the place soon. And now poured each of them a cup.

"It's absolutely beautiful, guys," Matt said as they sat. "The view. The location. Everything. To be honest, though, I don't know if I can swing it."

"Considering what it offers...and being this close to the company in one of the better parts of New York...it's not bad, Matt," Pete said. "I pay two hundred and fifty a month. And the security and cleaning services are fantastic!"

Matt whistled softly. That amount tripled what they paid for the two bedroom in New Haven. He looked into the glowing living room, and the view beyond into the bedroom.

"What the hell," he said. "I've got to have it! This is the most impressive layout I've seen!"

"I thought you'd feel that way, Matt," grinned Pete. "Hope you don't mind...but I took the liberty of signing the lease over to you. The manager's name is Fred Grayson. Triad occasionally let's him fly free. He didn't object...even though there's a waiting list. It's as if you've lived here from the start."

Pete fetched the coffee pot. Over his shoulder:

"You'll have to arrange telephone service, though. Everything else is included in the rent. Oh yeah...you'll need towels, sheets, blankets and pillow for tonight."

"Thanks a million, Pete. I'll get down and meet Grayson and get on his good side."

"That shouldn't be difficult...knowing you pull weight with Triad. And a fifth of Cutty Sark at Christmas won't hurt much, either."

They drank another cup of coffee. Chatted about the weather, baseball, restaurants and nearby shopping. Pete outlined other items of interest about the apartment building, its location and goings-on involving it. On New Year's Eve, for example, many of the tenants customarily gathered in the conversation area at the opposite end of the building. They'd pop several bottles of champagne, and oversee celebrating in Times Square.

A few residents carried the tradition since the building's construction twenty years ago.

Bob left the two alone and returned to his office. Pete packed his final belongings while Matt unsnapped his two large suitcases. He hung shirts, suits and ties in the bedroom closet.

Afterwards, the two lunched. Pete led Matt to a department store nearby where he bought sheets, towels, plastic dinnerware, paper plates and cups. Necessities to tide him until he outfitted his home away from home.

At three o'clock, movers collected Pete's final load and began their West Coast haul.

In the short period he knew the man, Matt liked Pete. In a way, felt sorry the other wouldn't be involved with DG&B handling the Triad account.

Pete possessed a bright sense of humor. And Matt appreciated his easygoing, comfortable demeanor. Based on others he'd met from California, he guessed Pete would mesh easily with the harried West Coast lifestyle.

Matt learned that he hailed from Toledo. Attended school at City College in New York. Then, on graduation, became a management trainee for one of the major airlines. He buzzed quickly through the ranks, and in two years supervised the airline's operations at La Guardia. Where Bob Griffith spied him when Triad opened its ticket counter next door.

Pete's ability to manage people...customers and employees alike... impressed Triad's managers. They offered him the job of overseeing Triad's startup in New York.

Which, at the time, consisted of four sales reps, two pilots, two copilots, six stewardesses, ten aircraft maintenance men, bookkeeping and payroll.

He attacked the assignment vigorously, and again excelled. Now, he would travel to Los Angeles and establish and manage an entire branch office.

Pete would fly to California mid-morning the next day. So he booked a room at the airport hotel. And tonight marked his going-away celebration. To which Triad also invited Matt, as an honorary member of the organization.

Bob arrived at six and ushered the two to a private room in The Waldorf, Selby's favorite drinking and dining establishment. Most of Triad's forty New York employees showed up to honor Pete. The majority bringing gag gifts.

At midnight, the festivities moved to several other nightclubs. And the group became considerably smaller by three o'clock, and brandy in Don Stein's Fifth Avenue penthouse apartment.

At first, Matt felt he'd fallen off the turnip truck on Grocery Row. He felt uncomfortable over the locals' lifestyles. Before the evening ended, however, he found himself immersed in the openness, gaiety and devil-may-care spontaneity they exuded.

Most Triad employees received the next day off in honor of Selby's departure. Except a well-paid skeleton crew handling ticket sales and reservations.

When Bob pulled in front of Matt's apartment building, the sun torched the sky pink over the Hudson River. Beside Bob in the front seat, Pete rattled incessantly. Matt didn't mind. The chatter took his mind off how miserable he felt.

His mouth tasted like a month-old sardine can. His head throbbed from too much bourbon, brandy, wine and champagne. And his stomach churned from overindulging on hors d'oeuvres, beef, stuffed crab and cherries jubilee.

The cigarette he lit and held cupped in his left hand smelled like burning plastic. He guessed he'd smoked two packs tonight.

At least so many tonight he wheezed and whistled breathing normally.

"Here are the keys to your limousine, Matt," Pete said. He reached into the back seat and handing over two metal objects on a Triad key chain. "I parked it in a lower level slot by the elevator. Used it hauling my crap from the office, or I'd have left it there."

"Thanks, Pete," Matt replied. He dropped the key ring into a inside coat pocket. "And good luck to you in California." He gave the man's hand a firm, sincere grasp.

"Thanks, Matt. Good luck to you here. You'll knock 'em dead in the Big City. You're in an exciting, dynamic field. And this is one hell of a town to be enjoying it in. You may end up bigger than J. Walter Thompson!"

"Doubt we'll make it that far, Pete. It looks promising, though. Listen, I'll call when we have phones in our offices."

"Please do, Matt. You're dealing with a great bunch here. I'm glad you're coming on board."

"Thanks, Pete. Take care out West...and have a good flight."

Matt patted Bob Griffith on the shoulder.

"Thanks for everything, Bob. Really enjoyed it."

"Thank you for coming, Matt," he replied. "See you at the office Wednesday. We'll have a look at your new working spaces."

"Sure thing. Bye."

He trudged to the apartment, unloosening his tie as he walked in the front door. Went first to the bathroom and dropped two heaping teaspoons of Bromo-Seltzer into a glass of cold water. He carried the fizzing mixture into the living room.

He used the bubbly, salty tasting beverage to swallow two aspirin. Then stood and stared out the window. The sun rose a molten ball over the Hudson. Washing the Heavens in hues of blue and red before making its supreme appearance.

He stood at the window in the silence of the living room. Hearing the building stir with life. Fellow renters arising, beginning their days. He watched tiny dots of people moving along sidewalks and crossing streets far below.

The headlights and taillights of automobiles and trucks burned bright in the dark blanket hanging at street level. The sun's warmth and light had not yet penetrated the darkness there.

Suddenly, Matt felt terribly alone. Hollow in the pit of his stomach. An uneasiness replacing indigestion. He glanced at his watch. Six thirty.

"She'll be up," he whispered aloud. He hopped onto a stool at the bar. Lifted the telephone receiver and dialed the operator. He gave her Karen's telephone number. Soon, metallic clicks of circuits built a path to New Haven.

A loud snap came over the line as the connection completed. He heard what passed as wind blowing. Then soon the intermittent buzz as the telephone rang on the other end. Once. Twice. Three times. He imagined Karen startled awake. Now, scrambling out of bed expecting the worse. Racing to answer the telephone in the hallway between the bedroom and the bathroom.

"Hello," said the soft, sleepy voice.

"Good morning, sweetheart," he said, in his most fake cheery tones. Trying to disguise the discomfort he felt from burning guts and thumping brain.

"Matt? Honey, what's wrong?" she immediately became alert. He noticed her voice reflecting concern. It moved him.

"Nothing, baby, nothing. Don't worry. I just got in from an all night bash for the guy whose apartment I've taken. I was just standing here... looking over this sleeping giant...and suddenly felt small and lonely. Sorry for waking you."

"That's okay, darling. I needed to get up anyway. Must wash my hair before work. Held off doing it last night. Thought you might call. Didn't want to be in the shower."

"Sorry about that, too," he said. "Didn't have a telephone until the last minute. Then we went out, and I never got around to calling."

"What's the apartment like? Do you have a view?"

"Smaller than ours...and more expensive. Yes...the view is magnificent. I see the Hudson on the left...Manhattan on the right. You'll have to come up for a few days. You'll love it."

"Oh, I'd like that, Matt," she said. She detected the excited inflection in his voice. Instantly felt uneasy about it. "What are your offices like?"

"I don't know, hon. Haven't seen them yet. Bob and I take a look tomorrow and see what's needed. He knows a good furniture store close by. And can get us a discount."

"How soon will you start hiring?"

"Might start interviews next week. Depends on production on Triad's new materials. After I get some sleep, I'll call Hoot and see how things are going. Need to talk with Eddie, too. See if he's been in touch with a couple of people we want to interview."

"Guess what?" she asked. The pitch in her voice rose slightly... crackled with excitement.

"What?"

"Remember my work for Hal Sappington...the doctor friend of dad's? He liked it so much he recommended Peck & Peck to the other doctors in the medical complex. We get to do the entire building. That's twelve offices...examining rooms, waiting rooms and a large lobby. The whole works! Plus, they want an atrium with greenery for the lobby. What do you think?"

"Honey, I'm proud of you. I could split! Way to go...Mrs. Vice President."

"Well...that's my good news for the day. I've been hopping up and down, waiting to tell you."

"I think that's great. I'm sure Charlie Enright is pleased finding his protégé succeeding so magnificently. Listen, sweetheart, I'd better go. My body is in revolt. I feel like water buffalo spent the night wallowing in my mouth."

"Okay, Matt. I need to run, too. Call me tomorrow?"

"It is tomorrow! But, yes...count on it."

"I love you."

"I love you, too, baby. Bye"

"Bye."

He placed the handset back on its cradle. Finished unknotting the tie as he walked into the bedroom. The sun had risen, and streamed through the window to his left.

He pulled both the liner and drapes closed. Switched on the desk lamp and undressed. He hung his suit and tie in the closet. Then pulled on pajama bottoms and went into the bathroom to brush his teeth.

The seltzer water and aspirin were taking hold. The throbbing headache subsiding. He scrubbed his mouth, switched off the lights, pulled the covers back and slid into the bed. Without looking, he tuned the radio on the nightstand to low music. Lit a cigarette and leaned on his left elbow, flicking ashes into an ashtray close by.

In the half dark...with only the cigarette's orange glow as company... he again felt loneliness welling. He smoked, and the radio played a song from the Forties. His mind flicked to the first time he'd seen Karen at The House. He chuckled to himself, remembering the knobby kneed, freckle-faced urchin staring through the stair railing from above.

He stubbed the smoke. Pounded the pillow firm beneath his head. Then drifted to sleep, recounting their early beginnings. Smiling happily.

Chapter 18

The New York Office

MATT'S FIRST MONTH IN NEW York sped in a flurry of interviews with job seekers. Wining and dining prospective clients. Meetings with Triad officers. And trying to keep his mind off Karen and the New Haven shop.

In the latter regard, Hoot and Eddie performed admirably. Staying abreast of new developments and endless deadlines.

On the surface, Matt speculated the arrangement might work. Once it became routine. Still, he felt uncomfortable leaving Karen on Sundays. And relying on tireless exertion to fill the void until Thursday evening. When he could be with her again. Which, too, eventually would become routine.

He created a well-ordered existence in his new environment. Everything in its proper place. Lined and ready for inspection. Probably resulting from the role military upbringing played in his life. Too, he believed that when things settle into a framework, anxiety ceases.

He spent most of his first week furnishing the offices leased from Triad. And finding that one indispensable person around whom efficient offices gravitated...the secretary.

At Sid Masters' recommendation, he interviewed a middle-aged lady who worked for Triad. She immediately impressed him as a New York equivalent of Ollie Park.

He hired her on the spot after talking for slightly more than an hour. Then delegated her with selecting furniture, office equipment and "any of the other paraphernalia" required for an efficient operation.

Her name was Dorothea Weymoth. Dot to friends. She willingly and happily took command of Matt's half of the sixteenth floor of the office building.

The television professional Eddie arranged Matt to meet proved just that. The two talked three hours about the new and upstart medium. Before Matt even asked the man about his background.

Greer McCall stretched high and appeared wire thin. He looked much older than thirty-two. Sunken cheeks outlined his rough hewn face. Which creased Victor Mature fashion when he smiled or frowned.

Matt's attention fell to the man's hands. Always in motion. Smooth, flowing gestures highlighted his words. Chiseling the ideas that poured from the producer's mouth. Continual, and animated creativity.

Matt appreciated how Greer broad-brushed the future importance of television. And found himself caught in the excitement the long slender hands and deep, resounding voice emulated.

After lunch, they discussed the proposed Triad commercials. Greer provided a brief history on filmmaking, cinema verite and production techniques. And when five o'clock arrived, Matt realized they had not talked about a particular job. Or what salary McCall drew. Or would ask.

He did know the day's rapid, ebullient conversations had siphoned his mind. He raised his hands abruptly, signaling a momentary halt to their conversation. Then asked:

"What sort of salary do you need to come work with DG&B?"

"Why hell, Matt. I thought I already was!" The reply sounded mockingly earnest. "I haven't set the film world ablaze yet. I've been shooting pictures for ten years. I don't require much. Probably get by on a hundred a week."

"How about one fifty?" Matt replied. "You'll work your butt off as our television expert."

"Holy shit...I've died and gone to Heaven," exclaimed Greer, looking upward, holding his hands as if in prayer. "Thanks boss."

"Which one are you referring to, Greer?" quipped Matt.

They talked another hour about Triad's commercials. And walked to a small bar near Matt's apartment building for a drink. Then went their separate ways.

Greer worked as editor and producer for live television shows at NBC. Which struggled maintaining its foothold. He visualized the uphill battle before becoming well known enough to produce a show.

He guessed, conservatively, five years. For him to become well enough known in the industry. Even though he garnered respect now.

The technology of television did not pace the creative applications and aspects dwelling in his mind. Waiting for the perfect means of expression before surfacing.

Greer scored, of course, as a stellar behind-the-scenes performer on Ernie Kovac's show. Had provided camera work for "Your Show Of Shows" with Sid Caesar and Imogene Coca. Early on, he recognized big dollars beckoned in television advertising. And he happened to be in the right spot when Eddie called to arrange the meeting.

When the two men parted, Matt returned to his apartment to call Karen. She empathized with his excitement over Greer's intimate tour of the fantastic and zany business of television.

Matt's new television specialist also introduced him to several young, bright and hungry copywriters. He quickly settled on two with particularly good-looking credentials and promise.

Out of college for a year, they worked for part-time slave wages at a larger agency. When Matt cast fifty dollars more a week in front of them, the two pounced on the bait. Within the week, they drew salaries from Durham, Gibson & Bauer. He also interviewed and hired the illustrator recommended by Eddie.

During the first month, hustling new business paid dividends. The Triad men introduced him to the chief executives of Cartiff Perfume & Toiletries, Standish Electronics Industries and Musgrave Manufacturing. The latter led in designing, developing and manufacturing large diesel tractors and earth-moving equipment.

The three accounts felt disillusioned with their current agencies. Tried in vain handling advertising and promotional work in-house. Or lacked expertise to do so. Too, the three had expanded their markets to include international sales.

Inside two weeks, Matt and his team called on the prospects. Met, wined and dined the decision-makers. Produced and delivered a DG&B capabilities presentation. And copped one-year client-agency agreements with all three. Including receiving go-aheads to produce marketing and advertising strategies, copy platforms, print ads and radio and television commercials.

He called Hoot and Eddie with the good news. And begged help in meeting production schedules. Then took his staff to dinner at "21," and nightclubbing at watering holes strung along Broadway to celebrate the good fortune.

Professionally, Matt's arrangement of flying to New York on Sundays and returning to New Haven on Thursdays became little more than routine. Personally, however, he missed the hell out of Karen when he boarded Triad's Flight 482 for New York. And accomplished little Thursday afternoons anticipating Flight 627 home.

An early riser, Matt's days stretched from six forty-five in the morning until around six thirty or seven in the evenings. Depending on weather, he walked to and from his apartment building. He fixed dinner or grabbed a bite along the way. Skimmed the paper, and watched television or read until bedtime at eleven o'clock.

Often, he dined with clients from the new companies for which he and the New York staff handled marketing, advertising and public relations needs. Attending plays, movies, the ballet, creative meetings or hitting nightspots clustered around his neighborhood or throughout Manhattan.

At first, he missed Karen desperately. Over the period of a few months, however, things became hectic during the day. And he regularly entertained at night. The resultant schedule left little personal time to consider goings-on in New Haven.

He called daily. And evenings on the town. The city, however, became his pulse beat. One thumping faster, wilder, and twenty-four hours a day. It caught him in its blurry white aura of hustle and bustle. And immediately represented to him the one spot in the world where anyone or anything might be found and used at anytime. Glamour. Adventure. Excitement. Challenge. Fulfillment. Abounding everywhere. Plucked by those with guts and drive. Which he knew he possessed in spades. Beyond infatuation...Matt fell completely for the gilded maiden's shiny, noisy, boisterous, allure.

He disliked New York when it rained. That ranked the only time. When gloomy dank days faded into dark damp evenings. If he was in the apartment alone, he would throw wide the curtains. Switch off the lights. Wrap solitude like a cloak around him. And keep company with sour mash or Russian vodka.

At such times, he felt the only person in the world. Cars below with flashing headlights...yellow-white jagged streaks on rain-slicked streets...possessed minds of their own. Alien creatures minding their business with minimal help from mankind.

On these evenings, he finally drug himself to bed and flopped prone on his back. The room glowing in Manhattan's lights. Like faces around a midnight campfire. He'd drift into troubled sleep...wishing, vainly, the new day would come bursting with brightness and cleanly scrubbed demeanor.

He changed, noticeably. How he talked, thought and acted. Karen, Hoot, Bobby and Eddie reflected on differences they perceived. He became quickly impatient. Bordering on nervous. And seemed to make more snap judgments. Rather than methodically thinking things through as before.

Not that his actions seemed rash or half-cocked. They just didn't mirror the same man they knew and loved. Karen also suspected he drank more than usual. And most days smoked two or three packs of cigarettes.

Her work progressed extremely well. Most focusing on the small medical complex that selected her company as its interior decorator.

On her own, Karen selected carpeting, furniture, plants and wall-coverings. And stayed well within the agreed-upon budget. Workmen began painting the first week in September. Now, they applied finishing touches.

She performed her yeoman's tasks admirably. Coordinating festive pastels that brightened building interiors. Her artist's flair introducing a cheeriness the residents received warmly. Doctors staffing the complex stopped by continually and commented favorably on work in progress.

Hal Sappington emerged her biggest backer. Even escorted her and her parents to the Resident's Formal Dance at the Yale School of Medicine.

Karen spent most evenings away from the apartment. Out with Hoot and Bobby. Or at her parent's talking or watching television. Nighttime was for sharing with Matt. Four nights alone in the small apartment rated too depressing to endure.

She knew at the outset having him gone more than home would be difficult. However, she underestimated the empty feeling that crept in on Sunday evenings as he drove away toward Hartford. Frequently, she reached across the bed and patted his pillow, then cried herself to sleep.

Matt worked closely with Greer McCall after hiring the young filmmaker three weeks earlier. He wanted to understand, absorb and learn as much as possible about television production.

Greer rated as a wizard for special effects. He singlehandedly nabbed Triad's television business for DG&B. The sixty-second commercial that clenched the contract opened with Bob Griffith on camera. Bob introduced Triad's "flying with the finest" theme by lauding employees... the luxurious, dependable Cometliner...and the airline's passengers.

When he finishes talking, the camera zooms to a tight close-up on a Cometliner model on his desk. The plane, brandishing Triad colors, suddenly becomes a real one flying over New York. And heading into a glorious sunset. Completing the promotional package, they filmed the closing sequence over all cities served by Triad.

Matt gathered his staff in the sixteenth floor conference room to preview rushes of the commercial before showing it to Triad. He and Greer mainly hoped the small group would find it did a credible job portraying the airline's commitment to customers and employees.

The two didn't realize how credible until DG&B employees watched the commercial the first time. Afterwards, Dot Weymoth...not one for emotions...approached Matt with misty eyes. And allowed that it scored as the most believable sixty seconds she'd ever watched.

By the end of September, Greer felt comfortable with his editing of the commercial. Hoot and Eddie flew to New York for the presentation to Triad.

Neither saw the commercial before airing for the clients. However, they recognized at once it would be a winner. First impressions confirmed when Bob asked Greer to rerun the videotape.

Then stood and announced: "Even featuring me...it's the best damned television work I've seen. Greer. Matt. Hell of a job!"

Throughout the assemblage clustered in the conference room the feeling was unanimous. Bob, Don Stein, Sid Masters and Larry Harst excitedly gave DG&B the nod to proceed with follow-up commercials. A dozen spots amplifying the "travel with the finest to where the sports are" theme.

Eddie already developed storyboards for skiing in Aspen...tennis and golf in Nassau...and fishing in Florida and California. Now, they could polish copy and shoot film.

With a winner's confidence under its belt, DG&B's New York staff attacked creative assignments with fanatic fervor. And when Matt boarded the Thursday evening flight to Hartford, his briefcase brimmed with rough copy. He also toted a portfolio of storyboards for Hoot and Eddie to examine and approve before beginning production.

Matt and his four New York staffers worked from early morning to ten at night all week getting campaign and marketing strategies smoothed. Now, he intended enjoying a long weekend and Fall Festival at Huntsdale.

The dash clock registered eight-thirty as he pulled the Buick onto the parking lot beneath the apartment. He saw the living room light as he switched the headlights and ignition key. He stepped out, gathered the briefcase and leather binder from the backseat. Then saw the outline of Karen through the drapes at the window. Her face filled the parted curtains, a wide smile brightening it as she waved to him.

She held open the door as he climbed the stairs. A tall golden goddess in a light bulky sweater and bluejeans. Her smile beaming.

Weekly when he returned for their three-day reunion, she seemed more beautiful than before. Now, taking the final few steps hurriedly, the invitation shining on her face made his heart pound. He sat the case down. Wrapped his arms around her waist. Kissed her full on the lips, and firmly. Her arms encircled his neck.

"Hi darling," he said. He looked down and bussed her forehead. "How's tricks?"

She picked up the briefcase, and he the portfolio, and they walked inside. He changed clothes, and Karen mixed them drinks.

"You hungry?" she asked from the kitchen.

"Famished!" he replied.

He buttoned the decrepit red and black lumberjack shirt he loved and wore with the first crispness of fall.

"We worked until the last minute on the Musgrave materials. They're pitching for business from a large construction company here. Does work in Europe and the Far East. Wanted sales literature and product films done toot sweet. So, we've been scrambling like crazy. In fact, Greer and the copywriters will work this weekend meeting deadlines."

"Shouldn't you be there Matt?" she asked. She handed him a glass. "Not that I'm chasing you back to New York."

"No...not really hon," he answered. He took a long pull of bourbon and water. "Not much for me to do. Greer and the writers have got most of it done. Needs polishing. Besides, I've looked forward to Fall Festival since the First of September."

"I'm glad, Matt," she said, kissing his cheek then nuzzling his face. "You deserve relaxation. You and Hoot can tramp the woods and shoot poor defenseless squirrels. That'll cheer you up."

266

"Yeah...you're right about that. It will be nice out in the fresh air with dad, Damon and old Hooter. New York may be exciting...but once in a while I feel boxed in. Sorta stuffy. I think how nice it is at The House."

His thoughts and words trailed into a distant image conjured in his mind's eye. Then:

"Hey...thought you said something about eating!"

They walked into the kitchen, arm in arm. She ladled two bowls of beef stew and gingerly fetched French bread from the oven. He sat at the kitchen table, and watched admiringly.

Karen again relaxed now that he was home. Suddenly, the apartment appeared warmer. Softer, as if she were seeing through a foggy lens or orange dusky glow of sunset. Comfortable. Peaceful. All is right, once again.

They dined by candlelight. Matt caught her up on the week's happenings. Especially the excellent tribute Triad paid their commercials.

Afterwards, the couple climbed into her MG and drove to the Uptown Theater for a late movie.

They waited in line a half hour to see "Giant"...a movie creating box office hysteria and touted for several Academy Awards.

When they returned to the apartment they made love. Afterwards, Matt fetched brandies. Then they lay in the darkness and talked. The glow from his cigarette comforting as she leaned her head on his shoulder.

"I miss you terribly, Matt. I really do." She whispered the words softly. Then silence.

"I know, honey. I miss you, too."

He stubbed the cigarette.

"Let's get some shuteye. Big weekend ahead."

"Okay. I Love you."

"Love you too, hon."

When Hoot pounded the apartment door the next morning, Matt stood in the kitchen frying bacon. Karen was in the bathroom, fussing with her hair.

"Hey, you in there! Durhams! You guys up and decent?" he shouted. His deep voice reverberated in the enclosed stairwell.

"Good grief, Hoot!" Matt exclaimed. He shook his friend's hand, ushered him inside. "You'll wake the building! It's just eight o'clock."

He kissed Bobby lightly on the lips. "Hi babe."

"Well, Matthew," Hoot tapped a cigarette from a fresh pack. "It's a workday. People ought to damned well be up by now." He cupped his hands around his mouth and shouted: "Reveille! Reveille!"

"Great gods, what's the commotion out here!" Karen poked her head around the doorway that lead to the bedrooms.

"Just Hoot, honey," said Matt. "Fall fever just bit him!"

"Are you kidding?" piped Bobby. "He hasn't talked about anything besides this weekend for weeks. You guys get really weird this time of year!"

"Yeah...and it's contagious, too!" Hoot said. He lifted his wife off her feet. Spun her while she protested.

"C'mon guys. Have coffee while I scramble my infamous eggs." Matt handed them cups. Refilled his own and passed the coffee pot to Hoot.

Karen appeared from the bathroom, hair in ponytails on both sides.

"Mornin' ma'am," Matt said, bowing low with a deliberate drawl. He pecked her cheek.

They laughed and chatted over breakfast. Then Matt and Hoot carried luggage and groceries to Hoot's car. Karen and Bobby washed and rinsed the dishes, and stacked them in the drainer.

The two men would drive in Hoot's car so they could talk business. Which suited the ladies. In minutes, the small convoy pulled from the parking lot. Karen's shiny red TD preceded Hoot's new company car. A Buick like Matt's. Matt lit two cigarettes, handed one to his partner.

"Hard to believe I've been in New York for more than a month, pal," he said. He took a deep pull of smoke. "Seems like a weekend ago that I moved. My days have been so damned busy I can't track them."

"I know Matthew. It's been really active here, too. We get caught up. Then someone's rush project is due yesterday, and the place goes bananas. Fact is, we've crammed your office with newspaper ads that need placing next week. Hell, it's the paperwork more than anything else slowing us down."

"That's the nature of the advertising beast, Hoot. You ought to know that by now."

"Oh, I know it okay, Matt. Doesn't mean I have to like it, though! Level with me, Matthew. How's the New York commute working out? Karen doesn't like it one iota, does she?"

"As far as work is concerned...it's outstanding! The people at Cardiff, Standish and Musgrave give us a free hand. We do what's in their best interests. They make damned few changes. And the service and products we provide impress them."

He lit another cigarette off the stub of the old smoke.

"More important, they like the results they're achieving. And the Triad bunch...well, still the same guys. A great client. Bob and Don appreciate one of us packing and moving to New York."

Hoot placed his hand on Matt's shoulder.

"You still haven't mentioned Karen, amigo."

"Hoot, near as I can tell she's adjusting. Hell, you know Karen! An atom bomb could fall on New Haven and she'd figure how to make the most of the moments left. She's scrappy gal. And I've never seen her discouraged. Or she puts on a hell of a front!"

"They poured her and Bobby from the same mold, Matthew. We couldn't have done better if we'd spent our lives searching. We're just plain lucky, I'd say."

"Agreed...and you can say again, pal."

Summer had been dry. The near drought became more evident when they turned north onto Highway 9 into the Paginaw River Valley. Instead of showing off blazing colors, the trees seemed ashamed of their reddish brown coverings. Determined to shed the rusty leaves as quickly as possible.

Hardwoods along the road into Huntsdale already lost their foliage. Now appeared sticklike creatures against a chalky noonday sky. Dust kicked by the MG ahead made it tricky for Hoot to see approaching vehicles. Or shoulders for that matter. He let off the accelerator and trailed a quarter of a mile behind the two women.

Matt gazed toward the river out of habit. Hoping to see birds on the wing. None flew. Save for several crows creating a ruckus in a giant cottonwood that clung to the river bank half a mile away.

"Extremely warm for late September," Hoot said. He switched the air conditioning to low. Closed the windows against the ruddy grit coating the inside of the car. "Bet the ducks move in later this year."

"Yeah, you're probably right. Second season in a row without good rains. Paginaw's probably even lower this year. Blind will stand high and dry in the shallows if we don't get water soon."

"Wonder how the squirrel hunting will be?"

"Probably okay along the creek, Hoot. It's spring fed. And I'll bet the old boys from Huntsdale have stocked up. And, we've got a dozen or so in the freezer at The House just in case."

In twenty minutes, the hood of Hoot's car peeked over the hill cradling The House. The frame structure stood five hundred yards away. Looming larger than usual because of the naked trees surrounding it.

Still, its beauty caught Matt's breath. He felt his pulse quicken. A wide smile painted his face with pleasure. He saw his father's car and Damon's stationwagon in the semicircle drive. Karen and Bobby were unloading the MG.

Off to one side in shade near the creek stood Raymond Daley's pickup truck. Matt and Hoot imagined Raymond by the creek in the hickory grove a quarter mile distant. Back against a tree. Listening to a tough old fox squirrel cutting a nut. Hoping it would invite several friends to its feast.

Minutes later...after paying respects to the Durhams and Forsythes... Hoot and Matt returned to the car. They hauled luggage, rifles and groceries to the proper room. And chuckled over the sharp popping of Raymond's pump-action twenty-two in the distance by Magusett Creek.

"Sounds like there'll be at least three fresh squirrels tomorrow," smiled Hoot. He stared in the direction of the gunfire.

"That's for sure, partner. Old Raymond doesn't miss."

After unloading the cars, everyone gathered in the kitchen for a brief chat. Evelyn Forsythe brewed a fresh pot of coffee.

The four couples comprised a warm, friendly group. And got along well with one another. Often, Walt and Damon agreed how lucky they were to have kids grow up like Karen and Matt. Now, they accepted Bobby and Hoot as part of the family.

The four women prepared tuna and chicken salad sandwiches for lunch. Meanwhile, the men cleaned a large area beside The House; site for this year's gathering.

Chores completed, they reassembled around the kitchen table for lunch. Afterwards, the ladies took Damon's wagon for last minute groceries and supplies. The men collected their rifles and went squirrel hunting.

Walt and Damon hiked Magusett Creek to rendezvous with Raymond. They brought sandwiches and a couple of bottles of Coca-Cola for his lunch.

Matt and Hoot drove to a large walnut and hickory grove in the river valley not far from the boathouse. A large field Damon owned bordered the copse on the west side. This year, Raymond planted it in corn.

Each took his respective place. Sitting on the dark soil beneath the tall hardwoods. Backs against rough bark. Watching and listening in the silence. For nuts or chips to fall. A branch or twig to snap. Or a fox squirrel to stand and scold them for interrupting his solitude.

Matt lit two cigarettes, passed one to Hoot. Savored the taste of nicotine blending with spearmint gum popped into his mouth at the car. Over the next three hours they talked little, and in hushed voices.

Mostly, they sat in the quiet and enjoyed the comforting peacefulness of the woods. A slight breeze picked up, and brought to them the dirt fresh smell of river and farmland. Dry leaves tossed around the ground like bits of brown, rustling paper.

They picked off three squirrels apiece with their rifles. And by five o'clock, skinned and gutted the harvest and headed to The House. They pulled into the drive and parked. As they stepped from the car, Hoot touched Matt's shoulder.

"Look there," he said quietly. He pointed toward the river.

Matt turned and made out the long wavy line of black dots. A vee of Canada geese going to feed. He cupped an ear, and in the distance heard the dog-yapping sounds of the flight. It moved slowly upriver, approaching the cornfield the two had left.

"That's a pretty sight...and welcome one," Matt said. He watched the formation disappear into the setting sun. "Won't be long now!"

Behind them, other voices rang. They spun to see Raymond, Walt and Damon approach from the creek bed. Each carried plastic bags containing fresh squirrel portions.

"Looks like we have something for the larder," said the general. "How many you boys get?"

"Six," Hoot replied. "You?"

"Eight," answered Damon. "Fair for an afternoon's hunt. Of course, Raymond collected three before we joined him!"

That evening, they dined on fried chicken, mashed potatoes and gravy, biscuits, Cole slaw and pecan pie. Later, Damon lit the first fire of the season. They sat around the living room talking and watching television. The two older women rising occasionally to peek at the cooking squirrels.

The game stewed in a sweet, hickory and brown sugar barbecue sauce common around Huntsdale. It scored as the doctor's favorite squirrel dish. And when meat fell from the bone with steamy succulence, it was easy to understand why.

Most of Huntsdale, typically, attended the next day's festivities. Slightly cooler temperatures blessed the congregation, and a slight overcast hinted rain might be forthcoming.

Also, typically, most menfolk overate. A few...Matt and Hoot among them...got slightly tipsy on beer by day's end. Still, the event passed joyfully and too quickly for most.

And when the last family bid farewell, the four hosting couples returned to The House and collapsed in exhaustion. On chairs, on couches, and, in Matt's and Hoot's cases, on the living room floor.

Fall Festival, 1956, like those preceding, marked another memorable, happy event for Karen and Matt. Ending too soon, as always. On Sunday, they returned to New Haven in the blissful rain, and that evening Matt flew to New York.

Although it marked the start of October...his birthday and favorite of all months...Matt did not look forward to Monday. He felt the slap of loneliness the minute he walked into the dark apartment.

October sped as quickly as it arrived, heralding his birthday, and a remarkable hunting season. Remarkable, since the Paginaw River roiled ten feet below its normal stage.

Matt and Karen enjoyed Thanksgiving dinner with Hoot and Bobby, and laid plans for spending Christmas together. The four decided on an entire week off, and reserved rooms at a Vermont ski lodge.

The week before they left, Matt returned to his office from Christmas shopping. His staff waited in the outer office near Dot Weymoth's desk. Also gathered there were the four Triad partners.

"What's this all about?" Matt asked, smiling. He set his bags of packages on a coffee table to one side, and noticed three buckets of ice with towel-wrapped champagne bottles protruding. He removed his overcoat, hung it in the closet, and stood before the silent group.

Greer hoisted a bottle from its holder, wrapped the towel around its neck and loosened the cork. Dot passed out champagne glasses.

"We just heard the news, Matt," Greer beamed. He filled a glass and handed it to his dazed boss. "Triad's commercials earned a COCA Award from the Council Of Creative Arts!"

"We consider that worth celebrating," said Bob Griffith, clapping his shoulder. "We came up to tell you folks you've doing one hell of a job! Congratulations."

When Thursday evening arrived, Matt boarded the familiar Triad flight for Hartford, he couldn't stop smiling. An exceptional week passed, following a noteworthy hunting season, and capping an extraordinary business year.

Even better, he looked forward to the week ahead in Vermont with Karen, Bobby and Hoot. Indeed, he had a lot for which to be thankful... and he recognized that fact. He also acknowledged within that a more promising year loomed ahead.

When the airliner lifted from La Guardia's runway, he loosened his seatbelt, lit a cigarette and leaned back.

The Christmas lights of New York fell away beneath the aircraft, then disappeared in wispy clouds drifting past the window.

"Good-bye, Big City," he whispered aloud through his reflection in the window. "See you in 1957!"

Chapter 19

Matthew Corley Durham

IN NOVEMBER'S ELECTION, DWIGHT D. Eisenhower easily defeated Adlai Stevenson. Garnering a second term as President. And winning nearly fifty-eight percent of the vote. Ike unveiled 1957 with a triumphant State of the Union report. He reported the economy perking, trailing two eras of war.

Senator Joseph McCarthy began his Army-McCarthy hearings three years hence. He ended up discredited, then censured by the U. S. Senate. And died during late spring.

Polio vaccinations were commonplace throughout elementary schools nationwide. Publicity focused on Americans confined to iron lungs. Which increased the numbers of youngsters standing in lines, and receiving orange streaks of iodine and quick, fairly painless inoculations. Bobby Gibson's New Haven Junior High seventh graders stood among the first receiving shots.

"Around The World In Eighty Days" earned an Oscar for Best Picture. Even though Matt, Hoot and Eddie thought "Giant" the hands-down winner.

Durham, Gibson & Bauer opened the new year on an extremely happy note. The majority of its clients...like most late Fifties businesses... chalked up record sales and growth. And leaned toward increasing their advertising budgets significantly. Especially for television.

By mid-summer, Matt's New York group began specializing in television commercials. They scored four COCA Awards at the Annual Spring Convention in Los Angeles. Greer McCall hired three writer-producers to help part-time. And even after hiring them full-time three months later, he had difficulty matching the demand for DG&B advertising.

Madison Avenue became the dictum for advertising, public relations and marketing. And word spread rapidly among creative shops that some "upstarts on Broadway" were cornering television commercial production.

DG&B, in fact, produced two spots for every one canned by bigger agencies downtown in the high rent district.

And, much as he disliked doing so, Matt often passed on new business. DG&B stood firm in meeting its client commitments to Triad, Cartiff, Standish and Musgrave.

The New Haven office handled most of the print advertising. Under the scrutiny of Hoot heading creative, and Eddie directing visuals.

Their print campaigns for Triad and Conn Castings received numerous awards from the industry over the years. Creative individuals and groups alike respected and admired the work developed by DG&B. And the increased business success provided its clients.

The American Association of Advertising Agencies, or "Four-As," appointed Matt a junior officer on its advisory board. He took seriously his duties as a collaborator, legally and morally judging advertising's public image. The recent publication of several books critical of advertising led the industry to devise an internal watchdog structure. Four-As championed that cause, and emerged a powerful conscience for those stepping over the lines of credibility and taste.

Matt bumped into Lyle Bradley occasionally at New York Advertising Club meetings. The latter inquiring, "How's the little frog in the big pond?"

Matt simply replied his group stayed too busy for swimming... "because lots of new frogs were climbing on DG&B lillypads and bringing big accounts with them."

Fall Festival weekend flew past once again. On Thursday, Matt gave final blessing to ad copy he proofed. Then caught the seven-thirty Triad flight to Hartford. He arrived at the apartment shortly after nine.

Karen did not meet him at the door as she usually did. He let himself in. Then saw her across the living room, talking on the telephone in the kitchen.

"He's right here, Bobby. Just walked in. I better hang up. Can't wait to tell him!"

Matt tossed his suitcoat on the loveseat. Stood the briefcase on the floor beside it. Went into the kitchen, put his arms around his wife's waist and kissed her.

"Tell me what?"

"Wait just a minute, buster! You go in and have a seat. Then I'll tell you!"

Matt walked back into the living room. Sat in his favorite easy chair. Lit a cigarette.

Karen opened the refrigerator. Retrieved a bottle of champagne. Uncorked it, and brought the bottle and two glasses to where he sat. She handed him a glass. Filled it. Then poured hers full of bubbly liquid. She settled on the floor in front of him. Knees doubled under her.

"Okay...what's this about?" he asked.

"I saw Hal Sappington today," she said. Her face glowed mysteriously. Matt intuitively glanced at the bottle. Seeing if she'd imbibed already.

"Oh? What did he have to say? More decorating jobs?"

"No. Nothing like that. It wasn't a professional visit. At least for me."

"What do you mean, honey?"

"Quite simply, darling...you're going to be a daddy!"

"What? What?" he sputtered. He leaned forward, spilling champagne onto his knee, the chair and carpet.

He laid his right hand on her shoulder. Looked into the eyes that now sparked with happiness. Skin crinkling around them. "Are you...is he certain, Karen? I mean, positive!"

"Well, Hal's a general practitioner. Still, his specialty is obstetrics. He said the rabbit didn't stand a chance!"

"My God Almighty damn! This is incredible! It's wonderful!"

He placed their glasses on the antique marble-topped washstand beside him. Hugged her tightly.

"I love you, babe. I truly do."

"And I love you, Matt. More than anything."

He relaxed his grip. As if holding a fragile china doll. She noticed.

"I'm pregnant, Matthew Durham," Karen scolded. "Not breakable!"

He held her quietly for several minutes. The thought of fatherhood catching his spinning mind. And realizing another step taken into adulthood. Another branch sprouting on life's tree of maturity.

"When's he due?" he asked.

"Late May or early June as near as Hal can estimate. He guesses I'm pregnant by a month. And...what do you mean, 'He!'"

"You haven't acted differently."

"I haven't felt up to par the past two weeks. No morning sickness or anything like that. A little nauseous during the day."

"Honey, it's the most fantastic news ever! Can't wait to tell the folks. They don't know, do they?"

"No...only Bobby. And probably Hoot by now."

"Great. Let's wait until we're at The House telling them. I'll buy more champagne. We'll have a hell of a party!"

Matt pulled her onto his lap. They clinked glasses, and sipped the liquor when the telephone rang. Karen set her glass down. Eased from his lap and answered it.

"Hello?"

"Hi ya...little mother!" Hoot's voice on the other end boomed with excitement. Matt heard him from the living room. Stood, and went beside Karen in the kitchen.

"Congratulations, gal. Where's the old reprobate? He there yet?"

"Thanks, Hoot. Yeah, just walked in. Here he is." She passed the handset to Matt.

"Well, Houston, you're going to be an uncle!" Matt bellowed into the telephone. He clutched his wife around the middle. "At last...we'll have some kid doing the dirty work foisted on us. Putting out and collecting decoys. Cleaning birds and game. Running the boat downriver in freezing weather. It'll be nice, won't it?"

"You bet, Matthew. Hey amigo...my congratulations. I knew you two would figure what causes kids one of these days! Hell, you're like squirrels on a hot roof now. Can't understand why it took so long!"

"Good things you wait for, Hooter. You know that. Hey, what time do we pick you up tomorrow?"

"Dunno. How about eight?"

"That's fine. I need champagne for a little celebration tomorrow night. Then we can hit the road."

"Your folks don't know?"

"No. We're going to surprise them at The House."

"We won't say anything, Matthew. I promise. We're really happy for you two. We may have a kid now. Even if Bobby puts up with twenty or thirty during the day!"

Karen overheard Hoot's comment. From Matt's left shoulder she shouted: "Tell him they can rent ours from time to time!"

Matt relayed the message. Hoot responded with a loud guffaw. Then they hung up.

The couple returned to the living room. Matt refilling their glasses. Karen reclaimed her position on his lap. They sat that way for another hour before going to bed.

While she brushed her teeth, Matt smiled to himself. Thinking of having a son...or daughter for that matter...he really didn't care. His craving for Karen suddenly flooded. His heart fluttering, as if brushed by butterfly wings.

When she came to bed, he rolled over, pulling her taut against him. He kissed her hotly, openly, on the lips. Karen felt his readiness against her. Eased up her nightgown. They joined in the still darkness of the bedroom.

At exactly eight o'clock, they gathered Hoot and Bobby and their travel belongings into the Buick. Stopping briefly for chilled champagne at a nearby liquor store. Then heading for Huntsdale, The House, and Fall Festival. Sharing a thermos of coffee along the way.

Unlike the previous year, heavy and regular rainfalls dominated this one. Leaves on the ride along the Paginaw River already flashed crimson, orange and vivid gold.

The Durhams and Forsythes drove down the day before. Hearing tires crunch on gravel, they gathered at the front porch. Matt nosed the Buick into the semicircle drive behind his father's.

The two couples climbed out, unloaded the car, then went into the kitchen. Evelyn fixed Eggs Benedict, while Claire grilled breakfast steaks. When they gathered around the breakfast table, Matt and Karen relayed the news.

"That's wonderful, kids," said Doctor Forsythe. He hugged his daughter, and pumped Matt's hand.

"I'll live to be a grandfather after all," said Walt. He placed his hand warmly on his son's shoulder.

The teary-eyed mothers contented themselves hugging one other.

"I know the ticket to celebrate!" said Damon. He snapped his fingers as the idea popped in his head. "Peaches and champagne!"

He kept three or four bottles of champagne in the back of the refrigerator. Retrieved two bottles of pink. Then he placed peach halves in goblets, pouring bubbly over them.

The four couples raised their glasses in a toast. Drank and consumed their peaches. Damon refilled the glasses as Evelyn and Claire served the eggs, cottage fries and English muffins with fresh preserves. Matt fetched the champagne they brought. He opened one bottle, and chilled the rest.

After breakfast, the group sat in the living room and talked. The women prepared dishes to take to the Festival feast. The four men drove to the Paginaw in Damon's stationwagon. They readied the boat, and motored to the blind to see about necessary repairs.

The hideout withstood the torrents occurring over summer. And required only Johnson grass and smartweed camouflage to ready it for hunting.

By late afternoon, they motored upriver. The four returned the boat to its roost in the shed. Then went to find Raymond Daley. One of his sons returned home on leave from the army. And the four figured on joining them for a few hours of squirrel hunting before dusk.

They spread through the woods behind Raymond's place. And when the squirrels searched for water and food, ambushed a dozen. These, Raymond marinated overnight and barbecued for the feast the next day.

Fall Festival arrived exuberant as ever. This year, made even more joyous with news of Karen and Matt expecting a child. All of Huntsdale seemed packed in The House's shady side-yard. Partaking of delicious victuals heaped in dishes, platters and bowls on long, narrow serving tables. And stopping to wish the younger Durhams every happiness.

When Matt and Walt joined the menfolk in the walnut grove for spiked cider, he good-naturedly accepted chiding.

"Chances are, Matt, you'll have a pretty little girl or a 'sissy' boy who doesn't like hunting and fishing," one of the locals joked.

"The more I've considered fatherhood...the more it doesn't matter if we have a boy or girl," he answered. "I do know, however, no boy of mine will be a sissy. His grandfather would tan his butt. And he'll like hunting and fishing. That's part of Durham heritage...passed from generation to generation. Part of the genes."

"Well Matt...what if it's a little girl?" asked Raymond.

"Having four hairy-legged boys, you wouldn't know the answer to that one, would you? Well, Raymond, it's this way. Little girls love their daddies!"

Matt swigged the biting cider as those surrounding enjoyed a hearty laugh.

October ushered exceedingly crisp temperatures. And a new sense of fear and questioning. On the fourth of the month, the Soviet Union launched "Sputnik." The first earth-orbiting satellite created by man carried more than mortal aspirations on its voyage. It confirmed that isolation and security no longer could exist anywhere on the planet.

Autumn's radiant golds, oranges and reds faded to sienna. Matt witnessed a twenty-seventh birthday flashing past. Pulling the hunting season, Thanksgiving and Christmas along as if towed by time's chariot. New Years arrived at midnight. And seemingly, when the last chime fell silent, spring suddenly called from outside the apartment windows.

Frigid, rain-soaked, nasty temperatures marked the beginnings of 1958. More and more, Matt dreaded leaving Karen and returning to New York. Her beauty compounded by pregnancy's promise.

Interminable cold...highlighted by whistling winds morning through evening...kept him prisoner in the small, lonely apartment. When buds burst in the park across Fifth Avenue...and robins appeared on front lawns...he stood ready for summer. Even knowing, down deep, he'd be cussing the heat in two months.

Doctor Hal Sappington performed admirably predicting when Karen would give birth. On May 29, Matthew Corley Durham...named to honor the departed judge...had his pink bare fanny smacked, and came wide-mouthed into the world.

From the first, he became Corley. Doted over by both sets of grandparents. Although Hoot became the worst offender.

Corley proved an exceptionally even-natured baby. He slept through the two o'clock feeding after the third night. Usually awakening and babbling to himself for an hour before raising Cain for human attention.

Hoot rough-housed with Corley on the floor on nights when Matt was gone and he and Bobby dropped by. Often, changing diapers and volunteering to baby-sit so the two women could shop or see a movie, or so Karen could get away for a few hours.

Toward the end of June, Matt unexpectedly arrived at the apartment Thursday afternoon. He announced to Karen they were going house hunting. Then arranged for his and her folks to watch Corley.

He drove to his folks' home...cradling the baby in one arm, diaper bag and grocery sack full of formula in the other...and strode inside while Karen waited. When he returned, she expressed shock over what was happening...and so quickly.

"I can't believe we're buying a house!" she exclaimed. The quizzical look masked her face as he pulled from the curb. "I mean...isn't this sort of sudden? You haven't mentioned it before now!"

"I guess," he replied. "Hoot mentioned a house in Wellham Park. Sounds like what we want. I thought we'd go by and look. Maybe shop around."

"Wellham Park? Those homes are expensive, aren't they?"

"No, not really. It's an older, more established community. Lots of younger families moving in. Some of the houses need fixing up. Which is your specialty."

Wellham Park consisted of twenty-five homes. Built on ten acres of ground that in the early 1800s formed the private Wellham hunting and riding club. An enterprising grandson inherited the Park. And sliced it into one and two-acre portions. In the early 1900s, New Haven's aristocracy built homes there.

The moment they pulled in front of thirty-two Lockesley, each recognized it **was** the home he and she dreamed of owning. Matt knew from within that somehow, he would afford this property.

Wellham Park was a fitting name for the community. Only enough trees fell to place houses here and there. From the street, thirty-two was barely visible. Perched atop a slight rise, a hundred and fifty feet away. Passersby caught glimpses of the structure through the abundant growth of elms, maples and oaks in the front yard.

Matt eased the Buick onto a wide drive leading to one side of the house. Karen sighed rapturously as they approached and viewed the complete structure.

It was a medium-sized two story. White frame, and colonial in architecture. Its structure bore strong resemblance to The House. Which immediately appealed to them. The realtor parked his car in front of theirs. Parallel to the two-car garage that opened into the basement level. He came striding, smiling, to their auto. His hand jutted in front.

Matt shook with the man. Introduced Karen. And they walked to the front door to begin touring.

The conviction each felt individually over finding the home they wanted...and so quickly...strengthened when the front door opened. Before them stretched a mammoth living room, with built-in bookshelves and fireplace at one end. French doors on the other side opened onto a large screened porch.

In between, a wide oak staircase led to the second floor. Pausing midway and turning right from a five foot by five foot landing. Hanging high above the staircase was a crystal chandelier that, swore the real estate agent, dated the house's construction to 1902.

Around the corner from the stairway opened a formal dining room, featuring built-in corner china hutches and a mirrored butler's pantry. Another set of French doors led to the screened porch off this room. Further to the left appeared the kitchen and a good-sized half bathroom.

The second floor boasted four spacious bedrooms, three full baths, several walk-in cedar-lined closets and storage areas. Above that, a floored attic ran the length of the house, providing ample storage and room for adding on should one desire.

As far as Matt and Karen cared, the tour could have ended slightly beyond the front door. It was then she clutched his hand. Squeezed it. And silently transmitted her desire to own number thirty-two.

One generation of a New Haven family lived in the house since its construction. The widower father passed away a few months back. His children, situated in the Midwest with families of their own, put it on the market.

When the realtor announced the heirs sought thirty thousand, Matt and Karen exchanged troubled glances. Noting their concern, he added: "They'll probably accept twenty-five. After all, it needs some work and tender loving care."

Without speaking, the two again traded looks. This time beaming. Matt said excitedly, "We'll take it!"

On Friday, they signed the mortgage papers. That night, they provided their parents, Bobby and Hoot guided tours. With champagne afterwards.

"It's lovely, dear," Evelyn said to her daughter. "You two will love the Park. It's so quiet. We have friends nearby. So, you'll be seeing plenty of us."

"Us, too," agreed Walt, from his sitting position on the bottom stair. He rode Corley on his knee. "I begrudge you this place, Matt. We've kept our eyes open for a house like this one...and in Wellham Park."

"Dad...I can't believe that," replied Matt, refilling the glasses. "You're the one who said our house had everything you wanted. You had it built that way."

"Matt's right, dear," scolded Claire. "As I recall, you wouldn't leave the poor contractor alone. Rumor has it he may have started World War Two to get you out from under foot!"

Matt renewed the apartment lease through July. That way, the house stood empty while Karen wove her decorating magic. In only days, painters, carpenters, floor sanders and wallpaper hangers lined up to perform various chores.

When Matt pulled from the driveway for Hartford and his return flight, he left Karen busily listing items for handling for the next day. Starting with a trip to her favorite furniture store, and taking advantage of her Peck & Peck discount.

Evelyn and Claire stopped daily to watch Corley while Karen went about her duties or chatted over coffee.

"Honey...you'll need someone keeping an eye on Corley if you return to Peck & Peck," her mother said one day as they scrutinized fabric for curtains and bedspreads.

"I have a friend moving to Boston. She's letting her housekeeper go. An older woman. Around mid-fifties, I'd guess. Nearly raised my friend's three kids. She could help take the burden off running a home, a business, and raising Corley. What do you say?"

"Gee, mom...I don't know. I do love my work. And the money comes in handy. Still, I planned on being with Corley full-time until nursery school."

"Well, honey. Why not work half days at Peck & Peck? That would be ideal."

"Yes, I suppose you're right. I could work mornings. Spend the rest of the day here with Corley. I'll discuss it with Matt when he calls tonight."

"Fine, dear. And the housekeeper?"

"That too, mom. Tell her we're interested if she is."

Matt fixed an evening nightcap, when the telephone rang. Karen explained her decision about the housekeeper, working, and raising Corley.

"If you still want to work honey, that's fine with me. I thought you were staying home with Corley until he starts school."

"I was at first, Matt. Peck & Peck means a lot to me. Not that Corley doesn't."

"I know, Karen. Sure...if you think this gal is okay it's fine with me. Don't think you have to work because we need money."

"I don't, darling. It's just that giving up a career I'm good at...and enjoy immensely...would leave a terrible hole. One I wonder if even Corley could fill. Is that too terrible?"

"No, sweetheart. I understand. Look at me! Hell, I'm working in New York while my family's miles away! No...if it's that important, then do it!"

Karen met the housekeeper her mother recommended. And loved her at once. Anne Westfield had been born in New Haven in 1907. Married a carpenter she fell in love with in high school. Always dreamed of a home and children. That world collapsed when he died during World War Two. She kept house for one of New Haven's Grande dames part-time. When the War Department reported her husband dead, she started working full-time. Anne's first and only job had been with friends of Claire Forsythe's. And she did, indeed, watch after children, house, and contents with the eye of a peregrine.

"I'll tell you, honey...he's a little corker!" the housekeeper said. She bounced Corley on her knee. In return received wide, toothless grins. And a multitude of joyous burbles.

"He'll grow into a ladies' man. Got your eyes and looks. Must have your husband's complexion. Yep...a corker alright!"

Matt liked Mrs. Westfield at first sight, too. Thought of her as a modern day flapper. Short, graying hair bobbed in the fashion of that time. Long, ebony cigarette holder dangling from the corner of her mouth.

When she wasn't changing, scrubbing or polishing, she chain-smoked the new filtered cigarettes entering the market. And looked dourly at Matt when he stoked a Lucky Strike.

"My husband Carl smoked those," Anne spat. "Nearly coughed his fool head off. Filtered ones are okay. Not much taste...but mild. And they keep most of the crap out of your lungs."

She lit a fresh smoke from one almost burning into the charred holder. "Yessiree. If you have to smoke...oughta switch to these!"

"Well...thanks for your concern, Mrs. Westfield," Matt replied, overly gracious. "I'm quitting soon, anyway. Up to two packs now. Mornings I croak like a bullfrog."

Lately, Matt returned to New Haven Friday nights rather than Thursdays. He spent most evenings in New York entertaining clients. Even after a difficult day at the office...or in a studio scripting or filming...something about the brightly lit razzle-dazzle city instantly perked him. It pulsated with its own life. There were so many things to do...so many mysteries to solve...he couldn't get enough.

"New York offers everything you could ever want," he said one day to Hoot. "People. Restaurants. Shops. Entertainment. Work. Action. Magic. Yeah...it has magic."

Matt stared blankly as his mind structured words.

"There's something different to do every minute. Even different ways of doing things you've done all your life."

Hoot worried over Matt's infatuation with the place. He didn't say so. And much of the time regretted a hesitancy to do so. He figured his friend was going through a phase. Like a child with a new toy.

He'd grow out of it when the luster wore off. And the ugly side exposed itself. Then again, Matt didn't hit the New Haven office on Fridays anymore.

Triad Airlines enjoyed success introducing flights to major American cities. Now, it planned international operations. With this in mind, Bob Griffith called Walt Durham. His company ordered several of the innovative Cometliner 660s. This latest model seated forty more passengers than the original.

Not only that, Triad hired Jug Hale as Corporate Flight Maintenance Director. "Repair Head," the ex-pilot termed his new duties. He and his staff of sixty service personnel stayed busy at the large repair facility near the Boston Airport.

Matt and Karen were happy for Jug. Even took him for a celebration dinner and night on the town on learning of his new career.

"You'd better treat me with greater respect, young plebe," Jug threatened Matt. He tried to emulate a grave look of concern as he hugged Karen around the waist. Fighting to keep from erupting in laughter. "I'm now a big-wheel executive with one of your major clients. Isn't that right, little sister?"

They enjoyed the evening immensely. Matt was glad he'd see more of his pledge father when the big man visited New York on business.

Summer scorched slowly into fall. By late September, Matt looked forward to the annual festival more than ever. Besides a few long weekends, he and Karen had not vacationed together for nearly a year.

He planned to leave the office the last week of the month. Spend some days in New Haven piddling around in the yard. Raking leaves and playing with Corley. Then driving to Huntsdale for the yearly event.

With that thought entrenched in his spent mind, he boarded the six-thirty Triad flight to Hartford. And drove home in record time, filled with the excitement and anticipation of a restful week ahead.

When he steered onto the private blacktop road that wound around the houses nestled in the thick woods that made up Wellham Park, he smiled and hummed with the radio. The lights were on in the living room and upstairs.

Two gaslights illuminated the garage area turnaround.

He got out, raised the garage door, and pulled inside. Then he closed the door and dashed up the basement steps. Near the top, the door swung open. Karen rushed to greet him.

He kissed and hugged her. Then walked to the kitchen where Mrs. Westfield gave Corley his evening bottle. Matt bent and kissed the infant on his tousled blond head.

"Hi, tiger," he said. He turned to smile in Mrs. Westfield's face. "Hi Annie. How's tricks?"

Karen prepared drinks. Handed one to each of them. Sour mash bourbon and water for Matt. White wine for herself and Mrs. Westfield.

The kitchen had been Karen's favorite room to decorate. She scored a marvelous piece of work. Over the years, massive oak beams crisscrossing the ceiling had got painted white. She had these stripped, and returned to a natural burnished luster. In contrast to the flat white of the plaster ceiling.

She wallpapered the enclosure in bright yellow, green and orange-flowered paper. Used glossy white paint on the chair rail, baseboard, cove molding and trim.

She also returned a natural sheen to the light oak cabinets. As well as countertops around the cooking and cleaning areas, and serving bar opening into the dining room. The most stunning element of the kitchen was its authentic brick floor. Handmade, kiln-fired clay rectangles laid ornately in herringbone fashion. Over the course of sixty years, bare feet padded it smooth treading across it.

The full effect created a sunshiny, airy and happy spot. A welcome nook for morning coffee around a butcher block table. Or leaning against cabinets having a final nightcap evenings.

Karen decorated the rest of the house in her favorite autumn colors. A fondness Matt naturally shared. She left the interior as original as possible. Tastefully blending antiques with more modern pieces and quality reproductions.

Interminglings of logistically placed soft pile carpeting, throw and oriental rugs further complemented the various rooms' decors.

Mrs. Westfield proved invaluable to Karen in decorating the house. Over the course of the renovations, the two women shared many laughs, likes and dislikes, and innumerable cups of coffee.

They became even closer over the months. It heartened Matt knowing Karen had someone sharing the house in his absence. Anne planned to bus to Boston and visit relatives while the Durhams attended Fall Festival.

"You enjoy yourselves now. I'll see you Sunday afternoon," she said. Anne waved the three off before calling her cab for the bus depot. "Don't you spoil my little scalawag with sweets during your party! And be sure he eats his vegetables."

"Yes, we will, Anne. I promise," Karen said. She held Corley on her lap and waved as Matt pulled down the driveway. "You have fun yourself."

Their car brimmed with a bassinet, stroller and groceries in the backseat. So Hoot and Bobby trailed the three to Huntsdale and The House. Once there, Karen's old crib mysteriously appeared at the foot of the bed in their room.

Most of Corley's first Fall Festival found him passing from lap to lap. With numerous chin chuckings. And Karen watching intently from nearby.

Finally, the participants gathered the last paper plates and napkins and jammed them into trashbags. Then they folded the tables and stacked them for hauling to the church. Chores completed, the four couples gathered inside to recount another enjoyable gathering. And put an exhausted Corley to bed.

Later that evening, Matt, Karen, Bobby and Hoot gathered on the front porch. They enjoyed the cool quiet, and final cup of coffee. And momentarily, they were at Halen's Lake enjoying one of many Indian summer evenings shared years ago.

"These will be the most cherished years of my life, Matthew," Hoot said in hushed tones. Hoping not to stir the dark quiet. Bobby's head nestled his shoulder as they sat on the porch's top step. "I can never repay you for introducing me to this place. This woman. These happy times."

"No repayment necessary, partner," responded Matt. He and Karen sat in the darkness on the porch swing. "Nice to have close friends to share times."

Karen's head rested on his shoulder. Now, she squeezed his arm as silence wrapped them again. Beyond the porch, cicadas chirred in trees surrounding The House. A calf bleated somewhere in the distance below. And Whippoorwills trilled through the still night along the Paginaw River.

Chapter 20

Hillary Engineering

T HE FIFTIES...EXCITING, FULFILLING YEARS FOR Matt and Karen, Hoot and Bobby...closed busily. Both Durham, Gibson and Bauer offices waded into the beginnings of the Sixties' electronic decade.

During 1960, DG&B-New York captured four Council Of Creative Arts (COCA) Awards for television commercials. DG&B-New Haven collected three print campaign plaques. Between the two, DG&B fast became one of the sought-after agencies in advertising.

In January 1961, one of the worst snowstorms in history plummeted the East Coast. It began during President John F. Kennedy's January inauguration, and extended intermittently into February. In its wake, a ten-inch blanket of white stretched from Maine to Virginia.

It shut off New York, so Matt worked via telephone from New Haven. He soon suffered cabin fever and anxiety over work needing doing in the city. And drove Hoot and Eddie crazy with his irritableness.

"For Christ's sakes Matt, ease up, please!" demanded Hoot one Monday morning. The other recently raked several copywriters and illustrators for typos inadvertently slipping through and appearing in a print ad.

"Granted, it's a page in Time," Hoot continued. "Still, the misspelling doesn't change the message meaning. It's no big deal."

"The hell it isn't, Hoot!" came the angry reply. "Damn it, that's unprofessional work. It reflects on all of us!"

Matt slammed shut his briefcase. Without another word, stormed from the conference room. He grabbed his overcoat from the closet and walked from the office.

Stepping off the elevator in the parking garage, the lower level chill soaked his overcoat, cooling him. He felt embarrassed over the scene with Hoot. He walked to his new Buick, tossed the briefcase into the backseat and climbed in.

Matt sat for a moment in silence.

Then, aloud: "Ah, shit!"

He pivoted out, went to the elevator, and back to the office. Hoot stood at Olivia Park's desk. Talking with the attractive woman. When Matt reappeared, Hoot walked forward. Hand outstretched. Matt apologized.

"Sorry, Hooter. This damned weather. Flights grounded. The work I've got hanging in New York. Right now, I should be screening commercials with Greer and his people."

"I know, Matthew. Sometimes, we just do what we can."

Ollie brought them coffee, and they went into Matt's office. After sticking his head into the copywriters' offices to say he was sorry.

"You know, Hoot, Karen's got an appointment with Hal Sappington this afternoon. She's feeling sluggish lately. Maybe I'll ask him to check me out. I've been antsy. And haven't had a thorough physical since the military."

"Might not hurt, Matt. Hell, I haven't been to a doctor since Korea either!"

"Yeah...think I'll call and see what he says."

Hoot stood, walked to his friend. Put his hand on the other's shoulder.

"Quitting smoking turned us into bears, pal," he said. "Bobby and I have argued more since January First than in six years of marriage."

"Same with Karen and me. We've grown used to the commuting. However, she likes it less and less. Just isn't enough space in two days for three of us to do what we want. Hell, it takes Saturday to slow me down...and I leave Sunday!"

Hoot sat on the edge of Matt's desk. His voice suddenly grew softer and serious.

"Matthew, if New York's wedging between you and Karen...then pull out. It's not worth it. The Triad guys would understand. Now you've got it set up, let Greer and the others run the shop."

"I've thought about it, Hoot. Honestly I have," Matt looked up, eyes pleading for understanding. "I can't quit. I love it. New Haven is a rest home compared to New York! I feel lethargic. Like I'm not doing much. Everything moving in slow motion."

"Well, amigo...you know what's best. I won't meddle. It's just I'd hate seeing you and Karen run aground."

"So would I, Hoot. Believe me."

Karen had booked a two o'clock appointment with Doctor Sappington. Matt arranged a physical for the same time. Figuring he'd take blood tests, x-rays, urinalysis and an EKG during her examination.

He had never met the doctor before. And the efficient manner in which the handsome young practitioner dispatched nurses performing the duties impressed him. The last nurse drawing blood told him the doctor would provide a prognosis within the hour.

After forty-five minutes of reading x-rays, mixing blood sample and evaluating EKG printouts, the two men met in Hal's office.

Matt straightened his tie when the doctor entered. Clipboard under his left arm. Stethoscope dangling around his neck. Embodying professionalism in his white cotton lab coat. He offered his hand.

"Matt, I'm Hal Sappington. Good meeting you."

"Nice meeting you, doctor," Matt replied. He returned a firm clench.

Hal leaned against the edge of his desk. Indicated for Matt to sit in front of him. He glanced at the clipboard. Flipping through sheets of paper and printouts.

"Overall, you're in fine shape, Matt," the doctor said. "I see you suffered serious injury to your right shoulder in high school. Ever bother you?"

"No, not really. Once in a while...if it's raining or damp. Aches a bit. That's all."

"Good. And I hear from Karen you've quit cigarettes."

"Yes. My partner and I stopped on New Year's Eve."

"That's good, too. X-rays show clear lungs. That'll keep 'em that way."

Hal glanced through the pages again. Stretched the EKG printout at arm's length. Folded it, accordion-style, on the clipboard.

"Well Matt...like I said, everything looks fine. Do you have any complaints?"

"Not really, Doc. It's been a while. Thought I'd check."

"Okay, Matt. It's been a pleasure." The physician stood, again held out his hand. "Karen's waiting outside. I think she's got good news for you."

"Oh...okay. Tell me Doc. Do people always get edgy when they stop smoking?"

"You bet. Notoriously! It's lack of nicotine in the blood. Tell you what, cut back on coffee and it'll help. Caffeine makes the effects of quitting even worse. And coffee typically is part of the habit. Hang in there until your system flushes. In a few months, you won't think about smoking."

"All right...thanks," Matt said. He shook Hal's hand and walked into the waiting room. Karen sat there. She rose to greet him. A beautiful smile lighting her face.

"Okay Chessie cat...why are you beaming?" he asked.

"Hal tells me you're healthy," came the reply.

"Sure. I knew that before coming here...more or less. Wanted him to tell me why I'm such a grouch."

"He couldn't?"

"Oh, sure. It's being off smokes. At least he thinks that. Anyway...I'll live with it. How about you? Is it irregularity?" he joked.

"In a way, wise ass!" she poked his arm playfully. Then took it in hers. "I've missed a few periods. Hal confirms it. I'm pregnant again!"

He stopped in his tracks. Took her shoulders in his hands. Looked into the smiling upturned face. His eyes wide. "Really! Again? You're kidding!"

"Nope. Corley will have a little playmate."

Matt hugged her to him. Kissed the top of her head.

"Honey, that's great. That's wonderful."

He held her at arm's length as the elevator door opened for them to enter.

"I'm really happy. And lucky I married you. I love you, Karen."

"And I love you...Matthew Durham."

Doctor Sappington estimated the baby's arrival in October or November. Which gladdened Matt and Karen, knowing she wouldn't be too uncomfortable during steamy summer months. He secretly hoped the baby would be born on his birthday.

Spring moved into the New England area. Greenery sprouted where weeks before packed twenty inches of soot-stained snow. Matt's humor and patience returned. Although the fresh year's blooming brought more accounts seeking his agency to represent them.

On the East Coast, word of mouth trails a successful agency like the wake of a small boat. It spreads wider as recognition increases. The growing number of firms craving DG&B services flattered Matt. And frustrated him. Inherently, he found it almost impossible to turn away business.

Matt already leased the entire sixteenth floor of Triad's office building. And finding space for additional employees continually occupied his mind. His staff had grown to twenty.

The New Haven operation faced a similar situation. Additional work meant hiring more employees. And finding more work space.

Hoot and Eddie sought to expand their operations. However, they worried about overstepping the boundaries of accepting and holding additional accounts.

The three met in April. Over two days...sequestered in the New Haven conference room...they outlined the near and long-term growth strategies for DG&B.

New Haven produced the bulk of print advertising, printed at Hoot's father's plant in Middletown. They opted for locating office spaces in Hartford, and setting up a new branch headed by Eddie.

He long wanted to live in Hartford. Now, the opportunity to do so arose. Which left Hoot and current staff members running the New Haven office. And enabling the organization to create another profit center in the growing and lucrative New Haven, Hartford and Boston triangle.

Matt searched office space in earnest on Madison Avenue. Closer to the heartbeat of New York's creative district. And quickly found two vacant floors at a prestigious two hundred address.

Within two weeks, DG&B-New York moved desks, equipment and people into new offices. Gearing itself to gaining new accounts.

In early June, Frank Musgrave called Matt. He owned and presided over Musgrave Manufacturing. It fared as a favorite account of Matt's. Mainly because company principals insisted the agency receive carte blanche creative, marketing and public relations authority. Musgrave Manufacturing appreciated and respected DG&B's strengths.

In return, DG&B provided Musgrave Manufacturing with consistent award-winning campaigns and outstanding sales histories.

Dot Weymoth buzzed Matt that Frank waited on the telephone. He answered at once.

"Frank? Matt here. How are you?"

"Fine, Matt. And you?"

"Pulling hair...but that's typical. What can we do for Musgrave Manufacturing?"

"It's what I can do for you, Matt. Or to you. Got someone for you to meet. You free for dinner this Thursday...the eighth?"

"Let me check, Frank." Matt thumbed ahead on his desk calendar. "Sure, looks okay. Can you tell who I'm meeting?"

"You bet, pal," the other replied excitedly. "Ever heard of Hillary Engineering?"

"Sure...they're big! Do business all over the world. Why do you need me?"

"I'll tell you, Matt..." Frank fell silent for a moment, underscoring the conversation's importance. "Hillary is disenchanted with its agency. Looking for a service-oriented group. You know any that fill the bill?"

Matt whistled through his teeth. His spine tingled with heady excitement. Or fear.

"I don't know if we could handle someone that big, Frank. I just don't know. Sure would like to meet 'em, though. For the hell of it. And ego, I suppose."

"Bullshit, Matt! You can do it. You've talked of hiring more people. And your second floor will accommodate them. Have you forgotten the open house we came to...and the personal tour?"

"Okay, Frank, okay. I'll meet Hillary. Honestly, I appreciate the reference. I'm gun-shy over such a big account."

"I knew you'd find balls and go for it, Matt. I already told them 'yes.' By the way, it's Keith Hillary. He's the head knocker. How about that?"

"Damn! That's incredible! Again, thanks."

"You've done us lots of good turns, Matt. Time to repay long hours and hurry-up jobs. All outstanding, by the way."

Frank paused for a moment, Matt heard him light a cigarette, then his client continued.

"Besides, Hillary purchased an entire fleet of earth-moving equipment. Needs it for a project in Italy. It'll keep us in the black for years. And he wouldn't know about our capabilities if not for your promotions. I'm just spreading the wealth around! Listen...got to go, Matt. Meet at Sarni's at eight...okay?"

"You got it, Frank. Thanks again."

He cradled the handset. Head spinning. Eager to call Hoot with the news.

"Funny thing," he thought, dialing. "Used to be I'd share the good news first with Karen." He felt a pang of guilt. Vowed he'd call her next.

Hoot and Eddie delighted over the news. Greer McCall heard their excited voices over the telephone as he walked into Matt's office.

"You wanted me, chief?"

Matt motioned for Greer to sit. Then ended the conversation with the others.

"Keep it under your hat, Greer. I wanted you to know we've got a shot at Hillary Engineering."

"Jesus!" came the reply. "The Hillary Engineering?"

"Yes. Learned a few minutes ago."

"Goddamn, Matt! They're huge. We'd need to hire half of Madison Avenue to do their sales literature!"

"Certainly would be worth it...right?"

"Oh hell yes! I'm speechless."

"I wanted you to know, and prepare yourself. I'm dining with Keith Hillary and Frank Musgrave Thursday evening. I'll learn the program then."

"I can't wait to hear, Matt. A chance at landing that account is exciting enough. Wow! What a compliment!"

"Yeah...that's how I feel. Guess we're a recognized agency."

When Greer left his office, Matt checked his watch. Calculated Karen was at work. Dialed the number.

Her secretary greeted him cheerfully. Then put him on hold while she fetched Karen. In a moment, he heard the soft voice.

"Hello, Matt?"

"Hi sweetheart. Listen...wanted you to know we have a shot at landing one of the biggest accounts ever. Hillary Engineering. I'm dining with the owner and Frank Musgrave on Thursday. What do you think?"

For milliseconds, she hung silent. Long enough he intuitively knew what would follow.

"Matt...I thought you had more business now than you could handle. That's why you gave up Fridays here. Does this mean even less of you?"

"No, honey. Not necessarily. What a plum if we snag Hillary Engineering! Aren't you excited for us?"

"Yes, Matt, certainly," she said. He knew the indifferent tone meant she wasn't. "Listen...I was out the door when you called. Anne has shopping to do. I'm watching Corley. Bye, darling."

Matt replaced the handset. Felt the pit of his stomach lurch roller coaster fashion. He leaned back in the chair. Wished he had a cigarette.

Wall-to-wall humanity jammed Sarni's when he entered precisely at eight o'clock. He scanned the dimly lit, candle-scented, smoke-fogged dining room. Past the maitre d'hotel he spotted Frank Musgrave at a table with several others. Frank waved to attract his attention.

"That table expects me," he said. He brushed past the major domo and to where they sat. Approaching, he distinguished four men and a woman. And assumed, correctly, Keith Hillary was the man on Frank's right. They rose to greet him. Keith spoke first.

"Matt Durham...glad to finally meet you. I'm Keith Hillary." The man's stature surprised Matt as he stood shaking hands. He was nearly six feet tall. And guessed Keith at six-five or six.

"Nice to meet you Mr. Hillary," Matt said. He returned a firm grip.

"Call me Keith...please. I also want you to meet my right hand...and daughter...Suzanne. Suzanne Whittier."

Matt took the graceful hand offered. Noticed long, immaculately cared-for nails. Felt softness, yet strength, in her handshake.

"Very nice meeting you, Matt," came the low, mellow voice.

"My pleasure, Suzanne," he replied. He looked into light blue eyes that contrasted with raven hair. Feeling nearly the same shock as when he first met Eddie Bauer.

He hadn't noticed her when he approached the table. More intent on superficially categorizing Keith. Now he stood, struck speechless by a sudden onslaught of unleashed beauty.

Suzanne stood tall like her father. And the gown she wore outlined a well-toned, athletic figure. He didn't release her hand until Keith introduced him to the two other men. Vice presidents of construction and marketing. He shook their hands, also.

Whether he imagined it or not, Matt thought he noticed her reluctance to surrender his hand.

"Well, Matt...I understand Frank filled you in on our predicament," Keith said after ordering drinks. "We've had a couple of agencies work for us over the years. Never really satisfied with the results. They think of major construction as sweaty men in hardhats. Pounding nails, laying bricks and drinking a case of beer a day. And it's not...at least anymore."

The drinks arrived. When everyone received his and hers, Keith lifted his glass in an informal toast. Joined by the others. Then he continued:

"Hell...the projects we involve ourselves in are as much a part of American politics as what happens at the White House!"

"Dad means companies like ours are like pawns in international politics," Suzanne added. "Dams constructed in Egypt last year represented gifts for getting negotiations under way with the United States."

"That's right, Matt." Keith commanded his attention again. "The Washington people figure the best way to talk terms is by offering American construction technology upfront. Then dangle it like a carrot to illustrate nice things done for those friendly toward us."

He took a sip from his drink. Studied its monogrammed container a moment. Then continued.

"I'm not knocking how they run the country, mind you. This finagling goes on in business every day. It's just we've got into tight situations living up to promises."

"They shot at us regularly building an oil pipeline across Libya," said the construction boss, shaking his head from side to side.

"Several different Arab tribes had feuded for centuries. They stopped fighting each other when we showed up. Made our lives miserable!"

"We lost a few people," added Keith. "Several others refused to work until we nearly tripled their salaries. In the end, the job cost twenty million bucks more than it should have."

"There are subtleties and nuances involved in our advertising and public affairs, Matt," said the man heading marketing. "Our work in the States is first-rate. And we intend to become well-known nationwide. Off the continent, however, it becomes a political hodgepodge."

Fresh drinks arrived. They ordered Sarni's house specialty, fresh swordfish steaks. Grilled in a light and tart anchovy, garlic and butter sauce. Broccoli spears, crab salad and cool cucumber soup served on the side. And chocolate mousse for dessert, followed by strong coffee and ten-year-old brandy.

Frank ordered bottle after bottle of expensive white wine. Toward eleven o'clock, Matt found himself caught in the excitement and sometimes, danger, involved with Hillary Engineering projects.

During the evening, his eyes several times embarrassingly locked with Suzanne's. Each smiled stiffly at the obvious attraction perceived by the other. Then sheepishly looked away.

He felt pleasantly uncomfortable. He chalked it to the wine. Plus, the excitement and flattery of a woman as stunning as Suzanne finding him attractive.

"Well, Matt, I hope we've given you insight into the devious dealings of Hillary Engineering," said Keith. "Frank speaks highly of your group's capabilities and talents. Which puts you in good stead with us."

Keith looked inquisitively at his daughter...then the two other Hillary executives. Confirming what he felt, deep down, he turned back to Matt.

"Think you could take us on as a DG&B client?"

Matt sat dumbstruck. The question he desperately wished for rolled across the table into his lap. For hours, now, he knew Keith would ask it. He knew the fluttery, victorious feeling long ago. Some inner, positive inkling telling him the account could be his.

Yet, he hesitated. He already should have formulated an answer. Here he sat...now...rolling it in his mind. Concerned over passing the opportunity.

Fearful over not living up to Hillary's expectations. And also finding in the pit of his stomach...for some reason...a gnawing realization that declining the account meant not seeing Suzanne again.

For some reason...the warmth of the brandy...sumptuous meal...or the heady camaraderie...he didn't want to consider that prospect.

"You've been honest with me, Keith," he finally replied. "I'll be upfront, too. We're stretched too thin to swing an account as large as yours. And do the work you deserve and should expect. Give me a few days to discuss this with my partners. I'm certain we can find a mutually beneficial approach."

"Okay, Matt. It's a deal. I appreciate your candor. Don't keep us hanging too long, though. We haven't anyone getting our message out. And there's lots we need to do and say."

"I'll catch the early flight to Hartford tomorrow morning. We'll look at the alternatives. Maybe assemble a separate staff to handle your account. New York crawls with top copywriters and designers."

"I want you handling the account though, Matt. That's the deal. If I'm paying several million dollars for DG&B's expertise...that's what I expect."

"You flatter me, Keith. Yes...we'd make that a contingency of our client-agency contract. I'll call Monday...promise."

At midnight, they represented the only ones in the dining room. Keith suggested they call it an evening. Friday portended busy for everyone. As they rose to leave, Matt shook hands with the other men. Then took Suzanne's.

"I enjoyed meeting you, Matt," she firmly squeezed his hand. In the dusky candlelight, her teeth glistened...as Karen's always did. "I hope you'll find some way of handling our account."

"We'll try, Suzanne. For certain. Hillary Engineering would be a benchmark account for us. Means we're a successful shop. Which is important in New York."

He cupped his left hand warmly over hers.

"I certainly enjoyed meeting you, too. Believe me." Afterwards, he hoped he didn't appear too forward over the suddenly surfacing yearnings he felt toward her.

Matt caught a taxi to his apartment building. Once upstairs, he undressed. Then poured a double shot of Gran Marnier over the rocks. He walked to the southern-facing window and looked down onto Fifth Avenue.

He couldn't blot Suzanne's face from his mind. Especially the sensuous pout as he left. Deep down, he knew they'd meet again. And soon. He smiled, fumbling with the mental list of chores needing doing tomorrow. The Gran Marnier causing his brain to slur.

"Hell!" he said aloud to the window. "It already is tomorrow."

The excitement of handling the Hillary account jangled his spine again. He tossed down the remainder of the liqueur, brushed his teeth, and slipped into bed.

Matt walked into the office at nine. He asked Dot Weymoth to book flights to Hartford for him and Greer McCall. Then called Hoot and Eddie and arranged the meeting there. Hoot could drive up.

When Greer arrived, Matt briefed him on the dinner the night before. And, most especially, the offer to manage Hillary's account.

Dot booked the two on the eleven o'clock flight. Hoot met them at the airport, and drove to DG&B's Hartford offices. Eddie stood in the receptionist's area when they walked through the door.

"Hello, Matt," he said, taking his handshake. The clear blue eyes sparkled with excitement. "Congratulations, too. My God...I don't know whether we're going to be rich or dead!"

"They seem to go hand in hand, don't they, Eddie?" came the answer.

Matt and Greer greeted the other employees in the office. Many of whom they had not met. Hoot and Eddie hand-picked the group. So obviously, its members ranked among the brightest and most creative available.

Lunchtime arrived by the time Matt and Greer introduced themselves. Eddie suggested a quiet restaurant nearby where they could discuss options uninterrupted. Matt agreed heartily. His head stopped throbbing from the previous night's affair. A beer or two might pick him up.

"Matthew, my main concern is you're covering too many bases yourself," said Hoot. "It's not the best time for a gigantic account to come along."

Hoot put his hand on his friend's shoulder.

"I mean...Karen's pregnant...and two of our offices are just getting organized. We may be biting off too much."

"Hoot's right, Matt," added Eddie. "The guys from Triad might not appreciate you spending all your time with Hillary. Which is probably what it will take. Plus, you've still got several other accounts."

"First off...I've passed most of Triad's work to Greer," Matt responded. "They're into television. And that's his specialty. We've got shit hot copywriters handling everything else needed. They all know Triad. And they know it's their asses if anything queers the account."

"What about Karen, Matthew?" Hoot repeated. "How will she take this?"

"I don't know, Hoot. She knew the commitments I'd make for us to be successful. Back when I moved to New York. She'll come to terms with this, too. It'll work out, I'm sure. Once things are up and running smoothly. Then, we'll have money and time to do anything we damned well please."

The four lunched on hamburgers, fries and a couple of beers apiece. Then returned to the office. The brews relaxed Matt's mind. Already he contemplated staffing challenges. Eddie raised that issue.

"Your New York office is shorthanded, Matt. How can you handle Hillary without adding people?"

"That's what I want to talk about," he answered. "I've given this a lot of thought. One way to get talented people is by merging with another successful agency. It's done all the time. Every day I read where one shop absorbs another. Not only combining work forces, but also accounts. If accounts conflict, they drop the less promising ones. It's a 'win win' situation for everyone."

"Did you have a particular agency in mind, Matthew?" asked Hoot. Already concerned over his partner's recommendation.

"Yes, Hoot. You know...I keep running into Lyle Bradley. He keeps asking the same question: Why don't we team up and storm Madison Avenue? Maybe, it's a good idea, Hoot."

Hoot stood. Walked to the window overlooking downtown Hartford. Hands clasped behind his back. Matt remembered his friend's contemplative exercise from Korea. Typically before a hairy mission. Hoot remained silent a full minute.

"I don't know, Matt. Damnit, I don't know."

He turned, faced the three at the conference table.

"I remember what your dad said years ago...when we pitched against Lyle and his dad for Conn Castings' business. Remember? 'Don't trust the son of a bitch!' Isn't that what he said?"

"Sure...I remember, buddy," Matt said. He rose, walked to the other, put his hand on his shoulder. "That was a long time ago, Hooter. I've worked with Lyle on advertising committees since. He's not what we first thought. He's got a good creative shop. They're latching onto neat accounts. I think his folks would complement ours. What do you say? Shall I call him Monday? Have a sit-down?"

Hoot looked directly into Matt's eyes. Saw anticipation there. Said: "Sure. It's okay with me, partner. If it's okay with everyone else. However, please keep your eyes on the bastard."

Matt put his other hand on Hoot's left shoulder. Looked at him squarely. "I will, partner. Don't worry about that."

That afternoon, Greer flew to New York. Matt collected his car at the airport and followed Hoot to New Haven.

It was nearly four o'clock when he pulled the driveway beside his house. He got out, walked around to the back door that opened into the kitchen.

Anne Westfield heard him drive up. She yelled upstairs to Karen who was laying down, reading a book. The latter arose, walked the stairs as he came into the living room.

"Hi, honey," he said. He clutched her to him gently, kissed her forehead. "How you feeling?"

"Pretty good, Matt," she said. She looked up at him. The quizzical look flickered across her face. "You look tired, darling."

"Yeah, I am...a little. Late night last night. Been a hectic week. Hillary Engineering offered us their account. So, we're figuring how we can get enough people to manage it."

"Matt...do you honestly need more business? Really? I mean, you're working twelve hour days. Corley and I only see you for a full day. And you're tired, then. We've got another baby on the way, you know." Karen patted her protruding stomach for emphasis.

"Please don't start, honey," he said in a low, flat and deliberate tone. He walked to the antique walnut chifforobe that served as a liquor cabinet. Poured an inch of bourbon in the bottom of a glass. Tonged ice cubes from a bucket on the breakfast bar and splashed them in.

He loosened his tie, dropped onto one of the living room couches. In the kitchen, he heard Mrs. Westfield whistling to herself as she started preparing the evening meal.

"When I return to New York, I'm seeing if Lyle Bradley still wants to merge our two groups," he said, rather matter of factly.

"Lyle Bradley? You've mentioned him before. Who is he?"

"Someone I knew in school. Has an agency in New York with his dad. Pretty heavy into managing political campaigns. We went head-to-head over the Conn Castings account several years ago."

"Well...I'm for merging if it means you'll have more time to take it easy. And for us to see you more often."

"It will, honey," he grasped her hand as she sat next to him. "Hey, where's that kid of mine?"

He helped Karen from the couch, and they walked the stairs to where Corley napped. Matt leaned and kissed his sleeping son. Then held his wife as they watched the youngster peacefully sprawled in the baby bed.

Matt telephoned Lyle Bradley almost immediately after reaching the office Monday morning. They made a luncheon date. Over drinks after ordering, he explained to Lyle the opportunity available by forming a partnership. Then briefed him on Hillary Engineering.

"I've been trying to get our groups together for quite a while, Matt," Lyle said. "Dad feels the same. He's more interested in doing lobbyist work in Washington than riding herd on clients. This would work well for him. We'll discuss it when I return to the office. By the way, what will we call our new group?"

"It only involves our New York operations. So how about 'Bradley, Durham and Associates?'"

"Sounds fine. Like I said, I'll run this past the old man and get back to you this afternoon. Then we'll have the lawyers put it in writing."

During the remainder of lunch, Lyle apprised Matt on activities in which he and his father involved themselves. Matt updated the other on his group's work for Triad, Cartiff Perfume, Standish Electronics and Musgrave Manufacturing.

He left Lyle with several brochures providing background on Hillary Engineering. As well as illustrating the various international projects in which the company played an active role.

It was nearly three o'clock when they shook hands and left for their respective offices. An hour later, Lyle called saying his father approved of the consolidation. They should meet Wednesday and contractually formalize the agreement.

Matt called Hoot and Eddie. Gave them the news. Then called Larry Harst at Triad, who still served as his corporate attorney. Larry agreed to meet with them, and help draw the contracts.

Arrangements made, Matt called Hillary Engineering. He hoped Keith might still be at the office. Instead, Suzanne answered.

"Matt, I've been hoping you'd call," she said. Her voice carrying an unmistakable tinge of excitement. "Dad left for a meeting that came up. I'll see him later. What may I tell him?"

"You've got yourselves a new agency, Suzanne," he said. He felt his heart pounding in his ears. His voice caught in exuberance.

"We've formed a new group...primarily to support your account. Named it, Bradley, Durham and Associates."

"That's wonderful, Matt. It'll really please dad. We should celebrate, you know."

"I agree," he said. He imagined the beautiful face behind the cool voice on the telephone. Mentally pictured the smile. "How about dinner at Sarni's Wednesday night? We'll legally form the new agency by then. Really have cause to pop a cork. I'll bring our new partners...Lyle and George Bradley. You dad should meet them."

"I can't wait, Matt." she breathed into the phone.

"I can't either, Suzanne," he answered. He deliberately put as much feeling as possible into the words. Then hoped he didn't sound like some giddy, love-struck highschooler.

When Matt disconnected, he twirled in his desk chair. He looked out over the city, leaning back with arms folded behind his head. He wished it already were Wednesday. And smiled over the thought.

Chapter 21

Diana Lynn Arrives

HOOT AND EDDIE WALKED FROM Triad Flight 658 into the sweltering, humid breath of late June at La Guardia in New York. Both instantly began rubbing watery eyes. Stinging from fumes of expended jet fuel. Coupled with traffic smog from the city. And held like a carpet near the ground. Not a hint of air stirred to sweep it away.

They hurriedly walked toward the terminal door. Escaping the burning pollution and prickly heat. When Matt appeared and strode toward them, arm outstretched.

"Morning gents," he said to the pair. "Good flight over?"

"Smooth and uneventful, Matthew," answered Hoot, shaking his hand. "Triad's a good, dependable airline."

"I'll second that," replied Eddie. He pumped Matt's outstretched arm. "I'm glad to hear it," replied Matt. "That's what we've told folks for years now. Hey, wait'll you see Greer's ideas for the international flight kickoff! I'll give you a peek at the clips when we get to the office and finish with the Bradleys."

"Can't wait, Matt," said Eddie. "Boy...wish they'd do something about this damned pollution!"

"You don't notice if there's a breeze, Eddie," Matt said, holding the door for them. "Only on quiet days like today. They're planning a new airport nearer the Atlantic. Won't have this problem. Here...parked my car in the Triad spaces. I'll fill you in on the campaign on the way downtown."

The three climbed into the Mercedes sedan Matt bought for a company car. He steered West on inner belt 268. Straight for the city and Madison Avenue to meet the Bradleys and their lawyer.

Larry Harst, representing DG&B, also would be there. On the way, Hoot and Eddie briefed Matt on the latest goings-on in New Haven and Hartford. In return, he explained the concepts underscoring Triad's new promotion.

He barely finished when they arrived at the new offices at 270 Madison Avenue.

Matt eased into the lower level parking garage. A black attendant disappeared with the car as they boarded the elevator for the twenty-fifth floor. When they stepped off, Hoot whistled softly.

"Man...they didn't spare expenses decorating this place, Matthew!" he exclaimed.

Indeed, the builders used walnut paneling and light granite and marble tastefully. Complemented by lush, deep pile carpet. An atmosphere of wealth and power hung in the small vestibules forming entranceways for offices on each floor of the building.

Twelve elevators served the entire complex. Only six to a side, traveling to certain floors. Odd numbers on the left. Evens to the right.

Matt led them to a door in the hallway centered between two stainless steel and glass panels. Emblazoned on the door in large bronze letters: "DG&B And Associates, Advertising." Through the glass panels, the visitors spotted a pretty receptionist. Matt pushed a white button near the doorknob, and smiled at her. A soft buzzer sounded...the electronic lock clicked...and he opened the door for the other two.

"Morning Janette," Matt said to the young woman behind the desk. "I'd like you to meet Hoot Gibson and Eddie Bauer. Our other two partners in crime."

She beamed at the two, perkily offered her hand.

"Nice to meet you, gentlemen. Welcome to New York."

They returned her greeting and chatted briefly. Matt inquired about the Bradleys.

"They're inside, Mr. Durham," she replied. "Mrs. Weymoth took them in for coffee. Oh...Mr. Harst called. He's on his way."

"Thanks, Janette. Show him in when he arrives."

Matt preceded his friends into the inner offices. On the wall to their left, walking toward his corner office, appeared several color enlargements of DG&B ads. Framed still shots from television commercials hung amongst the print ads. And the many COCA Awards won by the agency over the years.

Dot Weymoth intercepted them heading toward Matt's office.

"Good morning, Matt. Hello, Hoot and Eddie. Nice to see you again."

"Same here, Dot," said Hoot. "Always nice to see you." He took her hand warmly. "How are they treating you?"

"Terrible...as usual! Overworked and underpaid."

"Come to New Haven, Dot. Land of opportunity and wealth for the taking!"

"I may take you up on that some day," she said. "The Bradleys are in the screening room. There's fresh coffee and rolls."

"Thanks Dot," said Matt. The three walked to the double doors across from his office. As they entered, George Bradley stood to greet them. Lyle was examining the laminated ads and product photographs adorning the walls. Accompanied by several other notable awards earned by the firm.

"Matt...good morning," said Lyle. He walked to the three of them. Turned and introduced his father. "This is my dad, George Bradley. Dad, I'd like you to meet Matt Durham and his partners...Hoot Gibson and Eddie Bauer."

He then introduced their attorney. After exchanging handshakes and niceties, the newcomers helped themselves to coffee and rolls. Then joined the others around the walnut conference table.

"Our attorney, Larry Harst, is on the way here," Matt explained to the elder Bradley. "Until he arrives...maybe you and Lyle could brief Hoot and Eddie on your clients and activities."

George Bradley opened an alligator skin attaché case. He pulled out a matching leather notebook and paper-clipped sheets of paper. These, he passed around the table.

Each page contained a condensed client description, and details on the Bradleys' duration as agency of record. Status reports included described campaigns under way or in the works.

Matt glanced at several papers disclosing lobbyist activities. Most for hotly contested political causes. He casually wondered aloud the best methods for agencies to select proper causes and candidates to back.

"It's like everything else, Matt," explained George. "You go with what you feel. What you believe."

"We've got too much agency exposure here, George," countered Matt.

He tapped on the stack of papers.

"Suppose we go balls to the wall behind a politician or some cause. And it blows in our faces. Everyone on Madison Avenue will know about it before the dew settles. And so will clients!"

"You simply don't let that happen, Matt," chimed Lyle from his seat across the table. "Everything in politics has its price. Popular causes.

Parties. Even people. You find out what it is. And it'll be negotiable, believe me. Whether a full-blown media program free. Or a hot young ankle for a senior senator. Changing people's minds is easy. Hell, you ought to know that. You've manipulated people into believing rubbish for years!"

Matt flushed, slightly.

"One difference, Lyle. We won't work for a client whose product is shit. The Four-As take a dim view of deception. Whether you're pushing inventory or images. There's still something sacred about politics. It's almost un-American foisting some half-baked politico on a gullible public. That's hitting below the foul zone!"

"C'mon Matt. That's naive bullshit!" countered Lyle. "If we don't hype a political aspirant or cause...some other agency will. The result's the same. He gets the nod. The porkbarrel project passes. And the public pays heavier taxes. The big difference is we don't get paid...or have favors coming."

"Favors?" inquired Hoot. "What do you mean favors, Lyle?" He leaned forward anticipating the answer. Tensing over the conversation's direction. And the proposed merger. He recalled vividly Walt Durham's words of years ago.

"Wake up, Hoot. Don't feign naiveté, too!" spat Lyle. "Everyone knows the Federal Trade Commission cries 'deception' over nearly everything advertised today!" Lyle stood, paced to the window and back.

"Right now...liquor advertising isn't allowed. And they're going after cigarettes. Who do you think keeps the FTC in line? The politicians, that's who. And if they screw up, they know the big distillers and big tobacco growers will hold the big bucks. On the other hand, if they see things their benefactors' ways...give a little here and there...their campaign coffers magically overflow."

"I'm not as blunt as my son, gentlemen," said George Bradley, squirming slightly in his chair. "Washington means more than the outfit running the country. Capitol Hill abounds with thousands of special interest groups. All supporting personal causes. We call them politicians. If you convince them to pick up the banner and support your cause...or that of a client...that's good business. Like Lyle says... everybody's doing it."

"That's fine, George," said Matt. "If that interests you and Lyle... then go to it. We're bowing out of political undertakings. We've more than enough work handling client projects without tilting at windmills."

Matt rose...walked behind Hoot and Eddie...placed his hands on their shoulders.

"If we combine groups, it'll have to be so we can more effectively fulfill client needs. Not to expand political horizons. Or fill our book with favors owed."

"Whoa...cool your kidneys, Matt. Like I said the other day...dad will cover that end of the business. You won't soil your lily hands with politics."

"As long as we understand that, Lyle," responded Matt. He retrieved the coffee pot. Began filling cups. "Then...we'll be okay."

Larry Harst entered the room as Matt returned to the table. He introduced the lawyer around. Then the two attorneys shepherded the meeting. Explaining the contracts' binding terms before signing. And statutes under New York law legalizing the merger.

Contract conditions applied only to DG&B's New York office. With this in mind, Larry painstakingly scrutinized every document. Matt, Hoot and Eddie also read the instruments thoroughly. Making sure no codicil linked DG&B's Hartford and New Haven operations. Then, five pen strokes formalized the agreement.

The lawyers notarized, witnessed and signed the documents. That afternoon, Larry would file them with the city and state. Making Bradley, Durham & Associates a legal entity...and much larger advertising agency.

The new partners shook hands around. Then the Bradleys and their attorney left for their offices up the street. Agreeing to meet the others at Sarni's later that evening. To celebrate, and meet Hillary Engineering... the client causing the merger.

"Matthew...for a minute I thought you'd come unglued and about to throttle your new partner," said Hoot.

He, Matt and Eddie walked up the street for light lunch and cold beer.

"You flushed when Lyle mentioned political shenanigans," Hoot added.

"We need the bastards, Hoot. Or I'd have dropped them right then. I'll tell you this...like dad says, Lyle bears watching. He and George may enjoy the power and excitement of Washington. I don't want any part of it. My concern is our New York work. And especially our newest client."

The three walked into Smitty's. A kosher shop providing thick pastrami and Swiss cheese sandwiches. Potato salad and Cole slaw heaped in gigantic mounds. And served the coldest mug of beer in the city.

Matt ordered turkey with Swiss on white with Mayo. Hoot and Eddie opted for the tender pastrami. Over lunch, they discussed work under way at the three locations. Then Hoot and Eddie left to pay respects to Triad Airlines. Matt met with Greer at the studio, and previewed film on several new commercials.

At six o'clock, the trio met at Matt's apartment. They freshened, then enjoyed quick drinks. And at seven-thirty, seated themselves around the table at Sarni's that Dot reserved for them.

They barely got comfortable when Lyle and George appeared at the headwaiter's podium. Hoot motioned for them to join the group. When Lyle and his father sat down, they apologized to the others.

"I'm sorry if this morning's discussion offended you boys," said George. "I'm a crusty old son of a bitch. I do love the thrills and excitement of political chess in Washington. For me, nothing's more fulfilling. When someone I've helped mold gets named to an important post, it's part of me being elected. Damn, it's exciting! My mistake is thinking others get kicks doing the same thing."

"Dad's right, guys," added Lyle. "That's strictly his concern. Ninety-nine percent of our agency will devote itself to client work. I swear. After all, that's why I jumped at Matt's offer. Hell, we need your help to stay ahead, too!"

"Let's drink to that," said Hoot, motioning to the waiter. "And put this behind us. Bradley, Durham & Associates needs to start on the right foot!"

They ordered a round of drinks. And were toasting the merger when Keith and Suzanne appeared. Matt rose, and walked to where they stood. He shook hands with both. Led them toward the table.

"Looks like the wedding went well, and you're toasting the bride and groom," Keith joked. "Nice to see our agency's leaders in harmony... right, Suzanne?"

Matt looked into her glowing face as she spoke. Soft, melodious tones danced from a full mouth turned slightly at the corners, hinting a smile.

"Yes, dad, it is. Arrangements went smoothly, Matt?"

"Fairly so, Suzanne," came a guarded reply. He ushered them to the table. His hand lightly touching her back. Unconsciously guiding her to the chair next to his.

As they neared, the others arose. Matt introduced the newcomers. They shook hands and sat. He ordered drinks for Keith and Suzanne.

Over the next two hours, client and agency openly exchanged information about each others' operations. Keith candidly unraveled the scope of Hillary Engineering's worldwide projects. The more Matt absorbed, the more fascinating became the man who in only twenty years assembled a powerful, influential and international organization.

Hillary began as a construction engineer with the firm building La Guardia. When World War Two erupted, he ended as commanding officer of a Navy Construction Battalion (SeaBee) unit in the Philippines.

In only two months, his construction battalion dug and poured runways on Guadalcanal in the Solomon Islands. Constantly under fire from Japanese snipers. When they shipped to excavate Papua, Keith's wife was dying of cancer Stateside.

Suzanne was nine at the time. In 1942, she lived with Keith's favorite sister, Aunt Lowey. Short for Eloise. He never remarried.

"Never found the time," the man said, glancing into the bottom of his drink glass. "I'm way too old now."

Matt felt respect mixed with awe for Keith, whose daughter unfolded Hillary Engineering's story. And renewed excitement over the merging of the two agencies, and the account being his to handle.

He became aware, from the corner of his eye, of Suzanne watching him most of the evening. When he spoke, she seemed devoutly interested in what he said. Several times, talking among themselves, they touched with familiarity. An arm, wrist, hand or shoulder. And felt at ease doing so.

At one point, when Matt leaned to whisper, he thought she intentionally brushed her hair lightly against his face. Leaving a whisper of soft perfume lingering before his nose.

Hoot observed the interest each paid the other. At first, thinking little of it. Then becoming concerned as the evening matured. And exchanged glances and nuances became less subtle and more frequent.

He tried tracking discussions between Keith and the Bradleys, but kept losing his place. Attending, instead, to his best friend's infatuation with another woman. He decided on talking with Matt that evening.

Before he and Eddie caught the eleven o'clock flight to Hartford. And hoped Keith had not noticed the flirtations.

Hoot waited until they were enroute to the airport before broaching the subject.

"Suzanne's quite a looker, isn't she, Matthew?" he said. More statement than question.

"Oh yeah," Matt replied. "Extremely attractive."

Hoot formed the words in his mind as Matt swung onto the airport highway. Regretted the instant they left his mouth.

"You're not mixing a little pleasure with business are you?"

Matt's head jerked around sharply. Hurt and anger combined, twisting his face into a scowl.

"Hell no, Hoot! You know me better than that! Or at least I hoped you did!"

"Sorry, amigo. It's just you and Karen are special to me. Family. I'd hate to see anything jeopardize that relationship."

"We've been through this before, Hoot," Matt replied

He steered onto the La Guardia turnoff.

"Suzanne is charming. No question about that. It stops there. We're both married. The relationship is strictly business."

"Okay, pal. Sorry if I stepped out of line." Hoot put his hand on Matt's right shoulder.

"Accepted," answered the other.

Triad's flight lifted wheels at eleven o'clock on the nose. Matt headed toward his apartment building, singing along with a rock and roll song on WGNY, a popular station in the middle of Manhattan. Driving, he replayed the evening's events in his mind. Especially the friendly chiding and flirting between Suzanne and he. And her wonderful fragrance.

He decided to learn what she wore. Buy a bottle for Karen. It reminded him of freshly mown summer clover in early morning. Outdoorsy. Subtle. Sweet smelling. Natural.

He still detected its faint linger, or sensed it. His heart felt light over the evening's events. He sang even louder as another song began. A Beatles tune.

Suzanne graduated from Boston State College in 1952. She enrolled in its School of Law, and in 1956 earned summa cum laude honors along with her legal degree.

By then, returning vets occupied most jobs. Her father brought her into his fledgling company as a management trainee. She spent most of her time in the legal and contracts departments. When it happened.

The more familiar she became with her father's operations, the more exciting the job became. Soon, she wanted to function as an integral part of the company.

In 1958, Suzanne returned to college part-time. She attended day and evening classes at New York University's School of Engineering. By 1963, she earned bachelor of science and master of science degrees in civil and structural engineering.

Keith prided himself on his daughter's scholastic record. Lauded her for uncanny common sense, and a knack for efficient and effective ways of getting projects completed on time and budget. He appointed her his executive assistant, and dug into the business with fervor.

During her senior year at NYU, Suzanne married Lorne Whittier, an architect. He became a partner in a small firm on Forty-Fifth Street. She immediately set about learning construction, rather than having a family. Much to her father's chagrin.

"You should think about grandchildren for your poor old dad, Suzanne," he said, kiddingly. However, hinting at his true desire. "Let Lorne support you. He makes good money."

"No, dad. I've worked too hard. I love my job. If you won't keep me around, I'll work elsewhere. And you'll lose the best damned construction honcho you'll ever have!"

So ended the discussion. Keith knew she was right. The last thing he wanted was driving away the only person he cared for. The daughter who diligently, and probably knowingly, took the place of the son men hope for...but Keith never had.

Over the years, Suzanne became an irreplaceable asset to Hillary Engineering. A throbbing source of pride for her father. And a natural leader of rough-cuts accustomed to brute force. Making mountains yield, rivers change course and concrete structures grow dozens of stories into the skies.

Suzanne epitomized, as her father put it: "The iron fist in a velvet glove."

At the time...though neither she nor Matt knew it...her father intended that Suzanne head the company's European operations.

July and August proved hectic. Hoot and Eddie put final touches on Conn Casting's fall campaign for its Cometliner fleet. Matt and Greer worked closely and tirelessly on four thirty-second commercials for Triad. These would air in September, coinciding with kickoff flights to London, Paris, Lisbon and Denmark.

The officers of Triad chose to inaugurate international flights with profitable routes to Europe. And later on, introduce travel to the Far East when returns from this wing-stretching began mounting.

In early September, Matt flew with Keith to Australia. His firm constructed a huge electric power facility there. They continued to Naples, and participated in ground-breaking for an international airport.

"When we return Stateside, I'm going to ask Suzanne to run things here," Keith told him.

They sat drinking wine at an outdoor cafe on the Venida D'Putsio. He tried not to register the disappointment thudding in the pit of his stomach.

"She can handle the job," he answered. "What about Lorne?"

"Hell, Matt...she's making ten times what he is! He'll go where she wants to. Besides, it's a chance for them to learn Europe. And that's something every architect or builder should crave!"

Keith had become fond of Matt. He admired the young man's enthusiasm over work. And his earnest desire to make Hillary Engineering even more successful.

He especially enjoyed the talks the two shared about the construction industry before, during and after "The Big War." He looked forward to meeting General Durham, since Matt told him countless tales about Walt.

It did not surprise Matt to learn Keith served as project engineer constructing his apartment building. He invited Keith for nightcaps regularly, so the man could poke around the old building. He showed Matt his initials scratched in the foundation wall in the building's memorabilia-jammed basement.

Matt spent considerable time at the Hillary Building on Broadway near Columbia University. Examining project photographs and slides. Reading all he could on the company's background, current operations, and press clippings on file detailing the man who ran it.

On days at the Hillary Building, Matt often lunched with Suzanne. Occasionally, her husband joined them. From that first meeting, Matt felt comfortable around her. Enjoyed the way she made everything said or done seem interesting and important.

She regularly inquired about Karen, Corley, Hoot and Bobby. Their beginnings in advertising eight years earlier. She expressed most interest in Karen. What she was like. Her profession. The things she said.

That side of Matt seemed far away to her. However, it kept burning into her consciousness. For some reason, she felt jealousy's pique when he mentioned Karen's name.

Matt found himself behaving similarly when Lorne joined them. He inwardly resented the man butting into their serendipitous meetings.

Their regular spot became The Gashouse on Madison Avenue. Practitioners of advertising gathered there over mugs of beer and grilled ham and cheese sandwiches. Learning who was doing what, for whom, or to whom. And what accounts might be unattended for wily wolves to steal.

Matt also caught himself staring out the window of the Triad jetliner enroute to Hartford. Feeling emptiness in his chest. As if leaving a piece of himself below. Realizing it was Suzanne...more than the city... representing the excitement on which he thrived.

He felt it now. Flying home for Fall Festival. Looking down on bright strands of headlights weaving freeways around the city. Serpentine white strings snaking through the darkness below.

He wondered, hollowly, if one was the limousine carrying Lorne and Suzanne to the airport. To board a flight to Italy.

The routine journey to New Haven allowed his mind to wander from the task of driving. Suddenly, he would pass some landmark or building with a start. Realizing home was nearby. And as always, Karen greeted him in the kitchen as he entered the house. Mrs. Westfield had turned in.

"Hi darling."

She flashed her beautiful, sincere, loving smile. Kissed him lightly on the lips. He felt her protruding belly beneath the loose shirt she wore: One of his comfortable old button-down oxford cloths.

She gained more weight with this pregnancy than with Corley. Still, she showed far less than most women. Except her stomach and plump cheeks, she held her trimness.

Matt jerked loose the knot of his tie. Set his briefcase on the breakfast table. Put his arms around his wife.

"I love you," he said. And knew he did. Now, with Karen in his arms, feeling her loving warmth, her arms around his waist, New York slipped quietly from his mind.

He held her at arm's length. Looked at the tanned, perfect complexion. Her open, ready smile. The quizzical expression dashed across her face and disappeared in the silence. He kissed her forehead.

"Drink...or glass of wine?" he asked.

"Perhaps a glass of white wine, thanks."

He poured them both a glass. They walked arm in arm into the living room. It was uncomfortable for her sitting on the soft, low slung couches.

She sat on a large throw pillow on the floor at his knees. They talked about what occurred over the past four days.

The next morning...Corley and Mrs. Westfield occupying the back seat of Karen's new stationwagon...they departed for Huntsdale. Driving the winding blacktop leading to the small village, Matt reflected the hundreds of times he'd made this trip.

Yet each journey seemed as exciting as the first. As if this tiny fragment of Connecticut drew his soul like a magnet. When he turned onto the Seven Hills road, he experienced deep and gratifying feelings of freedom and relaxation. And the sight of The House still fluttered his insides.

Both sets of parents were drinking coffee when they pulled into the semicircle drive. They soon appeared on the front porch. Corley scrambled from the stationwagon and dashed the stairs to Walt. Who lifted and held him squealing joyfully over his head.

Damon tousled the young man's hair as Walt rough-housed him. Then passed him for the grandmothers to hug and kiss.

"Hello, honey. Hi Matt...Anne. Where are Hoot and Bobby?" the doctor asked.

"They'll be down tomorrow, dad," Karen said. She kissed her father on the cheek.

"That's good," he said. "I was afraid they were skipping out on us. How are you feeling honey?"

"Fat, daddy. And uncomfortable. Other than that, okay."

They went inside for coffee and rolls. Corley, accompanied by his father and grandfathers, walked to the creek. That afternoon, Matt and his father sat in the walnut grove behind The House. Walt inquired how his life fared in New York.

"Keeping busy, dad. Working late. Loving it."

"That's what I hear, son."

Walt leaned his rifle against a giant gnarled walnut tree. Eased himself down, his back against it. He looked at Matt.

"Matt...we don't want to pry. However, the Forsythes and your mother and I think you're over-stretching. Look at you. You've lost twenty pounds. Big circles under your eyes. You look beat, son. You need to slow down a little."

"Jesus, dad!" he slapped his palm against the rough bark of a tree. "You sound like Karen! Moaning that I want to be successful. Have the money to do as I wish. I'm getting close. And I won't be thirty-four for another month. I think that's pretty damned good!"

"I'm not begrudging your success, son. We're extremely proud of you. Always have been. It's just there are more important things. Beyond a big house, fancy car and money to piss away. Consider Karen and Corley. The baby on the way. They need you more than money!"

"Dad...in case you don't remember. I didn't see much of you growing up. You were flying off to battle somewhere. I didn't turn out too bad because of it."

"Hindsight is wonderful, Matt. Problem is, it comes too late. Looking back, I'd do things differently. Suddenly, I've retired. You're grown. It's an ideal time for us finally to do things together. And now, you haven't the time."

The general cradled his rifle in his lap. Studied his boots in silence for a moment.

"I'm just saying...don't be the same with Corley. Don't wake up fifty years later and wonder: 'Why didn't I grow with my family? Instead of away from them?'"

Matt leaned on one knee. Placed his hand on his dad's shoulder. Looked into misting blue eyes.

"We're as close as any father and son, dad. I love you. We've had lots of good times. And there'll be many more. Right now, my work is important. While I'm young and creative. Sure, it's all-consuming. That'll change, though. You'll see."

Walt put his hand on top of his son's.

"I hope so, Matt. I sure hope so."

Hoot and Bobby arrived the next morning. Sausage and pancake aromas encircled The House. The couple smelled the delicious scents the moment they stepped from the car.

Karen heard them drive in, and laboriously made her way to the front porch. She swung side to side as she walked, Corley holding her hand. Matt shaved upstairs. The others sat in the kitchen.

"Look, Corley, it's Aunt Bobby and Uncle Hoot!"

Karen beamed as the newcomers climbed the porch stairs. The youngster bashfully clung to his mother's skirt. Until Hoot scooped him off his feet and swung him amidst happy squeals.

"Hey, tiger, you're putting on weight," said Hoot. He sat the young man gently on the floor.

"I, or Corley!" Karen inquired, jokingly. She hugged her friends hello.

The four walked inside. Matt came down the stairs, slapping after-shave on his cleanly scraped face. He shook Hoot's hand. Pecked Bobby on the cheek. They went to the kitchen for breakfast.

Fall succeeded an uncommonly warm summer. One that lingered, and promised a colorless switch in seasons.

Fall Festival still provided pleasurable experiences for those turning out. Especially Corley. Like his father, he downed too much homemade ice cream. And had to lie down for comfort's sake.

A slight breeze finally stirred around dusk. The men gathered around one of the long tables. Drinking beer and listening to Roger Maris and Mickey Mantle pound the Yankees past the White Sox in eleven innings of baseball. The ladies attending sat on the porch and talked kids, clothes and family.

When October rolled around, Matt juggled his work schedule. Preparing for the hunting season. He planned on taking Keith Hillary pheasant, duck and quail hunting with his father and Damon in early November.

By telephone, he informed Suzanne of his intent to hold work on Hillary's spring kickoff until the first of the year. He foresaw no challenges at having the campaign completed in time for the heavy construction months.

She protested slightly. At first, feeling something akin to jealousy over his being away from New York. Then, learning his delay involved hunting...and with her father...agreed happily that he needed relaxation. Work on the campaign could hold until January.

On Saturday, October twenty-first, a week before his birthday, Matt raked leaves in the front yard with Corley. The two listening to Yale versus Brown University football. Mrs. Westfield rushed from the house to where they worked.

"Matt, Matt! It's time. It's time!"

"Oh my God," he said. He dropped the rake and ran toward the front door. "Watch Corley, Annie. And call Doctor Sappington!"

Karen busily gathered her hospital luggage. She wore his flannel bathrobe.

"I'm sorry, Matt," she said. He noticed the front of the blue robe was darker than the rest. "My water broke! It was the closest thing I could find."

"Don't worry about it, darling," he said. He eased her into a chair in one corner. "Are you in any pain?"

"Only occasionally. The contractions are coming closer together. Good thing I showered and did my legs!"

"I asked Anne to call Hal. He'll meet us at the hospital. Anything else need packing?"

"No, I've had a bag ready for weeks now. I've packed and repacked it dozens of times. Just wanted to make sure I packed my toothbrush."

He helped her put on another bathrobe. She cradled a towel between her legs to absorb further seepage. Then, arm around her waist, he helped her to the car. Mrs. Westfield followed with the overnight bag. Corley asking what was wrong with his mother.

They arrived at New Haven Memorial at one o'clock. Karen immediately went into labor. At two-ten, Diana Lynn Durham received a slap on the rump. Like her older brother, she turned pink from blue, and immediately screamed at the world into which Hal brought her.

They had not bathed Diana when Matt saw her and his wife wheeled from the operating room. He walked alongside a groggy Karen. Holding her limp hand. Kissing her sweat-shiny forehead. Babbling nonsensities about the beautiful little green-eyed girl.

She rested in a glass-enclosed room, surrounded by dozens of other babies. Parked in rows, swaddled in clear plastic bassinets. Five abreast.

Her early resemblance to his wife struck him...and warmly.

"It's only fair," he said, half aloud to his reflection. "You should look like your beautiful mother. Poor Corley's starting to look like his ugly old man."

An hour later, he walked back to the room. Karen sat in bed. Still sleepy-eyed.

"I've prayed you weren't hoping for another boy, Matt," she said.

He saw her wan face reflecting the ordeal she'd been through. Worry added creases to the quizzical look that flashed across her features.

He walked quietly to her. Sat gently on the edge of the bed. Softly stroked a ringlet of hair away from her eyes.

"All I've ever wanted was a healthy baby, honey. And for things to go smoothly for you," he whispered. "I've been down to the nursery. Looking through the window at the way they display the babies. She's the prettiest of the lot. Even with a red face and cavernous mouth!"

He took her hand. Felt her squeeze weakly. Looked into eyes fighting drug-induced sleep that pulled the lids heavily. He kissed her lightly on the cheeks.

"Like I've always said..." he whispered as Karen nodded off again. "'Little girls love their daddies!'"

The year had been bountiful for Matt. Personally and professionally. It came to a close with promises of more of the same.

For his birthday, Karen bought him a matched pair of Browning automatic shotguns. In twelve and twenty gauge. And in the ensuing months, he made excellent use of them on ducks, pleasant and quail.

By December first, they purchased a large deep freeze. They kept it at the foot of the stairs in their garage. Wild game soon filled nearly half of it. Either that Matt shot or friends gave him knowing his fondness for the taste.

Doctor Forsythe felt squeamish for several months. His colleagues at Yale Medical School checked him thoroughly, but detected nothing out of the ordinary. Still, Damon sensed something wrong, and intended seeing specialists in Boston early in the new year. He canceled the Christmas trip to Florida with Matt's parents. Preferring to remain in New Haven.

The doctor asked Matt if he, Karen, the children and Mrs. Westfield wanted to use The House again during Christmas. And he immediately accepted the offer. Much to Karen's delight. Since Christmas fell on Monday, they decided to drive down Saturday and spend the rest of the week in Huntsdale.

The sky offered a dull grey overlay as they pulled into the drive in front of The House. Matt unloaded the car, and noticed snowflakes drifting earthward.

So far, winter had been dry. With only occasional flurries and no buildup. This time, however, threatening skies meant business.

By the time he unloaded the car, Mrs. Westfield had lunch prepared. Snowflakes increased in size and intensity. And the near zero temperature enabled the white fluff to stick to grass, shrubbery and trees.

Matt laid a crackling fire in the living room fireplace. He stowed clothes, presents and food, then joined the others there. He rode his daughter on his knee, and welcomed the warmth permeating the room.

That evening, he prepared a large sirloin steak in the broiler beneath the range. He topped his entree with French fries, fresh peas and Mrs. Westfield's tart cherry cobbler and ice cream.

When the others went to bed, Matt and Karen sat on the couch before the glowing hearth. She tucked her feet under, and laid her head on his shoulder. They drank the sparkling red wine uncorked for dinner. Listening to soft music, and remembering the last evening spent on the couch. And making love before the dying embers.

Matt reached behind her, lifted a curtain with one finger. Outside, snowflakes cascaded between The House and light standard by the road. He knew tomorrow would arrive wrapped in clean white powder.

Sunday morning, they awakened and readied for church. Mrs. Westfield stayed to watch Diana.

Snow still drifted down. Adding to the five inches already blanketing the countryside. Matt started the stationwagon to warm it up. Then went inside for a broom. He swept the dry snow off the windows. And he, Karen and Corley piled inside for the drive to the First Presbyterian Church.

Matt loved driving on freshly fallen snow. Making first tracks, and looking over the hood at the pure white covering. Between he and Karen on the front seat, Corley excitedly chattered about playing in the snow and sledding when they returned from church.

The fourth quarter of the year was Corley's favorite, too. His excitement over Santa Claus' upcoming visit made him a willing volunteer for bedtime.

"When can we cut a Christmas tree, daddy?" asked the red-cheeked three-year-old seated between them. He leaned against his mother's left side. "When we get back? Huh? Huh?"

Matt looked over at his boy. Ruffled the silken hair with his right hand.

"Sure, tiger. Soon as we get back we'll change into warm clothes. Then go cut a big one!"

The youngster looked up at Karen. Blue-green eyes wide and pleading.

"Come with us, mommy. Okay?"

"You bet, darling," she leaned and kissed the top of his head. "After all...I'm the official tree picker-outer. Your dad couldn't do a thing without me!"

"She's right, son. She's exactly right."

Attendance at the morning service was sketchy because of the weather. Still, it provided them an opportunity to greet folks they hadn't seen for a month or two. Each of whom clucked over Corley's growth. And how he took after his father. Which made Matt proud.

When they returned to The House, Anne bent over a large pot of New England clam chowder bubbling on the stove. Grilled ham and cheese sandwiches warmed in the oven. And the ever steamy pot of coffee perked nearby. She guessed she drank at least fifteen cups a day. Sometimes twenty.

"Keeps you regular, if nothing else," she said when someone commented on her caffeine intake. "And besides..." she'd continue around the cigarette holder dangling precariously from one corner of her mouth: "...no calories, no alcohol and won't stain my teeth if I powder regularly!"

Mrs. Westfield spooned prepared baby food into Diana's ever-open mouth. A damp washcloth in her left hand, quickly wiping dribblings. And left eye squinted tightly against cigarette smoke curling over her cheek and watering it.

"You take a break...I'll finish feeding her, Annie," Karen said. She laid her hand on Mrs. Westfield's shoulder. "You're probably hungry anyway."

"Thanks, dear. Think I will have some coffee and soup. There's a chill in the air today."

"I'll check the thermostat," said Matt. He walked to the circular glass dome fastened to the dining room wall. "It's sixty-eight. I'll push it up a bit."

After lunch, Mrs. Westfield put Diana to bed for a nap. Then stretched out herself on the living room couch to read magazines. The others bundled and went outside.

Matt fetched Karen's trusty "Western Flyer" sled from the tool shed. Lifted Corley onboard. And hand-in-hand with Karen, towed him toward the cedar cluster half mile up the creek.

He intended cutting a tall balsam he spotted two years earlier when they Christmased at The House. Imagining it to be the right size now. However, Corley spotted a bushy Scotch pine. And Karen sided with him, voting down his father.

Matt took the bandsaw off his shoulder. Under protest, he cleared away snow and cut the trunk of the fat pine two inches above the ground. Its girth spread too full to fit the sled. So Karen pulled Corley, and Matt half-carried, half-dragged the tree.

When the three arrived...puffing and panting...they sat on the front porch steps a minute or so to catch their breaths. And sweep the snow off themselves and the tree.

Matt attached the tree stand outside. Then wrestled the conifer to the corner of the living room. The spot Christmas trees graced for more than one hundred years. He and Karen collapsed on the couch, while Corley unpacked bright ornaments and bulbs.

"You two probably could use these," said Mrs. Westfield. She appeared from the kitchen carrying a tray and two mugs brimming with hot-buttered rum. Matt took one of the containers. Handed the other to Karen. Clinked his against hers.

"Merry Christmas, sweetheart," he said. "You too, Anne and Corley. Here's to us."

Karen hefted her mug in toasting. Took a careful sip of the steamy liquid. Mrs. Westfield returned to the kitchen and reappeared with a bottle of Pepsi for Corley, and fresh cup of black coffee for herself.

That evening, they popped corn. Decorated the tree. And piled the glittery presents beneath. After wishing everyone season's greetings, Mrs. Westfield put Corley, Diana and herself to bed. By ten, only Matt and Karen remained downstairs.

He fixed them both brandies. Then switched on television. They sat with legs propped on the coffee table. Watching "White Christmas" and "A Christmas Carol" until past two.

In the shadowy room...illuminated only by a rosy glow from the hearth and milky picture tube glare...he felt her warmth beside him. Leaning against him. And recalled the many, many times in the exact same positions.

She dozed off and on. And tomorrow promised a full day. So Matt rousted her gently, and helped her up. He switched the television, and led her up the stairs to the bedroom.

Enroute to the bathroom to brush his teeth, Matt looked in on Diana in her crib. And Corley, sleeping in a full-sized bed with retainer railing. He kissed them both as they slept. His heart pulsing with the love he felt. Blended with the spirit of the season. And, probably, two large snifters of brandy.

Christmas day began with Corley tugging covers at seven o'clock. And again ended with them asleep on the living room couch at nine that night. Crowded between the hours came visits from Raymond and Helen Daley. And other of Huntsdale's townsfolk.

They received telephone calls from both sets of parents. As well as Hoot and Bobby, Eddie Bauer, and the Bradleys. In concert with Lyle, the previous Friday Matt arranged a catered party at the New York office. His other partners did the same at DG&B offices in Hartford and New Haven.

In Huntsdale, the three adults at The House teamed to prepare turkey with cornbread dressing, mashed potatoes, giblet gravy, green beans, cranberry salad and buttermilk biscuits. Afterwards, they made themselves even more miserable with large wedges of fresh baked pie. Minced meat for Matt and Anne. Pumpkin, for Karen, Corley and Diana. Topped with puffy mounds of fresh whipping cream.

Between their two incomes, Matt and Karen enjoyed a comfortable lifestyle...but not ostentatious. They could afford the things they wanted. Especially, nice Christmas gifts for each other, their children, their folks, and Mrs. Westfield.

As a Yuletide bonus, Matt gave the housekeeper a week off with pay...whenever she wanted. Plus, he would pay for her flight and first-class accommodations at the location of her choice. She accepted his offer. Only for a visit to her sister in Boston. And, by train.

"God didn't mean us to fly, Matt Durham," she scolded when he mentioned thirty minutes versus two hours. "A half hour turns into a lifetime if you plummet from the sky like a rock!"

Tuesday, Matt spent the day playing outside with Corley. And driving snow-covered roads around Huntsdale. The two visited Arch's store for a beer for him...and Pepsi for Corley. And chatted with the locals.

That night, with the children in bed, the three grown-ups played Scrabble. Until each of their eyes drooped closed, and they called it a day.

Wednesday dawned bright, sunny and much warmer. By the time they'd finished breakfast, large glops of melting snow splatted the ground from the gutters above. Making loud splopping sounds, and burrowing circles in the snow below.

Karen and Matt busied themselves removing ornaments from the tree in the living room. Corley helped. When the telephone rang. They heard Mrs. Westfield answer in the kitchen. And barely made out the hushed tones of conversation.

"Yes, just a minute please. I'll get him," she said.

Anne appeared in the living room. Beckoned to Matt. And shrugged her shoulders when asked who it was. He handed a string of lights he untangled to Karen. Disappeared into the kitchen to answer.

"Must be Hoot or someone," he said over his shoulder.

He lifted the handset from the countertop.

"Hello?"

"Hello, Matt. This is Hal Sappington." The doctor's voice on the other end sounded flat, strained. Matt's chest twinged, and goosepimples stood on his exposed forearm. "I've got terrible news. Is Karen nearby?"

"No, doctor. She's in the living room," he replied. His voice choked almost to a whisper.

"It's her father, Matt. Damon died a few minutes ago. Massive coronary. We tried everything. Couldn't get his heart beating. Damn, I hate telling you this but..."

"How's Evelyn, Hal? Does she know?"

"Yes. She's in shock. I think you two need to get back quick as you can. I've given her a sedative. Your folks are with her. She needs Karen. I'm so sorry. There just wasn't any more we could do.

"I'm sure it wasn't anyone's fault, Hal. I know you loved him like the rest of us."

Matt immediately thought of his father. Wished he was with Walt, sharing his grief. Even after the killing he'd seen, the general would take it hard.

"I'd better tell Karen, Hal. If the roads are clear, we'll be there in a few hours. Is Evelyn home?"

"Yes, Matt. We're with her now."

They hung up. Matt slumped into one of the chairs around the breakfast table. Buried his face in his hands. Thought of how best to tell her.

His stomach knotted. Hands trembled. And throat constricted to a choking tightness. Slowly, he rose from the table. Walked into the living room. Karen looked from where she and Corley placed shiny red ornaments in cardboard crisscrosses. Saw his ashen face. And her voice cracked with hoarseness.

"Matt? Matt? What is it?" She stood. Walked to him. Saw his eyes fill and overflow.

"I'm sorry, darling. That was Hal Sappington. Damon suffered a heart attack," he blurted. He clutched her tightly in his arms. Talked softly through her hair. Felt her tightening with sobs. "Hal said they tried their best...just couldn't save him."

Karen now sobbed hysterically. Trying to ask questions through choking gasps. Voicing only guttural sounds. He held her tighter. Stroked her hair and back.

Corley came to where they stood. Crying and concerned himself. Mrs. Westfield lifted and hugged him to her shoulder.

"We have to head home, honey," he said. "Hal says your mother needs you as quickly as we can make it. My folks are there. It's you she wants. We'll get started when you feel better."

Matt steered her to the kitchen. Poured them jiggers of brandy. Asked Karen to sip hers. The sobs came from deep within. Tears subsiding. The worst passed. Although several times, the fluttery light, sad feeling would return to her over the next few months.

They hurriedly packed the stationwagon. Matt planned to return for the remainder of their clothes in the next couple of days. By noon, they drove Highway 95 for New Haven. Riding the thawing roads in silence. Except frothy slush splashing in the fender wells.

Corley and Diana sat quietly in the back seat with Mrs. Westfield. Karen stared out the passenger's window. Eyes perpetually brimming.

Matt placed his hand on her knee. Offering what comfort he could.

They held Doctor Forsythe's funeral on Friday. Which, unlike the earlier snowy part of the week, turned unseasonably warm. Walt, Matt, Hoot and Hal Sappington counted among Damon's pallbearers. Wearing only dark suits.

Walt performed the eulogy. Paying fitting tribute to his closest friend for nearly half a century. Afterwards, he and Claire consoled Evelyn. Vowing always to be nearby if she wanted for anything.

"I loved him like a brother, Evie. Even more so. I know he felt the same about me," said Walt, as the black Cadillac limousine cruised smoothly along the inner belt from the cemetery to the funeral parlor. "In all our years...we never asked each other 'Why?' Or told each other 'No.'"

Karen and Matt asked her mother to stay with them. She accepted the offer. Moving a few of her things into an upstairs bedroom the next day. The two hoped her being around Corley and Diana would provide something to occupy her time and mind. Help her get over the man with whom she'd shared her life...good times and bad...for more than thirty-five years.

Matt planned on flying back to New York Tuesday evening, after spending New Years with his family. That afternoon, he, Karen and Evelyn enjoyed a glass of sherry.

"You two can have it, you know," Evelyn said, monotone. "I don't care about ever going back."

"What are you talking about, mom?" Karen asked. She slid to the floor to sit at her mother's feet. Looked up, and took both the woman's hands in hers.

Evelyn glanced sadly at her daughter. Then at Matt.

"The House. You two love it. Like Damon. Like I did. I can't go back there. It embodies a big part of him. Things connected with it are too tender."

Karen rose to her knees. Cradled her mother's head against her breast. Stroked her parent's hair. Tears welling.

"You'll be fine, mom. Don't worry. They cut Forsythes and Durhams from damned hardy stock. We'll get through this. And when we do, most everything will be the same. It'll take time. However, it'll happen."

"Karen's right, Evelyn," added Matt.

He stood and walked to the two on the couch. "We'll always be here. Please remember that. My folks, too. All of us love you. We'll work to fill the gaps. Believe me."

She looked up at them. Smiled a quick little smile through the tear-stained cheeks. Took their hands.

"You're right, of course. I loved that man more than anything. Now, there are many others to spend my love on. I'll be okay. Karen. Matt. I promise."

Later, pulling from the driveway, Matt watched the rearview mirror as his home receded in the distance. He felt a twinge of loneliness spark his stomach. A tingle rippled his chest.

Then he thought of work waiting at the office. Instantly, his temples compressed and neck taughtened with anxiety. Then he thought of Suzanne no longer there. The yearnings for New York faded.

He easily could make Triad's flight from Hartford. So he let off the accelerator, and drove quietly and slowly through the darkness of northern New Haven.

Chapter 22

Keith Hillary

"A LOT HAS HAPPENED IN THREE years, Greer," said Matt. Outside the office, a sunny September day shaped itself. The two looked over throngs of tiny people below. Parading around traffic on Madison Avenue.

Everything's happening too quickly, he thought to himself. President Kennedy killed two years ago. Everybody's up in arms...protesting about something. And this damned conflict in Southeast Asia. It's turning into a skirmish Johnson doesn't know how to handle.

Greer McCall took a long pull from his can of Pepsi. Shrugged his shoulders, and studied the container's words while he spoke.

"Agreed, Matt. It's all going too fast. Still, not much we can do but flow with it. Business is going great guns here. And in Hartford and New Haven."

He took another sip of the soft drink.

"Old man Bradley's with the public affairs corps in Washington. He's on the news almost every night. Plugging Bradley, Durham and Associates. Hell, look at Lyle! One of the top media buyers in New York. A veritable wizard at putting together television buys for our clients."

Matt walked to where the other sat. Lowered into an easy chair across from him.

"That worries me, too, Greer," came the comment. "Lyle and I seldom discuss what he's doing. I know he's at the networks. Or dining some bigshot. I haven't got a handle on how he arranges such fantastic television buys."

Matt leaned his head back. Turned it slowly, side to side. Heard and felt tension grind in his neck.

"Mind you, I shouldn't bitch. He wangled three minutes for Triad on 'The Virginian.' That show is booked solid well into next year!"

"Like I say, Matt. That's his specialty. He may have photos of network executives screwing goats! Whatever, he gets what our clients want."

Hoot's workload reached eye level proportions, too.

He oversaw the New Haven office of DG&B. Splitting time between Connecticut Castings and other local accounts. And also handled Middletown. Where his father's modern and mammoth four-color presses printed most of their ads and collateral materials. Hoot additionally tried sharing as much time as possible with Elizabeth...the daughter to whom Bobby had given birth in early June. Bobby opted to close her teaching career a few years and raise a family. Hoot favored the idea. And they posted a successful start.

Ed Gibson...like Walt Durham...tried desperately to retire. However, he loved work so much he still spent half days at the plant. Overseeing various and sundry jobs. Especially those Hoot and Eddie brought. Making certain they bordered perfection.

Over the past two years, Ed shifted most responsibilities to a man who worked beside him for a decade. He promoted him to general manager only recently. Leaving the decisions of running a huge plant with several large web and smaller sheet-fed presses in capable hands. Still, Ed felt useless just getting up every day. Reading the paper. And figuring what to do with the waking hours from seven o'clock on.

Walt fared as badly. Never a country club athlete, he once scorned tennis and golf. Considered them "sissy" games. Now, however, he enjoyed lessons in both sports. Hoping he'd fill the void in his life after retirement from Conn Castings.

Walt served as a Conn Casting's consultant and board member. Receiving top wages performing these duties. However, when the company introduced its new fleet of jetliners...now into the 700 and 800 series, carrying up to one hundred and sixty passengers...he felt tinges of regret for not having more involvement in their development.

Claire joined him in golf and tennis lessons. Attempting to keep her own mind occupied and body healthy as she could.

"God knows, our son isn't," she complained frequently. "What with smoking again. And probably drinking too much." She convinced herself of the latter. Several times when Claire reached him late at his apartment, he seemed thick tongued and irritable over her inquiries.

"Besides, Walt, he doesn't seem to come back to New Haven as regularly as he used to," she added. "And he should. His children are growing up under his nose."

"Yes, Claire," Walt admonished, patting her back.

In truth, she was right. Corley began second grade the week before. And Diana started nursery school. Karen worked full-time at Peck & Peck the past year and a half. Leaving Mrs. Westfield shepherding the children.

When Matt returned to New Haven for weekends, he spoiled them terribly. Providing toys, candy, movies, clothes and everything else they wanted.

And there was The House. Every other weekend...on his reappearance...Matt took Karen, their kids and Anne to The House. There, he disappeared on long walks during the days: "Clearing his mind."

Then muddling it again until morning's early hours with bourbon and water. When he half passed out and fell asleep on the living room couch. Watching "The Tonight Show," and cheering loudly when Triad commercials aired.

They hired a Huntsdale couple...Guy and Opal Simpson...to watch after The House. Make sure squirrels didn't get into the attic through the ventilation windows. Or pipes didn't freeze. Or weeds take over the manicured yard; of which Damon Forsythe was so proud, and fussed over like a Boston fishwife.

Guy stretched tall and lean as a leather whip. Skin tanned taut by seasons in the fields. Plowing, planting and harvesting. Then starting over. This time, perhaps, breaking even. Or making enough to pay another semester's tuition for a son in college.

When Matt inquired about someone looking after The House, Raymond Daley recommended Guy. An honest, hardworking farmer.

Matt met the couple two weekends later. Liked them immediately. And offered five hundred dollars monthly to keep the place in good stead. Not only that, but gave Guy permission to farm any land if he wanted. As long as he left untilled acreage and spilled grain for wildlife.

"Buy whatever equipment you need to make the land profitable," Matt concluded after they shook hands.

Guy took him at his word. Purchased a large John Deere tractor and combine. And ancillary equipment...plow, disk, planter and bailer.

The previous year, Guy planted soybeans, corn, sorghum and tobacco.

Each crop producing bumper yields. And profits from the land. That for several years suffered neglect and provided minimal crops to support wildlife.

Guy also kept his eyes sharp for tracts of land in the area worth purchasing. Always negotiating shrewdly, but fairly, he acquired another two thousand acres with Matt's blessings.

Matt's holdings of prime bottomland bordering the Paginaw River exceeded five thousand acres. Every three years, for as long as he remembered, the Paginaw topped its banks and flooded most of that acreage. Lost crops turned into insurance payments. And when the waters receded, they deposited for free another four inches of fresh, black soil.

Guy and Opal came from farm families in central Iowa. When The Depression hit...and crops withered and blew away...the two struck out for the East as newlyweds. Unlike everyone else, heading in the opposite direction.

Guy's older brother engineered for the Northeastern Pennsylvania Railroad. He finagled his kid sibling a job as yard supervisor in New London, Connecticut. Overseeing a spur line that dead-ended there from Scranton, Pennsylvania.

He toiled long hours. In stifling heat, and bone-chilling cold. Performing tedious, sweaty and grimy tasks. However, they ate without begging handouts. Even saved for a parcel of land west of Huntsdale.

They bought five hundred acres at fifty cents an acre. Including a ramshackle two-story farmhouse. In 1939, they moved there with their meager belongings.

When World War Two began, Guy enlisted in the army with several others from Huntsdale. He immediately shipped overseas, and drove troop transport vehicles. Where he demonstrated an ability to think under fire. And soon found himself as driver for a field commander.

In the fall of 1943, a mine exploded under his jeep at Salerno, Italy. It ripped off half of his colonel's left leg. And punctured Guy's right lung. Somehow, he bandaged the officer's wound and carried him piggyback for two miles. He stumbled into an Allied outpost behind the main line of defense before passing out.

The Secretary of the Army presented Guy the Silver Star and Purple Heart medals. And, because of his physical condition, released him from active duty with a lifetime pension.

The pension, combined with allotment checks he'd sent Opal, enabled them to buy used farm equipment and plant their first crops of corn and tobacco.

Over the years, the Simpsons frugally invested their profits from selling crops. They remodeled their home. Added a large dairy barn. And installed several equipment sheds and grain storage bins.

Each year, Guy set aside most of May or June to add a needed structure. Or paint and repair those requiring maintenance. The Simpson's farm presented a panorama of neatness. From white rail fence alongside the road, to the livestock windmill beyond the cornfield.

Beyond that, it stood as tribute and devotion to a way of life that brought satisfaction and happiness.

Opal appeared the complete opposite of her husband. Except in honesty, personality and humor. He reached skyscraper tall. Six foot three. And lean. Maybe one hundred and seventy pounds.

She was short, plump and apple-cheeked. Always smelling of freshly made biscuits and lye soap. And turned mustard greens and fatback into a gourmand's delight.

Her specialty was pastries. For which she possessed an obvious weakness herself. Her lemon meringue pies garnered blue ribbons at county fairs throughout the state. Eliciting sensuous moans of delight from those tasting them. And jealous grimaces from competitors when prizes fell to the victors.

Soon after discharge from the army, Guy met Raymond Daley at Arch's in Huntsdale. Over small talk and a bottle of beer, each developed a liking for the other. Over two decades, that happenstance friendship grew to tremendous respect.

So when Matt sought Raymond's recommendation for someone nearby watching The House, he immediately named Guy and Opal.

Matt looked forward to this Fall Festival for a month. At last, he thrilled catching the afternoon Triad flight to Hartford.

Two months ago, he bought a Mercedes convertible. Now, top down, its speedometer needle bounced against eighty miles-per-hour. And pressures of maintaining a leading New York advertising agency fell behind as the wind whipped his hair.

He collected a six-pack of beer in Hartford. Pulled from one of the cans as he sped south on Highway 91. Relaxing for the first time in months. Enjoying autumn colors creeping into the woods lining both sides of the road. He wedged the can between his thighs. Lit a cigarette. And let his mind wander to the promise of the long weekend ahead.

Matt crimped his third empty can as he stepped from the Mercedes. He walked up the drive beside his home. Stopped at the back door. Coat slung over his shoulder. Briefcase and three beers in a plastic holder in his left hand. Mrs. Westfield answered soon after his one-finger, beer-can-clutching ring.

"Hello, Annie Fannie," he said. He frowned at surprise sweeping the housekeeper's face. Recognizing he swayed to the left of tipsy. "Ready for the annual fall flim flam?"

"Matt Durham, you've got swacked!" she said. She jerked the remaining brews from his hand. Tossed them in the refrigerator. "You're lucky the highway police didn't catch you drinking beer! They'd run you in, you know!"

"Hell, Anne. They'd have to catch me first!" he slurred. He walked into the kitchen, set the briefcase and empty can on the serving bar. "Where's my happy little family?"

"Diana's upstairs napping. Karen's picking up Corley at school. She'll be back in a minute. Why don't you have a cup of coffee?"

"That bad, huh?" he asked, loosening his tie. "Yeah...you're right. I'd better, or Karen will jump me sure."

He took the coffee cup, collected his things, and went upstairs to the master bedroom. He shucked his business clothes, and pulled on a favorite shirt and faded jeans. Then packed a few casual outfits. Since most of his hunting clothes remained at The House.

He grabbed a shave kit from the bathroom, then brushed his teeth. Grimacing, as black coffee mixed with toothpaste. In minutes, the slight high began subsiding.

"Just in time," he thought, as Karen's stationwagon hummed in the driveway.

Moments later, he heard muffled voices in the kitchen. Then Corley shouting excitedly: "Daddy! Daddy!"

The thump of footsteps rushed the stairs. The bedroom door burst open. There stood his son. Nearly breathless from taking steps two at a time.

Cheeks tinged with red. Honeyed hair fluffed from exertion. Smile stretching ear to ear.

He ran to his father. Hugged as Matt lifted him up, and playfully tossed him onto the king-size bed.

"Hey, sport. Ready to plug a squirrel or two?"

"Yes, daddy. You bet! Think grandpa will let me shoot his rifle again this year?"

"I'm sure he will, son."

Matt tousled the youngster's hair. Felt his chest swell with pride over Corley's rugged good looks. The top of his head nearly reached Matt's chin. Of course, Karen was tall for a woman. He stood average height. He guessed Corley would hit six feet at least.

"Your stuff packed and ready, Corley?"

"Oh, yessir! Since last night! When do we leave?"

"Soon as Diana's up from her nap. And Uncle Hoot and Aunt Bobby get here. Why not carry your gear downstairs while I say hello to mommy?"

"Sure, dad," Corley replied. He hit the floor, both feet blurs for the doorway.

Matt walked down the stairs. Smiled, hearing his son rustle around his room. Happily talking to himself. Karen stood at the foot of the stairs. Talking with Mrs. Westfield. She looked up at her husband.

"Well...something must have tickled your funny bone," she said, meeting him on the last riser. She puckered her lips and squinted her eyes for a kiss.

He put his arms around her. Pecked her mouth.

"It's that kid of yours. Fall Festival excites him. Must be the food and ice cream."

"Not really, Matt," she replied, suddenly serious. Her voice dropped low and level.

"It's his only time with his father anymore."

Matt felt a warm flush spread over his face. Anger rising to her comment. Unsure, whether at her, or himself. The jagged edge of conscience ripped. And he regretfully realized she came too damned close to being right.

He started to agree. Then heard Hoot's car in the driveway. He turned and shouted upstairs.

"They're here, Corley. Bring your gear down, please."

He returned to Karen. Who now looked quizzically at him. Hurt glazed her eyes. She apologized.

"I'm sorry, Matt. I didn't mean it the way it sounded."

"Forget it," he said, subdued. "You're right."

He spun and returned upstairs to collect his things. No sooner reaching the top step when Corley raced past carrying a b-b gun in one hand, and duffel bag in the other.

"Let's go, you guys," the boy pleaded, racing for the back door.

Karen and Mrs. Westfield went upstairs and fetched Diana. Matt and Corley loaded the stationwagon. Hoot approached to offer help while Bobby stayed in their car, playing with Elizabeth. In a few minutes, Karen, Diana and Anne appeared at the back door, then entered the stationwagon.

"We need to stop for anything, Matthew?" asked Hoot.

"Maybe beer, Hooter. Don't think we've got any at The House."

"Sure thing. We'll hit that little liquor store on Maple Avenue."

Hoot backed down the driveway. He left room for Matt to assume the lead. The small caravan motored from Wellham Park and headed for the interstate.

Dusk tied their arrival at The House. And Evelyn Forsythe surprised the travelers by appearing with Claire and Walt on the front porch. Marking her first visit to the place for three years.

Karen's eyes glazed on seeing her mother standing there. Recovering from surprise, she jumped from the car and hugged the woman. Walt patted the two as he trod past on the steps, and helped Matt, Corley and Hoot unload the cars.

That evening, for the first time in a long while, the adults sat and talked until midnight. Then everyone sought bedtime, since the menfolk rose at dawn and headed for the squirrel woods.

Matt, as usual, was first up. Dressed, drinking coffee and scrambling eggs for the others. One by one, his companions arose, brushed teeth, washed faces, and straggled downstairs. Corley arrived second, and already jittered around the kitchen. He fretted impatiently to join the darkness outside that glowed blue-orange toward the East.

Matt smiled at the youngster's eagerness to get under way. Remembering himself at that age. Looking out that same window toward the Paginaw River. Imagining swarms of ducks that soon would circle noisily above their blind.

"Well, Burrhead...you two got breakfast ready?" Walt asked, entering the kitchen. He fussed with buttoning his wool plaid lumberjack's shirt. "We need to be in the woods by first light. Those squirrels will move early. It's nippy today."

By the time Hoot joined them, Matt set a huge skillet of fluffy scrambled eggs on a trivet in the middle of the table. The hunters dug in. And Corley politely circled the table. Filling glasses with freshly squeezed orange juice. As much keeping his mind and hands busy as helping his father.

When they finished eating, Matt and Hoot rinsed the dishes. Corley and Walt donned their canvas hunting jackets, then fetched the .22 caliber rifles from the locked gun cabinet in the library. Walt handed a box of cartridges to his grandson.

"Here, Corley. You carry the ammunition and rifle today. Old gramps is a mite stiff in the joints. Stayed up too late last night."

"Gee, thanks, grandpa," came the excited reply.

The sun painted the rear of The House as they entered the walnut grove at the crest of October Hill. Walt and his partner followed a game trail to the right. Matt and Hoot veered to the left, aiming for the hickory grove where the woods stopped and cornfield began. They hadn't sat ten minutes when the sharp crack of a small rifle pierced the stillness in the distance.

"Well, the general got one for the pot," Hoot said. Matt nodded. Offered his friend a cigarette. Hoot waved it off, not taking up the habit again. Matt lit and inhaled deeply. He raised the bill of his hunting cap. Let smoke drift from his mouth, and disappear into the clearing on his left.

The two discussed business. Families. The escalating turmoil in Southeast Asia. And, of course, good times had together.

From time to time while chattering, they heard a rifle pop in the direction Walt and Corley disappeared. And several times, Matt or Hoot would halt in the middle of a sentence. Then raise a rifle and collect a squirrel for their bag.

By noon, the two men stowed three squirrels apiece in their game pouches. They hiked toward the spot where they'd separated from Walt and Corley.

When they approached the other trail, Matt whistled like a Bobwhite. A similar trill sounded close by. And soon, Walt and Corley appeared. The young man carried the rifle military-style, over a shoulder and muzzle up. In his other hand, he clutched five large fox squirrels by their tails.

The number of folks celebrating Fall Festival grew smaller every year. Kids grew and moved away. Or farm families left for city work, rather than scratching livings from the rich soil around Huntsdale.

With Matt's nod, Guy Simpson acquired additional land as older families sold and moved. At last count, Matt reckoned he owned ten thousand fertile acres along the Paginaw. Much of it from Judge Corley's estate, auctioned a year ago.

Still, those attending the Festival partook of enjoyable times and full stomachs. The ruralists reckoned the hunting would prove exceptionally good this year.

Which it was...and for the next three, too.

Matt and Keith Hillary became comrades and close friends over the hunting seasons speeding by. Not that the latter could ever replace Hoot. Who frequently joined their hunts. As did Walt and, on reaching ten, Corley.

Keith recounted tales his daughter wrote or called from Europe. Eagerly exhibiting the many postcards she sent. Clearly, he expressed pride in the manner in which she stepped into an extremely challenging position. In what most called a man's world. Yet, Suzanne had become tremendously successful.

Matt listened with keen interest to Keith's conversations. In dealings and hunting ventures with the man, he also gained an intimate knowledge of international construction. Knew the ins and outs almost as well as Hillary Engineering managers. Which is why Keith kept offering him jobs at any salary, in any location. And Matt politely refused them, saying:

"I'm into conception...not construction. I build desires...not dams."

It became evident Keith thought of Matt like a son. Although somewhat jealous at first, Walt felt flattered and proud.

A respected and powerful person thought that much of the man he'd raised. Looking back, Walt guessed he hadn't screwed up too badly.

When Suzanne called her father with a report, or to discuss a problem that arose, Matt occasionally talked with her. Keith would politely busy himself doing something else. Or leave the room while they talked.

More and more, Matt detected something in Suzanne's voice. A certain note or inflection. An excited inner voice saying she talked only to him in this manner. And she ended conversations by saying she couldn't wait to see him again. And seeming extremely sincere in doing so.

He also looked forward to that reunion. Thinking of it excited him. And made his insides feel hollow.

Earlier in the year, lunatics assassinated Martin Luther King and Robert F. Kennedy. Riots broke in major cities throughout the United States. And Vietnam had escalated beyond a conflict.

When Matt read the year's death toll approached ten thousand, he became furious over the waste of being in "another war where we don't belong." And felt doubly thankful his son was too young for involvement.

With the passing years, Karen realized Matt managed to spend less and less time in New Haven with his family. In another year, Corley would finish grade school. Diana would be in the second grade. And they had yet to take a family vacation.

Matt stole away from New York five or six times for long weekends at The House. Which did not rank as a vacation for Karen. After all, she and Anne still cooked and cleaned. Plus, Karen yearned for more excitement. Something beyond sitting and talking while the kids played. And Matt either fished, hunted or got tipsy...or all three...with his cronies.

In New York, she knew he wined and dined clients almost every night. Or flew here and there for location filming and commercial production. He'd traveled to the West Coast for five weekends already. The last fell on June 20. Causing him to stand her up for their fifteenth wedding anniversary.

Karen dined with Hoot and Bobby. Then got pie-eyed drunk on champagne.

And extremely sick. Instead of showing Matt her displeasure, she suffered a thudding headache and turvey stomach that lurched for days.

Matt came home the following weekend. Wearing a sheepish grin, and presenting her with roses and an expensive gold Rolex watch. She icily refused to talk to him. Told him to, "Go back to the place you love more than us!"

That evening, Anne calmed Karen. And convinced her to talk with Matt, even though sobbing, and revealing red eyes and runny nose.

"After all, Karen," the astute housekeeper said. "The important thing is keeping the kids from getting hurt."

Matt sat in the family room with Corley and Diana. Reading the evening paper, and nursing Russian vodka on the rocks. The kids played Scrabble on the floor.

When Karen entered the room, his thick tongue greeted her. Angering her even more. She curtly asked the children to play upstairs. Then closed the French doors behind when they left.

"This boil has been coming to a head for a long time now, Matt," she said crisply, flatly. "I think we'd better air a few things."

She snatched the highball glass from his hand. Sat on the footstool directly in front of him.

"You're wealthy. You're successful. You head one of the top advertising agencies on Madison Avenue. And you're acting so goddamned stupid!"

Tears hung at the corners of her eyes. Her words finally penetrated his blank expression.

"I don't see you. The kids don't see you. Except maybe four or five days a month. How much longer can this go on!"

Her face flushed now. The tears welled in her eyes. Stained her cheeks. She wiped them away with the back of her hand. Stood, hands on hips, staring down at his silence. Exasperated. She continued, almost hissing the words.

"If you haven't time for your family Matt...that's fine. Just haul your ass out, and don't come back. I've had it with our children crying because daddy's never around. I sometimes think they blame me for not making you happy enough to come home."

At first, he grew angry. Ready to fight. Then realized she nailed him dead to rights. Somewhere deep inside he felt regret burning a hole in his guts.

"I don't know what to tell you, Karen."

He dared not look into her face. Under intense pressure as he now experienced, his face sometimes beamed a weird smile. Beyond his control. And to do so, now, would set her raging. He looked at his feet.

"I've tried cutting the amount of work I do personally. I thought merging with Lyle Bradley would help even more. I can't distance myself further. I love what I do. The excitement...the challenge of winning new accounts. Taking a nothing campaign, and making it sing. No matter how much we accomplish, there's always more needing doing. And in many instances, I'm the only one to do it."

"Bullshit, Matt!" she turned sharply. Clapped her hands against the sides of her thighs. "You do it mainly because you want to! You've got twenty other people to do the work. You could have any of them handle your assignments. In fact, you could delegate damned near everything you do...rather than tackle it yourself. You know that!"

"Hold it, Karen. My work is not that goddamned easy! And I doubt anyone is more knowledgeable about Hillary Engineering. Besides, Keith won't deal with anyone but me. Won't listen to someone else's ideas."

He raised off the couch. Fetched his drink glass. "Triad's the same way. Greer does most of the work. Still, those guys expect my touch. That's part of the deal. I keep at least thirty clients happy. Damned near one for every day of the month. That accounts for my time away from my family. It paid for this house. That watch. Your new car. And it'll see Corley and Diana through the best schools in the United States...or Europe for that matter. First class all the way, too."

"Okay, Matt." She held her palms toward him. Signaling the discussion's end. "You're right. You're the indispensable leader of Bradley and Durham."

She walked toward the door through which Corley and Diana exited.

"Well, fine. Let me tell you this, though. When you wake up someday...slow down and look around...you'll be by yourself. Your kids will be grown...and gone. I'll be past caring."

She turned on her heel, and softly said over her shoulder, "If that's what you truly want...better leave for New York now."

Then, she walked out of the room and up the stairs, leaving the double doors standing open.

Matt stood silently for a moment, then followed her upstairs.

She lay on the bed, facing the windows.

"I guess you're right," he said. His voice assumed monotone. "I'll catch the nine o'clock to New York. First, I'll look in on the kids. So long, Karen."

He turned and walked from the bedroom. Karen felt convulsing sadness flood her body. And sobbed into her pillow. The bed bouncing under her emotions.

Eventually, she cried herself to sleep. And before he climbed into bed, Corley tiptoed into his parents' bedroom and pulled a comforter over his mother.

Chapter 23

Hoot's Turn To Hurt

Richard M. Nixon served nearly two years as President. The conflict in Southeast Asia spread carcinoma-like into Cambodia. The "Chicago Seven" crossed state lines and incited rioting at the Democratic Convention in Chicago. Earning indictments. And on May 29, Corley Durham celebrated his twelfth birthday.

The youngster twitched with excitement riding the gravel road that led from The House to the Paginaw. He stared into the darkness, already imagining events that would occur. Knowing he always would cherish this first duck hunt with his father, grandfather and uncle Hoot.

Matt drove. His dad and Hoot sat in the back seat. Conferring over the many birds seen the day before, while setting decoys.

"I'll tell you, Corley...you'd have gone bananas!"

Walt tapped his grandson's shoulder to turn him around. The young man hiked his knee into the car seat. Faced his grandfather, mouth gaping.

"Yessir, it's a shame your dad couldn't drive down until last night. Bet Hoot and I flared five thousand ducks in front of the blind!"

"At least that many, Walt," agreed Hoot. "Reminded me of first hunting on the Paginaw with you. Must have had a great hatch up north last spring."

"It was a record, Hoot," Matt piped. "According to 'Ducks Unlimited,' the prairie states registered plenty of rain...and that helps the brooding."

He swung the car onto a dirt road bisecting the bottomland cornfields. Guy Simpson had been busy harvesting. The headlights flashed the stands of brown stalks. And reflected stark white against large birch trees lining the river bank a quarter mile away.

They drove the soft silent delta soil to a clearing. Where woods butted against corn rows. Matt steered beside the wooden walkway leading to the boathouse.

They stepped from the car, breaths hanging in clouds before them.

In the early morning stillness, the river current roared between its banks. Gurgling against pilings on which the boathouse and walkway sat.

The darkness pressing around them amplified the noise of unloading knapsacks, waders and shotguns from the back of the stationwagon. Matt flipped on a large spotlight and lit the way to the boat.

The four walked Indian style down the wooden jetty to the secured aluminum johnboat. Matt assumed his place at the helm. Held the light as the others climbed aboard.

When all sat...lifejackets in place...he switched the light off. He listened to silence for a minute. While his eyes adjusted to the engulfing blackness. In the distance...probably the cornfields up and across the Paginaw...they heard hundreds of Canada geese babbling. Sounding like dogs baying, as they fed on grain and awaited the sunrise to start their day.

Matt reached back and twisted the throttle handle to "start." He yanked the starter cord firmly, and the Evinrude fired. Racing wildly as it caught, then settling on a low growl. Spitting water and oil smoke behind.

Corley unhitched the bowline, and pushed the boat away from the dock. Matt pulled the gear lever into "forward." Cranked the gas handle slightly, and the johnboat lifted its nose. Skimming forward into the heart of the Paginaw.

They had plenty of time. It was not yet five thirty. So Matt gave the outboard quarter throttle and lit a cigarette in his cupped hands. The wind spanked chilly enough to make his eyes water. The sky showed a tinge of pink over Hoot's left shoulder. In half an hour, it would glow bright orange.

They motored downriver in frosty silence. Water slapping the flat nose of the boat ahead. Steady hum of the outboard behind. Until they spotted the decoy spread on their left. And square patch to the rear that would be the blind.

Matt shut the throttle completely. Dead-steered around the shadowy outlines of the hut on stilts. The craft drifted quietly, nudging the narrow walkway around the blind's perimeter.

Corley clutched a piling. Held the johnboat against the flooring as the others scrambled out. Taking tote bags, guns and waders with them. Then the young man pulled up onto the platform, and tied the boat beneath the overhanging cover of straw and Johnson grass.

Corley and Matt pulled on their chest waders. Hoot and Walt lit charcoal buckets that rested on asbestos pads atop sheets of steel. Then they arranged gear within the small enclosure. The two with waders walked down the three steps to the sandy bottom. Trudged among the decoys, untangling lines and increasing space between blocks. That done, they returned inside and peeled the waders.

Hoot poured cups of coffee for the grown-ups. A cup of sweet tea for Corley. Then they loaded their shotguns and waited for sunrise. While charcoal smoke stung noses and watered eyes until burning to glowing coals.

Matt looked to his right at his son. Thought back twenty-eight years to his first time. When he had become a member of The October Club. Privileged to hunt with grown-ups. Specifically, his dad, Judge Corley and Damon Forsythe.

A tinge of sadness flashed across his chest as he recalled the judge and doctor. Soon replaced by pride felt over his son.

A few hundred yards away, near the flooded timber, a mallard hen scolded the sunrise. Voicing to feathered comrades her disappointment over another day dawning.

Out of the corner of his eye, Matt saw Corley stiffen. Straining to hear and see the hen in the dark woodsy area where climbing golden sunlight had not penetrated.

Already, strings of waterfowl moved up and down the river. Several times passing low enough the men in the blind heard wings whistling. And the chuckle feeding call of mallards.

The general reached into the side pocket of his knapsack. Retrieved the traditional flask of blackberry brandy. Held it high.

"Gentlemen...to the hunt," he said. He took a quick swig of the biting liquid. "And to you, Corley. Welcome to the October Club."

He passed the container to Hoot. Who, likewise, performed the ritual. And handed it to Matt.

"Glad to have you with us, son. By the way...you do know who shags downed ducks, don't you?"

"Yessir...I imagine so," Corley replied. He took the decanter, put it to his lips, and took a sip. He coughed slightly. "Wow! That stuff's hot!"

The men laughed, then shuttled the brandy back to Walt. Who replaced it in the knapsack. Matt lit a cigarette, and dropped more charcoal into the fire buckets when wings whistled close and behind.

"Shush!" he whispered softly.

He eased out his call and trilled the "chucka-chucka-chucka" feeding sound. A thick mat of Johnson grass hung over the shooting slot at the front of the blind. Through it, the four spotted the waterfowl. About twenty mallards. Swinging wide to the left. Trying to get the wind against their breasts.

When the birds hovered straight away, two hundred yards out, Matt and Walt blew long, drawn-out highball calls. As if remote-controlled, the ducks swung sharply, cupped their wings, and pitched feet first into the outside edge of the decoys.

"Too far out," cautioned Walt.

He called with deep, pleading quacks. Then Matt joined him. Soon, the rafted mallards paddled within gunshot range.

Matt touched Corley on the right knee.

"Remember, son. You target birds swinging left of the blind. Hoot and I will shoot out front. Your grandfather will handle those veering right. And, greenheads only...okay?"

The young man nodded affirmatively. He lifted from the gun rest the twenty gauge automatic Matt bought him for his birthday. The others reached quietly for their weapons. In unison, the four pushed their ways through the camouflage and into the open.

When they did so, a hen close by sounded the alarm. In seconds, the quiet pool bobbing with decoys erupted in flailing wings and startled quacks as ducks beat for the sky in all directions.

Corley swung with a large drake heading his way. Undershot him first, the little gun smacking his shoulder. He heard the others firing. Took his time, however. Not rushing the shot. And when he touched off, the drake puffed feathers and cart-wheeled end over end. It splashed on the spread's outer perimeter. Floating lifelessly.

Corley's heart pounded so hard he didn't pick another duck and fire his last shell. His concentration focused on the downed drake. Making sure it wouldn't float away.

Matt watched his son through the ordeal. Culminating in the clean shot. Put his left arm around the youngster's shoulders. Hugged him to his breast. Corley's eyes teared.

"Damned fine shooting, partner," he said. "That's one drake we don't have to worry about."

Hoot led a fat male, and another crossed in front as he fired. He killed one cleanly, but broke the other's wing. He finished it with a water shot.

Stillness returned as remnants of the flight winged their ways in various directions. To regroup safely downriver. Five less in number. And more educated in river flying.

"Well, Corley, we've got our work cut out for us," said Matt. He leaned his shotgun against the shooting rack at the front of the blind. "Shall we?"

Corley placed his shotgun beside his dad's. And the two scrambled out onto the platform, retrieving the boat from under the structure. Matt locked its motor upright. Then they paddled around the blocks, collecting downed birds. As Matt had done hundreds of times before.

His mind fondly recalled the first day he and his dad retrieved ducks. Watching migrating flights blacken the sky as they oared about. And he remembered the words Walt said back then. Repeated them to his son:

"Makes you wonder what the poor folks are doing...doesn't it?"

Corley heard him. He sat at the front of the boat. Stroking the soft burgundy breast of his drake. Beaming ear to ear. And shedding happy tears.

They hunted several times. Then November faded into December. And suddenly, January. Then finally, spring.

Matt clocked even more New York time. Returning to New Haven one or two days a month. Hillary Engineering's campaign got under way in the United States and abroad.

Already, the company's name gained worldwide recognition. Hillary became the industry leader, with annual contracts totaling half a billion dollars. Spurring the company's reputation, Hillary built the unique John F. Kennedy Airport in New York. And, soon after, others of similar scope in Rome, Madrid and Naples.

With summer's arrival, workloads at Bradley and Durham, and DG&B, slacked. Enabling employees and principals alike to enjoy a few months of summer doldrums.

Before crashing to complete fall campaign chores.

Matt remembered his and Karen's seventeenth wedding anniversary. Flew her to the Bahamas for three days of celebrating. And topping that, bought her a flawless two-carat diamond ring with half-carat matching earrings.

Later in June, the entire family...including Mrs. Westfield...flew to Hawaii for ten days of fun and sun. All told, Karen saw Matt more in a month than in the last two years. And became accustomed to the proverbial man around the house.

"Don't let it fool you, though," he said, after an hour of long overdue lovemaking. "When August comes, the same old shit hits the fan. An annual report for Hillary Engineering. Commercials for Triad. Cartiff is introducing a line of men's cologne and after-shave. And wanting a big splash for the Christmas season."

Matt enjoyed spending time with Hoot at the New Haven office. And on several occasions, drove to Hartford and met with Eddie Bauer. Together, they visited a few of his earlier accounts.

Matt sometimes missed the action of driving the state. Calling on clients. Sketching ads and promotions on napkins. Or yellow tablets, late at night in drafty motels.

The melancholy fleeted, however. His thoughts eventually conjured New York. And he again craved the city's concentrated hustle and bustle.

Matt and Hoot firmed plans to take their wives to Halen's Lake on Saturday for the Fourth of July. As they had following Matt's wedding in 1953.

Matt flew into Hartford on Thursday, looking forward to meeting the Gibsons for the outing. And made record time to New Haven, arriving to partake of Mrs. Westfield's excellent, tender prime rib.

Corley had returned from softball practice. And Diana busied herself playing dolls with the little girl next door. The three adults, meanwhile, relaxed with drinks in the living room. When the telephone rang, and Karen answered.

"Hello? Oh, hi!" There was a silent pause.

"Hoot? What's wrong?"

She cupped her hand over the mouthpiece.

Turned toward Matt, already coming to his feet. A stricken look washed her face with pain.

"It's Hoot, Matt. Come quickly!"

He reached the telephone in three paces. Snatched it from Karen's hand.

"Hi, buddy. What's up?"

"It's dad, Matt." The reply came somber...strained. "He's dead. Suffered a massive stroke at the printing plant. The doctor just called from Middletown."

"Damn, Hoot. I'm sorry."

Silence hung momentarily on the line. Matt continued. "Does your mom know?"

"No. Listen, Matt, I'm going to drive up there. I hate asking...but would you go with me?"

"Sure, pal. Glad to. Have you told Bobby?"

"No, she's at swim camp."

"Tell you what, Hooter. Have a stiff drink. I'll be there in ten minutes. Karen will find Bobby. You and I will drive to Middletown and see your mom. We'll call Bobby from there. Okay?"

"Thanks, Matthew. My nerves are frazzled." Hoot's voice broke in a gasp. "Can't get my wits straight."

"Don't worry, Hoot. I'll be there pronto."

Karen overheard, and already collected her purse and car keys.

"We'll call from Middletown, honey," Matt said. He tossed down the rest of the drink. "I'd better get to Hoot."

"Drive carefully, darling," she yelled as he dashed out the door.

When he arrived at Hoot's office, the latter sat behind his desk. A half empty glass of whisky stood in front of him. His eyes still shone wet from tears flowing over the past half hour.

Matt walked to his friend. Placed his hand on his shoulder. Squeezed his neck affectionately.

"I'm really sorry, Hoot. I know how close you were to your dad. He was an honorable, well-loved man. He lived a good life. What more can any of us hope for?"

"He would have been seventy in another year, Matthew. Today, that's not too old."

"Damon was only sixty-eight, Hoot. It boils down to when it's your time...that's it. No missed appointments."

Matt helped his friend to the Mercedes. Held the door while the other climbed into the passenger's seat. Then entered himself, settled behind the wheel, and steered for Middletown.

When her husband didn't return home at five, Mary Gibson became concerned. Even though he'd gone to the printing plant later that afternoon. He didn't sleep well the night before. Complained of indigestion. And when he still hadn't shown by seven, she panicked.

She rang the plant, but no one answered. She called the young general manager's house. His wife said he had not come home, either. Which brought slight relief.

"That's it," she consoled herself. "He's out with someone from work."

Matt and Hoot arrived at seven-thirty. The minute her son entered the house...she knew. An expression of agony molded her face into a mask of pain. And she began crying, without actually knowing why. Just sensing why.

Hoot rushed to the frail woman as she started collapsing. Helped her to the couch.

"It's father, isn't it," she said. With surprising calm. Tears dribbled from her eyes, one after another.

"Yes, mom. I'm so sorry. They called from the plant. He had a stroke. Nothing could be done. He just went."

"Oh God, Hoot," she moaned from deep within herself. "Why? Why did that man work so hard? Even after retiring."

"Next to you...he loved work, mom. It filled his life. He built the business. Ran it for more than forty years. Nursed it. Cared for it. And he led the pack in what he did."

Matt remained with Hoot and his mother until nearly ten o'clock. Then drove back to New Haven. Asking his friend to call if he needed anything.

They reached Bobby at Karen's. She decided to pick up Hoot's car and drive to Middletown. And she and Matt probably passed going their respective ways.

They held Ed Gibson's funeral at nine o'clock, Sunday morning, at Middletown Memorial Cemetery. It appeared to Hoot that half the people in the state stopped to pay respects.

At least thirty limousines made up the funeral parade to graveside. And more than twenty men sought to be pallbearers. The unexpected turnout provided fitting tribute to a journalist well-liked and respected throughout Connecticut. And it spirited Hoot and his mother to realize so many strangers cared so much about the man they loved.

Still, the unhappy event overshadowed the Durham's and Gibson's Fourth of July. That evening, Matt drove to Hartford from Middletown to catch his New York flight. He left Karen and the children to ride back to New Haven with his folks.

On the drive, his intestines seemed tied in square knots. Subconsciously, he sensed something more than felt it. And it went beyond sharing his best friend's grief.

Something lurked that would change Karen's and his relationship. He knew it deep in his wrenching guts. Yet couldn't grasp exactly what gnawed at him.

He learned the next week. Hoot and Bobby stopped for a drink shortly after his return to New Haven.

"Mom asked Bobby and me to move to Middletown," Hoot said. A question half hung on the statement. "Wants us to take over dad's operations."

Hoot stood, paced nervously to the window. Turned, and looked at the floor.

"We said we would, Matt. Hell, she's alone up there. And he worked hard building the business. None of us wants to sell it. She can't handle it alone. So..."

Matt rolled the drink glass in his hands. His mind digested what his friend said. He looked at Karen, who flashed a quizzical look, saddening into a frown.

He stood, walked to his pal, put his arm around his shoulder.

"Well, Hooter...we'll miss having you guys close by. And, I'll certainly miss you at the agency. We have to do what we think is best. And this move probably is...for your mom, and you. I'd do the same, partner."

"Thanks for understanding, Matthew," said Hoot. He hugged his friend. "There's a good bunch here. They'll keep DG&B running smoothly. John Keller's been with us ten years. Knows the ins and outs. And our accounts. He could take over without problems. If you give the nod."

"You're probably right, Hoot. He's sharp enough."

Matt walked to where Bobby sat. Offered his hand. She rose from the couch, and they embraced. Eyes misting.

By the end of August, Hoot and Bobby packed and moved in with his mother. He adjusted easily to the new work routine. And knew enough about printing to learn the more technical aspects quickly.

Gibson Publishing printed two four-color magazines. The production of which had become routine, and the pressroom team handled these tasks with Swiss watch precision.

Most other printing work came from DG&B in Hartford or New Haven. And Hoot certainly reigned expert in handling those assignments.

He kept his interest in DG&B as a silent partner. Helping John Keller and Eddie Bauer through creative decisions when asked. However, taking his regular salary from Gibson Publishing where he spent his work days.

Over the years, Matt, Hoot and Eddie set up profit-sharing for principals and employees. Matt insisted Hoot continue receiving his portion of the plan proceeds.

Over the last five years, the three earned more than two hundred thousand dollars apiece. Money...and who accounted for what portion... never surfaced as an issue worth considering.

August dog days yielded to fall's colors. Soon, the East Coast braced for winter's arrival.

Matt, Greer McCall and Lyle Bradley brought their various campaigns in on time. And the New York office hummed with activity.

Hillary Engineering nearly doubled in size over the past ten years. Now, "Fortune Magazine" ranked it a multi-billion dollar operation. Much to Matt's pleasure, Hillary's business growth flowed to Musgrave Manufacturing.

Increased project work resulted in more frequent orders for massive earth-moving and construction equipment. Consequently, both accounts required bigger staffs servicing them.

Additionally, Cartiff's line of men's products penetrated its market at an ideal time. That account also expanded, and required additional people catering to its demands.

Even Standish Electronics outperformed market projections. The company invested heavily in high-tech plants and equipment, and developed transistors, microprocessors and myriad types of tiny integrated circuit systems.

Standish ranked as one of the first companies pioneering miniaturized electronics. And now found itself carried rapidly along with the burgeoning field of computer technology.

Keith Hillary joined the New Haven entourage making the Huntsdale pilgrimage for Fall Festival. He enjoyed himself immensely, and made fast friends with the townspeople. Who enjoyed hearing he, Walt, Guy Simpson and Raymond Daley swap old soldier's tales.

In November, he took part in a three-day pheasant and quail shoot with the general, Hoot and Matt. Climaxed by some of the best duck shooting he had ever seen.

They sat in the kitchen one evening, sipping brandy and reflecting on the day's hunt. Stomachs packed with venison steaks. Presented by one of the men from Huntsdale the day before.

"It would upset Corley if he knew the hunt we enjoyed today, son," commented Walt. "That boy loves being in a duck blind more than anything else."

"You've hooked him, all right," added Keith. "That's all he talked about during the Fall Festival. Said I'd love hunting ducks here. And he darned sure hit it on the head!"

"He's like his dad, Keith," Walt said. "On hunting days, Matt got up at three o'clock. He'd make tea, coffee and sandwiches. Couldn't sleep for excitement. Drove him crazy waiting for us old-timers to flush our kidneys and come to breakfast."

"Maybe I'll have a grandson to spoil someday, Walt," said Keith. "That is...if Suzanne and Lorne ever straighten their heads about starting a family."

"Where are they now?" asked Walt.

"England. Outside Burlington Downs. We're building new facilities for the Royal Air Force. Should be quite an air base from Suzanne's description."

"I remember the old airfield well, Keith," replied Walt. "Touched down on it a hundred times. That's beautiful countryside."

"Yeah...she sent me a postcard of the place. Said she and Lorne couldn't fly back for Christmas. Wondered if I'd join them there. I Probably will."

"You'll love it, Keith," added Walt. "Excellent time to be in England."

As the two talked, Matt stared into the snifter he held. His mind drifted into a fantasy of bringing Suzanne to The House someday.

Walking with her through the woods and fields of Huntsdale Valley.

He hadn't seen her in so long it proved difficult bringing her face into focus. Hoot's voice jarred his rhapsody, repeating a question he asked.

"Matthew! You awake? I asked if you were flying back to New York Sunday?"

"Huh? Oh, sorry Hoot. Yeah...Keith and I are flying the six-thirty out of Hartford."

"Why don't you folks spend Thanksgiving with us in Middletown?"

"Sounds good to me. I'll ask the family when we get back. Anne wants to visit her sister over the holidays. Might be the perfect thing to do. That is, if your family spends Christmas here with us. Your mom's welcome, too."

"We haven't done that in a long time have we, Matthew? Sure, make book on that. We ought to check with Raymond about borrowing his horse and sleigh."

"Hoot...I'm really looking forward to Christmas. Maybe we'll all find time to unwind. Get some things back in working order. Especially my relationship with Karen."

"That's sound thinking, Matt. You two are a real team. Your kids are icing on the cake. And I'd sure rest easier if you took things a little easier."

"Hoot, I just turned forty. Not eighty!"

"You know what I mean, Matthew. Slow down a bit. New York can survive without you a few more days a week."

"Hoot's right, Matt," added Keith. "I couldn't help overhearing. You're in New York because of me. Well, you've done a hell of a job over the last nine years. Seems to me, things are pretty much to the point where they run themselves. I don't want to cause any more family problems."

"Maybe you guys are right," Matt agreed. He took a quick sip of brandy. Set the glass down and lit a cigarette. "It would be nice spending more time in New Haven. Karen would be a lot happier. Corley and Diana, too. Okay, Keith...but I'll be on call when you need me."

"That's a deal, Matt. I know this is best for all of us. I suffered the same eager beaver syndrome at your age. It got me a lot of money...and even more loneliness. I don't want you suffering the same."

"I won't, Keith," Matt answered."

Thanksgiving in Middletown and Christmas at The House ushered two of the most enjoyable times Karen and Matt had known in nearly a decade. Sharing holidays with Hoot, Bobby and their daughter, Elizabeth, rekindled old times. The grown-ups spent countless hours laughing and reminiscing over past events.

Keith flew to England to celebrate the Yuletide with his daughter and son-in-law. Walt and Claire Durham escorted Evelyn Forsythe on their annual trek to Miami Beach.

When 1970 ended, Matt and Karen lay naked in each others' arms. Discussing the past year. And fresh one dawning. Trying to recapture the passion that ebbed in their lives...start it flowing again, before marriage dries and withers.

"Why can't it always be like this, Matt?"

She looked up at him from the pillow, as they clung together in the dark silence.

"It can...and will be again, Karen," he replied. "Somehow. I promise."

Chapter 24

Suzanne's Return

VIETNAM CLIMAXED IN A PERIOD of frenetic months the spring before. Leaving the final tally of U.S. servicemen dead at 56,555. Wounded at 303,654. Missing at more than 2,000.

Protesters at a Bicentennial celebration of the founding of the United States booed President Gerald R. Ford. He proclaimed the U.S. a military power which "stands in the front lines of the Free World."

Bradley, Durham and Associates captured the position as fifth largest advertising agency in New York for annual billings. Even DG&B in New Haven and Hartford ranked in the top one hundred.

After President Nixon resigned, his administration shifted gears. The Washington press corps ousted George Bradley from his job. Rumor had him linked with the Watergate cover-up. Earlier in the year, four Nixon aides also involved earned indictments.

In June, Bradley hurriedly retired from active participation in BD&A. And moved to Arizona to write about goings-on during the Nixon presidency.

Despite promises, Matt found himself deeply involved in marketing and repositioning programs for Hillary Engineering. He attended Fall Festival for only one day. Then flew back to New York that evening. Leaving behind, as usual, a crowd of displeased people. At the forefront of whom stood Karen.

Until the new year began, things progressed well between the two. In fact, they enjoyed exceptional moments together.

Matt returned to New Haven on his original Wednesday afternoon timetable. Working at DG&B's offices on Thursdays and Fridays. And coming home early before the weekend started.

They spent the past five Thanksgivings in Middletown with Hoot, Bobby and Elizabeth, and the Gibsons' new son, Houston Jr. In turn, Hoot and his family joined the Durhams' Christmases at The House.

These reunions became traditions enjoyed by all. And through familiarities shared, the two families nurtured and maintained love and respect for each other.

In February, however, Keith Hillary suffered a mild stroke. Soon after returning from a trip to South Africa. His company...at the "request" of the U.S. Government...constructed a refinery there.

In recent years, Hillary Engineering learned certain government projects demanded priority status and inflated cost proposals. Drawn up immediately. Or other work in which the company involved itself bogged in red tape. Newly enacted regulations. Labor difficulties. Or zoning and building codes.

It troubled Keith to no end. With tunnel vision, he worked days and nights with Matt. Trying to reposition Hillary Engineering for strictly continental U.S. projects. A distinct subsidiary, HILLCO, would assume responsibility for out-conus work.

The two men became even closer over the years. Matt, like a son to his older client. During the winter months, they hunted occasionally with Walt, Hoot and Corley. During summers, completed many business trips to projects scattered around the world.

Matt became as knowledgeable about Hillary operations as its chief executive officer. Often finding himself too close to the subject to maintain the objectivity. An attribute he found essential in developing realistic marketing plans.

In moments like this, he called meetings in Hartford with Greer, Hoot, Eddie, John and, occasionally, Lyle.

Lyle, to Greer's distress, ensconced himself as agency media director. Additionally, he headed political activities in which BD&A sometimes found itself involved. Mysteriously.

Soon, another major election would involve the country. If it survived the Bicentennial. And several times, local and national candidates approached Matt inquiring if BD&A might handle their promotion and publicity.

Matt politely declined on the excuse of workload. Plus, he did not wish his agency linked to a specific party or platform.

Lyle, however, openly sought and supported certain candidates. Providing agency time and materials to those whom he and his father felt could "provide favors down the road."

It had become obvious to Matt that Lyle, with his father's urgings, harbored political aspirations. If nothing more than behind-the-scenes finagling.

Often, the two argued over the agency's position of not backing candidates.

Many times, Lyle denied involvement with particular persons or causes. As often, Matt later would discover Lyle secretly and personally involved with a questionable politician getting elected. Or shady bill passing, often through out-and-out blackmail. Or what Lyle termed, "calling in markers."

Matt regularly questioned his judgment in merging the two agencies. Still, he rationalized it as the only means of landing Hillary Engineering. Although Lyle proved a nuisance from time to time. His employees demonstrated excellent skills at their craft.

Most of the time, Lyle kept to himself. Handling his accounts with almost secrecy. In the past six months, however, the agency mysteriously lost two accounts. Long-term clients at that. And they fell under Lyle's personal scrutiny.

By January, Keith and Matt decided to publicize HILLCO's formation. And kick-off Hillary Engineering's campaign as the nation's largest builder. Specializing in urban development, airports and high-rise office buildings.

The two convinced themselves and the board that more than enough work beckoned stateside. The focus on U.S. projects could keep the massive organization functioning. And simultaneously, enable Hillary Engineering, through its HILLCO subsidiary, to extract itself from work in other countries. And, the tremendous political pressures surrounding these jobs.

For the first time, Matt did not hunt opening day of the duck season. Instead, Walt and Guy Simpson took his eighteen-year-old son.

It ranked a bitter disappointment for Corley. Up until the last minute, he counted on Matt keeping his promise and showing. When the call came from New York, his mother answered it. His heart sank at her immediate anger. He knew his father begged off on yet another adventure planned by the two.

"I never see him anymore, grandpa," the young man said to the general.

The two hunkered over a charcoal bucket in the early November darkness inside the blind. Waiting for morning flights to begin scouting the river. Seeking solace from the cold.

"Dad hasn't been home a whole month over the past year. Diana and I are just additional worries for him."

"That's not so, Corley," Walt replied gruffly. "He's got lots on his mind, sure. Still, he loves you both very much. He hasn't learned how to slow down yet. Separate himself from his work. Always been that way. Even when he and Hoot worked in New Haven. Late nights. Early mornings. I sometimes wonder myself if he'll ever change."

"I don't know either, gramps. Appears to me if he loved us...and mom...he'd find a way to be with us. I'm a college freshman. Di is midway through high school. About the only time we see him is a few days during hunting season, and maybe Thanksgiving and Christmas."

"Believe me, Corley. It's neither you nor Diana. I got chewed on regularly by your grandmother for the same reason. Always stationed at a military base or overseas. Matt grew before we spent much time together. Hell, he was twelve when I brought him to Huntsdale and The House."

Walt's eyes glistened in the shadows within the hideout. He wiped them with his gloved hand.

"Charcoal smarts the eyes, doesn't it?" He paused a moment. "Corley, I can't believe that happened so long ago. It did, though. Father Time slips past when you turn your back."

Wings whistled over head. The three fell silent. A large flight of mallards circled the blind several times. Then flew to join a larger flight heading downriver. Toward the grain fields, and morning feeding.

"They'll be back mid-morning," Walt said. He replaced the duck call drawn from inside his shell vest.

"Will we ever be a family again, grandpa?" Corley continued. "You know...like when I was a kid and we came here Christmases? We had lots of fun. Always snowing. We'd go cut a family Christmas tree. Those are times I'll always remember."

Corley looked down, and sadly poked the bucket's glowing coals with a willow twig.

"I'd give anything to get them back."

"You will, Corley," said Walt. He put his hand on his grandson's back. "I'll make you that promise. Your grandfather will talk with his errant son. And I'll knock some sense into that burrhead if it's the last thing I do! Hey...look! Hush! We've got mallards landing in the decoys out front."

Nearly every weekend that season, Walt took his grandson duck hunting on the Paginaw near Huntsdale. Pheasant and quail hunting on farm land surrounding the village.

He enjoyed the teenager's company. Corley reminded him of Matt many years before. And the two often discussed manly things he felt too embarrassed to broach with Karen.

Corley loved his father. In most conceivable ways followed in his footsteps. And without much encouragement.

He quarterbacked the Huntington High Hornets. Served as president of the senior class. Belonged to several honor fraternities.

Even with a full extracurricular plate, he posted excellent grades. And Corley, too, discovered a bent toward writing. For that reason, he enrolled at Connecticut State. And expected to enter the School of Journalism in his junior year.

Corley dated several girls in high school. None seriously. And proved popular with females and males alike. Still, he felt an inward sense of grasping for something. Yet never reaching it. Like Sisyphus rolling his heavy boulder to the hill's top. Only to lose his grip, before pushing it over the summit.

He harbored within him feelings and thoughts he could only discuss with his father. A mother, or even grandfather, simply would not do. That, more than anything else, stretched the tenuous bond he shared with his father. And as more time passed, he deeply resented Matt's absences. Resentment that cropped in other areas. Affecting grades, his sense of humor, and overall attitude.

In mid-November, Karen received a letter from Conn State. Corley's grades had slipped dramatically. The terse warning stated his grades would improve by first semester's end in January. Or, he would start second semester on scholastic probation.

She tried approaching the subject with her son. Who immediately clammed up. And their discussion ended in a heated argument. With both of them frustrated.

Matt had not returned to New Haven for three weeks. He did promise, however, he would spend Christmas week with his family at The House. Once BD&A completed Hillary Engineering's repositioning campaign. Due for kick-off in March, with the beginning of the building season. He also promised Karen he'd have a serious heart-to-heart with Corley.

Christmas season arrived in New York. Wrapped in dark days and drizzle. Not bright lights, satin ribbons, smiling faces and pine smells. With only a week to the event, Matt had not begun shopping for Karen, Corley and Diana.

Guilt over that. Coupled with long hours. Handling too much of Hillary's campaign himself. And a strange numbness in his left arm. Skyrocketed his irritability level.

He jumped Dot Weymouth for accidentally filing an ad repro proof in the wrong folder. Several times, he snapped at staff members. Most of whom steered wide paths around his office.

Even Greer handled him with padded tweezers. Keeping conversations short. Friendly, but to the point. And hoping this represented a stage he would pass through. Due to the pressures of wanting Hillary's campaign perfect.

"You know what's wrong?" Dot asked Greer one morning as he left Matt's office. Gently closing the door behind him. Rubbing his rear in mock pain. "I think he's forty-six, knocking on menopause, and not admitting it!"

"Oh Christ...Dot! Don't tell him that! He's just under a hell of a lot of pressure. Can't find the relief valve. You'll see, though. Once we get Hillary's program under way...he'll be fine."

"I certainly hope so, Greer. Another month like these last six...I'm opting for early retirement! At sixty, I'm too old and crotchety to humor someone acting like a spoiled brat. And making Attila The Hun look like Little Orphan Annie!"

Christmas fell on Saturday. And Matt took off Friday. Flying to Hartford Thursday afternoon.

He collected his family and drove to The House that day. Figuring he, Karen, Corley and Diana could chop a tree the next morning.

As was the custom, Bradley, Durham & Associates held its Christmas party before everyone left for their holiday retreats. Dot selected the Wednesday before the holiday for the party. She then had invitations printed, and sent them to clients and business associates along with the agency's Christmas cards.

When Wednesday arrived, Matt appeared in better spirits. The long hours posted by him and Greer reflected in the agency's television commercials, radio spots and print ads.

The company's creative staff examined the separate pieces. And pronounced them, exceptionally well done.

The entire package emerged as Matt first had envisioned it. Right to the last word uttered by their businesslike announcer. And final period on the concluding page of copy.

The remainder of BD&A's personnel assembled in the creative review conference room the morning of the party. And also critiqued the campaign from beginning to end.

Each time he saw one of the commercials. Listened to a radio spot. Or flicked slides of the completed print ads. Matt felt more convinced than ever it represented the group's best work.

Proof the campaign would score more COCA Awards came after the final commercial aired. A hushed lull hung over the review room for nearly a full minute. Before seventy-five employees came to their feet, applauding and cheering.

When the critique ended, Dot turned the room into a lavish banquet hall. Tables of hors d'oeuvres magically appeared. As did champagne, and most other liquors. And ice-chilled bowls of red and black Beluga caviar. Per Matt's wishes.

"Our folks need and deserve pampering, Dot," he had said. "Let's do a first-class job of it!"

With that, she spent nearly ten thousand dollars. Partly out of spite.

Throughout the day...beginning at eleven o'clock...guests, suppliers, clients and employees filed in and out. Eating. Drinking. Scrutinizing the awards and advertising mementos hung on the conference room walls.

Some arrived at eleven. And remained at four. Feeling minimal pain. And hardly much more.

Matt huddled with Hoot, Eddie, Greer, Lyle and Max Standish... owner of Standish Electronics. They discussed the line of minicomputers the company prepared to introduce. When Matt spotted Keith Hillary enter.

He excused himself, and across the crowded space caught the other's eye. Matt raised his empty glass, signaling he'd fetch Keith a drink.

He stepped behind the bar, and poured two fingers of sour mash for his friend, and the same amount in his glass. He filled the containers to the top with branch water. Then wove his way through tightly packed bodies toward where he last had spotted Keith. When he at last came alongside the other, he handed him a glass. Then shook his hand and offered season's greetings.

"Great to see you, Keith. I was hoping you'd show."

"Quite an affair, Matt. They're lining the street outside to get in!"

As he formulated a reply to the quip, a fragrance caught him in mid-thought. He turned toward it, and looked into the sparkling, sea-blue eyes he had not seen for fifteen years. After all that time, he still felt soft wings brush his heart. "Suzanne!" he stammered. "What? How? My God...it's great to see you!" He felt Keith's hand on his shoulder. Faintly heard his voice from behind.

"Twerp flew in for Christmas, Matt. Arrived last night. Didn't think you'd mind if I brought her."

Matt turned his head slightly to face the man speaking. "Of course not, Keith."

He held out his hand. Felt the grip, still firm, yet soft.

"This is a wonderful surprise, Suzanne."

"Well, Mr. Durham...do I get a drink, too?" she asked.

"Sure," he chuckled. Put his hand on her back. "The champagne's ice cold. Excuse me, Keith...the lady says she's thirsty. I'll be right back."

Suzanne calmly reached down. Took his hand. "I'll accompany you...if you don't mind."

"It would be an honor," he said. And they waded through humanity toward the serving tables.

"Well, Matt...it's difficult believing so much time has passed since we last saw each other," she took the paper plate handed her. Placed peeled cold shrimp and chunks of crab meat on it. "You haven't changed at all. You look the same. Maybe a little thinner."

"Yeah. Your dad keeps me hopping. That holds the weight down."

His eyes swept her body as she reached for a napkin. He smiled to himself, approvingly. Suzanne had lost weight, too.

Yet through the beige slacks and blouse, he noticed the loss occurred in the right places.

The lady's raven hair accentuated her tan. She spent the last several months in southern France. Overseeing construction of yet another airport. Dark hair and skin made the blue eyes gleam even clearer.

"Europe obviously agrees with you, too, Suzanne."

She recognized the compliment. Flushed slightly.

"And how are Karen and Corley?" she asked, taking the glass of champagne offered. "Any more kids?"

They walked toward an empty corner of the room.

"Oh, fine...just fine," he replied, trying to sound convincing. "Yes, we now have a daughter. Fact is, we're going to the country for

Christmas. I'm flying to Hartford tomorrow afternoon. Then driving down. It'll be nice getting away for a while."

He took a pull of his bourbon and water. Lit a cigarette, and studied her features over the lighter flame.

"By the way, how are you and Loren doing? Any kids?"

He knew the answer to that question. Keith kept him informed. Still, for some inane reason, he felt the need to return her serve about 'Karen and the kids.'

She paused for a moment before answering. Fixed on her plate as the words formed.

"We're not, Matt. We split nearly six months ago. We finalized the divorce last month. I didn't tell daddy until last night. Loren's in Sweden somewhere. Designing apartment buildings or something."

"I'm sorry to hear that, Suzanne. Honestly."

"Don't be, Matt. We've known things weren't working the last several years. He envied the position my father gave me. Heading European operations. It really got to him. He couldn't adjust."

She looked him directly in the eyes. He saw pain, but behind it, longing.

"Especially when our projects became successful. And other countries wanted similar programs. Which meant traveling four days out of seven. I told him I'd resign. That we could start a family. That didn't please him either."

She drained the remaining champagne. Handed him the empty glass. Suddenly, flashed the smile he remembered.

"I went my way. He went his. It's that simple. Just tossed seventeen years of marriage in a brown paper grocery bag. Like coffee grounds, fish bones and grapefruit halves. And pitched the whole frigging mess into the dumpster."

"What are your plans now?"

"First, I'd like more champagne."

He steered her toward a table housing an ice sculpture and several chilled bottles of bubbly. Filled her glass to the rim.

"I've had enough of world traveling. So, I asked dad if I could help run things here. He said 'Yes!' I'll move back as soon as I wrap things in France."

"I'm sure Keith is happy as hell getting you back."

"Funny, Matt. You're all he talked about on the way over. I guess you know he loves you like a son."

"He's been a leaning post for me in New York. I feel the same about him. He's been patient while I learned your business. Always there with answers."

"Yeah...he says you know Hillary Engineering as well as he. You trying to steal my job?"

"Oh, God no!" he laughed. Again stunned by the radiant smile and gleaming teeth, against the browned face. "I represent little threat there!"

"Hey, you two are having too much fun over here."

Hoot suddenly appeared from the crowd clustered near the hors d'ouevres table. Offered his hand to Suzanne.

"Good to see you again, Suzanne. You're looking fantastic as usual. Couldn't help admiring you from afar."

"Why thank you, Hoot. The same in return. You and Matt must tell me your secrets of youth. I've traveled half of Europe seeking it...with no luck."

"That's certainly not true, Suzanne," the newcomer stated. "Is it Matt?"

"No," Matt replied with firmness. Taking Hoot aback. "It most certainly is not."

Hoot noticed the looks exchanged. Suddenly relived the discomfort he felt under similar circumstances many years back. "Well...I'll leave you two alone. I need a fresher anyway. You okay?"

"Yes, Hoot," they replied simultaneously.

He turned and left.

"Listen...I'd better spend time with other clients. Or BD&A will be out in the cold. How long are you here, Suzanne?"

"I'm flying back to France the first week in January."

"Okay, great! How about dinner after the holidays? I want to know everything you've done in the past decade. Jesus...that sounds like so many years ago!"

"It was, Matt. We'll cover everything in one night?"

"No. On second thought, we'll stretch it as long as you like. How about that?"

"Sounds better. I'm going to see what daddy's doing. See you later, Matt."

She took his hand. Squeezed it and smiled. He followed her graceful stride across the room. Her father stood talking with Greer and two other men.

Matt mingled also. Throughout the reception, occasionally stealing glances in her direction. And, many times, locking eyes with her's. And again experiencing the exciting, fluttery feeling.

Enroute to Huntsdale...after stopping in New Haven to collect Karen and the kids...he whistled happily to the rock song emitting from the radio. He looked forward to a quiet family Christmas at The House. And returning to New York to keep the date with Suzanne.

The instant thought of her caught him off guard. He glanced at Karen in the rearview mirror. She staring out her window. And felt a jarring pang of guilt.

In the passenger's seat, Corley strained his eyes, looking for ducks flying the Paginaw. As Matt had done many times himself. He was proud of the young man. Now even taller than he. This week, he would let him know.

Earlier in the day, it snowed in the southern part of the state. Along the coast. And threatened becoming serious about layering the ground with white around Huntsdale. Already behind the stationwagon, light, white powder swirled tiny dustdevils on the blacktop's surface.

When they pulled the hill to their destination...swinging into the semicircle drive in front of The House...Diana ticked off various chores to perform before Christmas Eve.

"Let's get up early. And have breakfast. Then go chop the tree like we used to, daddy," she said. Excitedly.

"Sure, sweetheart," he replied. "We'll have snow on the ground by then. Makes lugging a tree easier with a sled. And, of course, we have Corley the pack mule to help us!"

Matt switched the ignition. They clambered out of the vehicle. Each taking his or her respective suitcase from the back storage area. Now jam-packed with gaily wrapped presents.

Matt toted his and Karen's suitcases and clothing bags to the front door. Set them while he fumbled the keys from his pocket. Unlocked The House and went inside. Flipping on the entrance hallway light.

Opal Simpson did her job keeping The House shipshape. The floors gleamed, and everything seemed immaculate and in its place. Guy had laid wood in the fireplaces. Even restocked the circular log holder on the screened-in porch off the living room. They carried their luggage to their rooms. Then met downstairs.

Matt fixed Manhattans for himself and his wife. The kids poured glasses of Pepsi from huge glass bottles kept in the refrigerator. Then the four gathered in the living room. To unwind from the day and the drive. Corley switched the television to the evening news.

They watched the events of the day for an hour in color. Then Matt suggested dinner. He brought several T-bone steaks for the occasion. Took four from the deep freeze. Fired up the charcoal grill on the back porch, while Karen placed baking potatoes in the oven.

After dinner, they sat in the family room. Watching television and talking until nearly eleven. Then the foursome went to bed to rest for the day ahead.

When they arose the next day, Matt knew his prediction had come true without lifting from bed. Bright sunlight reflecting the snow's surface bathed the room in white light. Even with curtain liners drawn.

He looked at Karen. Stirring from sleep. Felt a throb somewhere within as her beauty took him off-guard. Her eyes opened wide. The quizzical look traveled her face.

"What is it, Matt?" she asked. Alarmed, and concerned over his stare.

"Nothing, honey. Sorry. Just admiring you." He pecked her on the forehead. Got up, and walked into the bathroom to brush his teeth. Stopping along the way to peer behind the shades at the newly fallen snow.

"Must be five or six inches down. More coming," he said. Then shut the door behind him.

Corley scrambled eggs his father's way. Mixed with mushroom pieces, Cheddar cheese and crisp bacon bits. Diana prepared English muffins and bagels with creamed cheese. After breakfast, they bundled and went into the crisp morning freshness. Country air chilled by winter's breath.

Matt unhooked the old sled down from its hanging place in the tool shed. Oiled its runners and sanded them shiny with quick sandpaper swipes. And the foursome started for the cedar grove a half mile away. Diana hopped on and off the sleigh. Laughing when her father kidded about the incredible weight his daughter gained.

At sixteen, Diana stood as tall as her mother. And carried herself in the same manner. Slightly thinner than Karen. And already exhibiting the maturity of a young lady approaching womanhood.

When the two women appeared together...as they did now looking at rabbit tracks...one easily spotted they were mother and daughter.

Matt called the duo, "A beautifully matched pair." As he often said, "A man could flip a coin for either...and come out a winner!" He also noticed Diana telegraphing the same quizzical look her mother perfected over the years.

As usual, Matt talked them into selecting a bushy, fragrant white pine. Corley made quick work with the band saw. And by Lunchtime, it stood, fully decorated, in front of the bay window off the family room.

To help celebrate lighting the tree, Matt made hot buttered rum for everyone. Which they drank from steaming porcelain mugs.

"Tell you what...let's hike the hill to Raymond Daley's," Matt said.

He divvied the remainder of the warm drink among them. "See if we can borrow his horse and sleigh. You kids haven't seen the countryside until you've crossed it horse-drawn."

"Ooh...that sounds like fun, daddy!" Diana exclaimed.

"I'm for it, too!" added Corley.

"I...three," chimed Karen.

Minutes later, the four pulled on boots and outer garments again. And walked through the snow to the Daley's. The Simpsons told Raymond the Durhams would come for Christmas.

By the time they arrived at his farm, he had curried the mare and cleaned the rig. Months of standing idle in the machinery shed coated it with fine dust.

He and his wife, Helen, spotted them from the living room window. Met them at the front porch.

"Howdy, Matt," the big man said, stretching out with his hand. "Hi Karen. Kids."

"Merry Christmas, Raymond," Matt replied, taking the handshake. "To you, too, Helen," he said to the apple-cheeked woman beside her husband.

They exchanged greetings and gossip among themselves. Chatted briefly. Then Helen, Karen and Diana went into the farmhouse while the men hitched the horse to the sleigh.

Soon, the bay mare swiftly towed the four through crunching snow. The men in front. Women in back. All snuggled in patchwork quilts and reveling in the fresh air. To the steady clump of hooves and jingling harness bells.

They sauntered the road south from the Daley's toward Huntsdale. Traversing the Paginaw beneath river bluffs painted stark white; save for scrub oak patches and evergreen copses that clung desperately to steep slopes and flat areas near the rock cliffs.

The little group enjoyed the trip to Huntsdale. Filing it away among fond memories. After hot cocoa at Arch's, they rode back to The House.

For Christmas Eve dinner, Karen and Diana fixed a large standing rib roast. Complete with jumbo shrimp cocktail appetizers. Parsleyed new potatoes, baked golden in butter. Fresh mixed vegetables. And, afterwards, blueberry cobbler smothered in whipped cream.

Matt uncorked two vintage bottles of cabernet sauvignon. And when they finished dinner...and retired to the family room...he prepared brandy ices for all.

By midnight, the fire's glow, wonderful meal, and after-dinner toddies spread drowsiness through the room. It enveloped them like silent fog. And one by one, they slipped to bed.

Matt tarried to poke the fire dead and lock doors. Then followed the others upstairs.

They exchanged gifts over coffee and sweet rolls Christmas morning. Then set about calling friends and wishing them holiday greetings.

The Durhams and Evelyn, as usual, sojourned to Florida until late January. They called early in the afternoon. Hoot, Bobby and their children still lived at his mother's home. And expected the annual Christmas call when Matt and Karen rang them up.

During the following week, Matt and Corley spent days roaming the woods. Or hiking the frozen Paginaw, plinking cans with their .22 rifles. Matt intended to gain as much ground as possible over the distance that came between the two. Corley, however, seemed reluctant to confide in the man he'd known only as an occasional friend and hunting partner. And, more often, as a guest to his home and life.

Corley intended using part of the week developing two term papers due when Christmas break ended. He never quite found time to do so. Instead, he procrastinated until Sunday before classes began. Then drove to the New Haven public library, and spent the day preparing his reports.

By New Year's, Matt and Karen recognized the cracks in their relationship had become larger. And they regretted admitting it was so. Each silently resolved to be more understanding. More tolerant of the other's needs.

Yet each also realized deep within that things had got out of hand. Regluing the pieces of marriage would require serious and concerted efforts. And each worried...without saying so...that the other might be beyond wanting to try.

Matt still loved Karen deeply. And she, him. Still, the all-consuming torrent of passion...the desire to be continually close to the other... trickled like liquid from a cracked bowl. Bit by bit, it disappeared. And refilling themselves with that kind of feeling again would be difficult... and require a long period of time.

Matt believed he stood at the pinnacle of having all he wanted. For himself, and for his family. Success. Money. Power. Prestige. Respect. And, security...from everything and everyone.

He no longer recognized the best part of attaining carefully sought goals...having someone with whom to share the accomplishments. Instead, while pursuing his objectives he abandoned the one to whom he devoted his mission.

Karen, on the flip side, felt torn by a dichotomy of emotions raging. She wanted Matt's success as much as he. For him...and herself. However, she had not recognized and permitted the freedom he required to operate within his realm of success. And she knew she would have to sacrifice him being within arm's reach to do so.

Shortly after returning to New York, Matt and Suzanne shared dinner. Spending the evening discussing what happened in their respective lives over fifteen years.

For the first time in many months, he felt excitement surge through his body. Just from talking, and watching her. Noticing little mannerisms enliven the beautiful face and iridescent blue eyes.

They dined together every night his first week back. Then Suzanne flew to France to collect her things. And tie loose ends on the project she completed.

Matt experienced emptiness inside. And when he recognized why, felt desperately ashamed. He loved Karen, yes. And also wanted Suzanne, yes.

Now the Seventies were ending. Another decade of accomplishment and disappointment. Of growing up, and growing older. Loving, and pretending love.

These things, Matt and Karen kept pressed between the covers of their lives' volumes. And each sincerely hoped...yet wondered...if their story would end happily.

Chapter 25

New York, New Years And Suzanne

S UZANNE RETURNED TO NEW YORK amid a wonderful spring. Sweet smelling, flowery breezes swept the streets. Even the alleys. Still grimy from an icy, snow-laden winter.

By summer's end, Keith involved her in major projects from East Coast to West. Keeping her traveling nearly three days of every week.

In between travels, of course, she and Matt lunched or dined regularly. Each enjoying tremendously the other's company. Making Suzanne's comings and goings more tolerable. And giving them a reason not to dislike her road time. Knowing when it ended they would be together again.

Keith over the past year met a lady named Grace Selkirk. An attractive woman in her late fifties, like he. And widow of the founder of a large New Jersey excavating company. They became friends almost overnight. Then infatuated with each other. And, more recently, close. Obviously lovers. Suzanne felt happy and excited for her father. Matt, too, enjoyed his friend's late-blooming romance.

Keith spoiled and coddled Grace with all the charm, possessions and gallantry musterable. And over several bourbons, told his daughter their plans.

"Suzanne...I've worked my butt off all my life. Making sure you had everything you wanted. Now, by God, it's my turn! As soon as you step in and run Hillary Engineering, Grace and I are seeing the world. Places I've visited as a businessman. As seen through the eyes of gawking, appreciative, American tourists!"

At this point, he slid his arm around Grace's waist. Pulled her against him.

"In fact...I don't know if we'll ever come back!"

"Now Keith," the new woman in his life protested. "Do these grandiose plans include making me an honest woman?"

"If you mean marriage, Gracie...the answer's an emphatic 'Hell yes!'"

"Well, Suzanne," the older woman looked at her prospective stepdaughter. "I take that to mean he's proposing. With your blessings, of course."

"You certainly have them, Grace," she replied happily. "Both of you. You're a cute couple. I think the world is ready for you. Give me until the new year, dad. I'll have Hillary Engineering under my thumb by then."

"That's a deal, honey," Keith replied. He held out his hand. "Grace and I will get married in early January. Getting hitched in the winter fits old coots like us. We'll be off to Paris in the spring. The perfect time of year!"

He shook with his daughter. Clutched her tenderly to him. Then slipped his arm around Grace. Held the two on either side. "What a wonderful way to wind a long career. Surrounded by women you love."

Matt's work on the Hillary account took him to nearly every job site. Arranging photographs. Publicity. Or shooting for commercials, films and print advertisements.

Slides, photos, film, negatives and artwork of Hillary projects crammed nearly an entire office at the agency. Along with exhibits and displays in various stages of completion.

Suzanne and Matt pored over these materials at least one day a week. She, trying to learn about her father's most recent undertakings. And Matt, providing details he could.

Keith also asked his daughter to work closely with the agency on a campaign for hospital construction. This undertaking would debut at the time she took the company's helm.

"If we make a dent in hospital and health care fields...we'll be assured work," Keith announced. "People always need these institutions. And like churches, their boards keep wanting to enlarge or improve them."

Keith had attended a health care convention three months earlier in New York. Hospital managers, doctors and administrators there lobbied him to get into building these specialized structures.

"Plus, advances in medical technology mean hospitals need to consider computer rooms and multi-function workstations," he continued. "I estimate you could revamp a hospital every three years or so. And then...consider nursing homes!"

HILLCO, Hillary Engineering's overseas division, had been landing fewer contracts. For which Keith was thankful. With completion of a small South American refinery, he hoped to dissolve the subsidiary. Most of HILLCO's employees would rejoin the holding company.

HILLCO had got involved developing military bases. Mostly throughout Europe and the Far East. And undertook several years of unpleasant tasks in Vietnam. Now under communist control.

Fall Festivals ceased. A gathering of Huntsdale's menfolk went squirrel hunting and whisky swilling. However, without the mammoth foodfest afterwards.

Matt and Karen traveled to The House many times. Spending uncomfortable, silent weekends together. Most of the time, he ending up drunk and passing out on the family room couch.

Matt had not hunted ducks the last four seasons. His father and son... often accompanied by Guy Simpson...kept the blind and boathouse in fit shape.

For years, the inconveniences of driving to The House far outweighed his enjoyment there. So he turned his back on Huntsdale and The House. As if they belonged to a period of life he wished to forget.

He had become imprisoned by the very things he loved. Work, and New York. And time. He no longer felt in control of seconds, minutes, days and years speeding by.

Instead, he labored under the pressures of too many tasks to do. Tainted by disappointment, knowing he could not get many done. Or done well. So he drank to forget. And seldom forgot to drink.

Corley entered school in California. His third college since quitting Conn State two years previously. Diana enrolled as a freshman at Boston College. Majoring in drama.

At their grandparents' requests, the two young adults decided against Christmas at The House. For a change, they would vacation in Miami with Walt, Claire and Evelyn. Karen also decided she'd fly down, after spending Christmas at The House with Matt.

October turned sullenly to November. Snow fell one day after Thanksgiving. And remained until Christmas week.

Matt hosted the annual BD & Associates Christmas party. And, after bidding farewell and holiday greetings to Suzanne, flew to Hartford. He collected Karen in New Haven, and drove to Huntsdale that evening. As usual, feeling his insides tug as he departed New York.

They didn't cut a Christmas tree. And when the day arrived, it brought wind and cold. And more snow. The House...even with roaring fires in two rooms...remained chilly and dark.

Compounded by two adults acting like strangers to each other. Hardly daring to speak. For fear of bringing into the open what had festered for years. Each, in his or her way, dreading to confront what happened to their marriage. Knowing that discussion could lead to an ultimate, clean severance of their ties.

The day after Christmas, Matt paced the kitchen nervously. Drinking coffee in steady gulps. Chain-smoking cigarettes, one after another.

"Matt, please sit!" Karen implored from her seat at the round oak table. Louder than she honestly intended. "You make me uncomfortable!"

He took the chair across from her. Stubbed his cigarette.

"Well...at least the snow stopped. You know, I hate to say it. I really should get back to New York. We've got loose ends to tie before Hillary's spring campaign. Not much time left. Suzanne's been doing lots of the work herself."

Karen got up, poured another cup of coffee.

"Oh? My, my. Poor little Suzanne. Working, when her dad has all those millions."

"Come on, Karen," he flushed with irritation. "She is a hard worker. Always has been. You know...she ran the European operations for fifteen years. And did one hell of a job, too!"

"Gee, I'm goddamned glad you told me that, Matt! Especially since I've done one hell of a job for about thirty years. And you've never said that about me!"

"That's not true, Karen. And you know it! I've supported your decision to work. Complimented you on outstanding things you've done. You know that!"

He looked into her hurt, angry eyes. And barged onward. "Besides, she runs a billion dollar corporation with two divisions. Watches over ten thousand employees. That's considerably different from managing an interior decorating shop with ten employees."

"Oh, it is, huh? Well, Matt Durham...if you miss your precious Suzanne and foul city so goddamned much, why don't you go back there. And for good, too, for all I care. It doesn't matter anymore, Matt. It just doesn't matter."

Tears streaked Karen's cheeks as she rose from the table.

She ran the hallway to the stairs. Hurried to the bedroom. He heard the door slam behind. Drowning the sobs.

"Shit!" he hissed to himself.

He arose, poured his cup half-full of brandy. Topped it with coffee. He went into the living room. Lit a cigarette. Then flipped on the television and sat on the large cushiony couch.

An hour later he went upstairs. Karen lay on her stomach on the king-sized bed. Staring out the window at white hills rolling into the distance. Merging with a grey-white sky. The view she cherished before. Now just looked at, not saw. He noticed tear trails glistening under her eyes and down her cheek.

"It's best I go back to New York, Karen," he said. His voice a low monotone. "We need breathing room for sorting things. You join the kids and folks in Florida. It'll do you good."

Without a word, she pushed herself from the bed. Wiped her eyes with a tissue. Picked up the leather suitcase near the closet. And began taking underthings out of her dresser. Folding them silently into the open luggage.

When she spoke, deep hurt tinged her words. Matt felt small, ashamed.

"This is where it all began. It's fitting this is where it ends. Wonderful while it lasted."

She patted silk undies into a square in the suitcase.

"I don't want it to end, Karen," he said. "Give it time to cool. We'll work it out, believe me. Let's not throw those years away."

She turned.

"How much time will it take, Matt? Another twenty years? You in one place...me in another. And our children? God knows where they'll be. Not that it matters to you."

He sensed her anger again. Rather than rekindling the argument with stupid remarks, he took his suitbag from the closet. Began hanging his clothes in it.

Karen quietly continued her packing. An hour later, he locked The House. They drove to New Haven in silence.

Only a few inches of snow fell in the city. When he pulled the driveway behind their home, she quickly stepped out. She retrieved her suitcase from the back seat of the Mercedes.

"Good-bye, Matt."

She stooped slightly to look inside the car.

"I hope the new year brings you more success. And you and New York enjoy it."

Matt clenched the steering wheel tighter against the sarcasm. He looked straight ahead. Knew her eyes were welling again. Did not want to see.

"And you enjoy Florida, Karen. Give everyone my best. Tell the kids and folks I love them."

"Sure, Matt," she said.

She pushed the door shut with a soft snap. Walked through the light snow to the rear door. He put the car in gear, backed down the drive following the tire tracks made coming.

At the end of the drive, he paused to look at the house. It sparkled in the clean snow. He saw the drapes part slightly as Karen looked out. Then close again.

He drove quickly from Wellham Park to the interstate. Then on to Hartford, making the six-thirty flight with time to spare. He spent it over martinis in the cocktail lounge.

The mantel clock chimed nine as Matt entered the apartment. He hung the suitbag in the bedroom closet. Pulled on a cardigan sweater against the chill. Soon, steam heat clanged the radiators. He poured a tumbler of vodka over ice with a twist.

He walked to the living room window. Sat on the arm of one of the couches. Looked out into the darkness. Eerily crisscrossed with strings of colored Christmas lights in the distance. And clusters of weaving automobile headlights on the other side of Central Park.

He sat. And watched. And drank. His mind in neutral.

No thoughts. No feelings. Staring into nothingness.

He stood, freshened his drink, and walked into the bedroom. He thought of reading, but the vodka's warmth and toasty steam heat began taking hold.

At midnight, he switched off the nightstand lamp and fell fast asleep.

Matt awakened at eight-thirty and brushed his teeth. He brewed a pot of coffee on his automatic maker, then called the office. Dot Weymouth answered.

"Bradley, Durham and Associates. Mr. Durham's office."

"Hi Dot, you gorgeous hunk of femininity! This is Matt. I'm back in New York. Anything going on?"

A long pause lingered. When she came back on the line, he instantly detected disappointment and anger in her voice.

"No...it's quiet here. How come you're back, Matt? And where's Karen?"

He stumbled. Tried to mold the correct words in his mind. Lost them somewhere on his tongue.

"It didn't work out, Dot. We had a tiff. She's off to Florida. And I'm going to cool it awhile. Be off by myself."

"I think that's a big mistake, Matt Durham! Damnit, you should catch a plane and go to Florida yourself! No sense hanging around this gloomy, cold and dirty city. All alone and feeling sorry for yourself."

"What the hell gives you the right to sound like Karen, Dot?" he bellowed into the mouthpiece. Then stopped short. Swallowing anger that tightened his neck near the base of his skull. Knowing instinctively she was right.

He apologized. Then turned his original question into a statement, changing the subject.

"So...nothing's going on. That's unusual!"

"Well...Mrs. Whittier is here. Looking at slides and photographs in the preview room."

He chuckled to himself. Mrs. Weymouth always called Suzanne, "Mrs. Whittier." As if reminding him of both their marriages.

"I think Greer's with her."

"Oh? Tell you what, Dot. Ask her to go into my office and pick up the telephone. I'd like to talk with her."

He heard an exasperated sigh. Dot put him on hold. Moments later, Suzanne's cool, husky voice filled his ear. Bringing a broad grin to his face and quickening his pulse.

"Matt? You're in New York? What on earth are you doing here?"

"Talking with you right now," he said. He lit a cigarette. "Listen, I played 'twenty questions' with Dot. Let's you and I pick up from there. How was your Christmas?"

"My, a little testy, aren't we? It passed quietly. Enjoyed dinner with dad and Grace. You should see them scrambling around, making reservations and wedding plans. It's exciting!"

"Yeah, I'll bet. Give Keith and Grace my best when you see them. Wish them a Happy New Year."

"Fact is, I'll see them tonight. We're going to Sarni's New Year's party. Why don't you join us, Matt? Please? Unless you've got other plans?"

He paused...only for a moment.

"Okay...sure. If you don't think they'd mind."

"Mind? Dad? He'd rather you show up than me! You know that. Besides, I think there's something he wants to ask you."

"Oh? What's that?"

"I'll let him tell you. Prepare yourself to rent a tux."

"Okay. Now then...what's the program?"

"Meet us at Sarni's at seven. We'll play it from there."

"Sounds like kicks, kiddo. I can't wait."

"I can't either, Matt. I truly can't."

When they hung up, he smiled to himself. Felt the tingle of excitement sweep his body. He poured another cup of coffee. Lit a cigarette and picked up the newspaper from the hallway. Already counting minutes until seeing Suzanne again.

As he bent to pick up the paper, the strange numbness tensed his left arm again. He mentally noted to find a doctor in New York for an examination. He hadn't had a physical for more than five years.

Even then, it consisted of a harried visit to Hal Sappington. Who gave him a penicillin shot for a nagging cold. Then promptly chewed him up and down for dropping so much weight, and consuming too much alcohol and tobacco.

"To hell with Hal Sappington, and doctors in general," he said aloud. He walked inside the apartment, massaging the arm. "Except old Damon, they're overpaid wise asses anyway."

Matt fried a couple of eggs. Flipped them onto a piece of white bread, next to three sausage links. He walked into the living room to read the morning news.

"Same old shit," he whispered. "Get a new president in, and before his plans take effect, everybody carps about everything he does!"

He voted for Reagan. Like most others, he saw the man dedicated to turning the country from submitting to commanding respect. Strengthening the United States' backbone and integrity.

He also knew, somehow, Lyle Bradley involved himself in the local elections. Bradley acted particularly despondent after hearing the winners announced. In fact, he took a week's vacation to Phoenix to visit his father.

Since returning, Lyle immersed himself in television programming decisions. Much to Greer's dismay. Still, he stayed out of the office...and out from under everyone's feet...most of the time.

Matt finished breakfast and scanning the paper. Then shaved, showered and dressed. And drove Broadway, shopping baubles for Suzanne. Not knowing what or why. Just wanting to buy her something.

At Tiffany's, he settled on a pear-shaped garnet set in a gold clutch. It sparkled brightly, revolving on an impressive serpentine chain. A simple necklace, honest yet elegant.

With boyish exuberance, he imagined it dangling from her long graceful neck. Competing for attention with the perfect smile she would wear. He asked the saleslady to box and ornately wrap the necklace. Then set about shopping for himself.

He returned to the apartment about four. Again telephoned his office. After checking Dot for telephone calls, he asked her recommendations for a local physician. She referred him to a young doctor not far from the office.

"If you'd like, Matt, I'll make you an appointment for early next week. Surely, you can clear your calendar for a couple of hours."

"No...that's okay, Dot. Thanks. No time to spare next week. I'll call the week after. Listen, you have a happy New Year's!"

"Thanks, Matt. You, too. And, please be careful."

He pondered her closing statement. Dismissed it. And read the evening edition of the New York Times. Then mixed a sour mash and branch water. Began preparing for the evening's undertakings.

By six o'clock, he finished shaving, showering and dressing for the second time that day.

And walked out the door to the elevators.

Several stewards in starched white uniforms set long tables at the north end of the hallway. There, annually for more than forty years, tenants held community parties. Feasting on lobster, crab, filet and prime rib. Drinking champagne by the magnum. And regaling from high above in the goings-on in Times Square.

Festivities didn't begin until nine o'clock. Still, he knew many of the old-timers would mill around the tables at eight. The servers better have things primed for "sampling" by eight-thirty.

He stepped aboard the elevator. And it occurred to him that in twenty years here, he'd only attended the building celebration twice. Both times for only a few minutes. He spent the majority of past New Year's Eves in New Haven or at The House. Thinking about them now...the elevator speeding past floors enroute to the basement...he felt remorse twinge over his brawl with Karen.

He felt the slim box containing Suzanne's necklace in the left breast pocket of his suitcoat. Patted it, and instantly regained his spirits. And renewed excitement over the evening's promises.

The drive to Sarni's involved bumper to bumper traffic. Many New York citizens already celebrated. Wandering aimlessly in groups throughout the strings of traffic. Slowing proceedings even more. Several times, Matt stopped completely for couples jaywalking in front of his car. Most sloshing champagne. Toasting all happening by.

His watch read a quarter of seven as he entered the restaurant. A waiter quickly ushered him to a table reserved for Hillary Engineering.

At least ten people clustered there. Including Keith, Grace and Suzanne. He knew most of them from over the years. Keith rose and greeted him as he approached the table.

"Matt, what a wonderful surprise," he said, extending his hand. "When Suzanne told me, I couldn't believe it. Nothing wrong at home, is there?"

He turned toward Suzanne momentarily. Knowing she would attend his answer.

"No, Keith. Not really. My wife was anxious to fly to Florida. She's spending some time there. And I needed to get back to New York. Figure on relaxing a bit."

He winked in Suzanne's direction.

"I couldn't pass up Suzanne's offer, though. Sounded like too much fun."

"Well, I'm glad you didn't. There are things I'd like to discuss with you. Strictly personal, mind you. No business tonight. Comprehende?"

"You got it, amigo," he replied. He lifted a glass of champagne from the tray held before him.

Over the course of the evening, they drank or spilled nearly a bottle of champagne per person. Consumed crab legs and tenderloin minuets by the basketful.

Six private parties enveloped Sarni's simultaneously. They mysteriously merged into one large, boisterous group shortly before midnight. Cheering, kissing and rehearsing "Auld Lang Syne".

Matt danced with Suzanne. And now, they stood to one side of the dance floor as the crowd started counting down New Year's.

Horns and clackers created an almost unbearable din within the packed restaurant. Matt looked into Suzanne's beaming upturned face and shouted: "Happy New Year's."

She echoed his greeting. Then locked her arms around his neck. Without hesitation, he kissed the willing, open mouth. At first, gently. Then hungrily. Pressing his lips tightly against hers. Thrilling to the tip of her tongue entering his mouth. And firmly brushing his.

When the Pandemonium subsided, they drew slowly from each other. Smiling knowingly. And returned to the table where Grace and Keith embraced.

"Happy New Year's, honey," Keith said to his daughter. He rose and bussed her on the cheek.

"Happy New Year's, Matt," he said, pumping the other's hand. "And many more to come."

Suzanne and Matt returned Keith's and Grace's wishes. Took their chairs at the table.

"Matt...now's as good as time as any," Keith leaned toward him. "I'm asking you upfront. Would you stand as my best man? Suzanne's all I've got left in the world. Except for you. It sure would mean a lot to me."

"Keith...my God. I'd be proud to," Matt responded.

He clapped his friend on the shoulder. "It's an honor knowing you'd let an old huckster attend the wedding. Let alone stand with you!"

They chatted another half hour. Then Keith suggested he and Grace "call it an evening." And asked Matt to drop Suzanne at her apartment on his way. To which the former responded positively.

After the others left, Matt draped his arm over the back of Suzanne's chair. Through the loud buzz of conversation and orchestra music, asked if she'd like to visit a quieter party.

"I'd love to, Matt," she responded.

They bid farewells to the others. And requested his car sent around front. Soon inside, Suzanne slid next to him. Took his right arm in hers, laying her head gently on his shoulder.

He detected the familiar scent of perfume in her hair. Wondered why it smelled so differently on Suzanne. And not Karen. He felt his pulse race excitedly with the moment. And the warm feeling of her nestled against him.

In contrast to Sarni's, the New Years Eve party at Matt's apartment building was quiet and relaxing. Lights glowed dimly, and soft music spilled from the built-in sound system. Only six couples remained seated in the vestibule at the end of the hallway. Talking among themselves. And hailing Suzanne and Matt to join them in a toast.

Matt took her arm, led her down the hallway toward the group. Beyond the large bay windows, they saw the twinkling lights of Times Square. The huge electric billboard blinked messages, and flashes of fireworks brightened the ebony surrounding Manhattan.

The two introduced themselves to the small cluster of people. Accepted the glasses of champagne offered. Then sat on a loveseat near the window.

"I heard daddy ask what he wanted, Matt," she said over the rim of her glass. Taking tiny sips between words. "You are sweet to agree. He thinks the world of you, you know."

"I feel the same about him, Suzanne."

"You know...he wants me for matron of honor!"

Matt tinked his glass against hers.

"You'll be absolutely ravishing."

They both laughed heartily. Then noticed the others turning to look at them.

Suzanne covered her mouth with a hand, stifling a giggle.

"Speaking of beauty," Matt said, reaching into his inner pocket. He retracted her gift. "This is for you. A New Year's present. I've been carrying it all evening. Forgot about it."

"For me? Oh Matt, how sweet. You shouldn't have."

"A token payment for the joy you bring when I'm in New York."

Suzanne hesitated opening the present, reached down and gave his hand a firm squeeze.

"The feeling's mutual, Matt."

She gingerly peeled the shiny paper from the silver box. Opened it. And lifted the necklace from its cotton padding.

The garnet teardrop sparkled brilliantly, even in the hallway's dim light. It spun lazily as she held it. A scarlet plumb bob dangling from a gold chain. His gift touched Suzanne. And she experienced difficulty voicing appreciation.

"Matt, it's exquisite! So delicate. Help me put it on, please."

She turned halfway on the cushion. Her back to him. She opened the clasp, and held both ends of the gold string behind her neck. With fumbling fingers, he joined the strands.

Suzanne turned around. Put her arms around his neck and kissed him. This time, even more longingly. Matt felt the lower part of his body stir.

"Let's finish the champagne at my place," he whispered. "There's even a fresh bottle in the fridge."

"Sounds delightful," she replied, pecking his lips. "Thank you for the stunning necklace. I love it."

They quickly downed the champagne remaining in their glasses. Placed the empties on a table with others. Bid good evening to their comrades. And walked the hallway to his apartment at the opposite end.

Matt unlocked the door, and switched on the living room light. He held it open for her, then closed it behind and flipped the safety bolt.

When he turned, she stood in the shadows of the dark room. Studying the lights of the city that sparkled through windows on both sides of the conversation area. He walked to where she stood. Hooked his arm around her waist.

"Beautiful view, isn't it?"

She put her arm around his middle. Her head on his shoulder.

"It's even better in the bedroom. You see most of Manhattan."

Suzanne turned her body against his. Entwined her arms around his neck.

"I'd love to see that view, Matt."

He pulled her gently, tightly against him. Their lips found each other's, tongues hot and probing. Matt felt his body reacting. And rubbed against her. Pushing firmly, as she rose to her tiptoes. Their lips clung, crushing their mouths wide apart. She felt his firmness. Moaned softly, deep in her throat.

Matt reached between her shoulder blades, tugged the zipper of her evening gown to her waist. Felt her feverish flesh yield soft beneath his fingers. He took her hand, and still kissing, led her to the bedroom. Once there, he slid the evening gown to the floor. She helped him out of his jacket. She didn't wear a brassiere. In the glow of Manhattan lights, he saw her full firm breasts rise and fall with excited breathing. Garnet necklace suspended perfectly between them.

He stood back as he unknotted his tie. Looked admiringly at her. Standing proudly in panty hose and undies. He unbuttoned his shirt and tossed it over a chair.

Suzanne unbuckled his belt and unzipped his fly. His slacks slid to his ankles. He stepped out, and her hand softly grasped where he jutted from his skivvies. She moaned again, as he lowered her hose and panties, stripped off his shorts, and they fell together onto the king-size bed.

In darkness atop of the bed covers...her body outlined by the faint glow streaming through the windows...Matt explored her with his tongue. Pausing when she writhed with ecstasy. Stopping between her legs, until she groaned and a body-wrenching climax flooded her in wonderful spasms.

He crawled on his knees between her legs. Until directly over her. Looking down into the face that still wore an expression of bliss. He lowered onto his elbows, and on top of her.

She guided him with her left hand. Wrapped her legs around his calves, pulled him tightly. Matt felt his entry. And her moan of pain and pleasure as they fit together, culminating time and again as they tossed in the light-strewn bedroom.

And when he felt the inevitable, pleasurable tingle overtake him, he shoved forward as she pulled, and they climaxed together in breathtaking convulsions.

For several minutes, they lay spent. Quietly wrapped in each others' arms and legs. Breathing deeply, heavily. He, feeling spent passion melt. She, the seeds of lovemaking, warm moistness between her thighs.

She pressed her head against his chest.

"Matt...making love with you pales any other sensuous experiences I've had. You're even better than I had hoped and imagined."

He didn't reply at first. Still enjoying the feel of her warm body against his. Bonded together by moonlight. He put his chin down on top of her head.

"Yes...it was marvelous for me, too. You are wonderful."

She looked up at him. Watched a flicker of concern sweep his face in the dim light. And realized.

"Don't feel guilty," she said softly. "It wasn't anybody's fault. It just happened."

"I know," he replied flatly. "Still...I saw it coming. In fact, hoped it would. I wanted you more than anything. Hungered for you. Still do, for that matter. From the first, I felt we'd end up like this."

"And...is that wrong?"

"I don't know what to think, Suzanne. Things turning sour between Karen and me. And the kids...I never know what they're doing. I can't handle more than my own life."

She cupped his face in her hands. Spoke to him in almost motherly tones.

"Matt, what we're doing is not wrong. We're alike in so many ways. Both boxed in. And needing out."

She raised slightly, leaned on an elbow.

"Need is a strong word," she continued. "It overrides intellect. Clouds judgment. And it can easily break the so-called commandments. For you and me, New York is an island. We're stranded on it. You needing me. I, needing you. I still do. And as long as I interest you, I still will."

Suzanne slid her hands around his neck. Pulled him over on top.

Cupped her lips on his, and eased her tongue into his mouth. She felt him clutch tighter. His tongue exploring. And between her legs, felt him stirring, then growing within. "Matt...Oh Matt...Oh Matt," she moaned.

He moved slowly against her body. She felt herself writhe, as passion's spasms again swept her. Flooding her senses again with pleasure and intense fulfillment.

Half an hour later, she arose to use the bathroom. Matt fetched champagne and glasses from the kitchen. Then they lay together...all night...talking, sipping champagne and making love. Sunlight streamed through the living room windows when Matt sleepily pulled the drapes to darken the bedroom. He and Suzanne drifted into slumber. Her head on his shoulder. Right arm draped across his chest.

They awoke shortly after one o'clock. Made love again in the shower. Then Matt drove her past her apartment to change clothes.

From there, they enjoyed late afternoon seafood on Long Island. Returning to his apartment early that evening.

As before, once through the door, they embraced hungrily. Then walked to the bedroom, undressed, and resumed lovemaking.

Thirteen hundred miles away, Karen stood on the hotel verandah. She looked over waves breaking against Miami Beach. Depositing white, foamy stripes on the shore. That the sand instantly absorbed.

She felt uneasy and hollow in the pit of her stomach. Wished Matt were with her. Her, Diana and Corley. Then the sensation subsided. As quickly as the breakers. And Karen felt the familiar rage and frustration well within.

"Damn you, Matt Durham," she said into the tropical breeze brushing her face. "Why did we let this happen? How could we?" She stood for another moment. Eyes moistening for the tenth time that day. Then went inside to join her mother, her children and her in-laws.

Chapter 26

Karen And Hal

B LIZZARD CONDITIONS PERSISTED IN NEW York through the first two weeks of January. Dumping fifteen inches of snow on the city. Immobilizing traffic. Snapping tree limbs. Leaving Central Park a tangle of shattered branches. And making sidewalk and street travel nearly impossible.

Luckily, the weather broke toward the middle of the month. Enabling Keith and Grace to repeat their nuptials at noon at Mary Queen of Peace Cathedral. Then depart on a three-month honeymoon through Europe. Climaxing in France in April.

Matt and Suzanne drove the newlyweds to the airport Keith built fifteen years earlier. And during the slow drive, the foursome sipped champagne from crystal goblets.

"Well, you two...how does it feel being young marrieds again?" Suzanne asked. She leaned her chin on her left forearm. Smiled wistfully at the couple in the backseat.

"Remember, Suzanne," her father cautioned. "We've both been here before. Just think of how great this union will be, since we're both practiced pros. Right Grace?"

"Yes, Keith. That's true," his wife agreed. Feeling giddy from excitement and bubbly.

When they pulled into JFK, Matt flashed his Triad pass. Then drove to the far end of the terminal. Making it a simple matter to check luggage and collect boarding passes at the gate.

Triad's London flight left at one o'clock. And touched wheels at Heathrow ten hours later. Allowing hardly enough time for jet lag to occur.

Matt and Suzanne watched the handsome couple board the jetliner. Stopping once, briefly, and waving enthusiastically from the portable ramp.

Then the motorized stair pulled away, and the jumbo jet rolled the taxi lane to the runway. In five minutes, the Hillarys lifted skyward. Heading for the fulfillment of their dreams and lives together.

Matt clasped Suzanne's hand. Caught her wiping a tear. Then smile broadly.

"I'm really happy for them, Matt. They're perfect together. Don't you think?"

"Yeah...I do. Couldn't happen to a nicer twosome. They fit. And they're going to have a fantastic life together."

"Yeah...I'm sure of it."

During the inclement weather, Matt picked up Suzanne at her apartment in the mornings. Dropped her off evenings. Sometimes, spending the night.

Most weekends, Suzanne stayed at his place. Each had his and her own keys to the apartments.

The two kept busy in the following weeks. Approving the creative materials comprising Hillary Engineering's spring construction campaign. His writers and designers performed brilliantly in crafting promotional items that would attract hospital administrators.

They targeted managers, directors and doctors involved in scouting new quarters. And remodeling or expanding current spaces.

They conceived print ads for the major trade publications. Rented space at several medical conventions. And Greer turned in superlative work writing, producing and directing several television commercials and film clips.

These aired nationally before the six o'clock news. And visually illustrated Hillary Engineering's expertise in building medical and health care facilities.

Greer's commercials appeared subtle, yet effective. They featured practicing physicians and medical administrators. Each proclaiming that spacious, attractive and technologically advanced facilities resulted in more effective and economical treatment.

Greer earned more COCA Awards than any other television producer in the city. And Madison Avenue pundits agreed his latest Hillary commercials would garner more plaques for his burgeoning collection.

Almost daily, Greer locked horns with Lyle. The latter involved himself in Greer's specialty...buying and scheduling commercial television time. Through intimidation, blackmail or both...Lyle weaseled into New York's circle of network executives. To his credit, for BD &

Associates' clients he wrangled time slots previously booked months in advance.

Greer, tired of butting against concrete, left time buying to his boss. Concerning himself only with the creative end of the business.

Soon after Hillary's campaign kicked off, Suzanne and Matt lunched at Smitty's...their favorite deli on Madison Avenue. So she could explain her new position and duties at the helm of the company.

They lunched together regularly. Mostly at Smitty's. Their favorite place. It served as a logical haunt and watering hole for agency people in the neighborhood. Specializing in fat sandwiches and standing-room-only crowds from eleven-thirty until past two.

"Tell me, beautiful lady...how does it feel captaining Hillary Engineering?" Matt asked jokingly over a thick hot pastrami and Swiss cheese on rye. "Controlling billions of bucks. Thousands of people. Making hundreds of crucial decisions daily?"

She didn't respond to his ribbing as he'd hoped. In fact, not at all. She seemed down. Fiddling with her potato salad. Ignoring her sandwich. He had hoped to draw her into conversation.

"It's not like you'd think, Matt," she finally volunteered. "Not at all." She despondently let the fork drop to her plate. Looked at him through concerned eyes.

"For instance...this morning I selected charities to support. People to promote. And what I'll wear to the New York Builder's Spring Ball!"

She took a hefty pull of dark beer.

"I can't waste time on nit-picky things! I should be on a project somewhere. Figuring how to bring in a job...on time, and under budget. That's exciting. This is boring as hell!"

"I know what you're saying, Suzanne. I faced the same problems... evolving from Indian to chief. Wanting to keep my finger in every creative pie. You can't do it, bunkie. Your new role is traveling in lofty circles. Making crucial decisions about buying half million dollar road-graders. Or accepting speaking engagements. Sitting on boards."

He refilled their glasses. Waggled a finger for another pitcher.

Believe me...my last important decision was selecting Dot Weymoth's retirement present! Hell, our place runs itself! Seriously. It's an automatic advertising agency. Push a button every morning, and it goes and soothes ruffled clients, or hunts new ones. It doesn't need me!"

"Well, at least it's a relief knowing I'm not alone. This bullshit must have driven dad crazy!"

"Oh, I doubt that, sweetheart. Somehow, guys like Keith and me find ways to pack fourteen hours in each day...and still leave stuff piled for the next morning. And you're just a chunk off the old cinder block. Right?"

"I guess you're right, Matt." She reached across the table. Took his hand. "You're a pretty smart fellow. Sorry for depressing you with my sob story."

"Don't be," he kissed the back of her hand. "Client service is what your agency guarantees. It's natural to feel you give up more than you gain, each step up the ladder. That's because from the heights of leadership...you see all the people actually making things happen. And you're not there anymore."

They returned to their lunches. From the booth next to their table, they overheard two men talking.

"I'm telling you, Jack," one said. "Nelson, Fane and McConnell hasn't a snowball's chance in hell. Not as long as agencies like Bradley, Durham and Associates are around. They just whacked our balls off by underpricing services on two accounts!"

"What are you talking about, Frank?"

"It's like this. We did volunteer work for Congressman Wilkes. BD&A backed someone else. They find out our guy gets elected. And chase every account we pitch."

Matt turned in his chair to see the two strangers as the conversation continued.

"They cover the costs of working smaller accounts by moving part of those expenses to their larger ones. It gets lost somewhere in a CPA's ledger. Nelson, Fane and McConnell doesn't have a prayer in this town. I'll tell you that much!"

Matt had even stopped chewing. He continued looking over his shoulder at the two young account executives in the booth. They turned briefly his way, then went on with their chatting over lunch.

Matt put the sandwich down. Took a healthy swig of beer. Suzanne whispered across the table.

"Is it true, Matt? What the kid said. You wouldn't have anything to do with it. But...?"

"I don't know, Suzanne. Suddenly, I'm not hungry."

He lit a cigarette. Jotted something in his calendar notebook. Tucked it in an inside pocket.

"I'll find out, though."

They finished their meals in silence. Pulled their overcoats on. And walked out into the frigid air.

Once again, the sky threatened snow. And the moist air hinted it could commence at any minute. He hailed a cab and dropped Suzanne at the Hillary Building on Broadway. Then walked the half block to his own offices.

He was mad as hell when he stepped off the elevator. And walked in the front door of the agency. The receptionist, Janette, started to speak. Then saw the dour look and thought better of it.

He took off his overcoat and muffler. Hung them in the closet in the outer office. Stuck his head into Lyle's office. The latter sat at his desk. Eating a sandwich, and reading The Wall Street Journal. He looked up at Matt. Instantly stopped chewing.

"Lyle, would you come into my office, please?" Matt asked with all the politeness he could muster. Lyle set the sandwich on a paper plate.

"Sure, Matt. Right behind you."

Matt asked his secretary to hold his calls. Walked into his office. Held the open door for Lyle, who appeared a few seconds later. They stepped inside, and he closed it behind them.

Lyle slumped at the round conference table across from Matt's desk. Matt camped on the arm of an easy chair. Lit a cigarette, and dropped the spent match into an ashtray beside him.

"I overheard an interesting conversation at lunch," he said, rather matter of factly. "Thought I'd relay it to you."

He pulled on the smoke. Looked menacingly at the other. "Ever heard of a small shop called 'Nelson, Fane and McConnell?'"

Lyle cast his eyes downward for a moment. Registered knowledge of the agency.

"Yes, I think so. Why?"

Matt tapped the ashes off his cigarette on the rim of the tray.

"Seems they recently presented to prospective clients. And we went in, undercut them, and pilfered the business. In fact, a couple of times."

"Those are the breaks of business, Matt. What the hell does all this have to do with me?"

"Nelson, Fane and McConnell worked for Congressman Wilkes. Got him elected. Now, they think we're ruining them because we backed some loser. Are we, Lyle?"

The other squirmed slightly in his chair. Crossed his legs effeminately at the knee. Tugged at his tie.

"Of course not, Matt. We agreed to steer clear of politics long ago. I kept my end of the bargain. And dad's completely out, you know."

Matt knew he was lying. As certainly as he sat across from him. He didn't push it farther. Just stood up. Ground the cigarette roughly into the ashtray.

"Okay, Lyle. Thought you should know. We don't need sleazeball tactics to win accounts. Hell, we've got more than we can handle now!"

Lyle stood, walked to the door. He halfway opened it, and turned back to Matt.

"This is a competitive street, Matt. You know that. You hit a lucky streak when you first came to New York. Now, it's milk or let go of the tits. If these little agencies want to play big league, they deserve to eat spikes."

Matt felt his neck stiffen. Face flush with anger. His fists doubled instinctively.

"Let's keep it clean, Lyle. That's all I'm saying."

Lyle shrugged his shoulders. Slipped around the half open door and disappeared. Matt sat behind his desk. Grabbed the pack of cigarettes and lit another. Seconds later, Greer McCall rapped lightly on the door. Then walked in, closing it behind.

"What was that all about, boss?" he asked.

Matt pointed Greer to a seat at the conference table. Stood, walked over, and sat across from him. Recounted his conversation with Lyle.

"Matt, he's lying to you!" exclaimed Greer, after hearing about the eavesdropped conversation at Smitty's. "He and an asshole politician have been tangled for years. Blanton, or a name close to that. Represents the Fourth District. Anyway, he stumped for another term."

Greer rested his elbows on the table. Clutched both sides of his face with his hands.

"Nelson, Fane & McConnell boosted Wilkes. Did a hell of a job, too! Blanton took it in the shorts."

"Blanton...didn't he come down hard on investing in the depressed areas. Bailing out minority businesses?"

"Yeah...the same. He painted the railroads as obsolete dinosaurs. Said they should 'Just go under gracefully.' Their time was done."

Matt jumped to his feet. Thudded his fist on the table.

"So, that's it!" he said. He pressed his forefingers to his temples, his eyes squinting. "No wonder we lost Eastern Freight Railways so suddenly and mysteriously! They learned BD&A backed Blanton. Hell, I'll bet Nelson, Fane and McConnell told them! Which is smart of 'em, actually!"

"That's what happened, okay," Greer affirmed. "We've kept it under wraps. Lyle doesn't think anyone else knows. Kept it hushed. He funneled Blanton's campaign materials through an art house in New Jersey. Eddie Bauer found out accidentally. Some original art ended up at his place rather than here. So he asked me about it."

"That sneaky son of a bitch!" said Matt. "Greer...why didn't you guys tell me about this?"

"By the time Eastern Freight got wind, it was too late. No use pointing fingers. The Hillary and Cartiff campaigns had you socked. We didn't want you worrying. Eastern didn't represent a lot of bucks. And they were slow paying. So, we kept it to ourselves."

"Well...thanks for that, Greer. I wish I'd found out sooner. Lyle doesn't know any of us is aware of what happened?"

"No...I'm certain of that."

"And that's why he's going after Nelson, Fane and McConnell! They trounced his boy. That bastard. Okay, Greer. Let's still keep this close to our skin. Promise?"

"Sure thing, Matt. It won't go beyond me."

"Thanks, pal."

When he left the office that evening, Matt felt more depressed than he had in a long time. On reaching his apartment, he called Suzanne and invited her to dinner.

Hours later...over several vodka martinis, a bottle of vintage burgundy and a rare steak...he told her what transpired between Lyle and him.

"You obviously can't trust him, Matt," she said, without emotion. "You thought he swore off political shenanigans. And he didn't. Why put up with his crap?"

"I won't much longer, Suzanne. That's certain."

"You and Greer should pull out. Between my company and Triad, you've enough to stay busy and comfortable."

"Yeah, I know. Trouble is, I wanted us biggest and best. Lords of Madison Avenue. I've sacrificed everything with that in mind. I couldn't go back to a one-horse shop again. That's where I started twenty-five years ago!"

Suzanne read between his words. Momentarily felt a jab of jealousy. Knowing he meant marriage played the lead in his sacrifices. She reached across the table. Lifted his hand in the candlelight. Kissed his knuckles, one by one.

"Let's go to my place for a nightcap, Matt. You need a good rubdown. I still have that wonderful brandy you bought a few months back."

"That's probably the best offer I've had in days," he said. He peeled off four twenties and left them on the table with the check.

He side-stepped behind Suzanne. Held her chair while she lifted gracefully. They donned their overcoats at the front door, and arm-in-arm walked from the restaurant into icy gusts outside.

The wind also blew in New Haven. Dust clouds of powdery snow skittled across the driveway as Hal Sappington pulled behind Karen's home.

"Come in for a drink, Hal," she said. She took the offered hand, and slid out on her side of the car as he held the door.

"I'd like that, Karen," he replied. "Thanks."

They walked to the back door, bathed in outdoor tracklights. He took her keys, unlocked it, and she flipped the light switch inside.

They took off their coats, and Karen hung them in the closet in the dining room. She clicked on the light by the bar.

"What's your pleasure, Hal?"

"Scotch...just a splash of water," came the reply.

Karen poured herself a white wine. And they proceeded to the living room. Sitting on a large couch in front of the fireplace.

The two dined and took in movies from time to time. Over the last few months, regularly. This night, they saw "A Chorus Line" at New Haven's Municipal Indoor Theater, starring the original cast from the Broadway musical.

Karen enjoyed Hal's keen sense of humor. Capped by his spontaneous, although sometimes caustic wit. Overall, he proved a gracious and courteous partner. He made her laugh, and feel comfortable.

Over the years, the doctor remained single. Preferring an opulent lifestyle that revolved around expensive automobiles. Hand-tailored clothes. A mansion in prestigious Vallmoor Woods Estates. And freedom to do as he liked, as often as he liked, and in the amounts he liked.

However, he would change on a moment's notice for Karen. Whom, he loved since their first meeting. And so many years ago he couldn't count. Her father reigned as his boss at Yale. In addition to being a close good friend and supportive mentor.

The remains of the fire Karen started earlier in the evening now glowed crimson. She slid open the glass doors, and rolled two small logs on the bed of coals. Soon, the logs snapped and spewed. And small flames licked from beneath. Steadily growing in intensity.

"I had a fabulous time tonight, Hal," she said. She slipped off her shoes, and tucked her left leg beneath her. Facing him. "I thought Chorus Line turned out to be spectacular. Thanks for taking me."

"You're more than welcome, Karen. Yes...I enjoyed it immensely, too."

He stood. Removed his sportcoat. Loosened his tie, then resettled into the soft cushions. Drink cradled in his lap. He looked up at her, noticing the flames reflecting in her wide eyes. And giving her hair an even more golden sheen. He marveled over how she mysteriously became more beautiful with each passing moment.

"It was my pleasure, Karen," he repeated, more to rock the silence. "Believe me."

She reached down and warmly took his hand.

"I appreciate all you've done for me these past several months, Hal. Really. It's been a difficult time. Now, with the kids back in college... and Annie with her sister in Boston...this big house gets too lonely for my evenings."

Hal affectionately brushed a dangling lock of hair away from her eyes.

"Karen...any time you need someone to talk to. Or go wining and dining. Just call. I'll be there for you. I mean it."

She sipped her wine. Set the glass on the end table beside her. Tenderly kissed the back of his hand.

"Thank you, Hal," she whispered softly.

He set his drink on the end table at his end of the couch. Still clutching her left hand in his right. He reached and gently laid his palm against her cheek.

Karen pressed her head against his hand, and he pulled her slowly toward him. When their lips met, he leaned back and she rolled onto his lap, facing him.

The liquor, warm fire, and shared feelings caught, and they clutched each other tighter. Tongues exploring others' mouths. Breathing, deep and husky. Tuned to one another.

Hal eased his right hand under her skirt. Slightly skimming her silken pantyhose, moving between her thighs. Karen shifted her legs slightly. Soon, he stroked between them.

She moaned hotly as he slipped his hand under the elastic band on her hose. And into her silk panties. Finding anxious moistness there. He caressed her gently. Softly. Tenderly. The length of her body now tight against his readiness.

Suddenly, she pulled her lips away. Buried her face against his chest.

"I'm sorry, Hal. I can't do this. Oh God, I'm sorry."

With his left hand, he gently raised her chin.

"Yes you can, Karen. Damnit, I love you. More than anything, or anyone else. Certainly more than Matt does. I want you. I need you. Please!"

He kissed her lightly on the forehead. And after a moment's silence, withdrew his hand from under her skirt. He felt her sobbing deeply.

"I'm the one who's sorry, Karen. I shouldn't have pushed this. I love you so much."

She looked at him. Eyes wet. Silvery trails streaking her cheeks.

"I feel strongly about you, too. I married Matt, however. And still love him deeply."

She stood, straightened her dress and lifted the wine glass to her lips. She took a few sips, then sat again.

"A moment ago, I wanted so badly for you to make love to me. Then I wondered if it were because of feelings for you...or anger at Matt. I don't know what will happen between Matt and me. I do know, though, that if we can't patch our marriage...I won't spend my life pining."

Hal took her hand, pulled her closer and kissed her cheek.

"Well, darling, I'd better leave," he said. He stood, straightened his trousers and hooked his coat over an arm. Karen put her hands on his shoulders. Kissed him lightly on the lips.

"Thanks again, Hal. For everything."

She walked him to the dining room. Helped him on with his jacket and overcoat. Then watched from the kitchen as he climbed into his car.

Under the outside light, exhaust drifted in thick puffy clouds as he started the Jaguar's engine. He waved good-bye over the dash, and backed down the driveway. Finally disappearing into the darkness.

Karen returned to the living room. Sat in front of the now blazing fireplace. Drank her wine, and thought of her husband.

In a way, she felt guilty over what occurred with Hal on the couch. Or was the guilt because of how he felt about her. Unrequited love, they called it in movies.

The more she thought of Matt, the lonelier she became. She poured another glass of wine. The telephone rang as she returned to the living room. She immediately glanced at the regulator clock above the mantel. Its hands pointed one. And her heart fluttered out of anticipation of someone calling at this hour.

Her first thought focused on something dreadful happening to Matt. In the next instant, however, she worried over Corley and Diana. Fear restricted her throat as she lifted the handset.

"Hello?"

"Karen? That you?" she experienced relief hearing Walt Durham's voice. Even though it conveyed a serious tone.

"Yes, it's me, Walt. Is something wrong?"

"I hate calling you at this hour. I tried you earlier several times... without luck. Thought I'd try again before turning in."

"I went with a friend to a musical at the Municipal Theater. Just got home an hour ago."

"I tried Matt, too. He's always with clients. So, no luck there either."

Karen felt a wave of anger sweep her. Learning he had not returned to his apartment.

"What's wrong?" she asked, rather impatiently.

"It's Corley, Karen. The Davenports called us...you know, the folks he stays with."

"Yes, Walt. What about Corley?"

"The police busted him for smoking marijuana, honey. He and his roommates. It's not serious. I mean...his first time. They're not going to prosecute him. Hell, in California marijuana's easier to get than fresh air!"

"My God, Walt! What will happen next? Will he get booted out of California State, too?"

"No, honey, I don't believe so. Phil Davenport will see the police Monday. He doesn't think they'll report the incident to the university. They were in an off-campus apartment. Apparently, someone snitched. An ax to grind against one of the other boys."

"Have you talked with Corley, Walt?" Karen asked. Tears blurred her eyes again.

"Yes, honey. He's ashamed of himself. Upset about the whole incident. Promised nothing like this will happen again. And he'd graduate in May on schedule."

Walt paused for a moment. Karen could hear an old movie on television in the background. Claire probably curled on the couch. His voice startled her when he spoke again.

"You know, Karen...my grandson's a bright kid. A dreamer, yes. A gentleman, too. And a damned fine writer. He gave his word to his grandpa. That's good enough for me."

"Thanks for handling this, Walt. I wouldn't have reacted well if the Davenports called me. I haven't had my head straight lately. I'll tell Matt. Or better yet, I'll write him."

"You say the word, Karen, and I'll jerk sense into that knothead. Claire and Evelyn worry themselves sick over you two. I'm not happy about the separation, either. Matt better come back to earth soon. Or he'll lose the things that matter."

Another long pause followed. Karen sighed, and thanked the general for calling.

She cradled the telephone. Returned to the living room to finish her wine.

In her mind, she replayed the carefree, wonderful times she and Matt experienced. Tonight, they didn't help. In fact, made her even more melancholy.

By the time the fire burned to bright orange coals, she finished her wine. She opened the glass doors on the firebox. Poked the glowing mounds with a brass poker. Reclosed the doors and chimney flue. Then gathered her shoes and walked the stairs to the bedroom.

She undressed. Slipped into a silk nightgown. And went to the bathroom to floss and brush her teeth.

Karen looked into the mirror at her swollen, red eyes. She splashed her face with cool water. Cleaned her teeth and went back into the bedroom.

The evening's events succeeded in exhausting her. And shortly after slipping between the sheets, she succumbed to a deep, dreamless sleep.

Karen arose slightly after nine o'clock the next morning. She visited the bathroom, then made a pot of coffee. And carried her stationery pad to the kitchen table.

By ten thirty, she had written Matt a four page letter. Outlining the details of what Walt relayed the night before concerning Corley. She also informed him that Diana dropped out of Boston College in January after her first semester, and now lived with a playwright at Martha's Vineyard.

She sensed her heart had bottomed out, somewhere near her ankles. She cried, penning unhappy milestones of her marriage. One that began with everything...and seemed ending somewhere short of miserable.

She instinctively signed the letter, "Love." Then looked at the funny word...so easily flowing from the pen...and asked aloud what had become of its meaning.

She folded the pages neatly. Slid them into an envelope, addressed and stamped it, then dropped it in the mailbox at the front door. She stood, looking over the snow-dusted front lawn. Barren, scraggly maples and giant elms resembled trees out of a cartoon forest. Sunlight burned through the overcast sky, and beamed warmth.

She turned, and went back inside the house. Deciding to shower and call Corley. Let her son know she loved him dearly.

Karen's letter arrived at Matt's mailbox two days later. He came straight from the office, after seeing Suzanne off to California. And worked until dinner, hoping to pack his time with activities and keep his mind off her.

When he pulled the thick envelope from his mail slot, he felt his heart flip-flop. Knowing, intuitively, it contained bad news. He mixed a stiff bourbon and water. Sat on the couch, and read the missive.

Each word Karen scripted in her neat handwriting chewed deeper into his conscience. When he read her closing lines, his eyes blurred and burned with remorse.

He lit a cigarette and walked to the window. Stood silently for a long while. Looking over the traffic below. Finally, he returned to the couch. And reread her writing. Again...then again.

Matt's left arm bothered him more lately. So much so, he massaged it constantly. Felt his grip becoming weaker, daily. And he seldom held anything in his left hand, which seemed shaky and numb.

He remembered the football injury many years back. Doctor Forsythe told him the arm would always bother him. Especially in cold, damp weather. Regardless, he decided to have it examined when the workload lightened. Although, three times before he made appointments for physicals and canceled when other commitments cropped.

Corley's arrest upset him. Diana dropping out of college crushed him.

He knew his son could pull himself together. Corley had grown into a strong young man. And fearless. Not a quitter.

Diana mirrored Karen. Trusting, open and vulnerable. He convinced himself she faced a shattering, agonizing experience ahead with the playwright.

He finally folded the letter back into its envelope. Tossed the remainder of his drink in the sink. And sprawled on the bed. He lay for an hour. Eyes full open. Staring at the ceiling that reflected Manhattan's golden glow.

He thought about Karen. His children. His parents. Hoot and Bobby. Relationships he'd taken for granted. And lives he'd carelessly shattered.

He swung his legs over the edge of the bed.

Grabbed the deck of cigarettes on the night stand. Fired another. He took a long and deep pull. Winced when the smoke seared his lungs. Instantly stubbed it in the ashtray.

Again, he spread-eagled himself on top of the comforter. His mind flashed events that punctuated the past decade. He sensed the room swirling like a whirlpool, with he caught in its vortex.

What Karen drafted kept echoing somewhere in the deep recesses of his being. Without conjuring, the thoughts swam freely to the top of his mind. To linger, and torment.

He filtered the consequences of his prodigal existence through his brain a final time. Then at last, closed his eyes into a fitful sleep. Swearing things would change.

Somehow...and soon.

Chapter 27

The Unraveling

T HE HECTIC PACE HERALDING SPRING'S coming carried through the summer for Matt. In May, the National Association of Advertising Agencies elected him to its Board. Heading the newly formed Committee for Higher Ethics In Advertising.

Now, he chiseled free time from crowded days. And spent it campaigning for, and helping govern, that organization's day-to-day operations.

During a day-long June seminar, two of his committee members informed him of rumors traveling Madison Avenue. In effect, Bradley, Durham & Associates engaged in unethical practices.

They volunteered the information casually. Still, Matt bristled at the insinuations. Especially since the others would not, or could not, attribute reliable sources for tales told.

"Don't take it so seriously, Matt," Lyle said when advised of the scuttlebutt. "The rumor mongers have been generating gossip overtime recently. Everyone's suddenly sprouting morals!"

As an Association Director, Matt suffered the gnawing compulsion to investigate the innuendo. And what more logical place to begin than within his own house. His mind kept flitting to his January conversation with Greer. And inevitably focused on Lyle. Which caused even more severe stomach churns.

He quietly interviewed BD&A account executives. Creative staff members. Clerical help. Even clients. Trying to corroborate accusations involving the company. Unsuccessfully.

Matt's temperament approached loose cannon magnitude, as attempts to find cause for the allegations proved futile. Such external strains...combined with internal misgivings...exacerbated his tension. Seeking solace, he grew reclusive and withdrawn.

Matt had not felt well for months. Now, disparaging comments on the street further aggravated his physical and mental anguish. By August, his nerves twanged like steel guitar strings. And his left arm trembled so noticeably he kept it tucked in his pants or coat pockets.

In the privacy of his office, he continually rubbed and massaged the arm. Nothing brought relief from the uncomfortable, tingling numbness. Not even squeezing a small rubber ball. Suzanne gave him one. Thinking he suffered a strained muscle that needed exercise and toning.

Additionally, he smoked two packs of cigarettes daily. Three when drinking and dining with clients. Which still occurred frequently.

At Suzanne's and Greer's urging, he consented to a doctor's appointment. And this time, vowed to keep it.

Greer stormed into Matt's office one particularly hot and humid dog day afternoon. Face redder than the ball Matt clutched in his left fist.

"Matt...you have to talk with that goddamned Lyle!" he sputtered.

Matt stood. Offered his friend a chair at the conference table. Poured him a bourbon over ice. One for himself.

"What's happened now, Greer?"

The other winced at the bite of the straight whisky. He looked at Matt incredulously.

"The bastard just fired me!"

"What!" Matt boomed, feeling the liquor and news heat his face.

"For misappropriation of funds! Can you believe that shit!"

"No, I can't. What's he talking about?"

"Our accountants crunched the numbers on television spot purchases and sales," Greer continued. "Compared these with escrow dollars in the account. And they don't jibe. They're off several hundred thousand dollars!"

"Holy Christ!" Matt exclaimed. He stood, closed the door to his office. Freshened their drinks, and sat quietly thinking for a moment.

"Lyle said you wanted out of time buying. That paper shuffling interfered with your producing commercials. Time buying has been solely his responsibility for a year! Did you ask him about that?"

"He has me sign buy and sell agreements as media vice president, Matt. I mean, purchases, insertions, contracts with stations selling us airtime...or reserving it for us."

Greer stood, walked to the window, looked out, shaking his head from side to side.

"It comes across my desk. Most of it, I sign without inquiring. There isn't time to nitpick everything."

"So, what you're saying is...maybe BD&A bought television time for a client. And didn't use it for his commercials? And, you wouldn't know."

"Exactly. It could be used for another client. Or logged as time owed us by the station. Like money in the bank to draw."

"Whose cockamamie idea is this, Greer? Or should I ask."

"Yeah, it's Lyle's. He figured we'd buy time at low prices when stations need to get rid of it. Then sell to clients at marked-up prices. If stations squawked, he'd give them part of the profits."

"Goddamnit, Greer! You knew about this! Hell, some auditor's going to castrate this agency. And there's nothing we can do!"

"I didn't know, Matt. Honestly." He took another sip of straight bourbon. "I only learned from the accountants this morning. That's when I approached Lyle."

He reached a notepad, jotted figures.

"Since January, we report television time sales topping eighty million bucks. We only have half that amount in the account."

"Jesus! Where'd the rest go?"

"Made up, probably. Sales entered...that never occurred. And keyed into media computers as if they had."

"I don't understand why, Greer."

Matt slid his chair back. Now he stood and walked to the window. He grew impatient...more with himself, for not grasping Lyle's motives for deception. Than with Greer's inability to define the situation clearly.

After a moment, he turned, fetched the whisky bottle, and again took his seat. Greer continued.

"In several instances, we bought worthless blocks of time. Often, that's the only way you can buy choice spots on the networks. You find chaff scattered throughout the wheat."

Greer picked up Matt's pack of cigarettes. Tapped one out. Lit it.

"A reasonable client doesn't expect his commercials to air at three in the morning. So, we sold prime time at prices that covered purchasing the bad. And then banked the worthless time. Later on, we sold it for a profit, too. The bean counters say we double-dipped. So, they called in an independent auditor. He's the one who uncovered the phony computer entries."

"And Lyle had access to the computer, right?"

"Sure, Matt. His group tracked what we sold. How much we bought. And, amounts of time banked at various stations. The whole tangled ball of yarn!"

"No wonder we're labeled the 'dirtbags of Madison Avenue!' How many other crooked deals involve us?"

Greer tossed down the remainder of his drink. Swallowed hard.

"I know of one more. The auditor cross-checked commercials aired with who paid for them. Do you really want to hear this, Matt?"

"Goddamned right I do, Greer. Don't hold back what you know or suspect. I want the bottom line on this."

"Prime time billed to Eastern Freight Railways actually carried promotional announcements for Congressman Blanton. Most of Eastern Freight's commercials appeared late night or early morning."

"Damn! You think Eastern Freight knows this?"

"I'm sure of it, Matt. They watch television. Lyle must have provided them a schedule showing what commercials are airing, and where and when."

"Of course, the devious bastard could tamper with schedules, and submit phony reports. Right?"

"You bet."

"If Eastern knows the time they bought went to the son-of-a-bitch trying to put them under...we're in deep yogurt! I'd better touch base with them right away!"

"It might be too late, Matt. Still, it's a show of good faith."

"I'll call Eastern and schedule a meeting. Don't worry about your firing, Greer. I've got something else to discuss with you later. Right now, there's a little task for me to do."

He turned on his heels, leaned down to the other, his hands spread on the table.

"Do you know where Lyle is?"

"Probably the Charthouse Restaurant...around the corner. He left for there after he talked with me."

"Thanks, pal. I'll see you later. Like I said...don't worry."

Matt stood, shook hands, led Greer to the door and held it for him.

"Thanks, Matt."

After Greer left his office, Matt called Triad Airlines. Luckily, he caught Larry Harst heading for lunch. He made an appointment for two o'clock. Then called Eastern Freight Railways and arranged a meeting the next day.

When he talked with Eastern's executive vice president, he detected guarded coolness restricting the man's once friendly manner. Gnawing in the pit of Matt's stomach confirmed his agency faced legal woes. Still, he did manage the four o'clock meeting. Hope existed.

He tossed down the remainder of his drink. Pulled on his light suitcoat. And informed his secretary he'd be gone until later in the day.

Matt walked to the Charthouse a block away. On entering, he spotted Lyle in a booth by himself toward the rear of the dining room.

A boisterous lunch crowd packed the restaurant, and several people stood in line for seating. Matt walked past them. Waved away the maitre d. Approached the table where his partner sat.

Lyle dabbed his mouth with a napkin. With a sweeping hand, motioned for Matt to occupy the chair across from him.

Instead, Matt stood. He leaned from the waist. His nose inches from the other's. In low, solemn tones he said: "Bradley...you rotten son-of-a-bitch. I'm dissolving our partnership...right now."

The force behind Matt's fist came at waist level. The leverage from leaning on his right leg. His clenched knuckles crashed under Lyle's jaw, lifting the latter out of his chair and spread-eagling him onto the table behind.

Lyle's limp body slid on the linen like a puck on ice.

Silverware, glasses, table lamps and food followed in the wake of his prone disappearance under the table. He fell to an unconscious rest in the darkness there. With napery and place settings covering him in an avalanche of accouterments.

Matt pulled his handkerchief out. Dipped it into Lyle's glass of ice water. Dabbed the bleeding knuckles of his right hand. Soothing the bruised flesh and ligaments.

He took a deep breath, slowing the adrenaline that made his heart pound like a jackhammer. And noticed in the sudden silence, all eyes riveted on his commotion.

He calmly turned and faced the diners. Wrapping his throbbing hand.

"A slight tiff between ex-partners," he said to the assemblage, loud enough that even those waiting in line heard.

He leaned over the toppled table. Looked down at Lyle, swathed in linen. Blood trickled from the side of his gaping mouth. Matt placed the crimson-stained damp handkerchief over the man's face. He turned, headed for the door.

"Please, folks. Enjoy your lunches."

He walked from the restaurant, sucking the raw, swelling fist as he went. Picked up his car from the parking garage. Then drove to the Triad Building, and his meeting with Larry Harst.

By the time he entered Triad's offices, the story of the Charthouse incident had preceded him by ten minutes. The company's four officers sat in the lobby, awaiting his arrival.

"Here's slugger now!" chided Bob Griffith. He stood and walked to usher Matt into the offices.

The latter instinctively held his hand to shake. Then quickly jerked it back, remembering the injury. His hand...swollen and bleeding again... resembled a catcher's mitt. He had wrapped it in a wet towel from the men's room. Already it weeped pink.

Bob placed his hand on Matt's back. Steered him toward his office. Stopped briefly at his secretary's desk.

"Louise, please ask Doctor Harris to come see Matt's hand," he said. Then the five walked into the president's office.

Don Stein went to the bar near Bob's desk. Poured them each straight bourbon.

"What caused this fracas, Matt?" Larry asked as they sat at the walnut conference table. "In nearly thirty years, I've never seen you lose your temper!"

"Lyle pushed me an inch over the top, Larry," replied Matt. He noticed relief as the bourbon burned his throat. Taking his mind off the sharp, jabbing pain in his injured hand. "For as long as we've been partners, he involved us in shady deals. This time, he mistakenly tried pulling a lot of us into the shit with him. That was more than I could tolerate."

"Does this mean BD&A is kaput, Matt?" asked Don.

Matt took another bite of the bourbon. Looked at the others. Fumbled a cigarette with the bandaged hand. Bob placed it in his mouth, and lit it for him.

"Sorry to say it does, Don. That's why I called Larry earlier today. I want to split my assets and ass away from Lyle Bradley. We can split our accounts as they were. Won't be difficult for bean counters to figure assets for each of us. What I really need are legal papers drawn quickly as possible. I need the partnership dissolved. And legal responsibilities fixed and carved in granite."

"I'll get cracking on that immediately, Matt," Larry replied. "Takes less time than divorce...believe me!"

"Okay, Matt," said Bob. "What happens to our account?"

"I'll tell you, fellows. Hate to say it, but I'm hitting the silks. I've enjoyed as much heat and dust from that immortal race as I can stand. Winning the garland doesn't matter, anymore. I've got enough money to do what I want."

Matt accepted a drink refill from Don.

"Don't worry, Bob. I'm going to ask Greer to oversee accounts we brought to the agency. Triad, Hillary Engineering, Cartiff Perfume, Standish Electronics and Musgrave Manufacturing. He's been handling Triad for years now. And the Hartford and New Haven offices are thriving. Besides a lot of our overload, they manage Connecticut Castings and dozens of other accounts."

"It's a relief knowing Greer will supervise Triad, Matt," said Bob. "Although, I'm sorry seeing you pack it in. We've weathered rough and easy for lots of years. Hate to see part of our winning team retiring. You know, if advertising's killing you...we need a marketing wizard."

"Thanks, Bob...but no. I'll dabble a finger from time to time. That's enough. I'll be there to consult with Greer, Eddie and John anytime they need my bag of tricks."

The five chuckled and Bob had poured fresh drinks when the doctor arrived. He looked at Matt's blood-stained hand. Cleaned it with a swab and peroxide. Then he wrapped it with gauze and tape. Saying he doubted it needed stitches, and to keep it clean.

Sid Masters offered the doctor a drink. He politely refused. He needed to see another patient before the day ended.

They sat and talked until nearly six-thirty. Then Matt joined them for dinner. He called Suzanne from the restaurant. She agreed to wait for him at her apartment.

It was almost nine when he arrived. When she saw his taped hand, she immediately asked what happened. He told her of his talk with Greer. Of punching Lyle at the Charthouse. And his decision to break the partnership.

A troubled look flashed across Suzanne's lovely features. She phrased the inevitable question: "Does this mean you'll leave New York, Matt?"

He accepted the snifter of brandy handed him.

"I don't know yet, Suzanne. Nothing makes sense anymore. I don't know where to turn. My mind feels like New York on rainy evenings. Everything melts into obtuse shades of grey."

Suzanne put her arms around his neck. His face buried between her breasts.

"Stay here tonight, Matt. I'll help you forget your problems. I promise."

He held her at arms' length. Looked into the beautiful face. The ripe, red, voluptuous, open mouth. The stirring began low within his body.

"I'll bet you could," he said. He pulled her to him. Kissed her roughly on the mouth. Their breath, tongues and lips merging.

After Matt left the Triad men at the restaurant, Bob called Hoot. He told him of the day's happenings. And voiced concern over Matt's depression.

"Hoot...I've known Matt almost as long as you. I've never seen him give up on anything."

Bob spoke loudly to hear his own voice. Over the dinner music piped above the pay telephone he used.

"You're right," agreed Hoot. "That doesn't sound like him. I'll fly to New York. Listen, Karen's visiting Bobby and me. We'll talk this over. I'll get back soon."

"Thanks, Hoot. I feel responsible for a lot of this. Matt came to New York because of Triad. I pretty much gave him the ultimatum...join us or leave us."

"That's not so, Bob. He decided based on the interests of the agency. His business...his work...has been his life and mistress. Don't feel responsible. Hillary Engineering created the biggest problems... demanded the better part of his time."

"I'll tell you, Hoot. He needs friends right now. I've never seen him look so bad. He's got the shakes. Chain-smokes. Hits the sauce pretty heavily. If you spent time here...or talked him into getting away for a while...it would help. I'm certain of it."

"I'll do it, Bob. I'll fly up tomorrow evening. I have appointments and meetings tomorrow afternoon. Still, I can catch your seven-thirty out of Hartford with no sweat."

"That's wonderful, Hoot. We'll meet you at the airport."

After they hung up, Hoot rubbed his face with his hands. Deeply concerned over sad news about his best friend. And wondering what to tell Karen. He opted for the truth.

"I don't know what to think," she said, after Hoot relayed his conversation with Bob. "Just like that...Matt split the agency? And punched Lyle Bradley? Of course, that's understandable. He mentioned sneaky things Lyle did before. So he had it coming, I'm sure. However, pulling out of the agency! Poor Matt. That's his heart and soul!"

"I'm flying over tomorrow evening, Karen," Hoot said. He retrieved the coffee pot. "I'm going to talk him into coming back with me. I want you two together again. This foolish episode has lasted long enough."

Hoot filled their cups. Returned the container to its perch on the coffee maker.

"If he craves involvement in advertising, he can head the New Haven office. From what Eddie says, they've got more business there than in Hartford. I'm sure John Keller would appreciate the help. He'd gladly move over as president. Let Matt be chairman and run the whole show!"

The three sat silent for a moment. Karen stood, kissed Hoot on the forehead, hugged him around the neck.

"You're a one in a million friend, Hoot. I don't know what we'd do without you."

The next morning, Matt awakened at seven. He dressed quietly. Kissed Suzanne on the cheek, and drove to his apartment. There, he perked a pot of coffee. Shaved, showered and read the morning paper. At nine o'clock, he entered the offices of Bradley, Durham and Associates.

"Joy, please ask everyone to come into the conference room at ten o'clock," he said to his secretary. "I've got an announcement to make."

Next, he poked his head into Greer's office.

"Come see me for a minute, would you Greer?" he asked his friend.

Matt walked into his office. Took off his suitcoat. Hung it in the small closet across from his desk. He asked his secretary to bring coffees, then held the door for Greer. They sat at the conference table, and Matt told him the previous day's events.

"You busted the s.o.b. after you left here!" asked Greer, his face breaking into a wide grin. "Jees...that must have felt great!"

Matt raised his bandaged hand. Rubbed it, and winced finding it still sensitive.

"Fact is, it hurts like hell! Must have caught a tooth or something."

He told Greer of his meeting with Larry Harst. And the others from Triad.

"They've got faith in you, Greer. Bob knows you can manage the account with no problems. What I want to know is...can you take over the others?"

"What do you mean, Matt?" Greer looked at him incredulously.

"I mean...our original clients. I'm calling it quits, old pal. I'm splitting the sheets with Lyle. If you'd like, I want you to run the New York agency. It'll be your ball of wax...the whole thing."

Greer fell silent a moment. Contemplating the proposition. Finally, he looked at Matt. Smiled broadly.

"Hell yes, I would!" he exclaimed. "I can do it, Matt. What accounts will we keep?"

"I'll call them this morning. Cartiff, Musgrave, Standish and Hillary. And, Triad of course. Those are the major ones. I'll call and ask if they want to stick with you, or go with Lyle's group. Of course, you'll also have overflow and video work from New Haven and Hartford."

Matt pulled a cigarette from his pack. Offered one to Greer, then lit them both. He snapped the match dead.

"I'm positive our accounts will remain, Matt," the other said. "We've been family for years. And, they've received quality work from us."

"I agree, Greer. Listen, I'm calling everyone in the conference room at ten. I'd like you there. And make the announcement. Okay?"

"Sure thing, boss," Greer replied. He reached across the table to shake Matt's hand. Remembered the injury, so clutched his left.

They talked a few minutes longer. Matt showed Greer to the door. Stuck his head outside and asked his secretary Lyle's whereabouts.

"He's in his office, Matt," she answered. "He arrived a few minutes ago."

"Thanks, Joy," he said. He walked to the opposite end of the room. To Lyle's door. He rapped, opened it and stepped inside.

Lyle stood behind his desk. When Matt appeared, he defensively moved against the wall.

"That's okay, Lyle," Matt said. He held his hands palms outward. "I won't do anything. In fact, I apologize about yesterday. I'm not a bad ass."

Lyle grimaced as he touched his chin. Which sported a deep purple patch, the size of a tennis ball.

"You nearly broke my jaw, Matt!" his voice rose. "And I lost a tooth somewhere. I ought to sue for everything you've got."

"I doubt you will, Lyle. Anyway, I came to say Larry Harst is drawing papers to split our happy relationship. The accounting people can work out the details of who owns what. At ten o'clock, I'm informing everyone in the conference room. Those wishing to stay with you may do so. The rest go with Greer. He'll handle the accounts we're taking with us."

"Now hold on a minute, Matt. It doesn't have to come to this. Sure, we disagreed over something. I think I've paid royally for my sins." Lyle rubbed his chin again for emphasis.

"It won't work any longer, Lyle. They didn't cut you and me from the same moral fabric. Pretty soon, the National Association of Advertising Agencies will smite you like God in the Old Testament. And Eastern Freight Railways is going to sue your ass off. Did you know that?"

"No, I didn't," Lyle hissed his reply. Matt felt his face flush. "What ever for?"

"They know about that cute scam you pulled with television time they bought. You know, when you gave away prime time supporting that fathead Blanton.

"What! How! Where...how did...who?" the other stammered.

"It doesn't matter how I found out, Lyle. Just know that I did. That's why I decked you. And believe me, I can do it again with my left hand!"

The ex-partner backed tighter against the wall. Looked down, shamefully.

"No...that's okay, Matt. Don't get pissed again."

"Anyway, Lyle, it's over. I wish you luck...because I think you're going to need it. Lots of it. See you around."

Matt walked from Lyle's office to his own. It was nearly ten o'clock. He pulled on his coat, and went to the conference room. Greer sat near the podium at the front of the room. The remaining agency employees sat or stood along the walls. Awaiting Matt's announcement.

He told them of the agency split. Without elaborating. And enjoined any wishing to go with Greer to do so. He also explained his leaving the company. And advertising altogether.

Matt explained he would remain temporarily in New York. Help form the new group, and arrange offices.

The meeting took about an hour. Afterwards, the bulk of employees shook Matt's left hand. Wished him well, and informed Greer they most preferred remaining with his agency.

"Well amigo," Matt said to him afterwards. "You've got an agency, clients and employees to do the job. Good luck."

The two shook hands. Then Matt spent the remainder of the morning calling accounts. Informing them of the change. BD&A completed the bulk of its work for the major accounts. The changeover would not affect them. And all felt secure knowing Greer would run the operation.

He finished contacting his last client when Suzanne called, inviting him to lunch.

"Sounds good, hon," he said. "However, remind me I've got a one-thirty doctor's appointment."

She agreed she would.

So they stopped at a seafood restaurant. Located around the corner from the medical building where he would take his physical. They devoured huge tomatoes stuffed with chunks of crab meat and garnished with a special sauce. Afterwards, she walked him to the doctor's office.

Jim Benedict looked much younger than his late fifties. Matt's physical state appalled him.

"How much do you smoke, Matt?" the doctor asked. He studied x-rays brought by his nurse from the laboratory where Matt posed for them.

"I don't know. Pack or so a day."

"I'd suppose more than that. Lots of dark area. Looks like congestion. Nothing out of the ordinary for heavy smokers. You should cut back, you know. Ideally quit. More for your heart than anything else. You exercise much?"

"No, Doc. Not for a while. Used to hunt and fish a lot."

"You should start again. Get involved in some sort of aerobic exercise. Bicycling, or maybe fast walking. Something to clear those lungs. Emphysema isn't much fun, you know. Breathing all the crap in this city doesn't help either."

Matt disliked receiving lectures.

"What's the prognosis, doctor?" he asked curtly.

"For someone who hasn't taken care of himself for a while, you're pretty well off. You need to do something about smoking. And watch how much you drink. Your cholesterol level's probably going to be higher than I'd like, too. Will it do any good telling you this?"

"Probably not, Doc. I'm old and set in my ways. What about my left arm? Why does it feel like the circulation's bad? Always tingly, throbbing. And trembling."

"I'm not certain, Matt. When I get the blood results in a week, I'll let you know. Okay?"

"Yes, doctor. That would be fine."

"Swell. You can get dressed again. Remember what I said about the smokes and liquor...okay?"

"I'll try to cut back. I promise."

"I'll accept that," the doctor said. He stood and made notes in the file folder he created for his new patient.

"I seldom delude myself into thinking I've converted another pitiful soul to healthful acts and thoughts. I'll settle for raising the conscious levels of a few. Good day, Matt."

The two shook. Matt changed into his suit, and went into the waiting room. Suzanne sat, reading a magazine.

"Well, Mr. Durham," she smiled. "What's the prognosis?"

"The doctor said to smoke filtered cigarettes. Increase my alcohol intake to ward off germs. And lay off sex completely."

"Ooh!" she exclaimed. "I know some sex you can lay on or off any time you'd like!"

They chuckled over her wit. She took his arm as they left the medical building.

"You know what I'd like to do?" she asked. They were driving the West Side Expressway toward Manhattan.

"What's that?"

"Take my convertible. Drive out Long Island where it's gorgeous. Look at fall colors, and eat lobsters at a little restaurant I love."

"Ms. Hillary that sounds like a winner to me," he said, veering off the freeway at the Fortieth Street exit. "I'll swing by the apartment. Change into something casual. Maybe toss on a light sweater. It's nippy out, and I don't want these old brittle bones getting chilled."

"I don't either," Suzanne replied, as he pulled into the parking garage beneath the building. She scooted over in the seat. Kissed him tenderly on the cheek. Matt shifted, and returned her kiss on the lips.

They went upstairs while he changed clothes. Then drove to her apartment, so she could do the same. Twenty minutes later, they motored Highway 465 east toward Long Island.

Since noon, Hoot tried to reach Matt. He called the office only ten minutes after Matt left. Wanted to announce he'd be on the seven-thirty out of Hartford. And needed to talk with him as soon as possible.

Hoot left word with Joy for Matt to call if he paged in. Then he tried the apartment three or four times. Rushing to telephone during breaks in the meetings he attended.

Hoot tried a final time at six o'clock. Then kissed Bobby good-bye and drove for Hartford to catch his flight.

Matt and Suzanne spent the bulk of the afternoon exploring coastal villages. Devoting two hours to an amusement park. Where, like kids, they smashed each other in bumper cars, and rode the Ferris wheel and roller coaster.

He won her a giant furry cat, shooting the red star out of a cardboard square.

From there, the couple drove to the restaurant she remembered. They consumed two one-pound lobsters apiece. Served with salad, corn on the cob, a dozen oysters, and carafes of house white wine.

Matt watched Suzanne tie her plastic bib. And his mind reversed thirty years to his honeymoon with Karen. A twinge of guilt tugged his chest. Briefly dampening his mood. Suzanne caught the flicker of concern sweep his features.

"What's wrong, Matt?"

"Oh...nothing, Suzanne. Just a touch of déjà vu?"

"You've been here before? Or feel like it?"

"No. Another place. Another time."

She couldn't put her finger on it. However, from that moment...and for some reason...the sparkle disappeared for the day.

Driving back, the setting sun changed the clear blue sky above Long Island to burnished copper. Matt hardly spoke. When he did, it was without enthusiasm.

She pulled in front of his apartment building at eight-thirty. He stepped out, walked to the driver's side, and kissed her goodnight. Then he walked inside.

As she pulled from his building, Suzanne detected the unsettling grip of concern pulling at her mind. She wished her intuitions would go away and leave her alone.

Matt approached his apartment, and a familiar sound suddenly dawned on his consciousness. Inside, his telephone rang onerously. He hurried to the door. Unlocked it. Bounded into the kitchen and grabbed the handset from the wall telephone.

"Hello?" he said, gasping for breath.

"Matt? It's Bob Griffith," came the deep voice on the other end. For some reason, Matt's stomach knotted deep inside. "Thank God you're home!"

"What's up, Bob?" he asked. Instinctively dreading his friend's answer.

Feeling something terrible would be forthcoming.

"You haven't heard or seen the news, Matt?"

"No, I just walked in. Car radio wasn't on. What gives?"

"Matt...one of our jets went down approaching Kennedy. The pilot of a small plane misunderstood instructions from the tower. He banked into our plane as it landed."

"Oh, no, Bob!" he exclaimed. "Anyone injured?"

"About forty passengers...near as we can tell."

"Oh, my God!"

"The small craft hit Flight 468 at two thousand feet. Our jetliner lost a wing. Cartwheeled into the marsh south of the airport. It's a mess out there, Matt! Search parties...rescue crews. It's a nightmare!"

"Bob...get hold of yourself! What can I do to help? You name it and I'm on my way."

"No, Matt...that's not why I called."

His voice trailed. Suddenly Bob seemed calmer, serious. Matt detected the change. Panic swept his body.

"It's Hoot, Matt," the other continued. "He was aboard 468. One of the first casualties recovered."

Black silence surrounded Matt. He stared into the handset, dumbfounded. When he finally answered, he cried, sobbed and tried to catch his breath. Pleading for more information. Trying to make sense of what Bob told him.

"Matt? Matt?" Bob shrieked on the other end. "My God, I'm so sorry."

When Matt partly regained his composure, Bob asked if he wanted him to call Bobby. Or would he rather do it himself.

"I'll fly there...talk with her face-to-face," he said. Still finding it difficult to believe his best friend died. Words did not exist to describe the innate emptiness burrowing into the bowels of his soul.

"Okay, Matt. Don't worry about a thing here. There's a funeral home nearby. They'll take care of Hoot until you make other arrangements. Again, Matt. I'm sorry as hell. I loved the guy like you do."

When they disconnected, Matt poured a glass of Napoleon brandy. Grimaced at the bite as he tossed down the full shot.

"Karen," he said aloud to himself. "I must call Karen. She'll know how to handle this."

He picked up the telephone. Dialed her number. She answered on the fourth ring.

"Hello?"

"Karen...it's me."

"Matt?" Silence. "What's the occasion?"

He sensed her voice harden. A quick flush of anger instantly turned sympathy. He dreaded telling her. And asking her to help him confront Bobby.

He halfway blurted it.

"It's Hoot, Karen. His flight went down at Kennedy. He's dead... our friend is dead."

Matt's eyes welled again as he mentioned his long-time friend. Silence came from the other end. Then he heard Karen drop the handset. It bonked against the nightstand. He knew she threw herself on the bed.

"Honey! Honey!" he shouted into the telephone.

He heard her crying in the distance. Finally, she returned to the line. Sobbing heavily.

"Matt, I'm so sorry," she said through teary gasps. "I know how you must feel."

"I haven't told Bobby. I hate to ask...but would you meet me in Middletown? Help me break it to her?"

"Certainly, Matt. Oh, poor Bobby. It'll kill her. This will be the hardest thing I've ever had to do."

"Yeah...me too. I'll catch the six-thirty to Hartford. Then drive down. Should be there by seven. Meet me at the coffee shop down the street from their place. We'll drive in together."

"Okay, Matt. I'll see you then."

When he hung up, Matt tossed down the last bit of brandy in the glass. Changed into pajamas, and went to bed. As he lay in the darkness, he pictured Hoot's face in his mind. Remembering times shared over thirty years they'd loved each other as brothers. Tears formed easily in his eyes. And rolled out of the corners.

"Christ, Hoot...you turkey!" he said aloud. "Why'd you have get yourself killed?"

Matt rolled on his left side. Buried his face in the pillow. And sobbed from his guts over his friend's passing.

Half an hour later, he got up. Washed his face, and brushed his teeth. Then slipped back into bed. Mind crammed with worrisome images and thoughts. And slowly, sleep carried his pain and worries away.

Matt caught the morning flight to Hartford. Collected his Mercedes at the flight service garage. And drove to Middletown.

Karen stood at the window of the coffee house when he pulled in. He parked, and walked inside. He hugged her to him. Started to release... but she held. He noticed her trembling. Knew the beautiful face would show tear stains when he saw it.

"I don't know what to say, Matt," she sobbed into his chest. "I don't know if there's anything I can say. Except I'm as sorry as I possibly can be."

He took her elbow. Steered her to a booth.

"Let's have coffee, Karen. Then we'd better talk with Bobby before she learns some other way."

They left her car at the restaurant. His pulled into the Gibson's driveway at exactly eight o'clock.

"The kids will be in school," Karen said. He held the door for her. "Bobby and Hoot's mother will be alone."

She pressed the doorbell button.

Bobby came to the door in her bathrobe. When she peeped through one of the tiny windows and saw them, she opened the door wide.

"What on earth are you two doing here?" she asked, eyes wide in amazement. Then she saw the looks on their faces. And sensed her heart crashing into a boundless chasm.

"What is it? What's wrong, Matt? Why are you here without Hoot?"

She looked at Karen frantically for reassurance. Saw the other's eyes suddenly flood.

"No, no! Oh, God no!" she cried, holding her hands over her ears, stumbling backwards. Matt caught her before she fell. Steered her to the couch. Mrs. Gibson appeared from upstairs.

"Why, what's wrong here?" she asked. "Matt? Karen?"

"Sit down, mom," Matt said. He gently seated her beside Bobby. Leaned on one knee, facing the two. "I've got terrible news. And I'd give anything not to have to tell you. Hoot's flight went down at JFK Airport last night."

Bobby looked up. Eyes red and misty.

"Was he hurt seriously, Matt?" she asked. Hoping against hope that was all.

"It's worse than that, Bobby," Karen said. She walked to her friend. Put her arms around her.

"He died in the crash," Matt stated flatly. Mary Gibson slowly lowered her face into her hands. Her back heaved against the deep sobs she emitted. Matt put his arm around the woman's shoulders.

When they regained composure, Matt described Bob Griffith's telephone call. On the drive to Middletown, he heard an early morning newscaster mention the plane crash. Reporting victims' names withheld until families informed. He remembered thinking how much he did not enjoy being the one doing the notifying.

Bobby arranged Hoot's funeral for the following Sunday. They buried him in the family plot near his father.

More than fifty people attended. Including Walt and Claire Durham. Evelyn Forsythe. Eddie Bauer. John Keller. The four Triad officers. Jug Hale. And several of Hoot's friends from the printing plant. All paid respects to Bobby and Mary. And expressed their deepest sympathy over their loss.

Matt provided the eulogy. Writing it proved his most difficult task, ever. Time and again, emotions hampered the simple act of putting pen to paper. He managed to finish it, though. And tasted tears presenting his tribute.

Bobby begged Karen to stay in Middletown with her and her mother-in-law. And she consented. After the funeral, Matt talked nearly an hour with the three at the Gibson's home. Then left to catch his flight to New York.

Karen walked him to his car. Straightened his tie as he prepared to climb in.

"When will we see you again, Matt?" she asked softly.

"I don't honestly know, Karen. I do know it's over between New York and me. I'm leaving the agency. Once we sign the papers, I turn everything over to Greer. And I'm gone. I don't know where. Or how. Just away."

"I'll still be in New Haven, Matt," she whispered. Her voice caught. She stood on her tiptoes. Kissed his cheek. Turned, and walked into the house.

The following Monday, Larry Harst presented the papers dissolving Bradley, Durham and Associates. And creating a new shop, "McCall And Company."

Lyle signed first, then disappeared. When Matt and Greer penned their names...erasing one agency and opening another...they sealed it with champagne.

Greer wound up with most of the accounts. And nearly all the employees as well. Lyle also surrendered his end of the lease agreement for the building. Opting for smaller quarters farther down Madison Avenue. Which cheered Matt and Greer.

Since legalities shot the day, they decided to celebrate opening Greer's agency with a party at Sarni's. Matt called Suzanne to join the festivities. And felt little pain by the time she arrived.

"This is where it started for us, beautiful lady," he slurred. Last call had sounded. And he nuzzled her ear in the dimly lit private dining room. "What say we silently slip away? Go abuse each other at my place!"

Suzanne interpreted his dragging words and unfinished sentences. He had finished celebrating. She agreed on shepherding him to his apartment. On the way, Matt slid next to her in the front seat of his car. Kissed her neck below her right ear as she drove. His right hand easing under her skirt.

"Now Matt," she protested. She lifted his hand back onto his knee. "Not while I'm driving...okay?"

When they arrived at his building, she parked the car in the basement garage. Helped him onto the elevator, and escorted him to his apartment. Inside, she prepared a pot of coffee while he slumped on one of the living room couches. He kicked off his shoes. Leaned heavily against the cushions.

"Bring me a brandy, Suzanne," he mumbled from the dark.

"No, darling. I'm fixing coffee. You've swilled enough for one night."

"Oh, bullshit!" he snapped. He tried standing, and fell onto the couch. On the second try, he found his footing. And reeled down the narrow hall to where she stood behind the serving bar.

He fetched the brandy decanter. Sloshed two inches in the bottom of a snifter.

"You want one?" he said, trying to articulate around a thick tongue.

"No, thanks," she said. She filled two cups with coffee. Led him to the living room. Where they sat across from each other.

"What's troubling you, Matt?" she asked.

Even through his stuporous state, he detected bewilderment and despair in her voice.

"I've never seen you drink like tonight."

"Well, seeing ain't believing yet, kiddo," he said. He took a sip of brandy, then scorched his tongue with scalding coffee.

"Why, Matt?" she pleaded. Desperate. "You can do anything you want. What makes you so unhappy you need to drown your senses?"

Matt tried to fix her with an unsteady gaze. His eyes refused to focus.

"I killed him, Suzanne," he blurted. Then hiccupped. "I sure as hell did."

"Who? Killed who? What in hell are you talking about?"

"Hoot...that's who!"

"That's ridiculous, Matt. Why say you killed him? You loved Hoot."

"Yeah...but I moved to this goddamned city. Turned my back on everything and everyone I loved. To make a lot of goddamned money. That's why. Old Hooter came here to take me back to New Haven. And got killed doing it! That's how it's my goddamned fault!"

Suzanne lifted from the opposite couch. Sat on her knees at his feet. Placed her hand alongside his face. Felt hot tears.

"It wasn't your fault, darling. Don't blame yourself for Hoot's death. You've done what you thought right. And never intentionally hurt anyone...especially Hoot."

Matt leaned on his elbows, face pressed into his palms. When Suzanne finished speaking, he collapsed against the sofa's back. His head flopped forward as he passed out.

She leaned him sideways until he lay horizontally on the couch. Undid his tie. Covered him with a bedroom comforter. Then sat in the darkness, watching him sleep.

Matt awoke at eight the next morning. Head pounding. Stomach swirling. When he tried to raise, the thumping quadrupled. He cursed the pain. Then noticed a sheet of paper on the coffee table under his cigarettes. He read its contents aloud:

Dearest darling Matt,

By the time you read this, I'll be on my way out of your life...headed somewhere. It's time you headed somewhere, too. Back to Karen. Your kids. What you left behind.

I love you, Matt. More than anything. And that's why I'm giving you up. I may grow accustomed to loving you and having you around. But, never to the fact that you love her more than me. You always will.

I've never mentioned it before, but when you stayed with me you often called me Karen in the middle of the night. I've heard it said that people don't lie in their sleep, darling.

I love you. I'll miss you. Good-bye.

Suzanne.

He read the note a second time. Then once more, while he fixed Alka-Seltzer and swallowed three extra-strength aspirin. Then he poured a cup of coffee. Sat on the couch in the living room. And read it once more. He still wore the suit from the day before.

He dialed Suzanne's apartment. Nobody answered. He hung up after twenty rings. Poured another cup of coffee and walked to the bedroom. He stripped the suit. Tossed it in the laundry hamper for cleaning.

Ten o'clock approached by the time he shaved and showered. His system recovered slightly in the steamy enclosure. Although his stomach growled harshly at the coffee. And he felt weak. Shaky. He likened it to an out-of-body experience gone awry.

Since he couldn't reach Suzanne by telephone, he decided to drive to the Hillary Building to see if she were there. As he walked out the front door, the telephone rang. He answered it. Doctor Benedict's nurse asked if he could drop by in an hour.

"Sure," he answered. "I'll be out that way."

Minutes later, he pulled in front of the Hillary Building. Suzanne's secretary said she'd called, and was leaving town.

"She didn't say where she was going, Mr. Durham," the young lady repeated. "Or when she'd be back."

Matt thanked her. Asked her to have Suzanne call if she paged in. Then went back to the car. Feeling desperate loneliness settle in his gut like morning fog over a river.

He had ten minutes to spare when he arrived at the doctor's office. An attractive nurse ushered him into an examining room.

Doctor Benedict appeared almost instantly. Gestured toward a chair. Asked Matt to sit. The doctor wheeled a rollered stool beside him. Sat there, holding a brown folder containing papers. Matt saw an electrocardiograph printout protruding from the sheath of medical forms.

"We've got your tests back, Matt," the doctor began. His voice steady, measured. "We think we know what's wrong with your arm."

"Oh?" Matt said. Curious...also dreading.

"It's Parkinson's Disease, Matt. Sometimes called Parkinson's Syndrome. That's what causes the tremors and weakness."

Matt sat silently for several moments. Then unconsciously noticed rubbing the arm. Which, as they talked, trembled noticeably.

"What's it boil down to, doctor?" he asked. Now alert and attentive. No longer hungover.

"It's not terminal, Matt. If that's what you mean. Parkinson's is idiopathic. In short, we don't know its cause."

The doctor straightened his patient's arm. Flexed its muscles.

"It leads to deterioration of muscle tissue in certain areas of the body. Mainly around elbows and knees. It's a gradual disease. And you can expect a normal life span. Providing cigarettes and liquor don't get you first."

The doctor stood, retrieved several pamphlets. Handed them to Matt. Sat down across from him.

"We can also treat Parkinson's, Matt. Artane does an effective job alleviating stiffness, and controlling tremors. Don't overdo your dosage, however. You'll start hallucinating!"

"That sounds pleasant," Matt replied stoically.

"Most things prescribed for Parkinson's have side effects, Matt. If Artane doesn't help, we'll try Parsidol. That might make you dizzy or drowsy. And Levodopa, or 'L-dopa,' may be okay later. Although it's rough on your guts at first. We'll see how the milder forms of medication work first."

"I guess it could be worse...couldn't it?"

"Oh, God yes, Matt! Who knows...in the next ten or twenty years, someone might find a cure. From what I read about DNA and genetic engineering, we're getting closer. That's about all I can tell you."

Matt stood, took the hand the doctor offered.

"Don't let this get your dobber down, Matt. You're healthy as a horse, otherwise. And you can live with that. It'll frustrate you at times. Possibly embarrass you. Still, you've got a lot going for you. The alternative is a real bear."

"Yeah...I know, Doctor Benedict. Thanks for everything."

"Let me know of changes once you're on medication, Matt. And check in more regularly...okay?"

"Sure...will do."

He walked out of the doctor's office and medical building, to where he'd parked the car. His mind a swirling turmoil of thoughts, emotions, feelings and questions. He drove to the apartment building. Pulled into the garage. Walked out the side entrance to Central Park across the street.

At midday, fresh air sluicing through the park carried autumn's bite. He pulled on the suit coat he'd thrown across his shoulder. Walked the asphalt jogging path around and through the forest of mostly maple and elm trees. Hardy stock for life in the middle of an over-carbon-dioxidized city. He skirted the murky pond in its middle.

Coots bobbed in a cluster of willows by a cut-bank on the opposite shore. He chuckled over the antics of the small birds.

When a mallard hen squalled from her cover of thick reeds in a slough to his left.

He stood still a minute and listened. Smiling to himself, he lit a cigarette. He breathed autumn crispness with the smoke. Noticed trees displaying fall colors. And heard his favorite waterfowl rhapsody.

Suddenly, nostalgia flooded his senses with a ferocity that caused him to gasp. It had happened before. So many times. In so many places. Always in the same way.

At that moment, Matt Durham realized...deep in the core of his being...the basic yet sensual love, enjoyment and appreciation he held for this season. Its creatures. Its sounds. Its smells. Its splendor. And its ability to start life's juices flowing again.

Parkinson's could rob him of steady hand, steel rod posture and basic motor functions. However, it could never dampen autumn's innate spark, filling him with unusually pleasant melancholy, time and again.

And Matt knew, then, what he wanted to do.

Go home. To Karen. To the kids. To The House. And to the rest of what he determined...from that point forward...would be meaningful, full, happy and exciting days.

And to hell with New York!

Chapter 28

Home To The House

MATT SPENT TWO EARLY MORNING telephone calls releasing the apartment: One to Greer McCall at the new agency, who envied Matt for the swank and convenient location, and snapped it up without hesitation. The other to his former landlord, Fred Grayson, to transfer the lease.

Fred protested briefly, saying he'd compiled a waiting list of twenty people over the years Matt lived there. He succumbed, however, when Matt mentioned a case of Cutty Sark was on its way, and also that his lawyer suggested keeping the long-lease apartment and subletting.

After Matt packed and booked reservations, Greer drove him to JFK to catch Triad's flight to Hartford. Two Triad executives...Bob Griffith and Larry Harst...met them at the terminal. Shared a last Bloody Mary in the Silver Prop Bar. Then saw Matt off.

In forty minutes, he headed the Mercedes south on Highway 91. Half an hour later, he pulled into the driveway of his Wellham Park home.

Karen's Mercedes convertible was not in the garage. He intuitively wondered why, then dismissed his quandary and lugged suitbags and cases into the house. There, he unpacked and changed clothes, elated he had made up his mind concerning his life. Excited over what he planned to do.

At Greer's insistence he had accepted an upfront earnest payment of a half million dollars, representing a fifth of his interest in the New York operations. And on impulse, he fulfilled a promise made to himself twenty years ago and called a New Haven auto dealer who specialized in imported cars. Over the telephone, he bought a flaming red Ferrari Testarossa.

Now, he telephoned the dealer and confirmed the car was ready. Then called for a taxi to drive him to the dealership. In an hour, Matt signed the title, arranged insurance and penned a check for eighty-six thousand dollars. After a few jerky starts, he felt at home in the sleek vehicle.

He returned to Wellham Park, tossed sweaters, jeans, loafers, shave kit and underwear into a soft travel bag, and wedged it into the small storage area behind the leather bucket seats.

Then he went back into the house briefly and left a note for Karen, explaining he'd be at The House a few days and wanted to talk when he returned. He taped the note to the back door, popped a can of beer and put another six-pack in a small cooler, which he placed on the passenger's side floormat.

Matt backed down the driveway, steered out of the Park, and onto Highway 91 again.

The Ferrari loped at seventy, its tachometer bouncing at five thousand revolutions-per-minute; pleading for him to loosen the reins. Its deep-throated tuned exhaust filled his ears with wonderful music.

In minutes, he intercepted coastal Highway 95 and turned northwest onto Highway 9. And forty-five minutes later, he churned narrow blacktop topping the seven hills leading to Huntsdale.

As the sports car droned effortlessly, Matt relaxed for the first time in months. His neck no longer steel cable stiff. Nor the back of his head feeling tremendous pressure building, and seeming ready to burst his skull at any moment.

It may have been the brews or vivid fall foliage lining the asphalt ribbon. Whatever, a burdensome weight lifted from his shoulders and he again felt at peace with himself and the world. He knew what he wanted to do. Knew what he had to do. And looked forward to completing his tasks with only minimal fear and anxiety.

After a few days unwinding at The House, he would return to New Haven. Patch the shattered relationship with his wife. Renew ties with his children, and with family and friends.

"The people I've turned my back on for many, many years," he said aloud.

He lit another cigarette. The Ferrari swerving sharply as he took his eyes from the road. He balanced his lighter and can of beer, heart instantly lurching. Tight steering easily brought the machine back in tow. And he mentally noted an old pilot's homage: "Keep your eyes out of the cockpit."

He secured the beer can between his thighs and held the cigarette in his trembling left hand. He studied the quaking arm. "What a worthless piece of crap you've become." He laughed to himself, and down-shifted to third as the car hugged a tight corner.

Huntsdale appeared as always for Matt. Almost as it had for nearly 200 years.

A quiet little village. Gas station. Church. Ten or fifteen homes. And Arch's grocery and hardware store, still Texaco gas out-front and dispensing bottled beer, sardines, Vienna sausages, cheese and sandwiches in the back room, near the huge potbellied stove, jukebox and pool table.

He again down-shifted at the stop sign across from the weathered store. Imagined several of the town's elders gathered around the stove. Sitting silently, or swapping tales of things that used to be. Awaiting winter's bite. And a cheery fire in the steel squatty-legged black sphere.

Many of Huntsdale's townsfolk raised what they called shade tobacco. Grown under long strips of silken fabric that formed awnings. Several survived as farmers, part-time trappers, hunters and commercial fishermen. A few worked at odd jobs in town.

Most younger Huntsdalians had long since packed and left. Realizing that a life working in the soil today accounted for heartbreak and misery...not a decent living.

Matt had learned that truth over the last two decades. Only big feedlots and corporate farmers could survive. Little farmers...less than a hundred acres...would have to consider hobby-farming. Working full-time in town during the week and farming weekends.

He turned right onto the rough, dusty, gravel-strewn road across from Arch's. Thought about the old man. Dead for twenty years now. His mind flitted to the antique jukebox inside. Railing screechy country songs throughout the day.

He asked himself again, then, for the hundredth time...what happened so quickly to so many years. Between the boy shooting firecrackers in the dust beside the store. And the middle-aged man coming back to the place he most loved. And with which he felt most comfortable. Yet deserted.

Coming back to reglue the shards of an existence that let its foundation crumble. Allowed everything held dear to crash around it.

Still, he smiled realizing he knew what was wrong. And hoped he had not discovered too late. Because, by damn, he could fix it.

He smoothly shifted the Ferrari into second. Popped the clutch. Listened to the feisty high-pitched engine unwind. Gravel and dust spewing in the middle of the road behind.

He slowed as he approached the rock road leading to the bluffs.

The Paginaw River wound to his left. He recalled the many times his dad and he prowled these fields. Visiting Arch's after hunting ducks all morning. Ambling silently through the squirrel woods beside the river. "Scrounge hunting," the general called it. Or plunking cans with their target rifles.

When Damon was alive, he and Walt enjoyed drinking beer with the men of Huntsdale. Most of whom they knew and mutually respected for nearly half a century.

Matt drank a Pepsi or Orange Crush. And sat quietly listening to the elders' tales. Or he'd buy a pack of firecrackers and explode them outside in the road.

He glanced through the Ferrari's tinted glass. Across a sea of brown soybeans. Ready for harvest. He imagined Guy Simpson would begin that chore over the next couple of weeks.

A strange sensation brushed his consciousness. Realizing the land he cherished had been Judge Corley's. Then Doctor Forsythe's. And now his. Sadness welled and subsided as he thought of the two gentlemen.

The Paginaw surged only a quarter mile away now. On the other side of the woods. In his mind's eye, he knew exactly what it looked like. Its channel had changed imperceptibly over the years. It flowed straight, deep and fast. The color of milk chocolate. Roiling great swirls and whirlpools. An endless current eating its way deeper and deeper into the earth.

"Someday, Matt, it'll saw the world in half," Damon used to tell him.

He passed the weed-choked road leading across the fields to the river. Its padlocked gate displayed a "posted" sign. He squinted against the bright sunlight, trying to spot the dark outline of the boat house in the distance.

Brush grew too wildly and thick to see beyond the edge of the woods. He knew, though, the shed would be there and in good shape. Thanks to Guy.

In a mile, he turned right again. Up into what once was the original river bottom. Carved and filled by glaciers thousands of years ago. Now the road inclined toward the promontory on which The House set.

He edged the Ferrari onto the gravel heap of a shoulder. Shut the motor off and stepped out. Hoping fresh air would blow his mind and heart clear.

In a tall sycamore to his left, a mourning dove issued its plaintive "ah-whoo, whoo, whoo." And a big fox squirrel chattered and scolded him for interrupting her noontime feeding routine.

He leaned against the car. Fired a cigarette. Cupped his hands and imitated the squirrel's bark to see its reaction. She ignored him, and he chuckled once again.

A light breeze wafting inward along the river from the coast boasted a salt water flavor. Mixed with the Cheddary smell of bottomland soil. The acidic smell of insect spray or fertilizer. And the sweet fragrance of willows lining the river's banks.

The breeze also carried a warning that winter soon would be at hand. It felt cool and refreshing against his face. Rattling dry leaves on the road beside him.

A flock of crows...tormenting an owl in the woods downriver... compounded the sharp din raised by the crotchety red squirrel.

"All right, all right," he said aloft to the chattering rodent. He crushed the cigarette in the thick dust under his heel. "I'm going! I'm going!"

He climbed back into the roadster and pulled away.

In a few minutes, he ascended the grade leading to The House. Soon, it materialized over the gracefully sloped hood. Bringing the same fluttery feeling it always had.

"Guy's been busy," he said aloud, noticing The House's fresh coat of white paint. He pulled into the half circle drive, stopped in front of the porch steps, turned off the Ferrari and stepped out.

He heard the "pop-pop-pop-oom-pop" of Guy's John Deere tractor a half mile away, and imagined him picking corn in his fields by Raymond Daley's place.

He retrieved the clothes bag from the storage space, walked up onto the porch, unlocked the front door, and left it open to air The House. Then Matt went upstairs and tossed the bag on the bed, then into the bathroom where he splashed water on his face.

When he returned downstairs, he opened windows in the family and living rooms for cross ventilation. Over the heavy ticking of the Regulator clock on the mantel, he still heard Guy's tractor laboring in the distance. "'Poppin' Johnnies' is what they used to call John Deeres," he remembered Guy saying. "Not a better tractor anywhere."

He went into the study. Opened another window there. Then mixed a stout sour mash and branch water.

He walked to the bay window. Looked through the walnut grove toward Magusett Creek. The breeze atop the hill swirled fallen leaves in ringlets along the ground.

"Going to be a good season for the squirrels," he remarked. He noticed the branches of the walnut trees sagging under heavy loads of nuts.

The peace he anticipated closed in on him comfortably. He smiled to himself as he studied the outside surroundings.

Matt set the drink glass down. Stoked another cigarette. Then chuckled once more over the tremor in his left hand. He sat on the cushions in front of the window.

On the drive down, a lot of thoughts stirred in his mind. Seeing the red fox churned up more. Now, they began germinating and taking shape. He had the money he needed. Everything he wanted.

"Even a new Ferrari!" he happily exclaimed.

He didn't need to work another day if he didn't want to. Not only that...Guy Simpson had turned Matt's land into an extremely profitable venture.

He decided to write a book. Perhaps about Huntsdale. Its lore, people and simple way of life. Enough tales abounded concerning Huntsdale's history and families to fill several volumes and barely scratch the surface. And he certainly could write about advertising. He'd donated thirty-five years to its cause. Not only that, he had contributed a chapter to the text marketed by the National Association of Advertising Agencies.

Matt cloaked himself tightly in reverie, thoughts drifting freely in and out of his mind like smoke from his cigarette, with no particular outcome sought. He heard a car door snap shut but paid little notice, figuring Opal Simpson had seen him drive up to The House and not recognizing the car, had stopped to see who was about. He sipped his drink, when a long familiar voice came from across the room and startled him.

"We're too late for Fall Festival this year, Matt," Karen said lightly. "You know that...don't you?"

He turned and looked appreciatively at the gracious, beautiful woman with whom he'd shared so much over so many years. His heart crowded his throat when he spoke.

"As long as it's not too late for us, Karen."

He raised off the couch. Without another word, crossed the room. Embraced her gently. Felt her stiffen at first. Then return his embrace.

"I've been such a fool. Such a son-of-a-bitch," he said flatly. Her soft hair brushed his cheek. Its clean, herbal scent filled his nostrils.

"I've got so much to make up for. So many people to repay for what I've done."

She gently pulled away. Took his hand. Led him to the bar in the study.

"Fix me a drink, too, Matt. Please. Then, let's talk like your note said."

"You got it," he said. He poured her a drink and freshened his.

They sat on the cushions by the window. Looking at each other. Recognizing what they hadn't seen lately. Love, reflecting in the other's face. Karen felt tremendous calm sweep her. And intrinsically knew he experienced the same emotions.

He fumbled with his pack of cigarettes. Tapped one out and lit it. Held it momentarily in his left hand. Then transferred it to his right, hoping she didn't notice the tremors.

She took the shaking hand in hers.

"I know about the Parkinson's, Matt," she said, softly rubbing his hand and arm.

"Oh?"

"Yes...Hal Sappington told me. He heard from your doctor in New York. Said he called to get your previous medical history. And thought I should know."

"He's a blabbermouth," he replied. "That's violation of confidentiality between patient and physician. I didn't want you to know."

"Why, Matt?" her voice pleaded. "Why shouldn't I know? You're still my husband."

He stood, back toward her, and head down.

"I want us back together, Karen. More than anything. Pick up where we left off. Repair what I almost destroyed. I don't want it happening out of pity, though."

"Pity!" she exclaimed, hopping up from the cushions. She grabbed his shoulder, roughly turned him to face her. "You and your stupid pride,

Matt Durham. If you can't distinguish love from pity...you're beyond help!"

He hung his head further. Placed his hand over hers. Smiled sheepishly.

"You do love me, then?" he asked. Dreading the reply.

She cupped her hand under his chin.

"Yes, Matt, I do. Don't ask me why, though. I probably always will. For some people in this world, there's just one other. I've tied my life to yours. That's how it's been. That's how it will be."

He smiled broadly. Cupped his right hand behind her head. Drew her lips to his and kissed her softly.

"I love you too, Karen. More than anything. I've got myself straightened out, now. And we can make our marriage work."

"I know we can, too, Matt," she agreed. "I know we can."

He lit another cigarette. His heart thudded in a combination of excitement and happiness. His face flashed a worried frown. She noticed.

"What is it?"

"Thinking of the kids. If there's a way of making up what I've done to them. No wonder their lives drifted off course."

"That's news I'm bursting to tell," she said excitedly. "That's why I rushed here after seeing your note. Figured you could stand some bolstering. I mean...after Hoot and all."

"Well...tell me, tell me," his voice implored. "If it's good news, I want it!"

"Corley graduated from Cal State in June. And stayed on with the Davenports. Remember? I wrote you in July."

"Yes, I remember your letter. And?"

"He voluntarily slaved for a film producer who spoke to one of his classes on script-writing and editing. That's why Corley stayed on the West Coast. He finished a screenplay he started a few years ago. And with the producer's help, he sold it. They're going to make a movie of it!"

"You're kidding!" he beamed, slapping the side of his leg for emphasis. "I knew that kid had it! Knew he'd be a good writer!"

"That's not all, Matt."

"There's more? Jesus, Karen, can my heart stand it?"

"You'll love it," she said. She gently placed her hand on his forearm. Tugged him beside her on the couch. "Corley's not the only successful writer," she continued. "It runs in the family. Remember Alex Gordon...

the young man with whom Diana has stayed at Martha's Vineyard? He has two plays running off-Broadway!"

Karen clutched his hands in her excitement.

"Not only that, one is a tremendous smash. And...the best part... Diana says the Boston Repertory Theater picked Alex to direct its performances! One of the country's most prestigious playhouses!"

"My God, Karen...I...I...uh." He was speechless. Completely.

"Diana returns to Boston College next semester, picking up where she left off. She's continuing in drama. And you'll also be happy to know they plan on marrying this spring."

He silently eased his arms around her neck. She felt his body wrench with sobs.

"I don't...can't...don't know what to say," he sputtered, tears streaming his cheeks and quivering off his top lip. "It's all I've prayed for lately. Even more. I don't deserve to be so lucky. And happy."

"Why not, Matt? We've worked hard all our lives for these moments. And we've got lots of life in us yet! Now we can do what we want. And enjoy it even more, because there's no worry about how much it costs or how long it takes."

She patted his back as she held him. After a moment's quiet, he leaned back, held her at arm's length. Moist tear trails lined each side of his face.

"I'll make it up to you...and to them, Karen. I swear it. Let's bring the whole group here for Christmas. Corley. Diana. What's his name... Alex? Maybe dad and mom, and your mom...could skip Florida for a week. What do you say? Let's do it up big!"

She watched and felt the excitement stirring within him. Transforming his whole being.

"Hold on, Matt," she said. She took his arm in her hand. Patted it, calming him down. "Are you certain about this?"

"More than anything before, honey," he replied. "When we get back to New Haven, let's create some invitations. Tell them about us. Ask them to help us celebrate Christmas."

He lifted off the couch, clapped his hands together, and snapped his fingers with an idea.

"I'll pay for Corley, Diana, and Alex to fly here and back! Hell, I've got friends in the airline industry. They can get me top rates!"

"It does sound like fun, darling. It'll be the first time in years the whole family has got together."

She turned her body sideways to his. Leaned her head on his shoulder. They sat for several minutes in the silence. Feeling occasional currents of wind around the bay window. October's breath searching its way through the tiny spaces between frame and glass.

He swallowed the remainder of the drink in his glass. Felt her body quake with subdued laughter. He turned toward her.

"What's up? What's so funny?"

She chuckled happily. "I just thought...want to help gather walnuts for the squirrels?"

He leaned his head back and joined her in laughter, then took her hand in his and kissed it gently.

"Damned right I do!" he stated. "Let's go."

They walked arm-in-arm out the front door. Two kids finding love again. Eager to be outside together.

She nodded toward the cherry red sports car parked in front of her's.

"I see you finally got your Ferrari."

"Yeah, cost me an arm and a leg. What do you think?"

She tugged him to stop. Looked him in the face, and quickly bussed his cheek.

"You'll have to get rid of it. It's not us."

They strolled the stand of walnut trees by Magusett Creek, ankle-deep in autumn's crisp, crackly brown leaves, hand-in-hand, her head resting against his shoulder. And as they walked, the gentle breeze flipped fallen leaves like playing cards on a table, covering the paths they made.

Matt looked into the grey overcast sky, stopped abruptly, and pointed out to her a large wavy vee of ducks, snaking its course along the Paginaw River, and confirming October's arrival at The House.

The End

31250552R00276

Made in the USA
Middletown, DE
24 April 2016